DETECTIVE LAFLEUR MYSTERIES

BY

STEVE ABBOTT AND JOHN FOUNTAIN

O.R.

Firesign

Hot Gold

OLD MAN in a HURRY

A Detective LaFleur Novel

STEVE ABBOTT

———

JOHN FOUNTAIN

This is a work of fiction. Names, characters, places, and incidents are the product of the authors' imaginations or are used fictitiously.

ISBN: 1545349274
ISBN-13: 978-1545349274

To Kurt –
Best man for a few
Best friend of many
Admired and enjoyed by all

To Jary –
For showing the way

The world is his who hastens most.

-- *Babar the Elephant*

CONTENTS

OLD MAN in a HURRY

PROLOGUE

1944: FORT ONTARIO, OSWEGO, NEW YORK

A damp chill seeps through the soles of Tamos Szabó's new shoes. He stands on the north side bluff of Fort Ontario, next to the lake, waiting and watching. The weather, earlier unsettled, now threatens.

Behind him, patient and cold, the lake takes no notice of his growing discomfort. In the dim light of late afternoon, the white curl of the waves breaking in shallow water imitates the glint of ice slowly building on the rocks scattered close to shore. Tamos turns and looks out over the lake, eyes burning, from the wind or the cold or from staring too hard at the sky, he cannot tell.

Storms in Oswego arrive unannounced and unrepentant. This one is a storm that has decided there is nothing left to lose, and it throws itself into the event like a rowdy kid at an amusement park, ready to try anything once – and so brings sleet, wind, snow, lightning, rain, all at once. The temperature drops so suddenly that the entire length of shore below Tamos begins to ice up. Gusts of wind send a frigid mist up and over the top of the hill.

Tamos sits, huddles down into his mackinaw, wrapping his arms around his knees, determined not to shiver, not noticing when he starts to rock back and forth rhythmically, humming a tune under his breath, staring out at the lake, sometimes leaning back, craning, still watching the sky. The cloud ceiling has now dropped so low as to be practically indistinguishable from the water, shifting the boundaries of water and ice and sky. It begins to snow harder.

As Tamos slowly sinks into near hypothermia, he hears an insistent droning coming out of the west, a low tone, pitching somewhat erratically. He stops humming, nearly stops breathing, and stands up, almost falling over as his legs refuse to unlimber as quickly as he demands. He momentarily loses track of the thrumming sound as the wind changes direction, then recaptures it, then loses it again.

Becoming more alarmed as the sound shifts, Tamos runs the few feet down the hill, across the railroad tracks to the very edge of the water, straining to see. But there is only the hard gray of the lake seamlessly merging with the horizon. He stands deathly still, staring in the direction of the sound as it moves from left to right.

The thrumming stops.

He pulls his hood back and listens intently. Nothing. Did he imagine it? He turns back towards the Fort. In that direction? Still nothing.

As the clouds lower and the light fades, the lake gives up its colors: first the last trace of blue, then the violet-green of eddies along the shore. Now in place of the lake there is only an indistinct mass, forcing him to strain even harder to see beyond the breakers. The dark green of the scattered bushes close along the shoreline soon follows the water and sky into obscurity.

Sound also seems to follow the light, disappearing as if into a vacuum, returning only in pieces, reluctantly. He hears the splatter of sleet on his jacket. The static of the wind. The grasping sound of waves on the sand.

He stands there a long time as the night and the cold close swiftly around him.

***

Seventy years later, Dr. Michael Fuentes is startled by a sudden noise. He looks up. Someone dressed in hospital scrubs and a surgical mask lunges across the desk and drives a scalpel deep into his chest.

The pain is blinding; his vision blurs as he falls face down onto the desk. There are a few loud, crashing noises, then silence.

"I'm sorry, Tamos," he says.

He closes his eyes.

BOOK I: HOW IT BEGAN

Oswegonian

OSWEGO, NEW YORK

Alonzo Carlton LaFleur had never met the two uncles he was named after, his mother's only brothers. They died in late 1944, three years before he was born, killed in Italy only two days apart, by pure chance less than ten miles from one another, in minor skirmishes that did nothing to further the war or even the liberation. Neither one had even known the other was in the country.

Alonzo's mother, Marie, married an ex-Navy pilot named Antoine LaFleur in 1946, moving from New Jersey where her grandparents had settled to Antoine's hometown of Oswego, New York. Her two sisters were her bridesmaids, but there was no maid of honor and only a virtual best man: she had asked the groom to honor the memory of her dead brothers by naming "Alonzo Carlton" as best man in the wedding program, relegating Antoine's brother and best friend to being groomsmen. Then when the baby was born, well, what other choice of names was there? Alonzo Carlton, it was.

Three good years was all the time the universe allocated to Marie and Antoine. In 1951, Antione was called up. It was not long after that his is F9F Panther fighter was shot down over the Yalu River, in Korea. And that is how it was that Alonzo Carlton grew up with only second-hand memories of his father; Kodak Brownie snapshots, a handful of letters on Navy stationary, and a faded Air Group Five insignia. Marie never remarried.

By the time Alonzo Carlton entered third grade, he had, to his great relief, become known as simply "A.C." (to everyone except his mother, who always called him by his full name, an indulgence he never denied her). His mother's stories of the exploits of his nearly mystical uncles and missing father enthralled him as he grew up; as did the few remaining artifacts of his father's service.

Never extremely outgoing or particular athletic while growing up, he avoided most social events and team sports, spending his time reading at the library, working on magic tricks in his room, and playing chess and other games with a few of the other less popular kids – submarine was a favorite – and was outwardly just another regular Oswego kid. He was a bit lazy at school, but due to disinterest, not lack of ability. When he got a little older, he spent a lot of time at Oswego's secular answer to the Knights of Columbus, the Fortnightly Club. While waiting tables and cleaning up, providing a fourth for bridge on slow nights, and performing the occasional card trick, which brought in good tips, he began to prefer the company of adults, which isolated him further from his classmates.

When he turned nineteen, in 1966, he didn't wait to get drafted into the Army infantry, which he perceived to be a losing prospect from all vantage points, but instead joined the Navy. But dreams of reliving his father's naval air career ended with an eye test. His mother's hopes of a safe stateside or European posting were not realized, and A.C. ended up in Vietnam on a swift boat. He seldom talked about it.

Oswego is a city locked into a long tradition of working class jobs passed from generation to generation; dock workers' sons went to the docks, factory workers' sons (while the factories lasted) went to Diamond Match, Oswego Shade Cloth, Kingsford Corn Starch, Oswego Car Spring, or to the textile and knitting mills. The Irish policemen's and Italian firemen's sons of course went into their fathers' respective departments.

A.C., after his return from Vietnam, didn't have a "family trade" to go into, no tradition to carry on. He was on his own. Still in a military frame of mind, and in spite of his status as an outsider, he got on the local police force, but not with the intention of being just another street cop; he had always wanted to be detective.

He still loved games, and what more challenging than the real-life game of solving difficult crimes? Anyone, after all, could deal with a domestic violence call, a traffic accident, or a bar fight. A.C. was more interested in using his brains. He worked his way up quickly and was soon a senior detective. Respected but never really "one of the gang," he remained somewhat of a loner.

So, he did his job, quietly and efficiently, bided his time, and after a time, got promoted to senior detective. Shortly after that, now secure in a career, he got married, to an almost local girl, but from up north, from Watertown; they had not known one another prior to their meeting at a shared second cousin's wedding. They moved into a nice house on East Third. Had two kids, daughters. A.C. settled down and stayed out of trouble, played cards at the Fortnightly Club, took his wife out to dinner and a movie now and then, went to school plays, and in general liked his life.

To keep himself sharp at work, he pursued oddball cases, for fun, during slow periods. Cases no one else thought were either solvable or worth the effort. The answer book theft at the high school (a lame attempt by a senior football player trying to sabotage the SATs). Another high school case, the disappearing janitorial supplies – no forced entry, no suspects – the janitor, "Old Swede," was as innocent as the day is long, he said, and no reason to disbelieve him. No one else on the force could be bothered, but LaFleur's curiosity got the best of him. He finally tracked it down to Swede's ex-brother-in-law, who had been hoisting his ten-year-old nephew into a small open window, the kid passing out supplies, which the brother-in-law then resold to the school, with Swede's assistance.

Then there was the case of the three kittens stolen from the Humane Society holding area (technically a felony theft, at a valuation of fifty dollars per kitten), soon known around the precinct as "The Great Kitten Caper." He took some ribbing over this and other similar cases, but shrugged it all off, and kept himself busy, unlike some of his fellow detectives, whose idea of a busy day was hitting three bars instead of the regular two.

LaFleur learned early on that one of the most important things was to maintain the status quo. This was brought home clearly in an infamous incident at Oswego Hospital: a young nurse had been found dead in an employee lounge, under mysterious circumstances, but declared a suicide practically before the body cooled. He and a more senior detective had been pulled off the assignment within eight hours, for political reasons. LaFleur had already made a reputation for himself as a self-starter, and the bosses were afraid he would start poking around, asking questions – doing his job, in other words – and solve the case, a case they definitely did not want solved.

The years went by, as years do, some eventful, most not, and suddenly A.C. found himself a statistical anomaly – his wife died before him, six months into his retirement. He had always been told that women outlive men, and now, feeling cheated, at sixty, alone (kids off in Florida and Boston) and a bit awkward in mixed company, A.C. quickly fell into solitary habits: reading, fishing, more reading.

He'd never been more than casual friends with most of the cops he'd worked with over the years – just not enough in common – and his best friend in those days was a retired professor he'd recently become reacquainted with; they got together regularly to play chess, and go out to dinner. Even so, life seemed to drag on, like a bad school play: uninspiring, bland, and occasionally painful.

Something had to change. LaFleur, never one to do things by half, abruptly moved out of his house and on to a small houseboat, for which he had somehow wrangled the permits necessary to allow him to moor it permanently in Oswego harbor. He adopted a cat, Newton. Although remarkably engaging, for a cat, Newton failed to provide much in the way of social stimulus. For a time, the stimulus of a more active life on the boat, which introduced him to an entirely new circle of friends – many having to do with the seemingly never-ending burden of marine maintenance – kept the demons at bay. But as routine gradually overwhelmed him, LaFleur again began to feel, appropriately enough, adrift.

And then life changed again.

1850 House

OSWEGO, NEW YORK

"Maggie?" A.C. called out loudly. There was no answer, so he walked over to the short passageway from the bar into the dining room in front, and called out again. "Maggie!"

"What is it?" came back from somewhere in the room.

"Did Salerno's ever call back about that delivery?" He walked into the dining room. "Oh, there you are," he said, seeing her arranging chairs at a double table back in the corner. They probably had a large party coming in, LaFleur guessed.

Maggie turned, brushed down the front of her skirt, then flipped a stray strand of auburn hair off of her forehead. Her hair, the color of plum-red paint on a rusted-out old Cadillac (as LaFleur described it), was only one of her attractive qualities, again according to LaFleur, but a fact generally acknowledged by just about everyone who knew her.

"Let me finish this and I'll come back to the bar and explain it," she said.

"Whenever you get a chance," he said, waving as he went back to the bar. "I'll be here."

The new owner and proprietor of the eponymously named 1850 House (built in 1850, as a boarding house) returned to the bar and absentmindedly continued taking stock. A tall man, but not obtrusively so, LaFleur moved through the bar with smooth deliberation, jotting down notes on a small pad as he went from shelf to shelf. He did not use an electronic tablet or smart phone; the feel of putting pencil to paper was much too satisfying, an ingrained habit impossible to give up.

Catching a glimpse of himself in the mirrored back wall of the bar, behind the array of bottles, he thought he detected a hint of smugness around the eyes, at the same time flinching a bit at the increase in the extent of the crow's feet. The gray hair he had grown accustomed to. Well, shouldn't he be allowed some small measure of smugness, given the past few years? It had not been easy, navigating a retirement that had proven as difficult – no, more so – than his years as a senior detective. But still – no regrets. Regrets, he believed, other than for those things not done for the wrong reason, were in general counterproductive. Those few he would admit to, he put on the Sinatra plan – *yes, I've had a few, but then again,* as the refrain went. And so here I am, he thought, brushing his hair back and adjusting his glasses, sixty-seven years old, trim and fit, with a beautiful woman to share my life – why not feel a bit self-satisfied? Maggie even teased him occasionally about the “affable swagger” he had when walking around the restaurant.

The restaurant sat inconspicuously in its stone and green clapboard face, its casement windows and ivy-covered eaves looking out onto East Bridge Street, just a few blocks up from the river. With the death of the owner, Joe Crisifulli, the restaurant had been shuttered for many years, just locked up and left as it was the day Joe died. Now it belonged to LaFleur.

From the outside, the restaurant was unremarkable. The interior, however, looked for all the world like a huge jumble sale, with all of the accompanying clutter, all of the requisite randomness. There were the obligatory cheap figurines – cats, donkeys, roosters – but also exquisite pastel-colored Lalique, French ladies and gentlemen in elaborately ruffled court dress; small antique barn implements and obsolete kitchen gadgets; oddly shaped and colored bottles, some with the original contents and stoppers – Lydia Pinkham’s Vegetable Compound, Dr. Keene’s Liniment; vintage medical instruments; statuettes and busts in various mediums and states of repair; all of this in the entry vestibule. One particular bust had a position of pride, however: in the Men’s restroom, a marble bust of Caruso sat on top of the toilet tank, lord of all he surveyed.

Inside, along the hall leading into the main part of the building, were more shelves, and items hanging on the walls: old paintings and prints, some rare and in good taste (a pristine Maxfield Parrish print of “Daybreak”), and some not so rare and in dubious taste (a shabby velvet painting of Elvis in a gold lamé frame); books, some beautifully leather bound, rare editions, but most of somewhat indeterminate binding; cut-glass kerosene lamps, delicately shaped and tinted purple with age; souvenir plates from France, Holland, Germany, Czechoslovakia, or closer to home, Niagara Falls; and other items of all description, all for sale – price as marked, no reasonable offer declined – surrounding an eclectic selection of small dining tables and mismatched chairs.

Newton, who of course considered himself part owner, could often be seen lounging in the front window, alternately watching the passerby on the sidewalk outside or surveying the diners at their tables. Some regulars came to visit Newton as much as for the food; at least, this is what they jokingly told Frank, the chef.

It was not as if LaFleur had been actively looking for a change. Owning a restaurant had come as something of a surprise. One day he was living a simple life, puttering around in retirement on his houseboat, more or less minding his own business, seeing Maggie occasionally, holding a regular poker game, and the next day the burned-out shell of the houseboat was at the bottom of Oswego Harbor. This had been the result of a cold case he’d taken on in retirement, a case being ignored by the department, and which had been urged on him by Maggie for personal reasons. Not the first such case she'd brought to him.

Buying the restaurant had given him not only the opportunity to move on from a past life that was only slowly releasing its hold on him, but the roomy apartment upstairs, after a complete remodel, had also given him a great place to live after the loss of the boat. Best of all, Maggie had moved in with him. Thank God for Maggie, he said daily.

Maggie had spent more than forty years as a nurse at Oswego Hospital – the last twenty of those years as head nurse – weathering all storms: administrative, professional, and personal. Her early years at the hospital had been during the golden era of male-domination in medicine, when senior physicians held nearly unlimited power over their "charges," – interns, administrative personnel, and nurses, whom they typically ranked in that order of importance. She'd somehow remained single, "narrowly escaping" marriage twice, she liked to say. She relied on her two sisters to provide several nephews and nieces on whom to dote, and was the favorite aunt.

Together, A.C. and Maggie had restored the restaurant to its former glorious life, leaving its flea market atmosphere more or less intact, though it was hell to dust and tedious to restock. Fortunately, the storage shed out back contained what appeared to be several years' worth of inventory.

They'd changed the menu slightly, as Joe had believed every dish should be floating in golden pools of garlic butter; otherwise they had been able to maintain a considerable continuity with the past. It was a little detail in the larger scheme of life, the changing of the menu, but LaFleur had found that the best course was to carry on forthrightly, in things both large and small, with good sense and grace.

And besides, he hated garlic butter.

Sentimental Journey

1850 HOUSE

The professor came in at his usual time. Formerly a physics teacher at SUNY Oswego, now long retired, Tamos Szabó was ninety-four years old, a wiry, five-foot-eight, one-hundred-and-forty-pound dynamo.

"Very robust for my age," he liked to say, with no exaggeration. "Twenty sit-ups a day, ride a mile on the exercise bicycle, and walk half a mile, or more."

Only slightly stooped, his one real disability was his eyesight. He had voluntarily relinquished his driver's license at age eighty-eight, claiming that no one as old as the number of keys on a piano should be behind the wheel of a two-ton, rolling mass of steel. "F=ma," he often said, "is the only thing keeping me from driving – disregarding the complicating factor of velocity, of course." He would gladly oblige the listener with a more detailed explanation of the various derivations of Newton's equations if one were generous enough to offer him the opportunity to expound; few took him up on the offer, to their detriment. The professor was a rare breed, a teacher who could make even the most uninterested of students excel; he was a great proponent of the Platonic dialogue as the best method of instruction.

Calling out a cordial, "Hello, A.C.," Tamos walked through the bar to his usual corner, back and to the left, toward a small round table. As he passed the end of the bar and turned to sit down, he tipped his hat, a quaint custom; the professor was typically very formal. The tip of the hat was not directed at LaFleur, however, but to an old black-and-white photograph hanging on the wall at the end of the bar above the jukebox, a vintage Wurlitzer Bubbler.

The photo portrayed rows and rows of World War II pursuit fighter planes, lined up adjacent to a long runway, situated in an open and unidentifiable prairie. The planes looked sleek and ferocious, gleaming in the sun, seemingly poised to leap straight into the air as if of their own accord. There was a small "Not for Sale" sticker attached to the frame. When LaFleur had asked Tamos where it had come from, the professor said he'd had old Joe hang it for him some indeterminate number of years earlier.

"But why?" LaFleur had pressed.

The professor smiled and shrugged it off. "Just something I came across somewhere. And Joe seemed to like it, so we thought it should stay up there."

Pausing at the jukebox, Tamos selected a few classic big band tunes, as always: Glenn Miller, Tommy Dorsey, Artie Shaw. And Les Brown.

Sentimental Journey. He never failed to include *Sentimental Journey*. The first tune filled the bar as the professor hung his hat on a hook on the wall and took his usual seat. He made a classic picture sitting there, dressed in his old-style striped suit and vest, black bow tie, and Florsheim shoes, as if he'd traveled back in time.

The professor had been frequenting 1850 House for many years; had become quite a fixture, in fact, eating most of his dinners there, as had LaFleur in those days. The professor, LaFleur thought, was without a doubt one of the most intriguing persons he had ever met. Considering that LaFleur had spent over forty years as a police detective in a town known for its interesting characters, that was saying something. Now that LaFleur and Maggie owned the restaurant, the three of them had become quite close.

Not that the professor lacked for friends, though he occasionally, and rather ruefully, commented on how many friends he had outlived. He'd lived in Oswego for over seventy years, after all, and while he'd always lived simply and quietly, he was far from being a recluse. In early days, there had been regular bridge games at the Fortnightly Club (he remembered seeing A.C. there, working as a waiter, when A.C. was just a kid); socials in the ballroom of the Pontiac Hotel; dancing and drinks at the old White Horse Inn. He knew everyone at the synagogue, went to every family function and celebration he was invited to – and even in a Jewish community as small as the one in Oswego, there were plenty of opportunities for parties – friends' birthdays, friends' kids' birthdays, bar mitzvahs, bat mitzvahs, and so on. And funerals (too many funerals). He made regular drop-in visits to the two or three nursing homes in the neighborhood, though he no longer knew anyone in residence, and was sometimes disheartened to see residents much younger than himself in poor mental or physical health.

No, in spite of his outwardly conservative demeanor and lifestyle, Tamos was not one to hold back when it came to socializing, especially in his home away from home, the 1850 House. It was his very formality, in fact, the reserve that he typically exhibited, that worked to his advantage when having a bit of fun. One April Fool's Day, for example, he'd conspired with Frank, the chef, to make all the burgers that day out of rabbit – Hasenpfeffer, he called it – and was amused and gratified at all the positive comments from the customers. It was obviously something different, and everyone had loved them! LaFleur toyed with the idea of making it one of the regular specials, but it turned out to be hard to find a reliable source of rabbit. Tamos and Frank had become friends very quickly after that, which had led to Tamos cooking a special goulash dinner every year on several Hungarian national holidays – both 1848 and 1956 Revolution Memorial Days, in March and October (sad to think there had been two revolutions, one with such dispiriting results); the May 1st Labor Day; and Hungary National Day in

August. The bar became particularly busy on SUNY reunion weekends; the Professor's old students always made it a point to meet him there, reminisce, and listen to Big Band tunes.

A.C. and Maggie loved listening to the professor's stories of the early years of Oswego, stories told in a voice that was both soft and penetrating; a smooth Perry Como-sounding voice, a voice tender but with an underlying strength; a voice tempered not just by age, but by a lifetime of lecturing. There was something else in that voice as well, LaFleur often felt, especially on those afternoons and evenings when the stories – half-finished stories, usually – drifted back to the war years: the timbre of a remote yet ever present loss.

But whenever pressed too hard about the old times – particularly the days of the war and those just after, the years before he had become a professor and settled into his comfortable, unassuming, professorial life – the professor would firmly change the subject, or maybe even quit talking at all.

And whenever that happened, he'd just tip his head, catch your eyes in his, flash a wry, sad smile and quietly take his leave.

Checkmate

1850 HOUSE

During a game of chess one afternoon, the professor took the opportunity to assure LaFleur that his friend's career hadn't consisted entirely of insignificant cases, as LaFleur sometimes claimed.

"I have observed that you often devalue your professional worth for the time you spent on the force, A.C.," he said at a pause in the action. "I happen to know that you were considered one of the best."

"Where did you ever get that idea?" LaFleur said, as he moved his knight in what he knew was a nearly random fashion. He was simply trying to maintain a presence; Tamos had been ruthless all afternoon, and had an impressive number of white pieces on his side of the board. LaFleur was on the verge of annihilation.

"Let me remind you of the campus safety committee we both served on; I don't remember the exact year; that doesn't matter. In my case, I was fulfilling an obligation sometimes foisted on tenured faculty. You were there representing the police department, as you had been the lead detective on the case being reviewed. I didn't really know you then, but recognized your name on the committee roster immediately, from the time you worked at the Fortnightly Club, years before."

"Yes, and I remembered you too, but you're right, we didn't really know one another then."

"The rape/murder case under review was initially judged by the department and the university administration to be fraternity related, and as such, had been essentially swept under the rug. But based on your preliminary investigation, you were not convinced this was the case."

"No, there were things that didn't look right to me. And they had rushed the investigation, as they often did in those days."

"But you persevered. Now, unfortunately, after all these years, the precise sequence of events isn't entirely clear in my mind. But as I recall you discovered contradictory evidence."

"That's right. Some of the things I'd observed at the scene – later confirmed by pictures taken by a campus newspaper photographer, which had been quietly filed away – pointed to an off-campus perpetrator. One thing in particular led me away from campus; a Redwing boot print. Not the usual preppie footwear in those days, not even in winter. And there had just been a dusting of snow, but the scene around the body was not disturbed the way you would expect. The outline of the body was too concise; no signs of a struggle, and so on."

"Yes, now I remember the boot print. And it led you to a nearby construction camp."

"And to a transient construction worker living in his pickup truck. That's where I found the real evidence – evidence that showed she'd been killed elsewhere and the body dumped on school property."

"Yes. And that is not the only case like that. The other case I remember – we reviewed quite a few police records during that time – was the murder of an elderly couple during an apparent burglary."

"The Barnwells."

"Yes, that was their name. I'd forgotten it. After the case had been put in the inactive file, you discovered that the burglary had been staged, and the murder committed by a long-lost relative in dire financial trouble who was trying to inherit the estate with a forged will. You were the only one who cared about them."

"I used to wait on them during bridge parties at the Club. They always treated me very kindly."

"And you repaid them in the end, as you did the murdered girl. Justice was served, as they say, and entirely due to your efforts. To your exemplary skills as a detective."

"Well, I appreciate the compliment, Prof. But that doesn't change the fact that in the past few years, everything I attempted to do, the three cold cases I jumped into, well, they all ended up inconclusive, or worse. And endangered Maggie, and then Michael, in the process. And letting the Ukrainian, Bondurenko, skip the country; not a great result there, either. No real justice."

"Didn't you once say that justice is where you find it?"

"Sounds like something I might have said, once. Maybe not now, not anymore."

"A.C., you are not making this easy. Let me remind you of something else. You were always known for a rather unconventional approach to your work. A philosophical approach not common to the Oswego Police Department. Something to do with a principle known as 'Occam's Razor,' I believe."

"I'm surprised anyone was paying attention," LaFleur said.

"You were considered something of a savant."

"Okay, now you're going too far."

"Perhaps I am making it sound overly dramatic. Please excuse it as failing of the elderly. Drama increases in inverse proportion to significance as you reach extreme age. Every morning is a revelatory event, every evening a triumph of will."

"It's your move," LaFleur said, trying to change the subject.

"Check."

"Damn. You distracted me with all that talk of my supposed skills as a detective."

"You still have a way out."

"One that will only lead to my ultimate downfall, I'm sure."

"Not necessarily. Not if you get serious and bring some of your analytical skills to bear."

Twenty minutes later it was LaFleur who was able to declare "Checkmate."

"You see?" said Tamos, gleefully. "You *are* a savant."

Rotten Drunk

ALEX'S ON THE WATER

It was a slow midweek night, so LaFleur had taken the opportunity to ask Maggie and their mutual friend Dr. Michael Fuentes to accompany him for a late-night drink at a bar other than the 1850 House; just for a change of scenery, he'd said.

It was an anniversary of sorts; three years ago, to the day, LaFleur had met Maggie at the Oswego Hospital, in Michael's office. That was the day LaFleur had taken on the first case of his retirement. As they walked to the restaurant, Michael reminded him of that meeting. "As I recall," he said to LaFleur, "you weren't too keen on the idea."

"And as *I* recall, Maggie was very persuasive. Something about justice, and all that."

"Oh, you were interested from the beginning," Maggie parried. "You told me later that you had always wondered about that case."

"Well, I don't know about that. It happened forty years ago, after all."

"That day in my office, that was the first time you two met, wasn't it?" asked Michael.

"We were just talking about that," LaFleur replied. "I remember going to the hospital the day the nurse died, back in 1964 – I was still a rookie – and Maggie claims she remembers me, but I don't remember meeting her. Even though she'd also forgotten all about it when we met in your office a couple of years ago, Michael, when you asked me to look into it."

"When Maggie asked you," Michael corrected.

A couple of years earlier, Maggie had decided, after decades of silence, that the time had come to exonerate Angie Frascati, a nurse who had died at the hospital under suspicious circumstances, way back in 1964, as LaFleur had just mentioned. In their meeting with Michael, Maggie had convinced LaFleur to take on a cold case so unlikely to be solved that she had only recently acknowledged that she'd had to rather cleverly orchestrate his involvement. She'd also admitted as well (but only to LaFleur), that she had been the one to post the obituary on Michael's anesthesia machine, piquing *his* interest in the case.

Michael Fuentes had been on the Oswego Hospital staff for almost five years at the time he'd met LaFleur, and they had quickly become friends. Michael was stereotypically tall, dark, and handsome, with brown curly hair (just starting to thin), and a physique like Michael Phelps. That, along with an exotic Latin/Sephardic look, made him (according to LaFleur) irresistible to every nurse at the hospital. Not that it had gained him anything in that department, he sometimes lamented.

"Well, it all worked out," LaFleur said. "Maggie was right, it was time to put it to rest."

The probable killer had been identified and had, albeit indirectly, paid for the crime. More important, the surviving family members were gratified that after all those years, some measure of justice had been served, and Angie's reputation cleared and her memory honored. Maggie's persevering and judicious nature throughout the investigation, even at the risk of her own life, had attracted A.C. then, and that attraction had only grown stronger over time.

It was an easy walk down to the harbor to Alex's on the Water, LaFleur's new competition. But a nice place for all of that.

They had not made it to their table before they were stopped by a loud call.

"LaFleur, you old bastard!"

LaFleur turned around to see a burly, dark-haired man approaching them, waving a drink.

"Ah. Giamatti," LaFleur said. "How are you?"

"God damn it, LaFleur, why aren't you at my party?" He waved in the general direction of the banquet room off to the side. "My retirement party. Why aren't you there? Everybody expected to see you, you know. Just not the same, not without old A.C., right?"

"Was I invited, Bob?" said LaFleur.

"Hell, yes, you were invited. Never got your RVS, uh, RSVP, though. What, too busy to celebrate with an old comrade?"

Maggie and Michael had stepped to the side while this exchange took place, both looking a bit bemused.

"Hey, really, I never got your invitation. I sure would have come if I'd known."

"Ah, LaFleur, don't shit me. Why would you?" He turned to Maggie and Michael. "We never really got along, on the force, LaFleur and me. Did we, A.C.?" He waved his drink at LaFleur. The bantering tone he'd been using shifted to one of drunken surliness. "Oh, no, LaFleur here never had too much use for me, or anybody else, for that matter. Always too good for us, yeah? Always trying to make the rest of us look bad." Giamatti's head wobbled as he looked around. "Pretty nice place, huh, for a slob like me?"

"Listen, Bob, I'm really sorry I didn't know about your party. Why don't you..."

Giamatti turned to face Michael. "You're that doctor, right, that

Spaniard?"

"Part Dominican, not Spanish," Michael said evenly, "but yes, I guess I am 'that doctor.'"

"You and A.C., you did that unofficial investigation, that thing about the dead nurse, the one who died way back in '64."

"Yes, that's right."

Giamatti faced LaFleur. "Didn't work out much better than it did the first time around, did it, A.C.? A real shame old Doctor Montgomery had to die like that, before you could pin anything on him. Sullied your perfect record."

LaFleur dropped his eyes. "Guess so, Bob."

"And then, if that wasn't enough, you had to get in the middle of that arson case. Couldn't let us handle it, oh, no. The great LaFleur had to come in, interfere in an active investigation, one that I was handling just fine, thank you so God damned very much, and you had to screw that one up too. Had half the town on fire before you were done. Even got your own boat burned out from under you. Oh, yeah, that was choice, LaFleur. Quite a performance."

"Listen, Giamatti –"

They were interrupted by a call from outside the banquet room.

"G-man! What the hell are you doing? Get back in here; we're cutting the goddam cake!"

Without another word, Giamatti turned away and went back to his party, closing the banquet room door behind him.

"Well," said Maggie, "what a pleasant man. Why have we never been introduced, A.C.?"

"He's right, you know," said LaFleur.

Maggie and Michael both stared back at him.

"What are you saying? Right? Right about what?"

"I could be a real pain in the ass, back in the day," he said. "I did push pretty hard."

"So, what?" said Maggie, forcefully. "You were the only one really getting anything accomplished."

"Oh, I suppose so. But still. And these unofficial cases I've been involved with over the past few years? Well, they really haven't worked out all that well, have they? No convictions, no real justice. A lot of confusion, no real resolution."

"A.C., that's not true," said Maggie. "You've made a huge difference, in people's lives, for the people affected. I know. I've talked with them. What you've done is to be commended, not condemned. Especially not by someone like him. He's just a drunk."

"Well, drunk or not…oh, I don't know. Maybe." He gestured for them to continue back to their table. "Let's not let Giamatti spoil what can still be a nice evening."

But as he sat down next to Maggie, he leaned in and muttered, "Never again. No more cold cases."

Call 999!

1850 HOUSE

The day it happened, LaFleur and Maggie were in the back room puttering around – doing inventory, reorganizing shelves, making lists: *where did all the tagliatelle go? Did we forget to order the dried porcini again?* Boring but necessary work, and they were glad to have a chance to get it done early in the day, in the middle of a slow afternoon, while they were both amiable and agreeable, rather than forced to do it at eleven at night, as was the usual case, tired, annoyed, and kvetching at one another.

It took some time for them to become aware of the commotion in the outer room. There was a scraping of chairs, a dull thumping of footsteps on the old oak floors, and unintelligible exclamations in several voices. At first, they paid little attention to it – probably just a rowdy group of SUNY students having a late lunch – until they heard the lilting soprano of their day-shift waitress, Imogen, a red-haired, energetic Australian girl who had been stranded in Oswego some months before by an unreliable traveling companion.

"Help!"

By the time they got to the dining room, Imogen had already placed a wad of folded-up napkins under the professor's head, elevated his feet with an old wooden Coca-Cola crate, and was wiping his forehead with a damp cloth, at which indignity he was vehemently complaining, swatting at Imogen's hand while at the same time trying to push himself up off the floor with the other hand, succeeding only in dislodging the cloths under his neck, causing his head to hit the floor with a thud, like an old cabbage.

"Oh, my God," Imogen cried, raising the professor's head back up, firmly placing it back on the napkins. "Oh. Somebody, call emergency, call triple zero, no, what is it here? 999!"

Maggie was already on her knees at the professor's other side, hand on his wrist. After forty years as a nurse, her reaction was automatic. "Lie still, professor. You've had a bad fall." Newton had run over to the Professor's side as soon as he had fallen, and was now watching over the proceedings with some alarm.

The professor kicked the Coca-Cola box away with a screech, alarming Newton even more, and waved his free hand in consternation.

"I'm fine! Let me up!"

LaFleur bent down to look Tamos in the face. "Prof, what happened? Are you sure you're okay?"

"Yes, yes, I'm perfectly fine. Just stumbled, lost my balance." He gave LaFleur an arch look. "It's these crooked old floors, A.C." He gave a short laugh, appeared as if he were trying to stand, and then sat back again, panting with the exertion.

"All right, all right," said LaFleur. From all appearances, the professor was actually okay, but obviously shaken. "Don't try to get up. Just relax a minute. Get your breath back."

LaFleur took Imogen by the arm and pulled her gently on to her feet. "It's '911' here, Imogen, but we might not need to call. "Maggie? What do you think?" he asked.

Maggie was still kneeling next to the professor. "Pulse is strong. Color good. I think he's okay." Maggie released his wrist.

"Tamos?" LaFleur asked. "Are you sure you're okay?"

"Yes, perfectly," he replied, awkwardly pushing himself up off of the floor, and with the help of both Maggie and a nearby chair, standing. "I am perfectly fine."

After helping Tamos to a chair, then sitting Imogen down at the same table, with the cold cloth to *her* forehead, Maggie and LaFleur sat down with them. They had shooed a couple of other customers back to their tables, and things were quiet again.

"What happened, Prof?" asked LaFleur.

The professor leaned forward, accusingly: "Where did *that* come from?" he asked, pointing to the dining room wall.

LaFleur looked over. "Oh, that? I found that back in the storage shed. Don't know exactly what it is, but it's pretty cool looking, isn't it?" He looked at the professor expectedly.

The professor just looked down at the table, shaking his head.

The object hanging on the wall had replaced a matched set of Ford Edsel hubcaps that LaFleur had sold to a collector from Peoria the week before. It was just a random selection from old Joe's collection, filling a blank space on the wall. It was a large piece of sheet metal, obviously old, somewhat corroded – one ragged edge looked as if it had been hammered smooth in the distant past – but it was intact and relatively clean. It was green, or had been at one time, and looked vaguely familiar; mechanical, no doubt, part of a much bigger piece of equipment of some kind, but otherwise unidentifiable. It had a large, red, five-pointed star painted on it.

The professor regained his composure as he sat and rested. A scotch and water was retrieved from the bar by Imogen, now also recovered. LaFleur, Maggie and the professor sat at the table in silence. LaFleur was watching the professor curiously, as if trying to decide what to make of the sudden and dramatic interest in an old piece of junk. Maggie, with a lifelong nurse's sensibility, was up and down out of her chair, hovering, obviously wondering what had caused the sudden collapse, and mentioning that, perhaps, shouldn't we run up to the hospital for a quick checkup?

The professor, for his part, had turned back to the object hanging on the wall, studying it as if it were a famous work of art, noting details of composition, color, and light: the subtle effect of olive green shading into oyster gray at the edges; an afternoon in the park slipping into dusk; narrow bands of dusty white sunlight streaking in from the front window, framing the star from above and below, like old movie premiere spotlights heralding the arrival of something monumental; and the star, mottled, blotchy red, bordered by thin strips of off-white, a bloodstain on an old shirt, a tattered bandage.

"Prof?"

Tamos blinked and looked over at LaFleur, returning to the present.

"What is that thing, anyway?" LaFleur asked.

"Can you take it down?" he replied, ignoring LaFleur's question. "I want to look at it more closely."

"Sure. Hang on a minute." LaFleur went back to the storeroom for a stepstool.

While they were waiting, Maggie asked the professor again if he was sure he was alright. "You look a little pale, Prof," she said. "Can't I just run you up to the ER?"

"No, no, Maggie. I am fine." Failing to keep a shrill note of annoyance out of his voice, he blushed, and immediately apologized. "Forgive me. I realize you are only concerned for my welfare. But I assure you, I really am perfectly fine."

The professor was always old-world polite, never uttering a cross word or a rebuke to anyone, even deservedly. The fact that he let LaFleur and Maggie address him informally as "Prof" was simply an indication of how close he felt to them both, and not something he tolerated from anyone else. The first time one of them had used it, he'd forgotten which one of them started it now, he'd admonished them, saying the only person he'd ever known to be called "Prof" was Alan Turing, and he certainly was no Turing. He'd tried getting them to call him "Tamos," but that hadn't caught on, and they had persisted with "Prof," and he'd gotten used to it, even coming to like it, but only from them.

"I'm sorry for pressing you," said Maggie. "But you let me know if you start to feel any differently."

"Yes, of course, Maggie. Thank you."

At this, LaFleur returned, and climbing up onto the stool, lifted the panel down from the wall and carried it over to the professor's side, leaning it against a chair. "Here you go." He did not ask again what it was, or what interest Tamos had in it; that would be forthcoming, he knew, in the professor's own good time.

The professor stood, and holding on to the top edge of the piece, turned it around to look at the back. It was somewhat more corroded on that side, the paint flaking and dirty. There were some marks in what looked like yellow carpenter's chalk on the upper corner.

"What are these marks?" he asked LaFleur, tipping the piece around to where LaFleur could see it. "I can't make them out."

LaFleur leaned the thing forward and adjusted his glasses. "Let's see…oh, those are Joe's notations. He usually marked his stuff with a date and location, when and where he found it. Don't know why, doesn't really seem to be that important, but that was Joe. Oh, there's also a price, below his notes – I marked that in pencil before I hung it up – twenty-five dollars."

"I don't care about the price – I'll take it, in any case – but what do Joe's notes say? Where did he find it?"

"Well…nineteen seventy-six, or seventy-five. The date's sort of smeared."

"But can you make out *where* he got it?"

"Oh, yeah. Mallard Farm. Sandy Point."

"Ah, yes. I know of it." He looked at LaFleur with a sudden urgency. "Please take me there now," he said, and started towards the door.

A.C. and Maggie looked at one another in alarm.

"Prof! Hold on!"

BOOK II: THE SEARCH

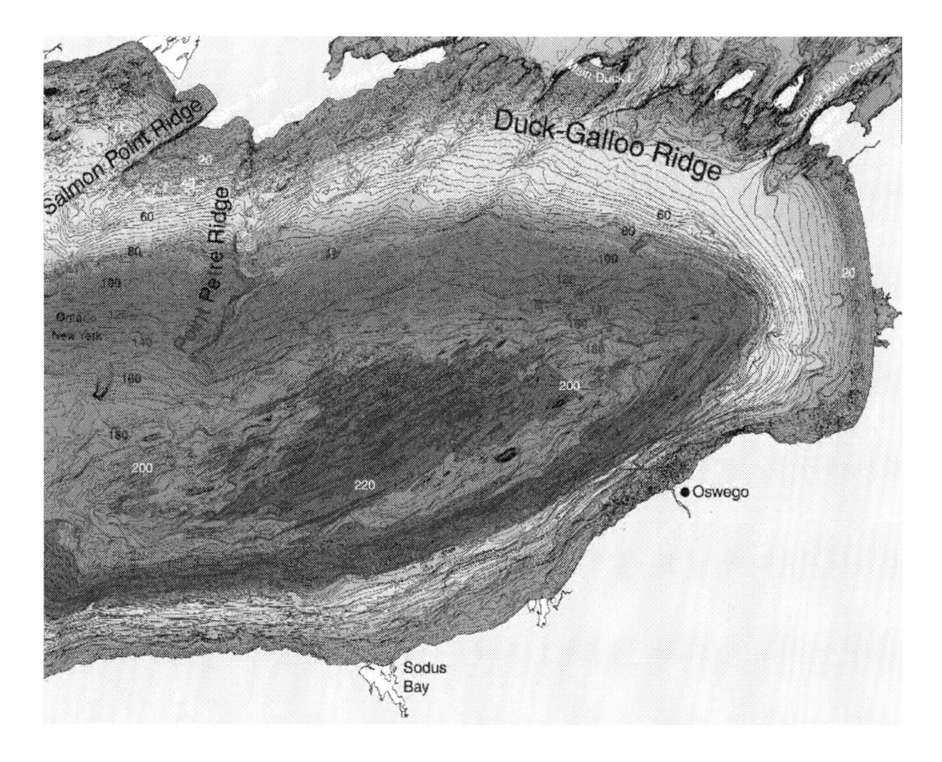

LAKE ONTARIO

Homer's Tale

RENSHAW BAY, LAKE ONTARIO

Lake Ontario is big. It is one of those can't-see-across-it lakes that people from drier, less watery places find nearly incomprehensible. It is just too big to be a lake. One cannot see across an ocean, of course – but a lake? Please! Lake Ontario is so big that it is affected by the earth's rotation, in the form of Coriolis forces. It has currents. And it is deep. Not fjord deep, certainly, but for an inland lake, still deep; eight hundred feet in the center, deep enough that it doesn't freeze solid in winter. An ice age era lake, carved out of soft Silurian rock tens of thousands of years ago, it is big enough that it creates its own localized blizzards – lake effect snow – that can bury Oswego and Pulaski in twenty feet or more of snow in a season, sometimes over six feet in a single day.

On the eastern edge of Lake Ontario, north from Oswego about half-way to a stubby peninsula called Stony Point, is a shoreline lake called Sandy Pond, separated from the main body of Ontario by a thin strip of sand. Sandy Pond is a fairly large lake in itself, or would be anywhere but next to Lake Ontario; large enough to have its own bay, at the north end, Renshaw Bay. It was a small farmhouse at the northern tip of Renshaw Bay that Maggie and Professor Tamos Szabó were on their way to visit.

They were heading north along Highway 3, air conditioning on high. The thick native woods and scrub bordering the road suddenly opened up to mowed fields, farm houses and yards, soon followed by the manicured fairways and carefully planted pines of the Elms Golf Course.

"We're getting close," Tamos said. "Slow down!"

Maggie looked sideways at him, scarcely taking her eyes off the road. Those greens were awfully close to the highway. She wondered how many golf ball damage claims were filed every summer.

"It's still a way up the road, Prof. We'll get there."

Tamos twisted around in his seat, craning his neck like a heron. "That place back there, wasn't that the road house? We need to turn at the roadhouse."

"That was just an old barn. Don't worry, I won't miss it."

The professor settled back into his seat, mollified for the moment, then arched back up as they passed another farm building.

"What was that?"

"Relax! I'll know it when I see it."

"All right, all right."

"We just passed Green Pointe Road. We're almost there." In a couple of minutes, she turned to him and said, "There. Just ahead, on the right. That's the roadhouse." She slowed and turned down Renshaw Bay Road, to the left.

As they passed the roadhouse, Tamos commented, "Used to be a hot little spot in the old days. I could tell you stories…"

Maggie glanced quizzically. "Oh?"

"Before your time, of course," said Tamos. "Remind me sometime to tell you about the time…well, never mind." He looked out the window. "Never mind," he said again, under his breath.

The woods had closed back down close to the road by now, and Maggie slowed, knowing they were close to the lake. And there it was, off to their left.

"Sandy Pond, Prof. We're almost there." They passed a combination marina and trailer park on the left, an open field on the other side. She veered off to the right, onto Parson's Road.

"What is this thing you're interested in, again?" she asked, even though the professor had never explained exactly what it was, or why he was interested in it.

"I've told you, it's just a...a relic, a bit of history. I'm interested in certain…historical artifacts from those years."

"What years?"

"Well, the old days, you know." She didn't.

She turned right, heading along the shore. "Start looking for numbers," she started to say, then realized her mistake. "Almost there, Prof."

They passed by some large, well-tended lots endowed with large, well-tended houses. Maggie slowed as they came to a clearing, where a dirt path broke off to the left, leading into a large open area with three or four old boats lying around, and several outbuildings in various states of dissolution. The Tobacco Road of North Sandy Pond, she couldn't help thinking. No, that wasn't fair. She mustn't pre-judge.

She drove slowly up next to the house, a large, paint-peeling house with a vinyl-sided add-on, a garage, maybe, and a plastic greenhouse tacked on to one side of the large screened porch. It would fit right in to any neighborhood in Oswego and no one would pay it the slightest attention. A large brown dog of no discernible pedigree slouched next to the porch steps like an oversized, overstuffed toy animal. It lifted its head half-heartedly as Maggie slowed to a stop, then dropped back to sleep.

"What was the name again?"

"Saltway. Homer Saltway."

She unbuckled her seat belt and opened her door. "Okay. Let's see what Homer has to say."

The woman peering out through the ragged screen door expressed an unexpected level of astonishment at Maggie's query.

"Homer? You're here to see *Homer*?"

"Yes, we talked with someone yesterday –"

"Homer Saltway," Tamos interjected. "Is he here?"

"Well, yes," the woman said slowly, "but he doesn't get all that many visitors."

"Didn't he tell you we were coming?" The professor's impatience made his voice as shrill as a lake tern's.

At this point, another larger, darker shadow appeared behind the screen. "It's okay, Loretta," a male voice said. "I'm expecting them."

The screen door opened and a large, middle–aged man with a round, benign face stepped out onto the porch. "I'm sorry, folks," he said genially. "We don't get too many visitors, like she said." He turned to Maggie. "Mother-in-law," he murmured, as if an explanation were necessary. "C'mon around back," he invited, gesturing off to his right. "Pop's waiting. I'm Harlan, by the way."

"Glad to meet you," they both replied, shaking hands in turn.

Harlan led them off the porch. "This way."

As they rounded the corner of the house, they got their first unobstructed view of the lake. Tamos faltered a step, then regained himself. Harlan led them to a small patio at the back, where a thin old man sat in an Adirondack chair, looking like an advertisement for a senior retirement home. Lake views, caring staff, all the comforts of home.

"Pop," Harlan said loudly, "these are the folks that called yesterday. About the thing you found in the lake."

The old man sat up, pushed himself to his feet, and stuck out his hand. "Homer Saltway. Glad to meet you."

Tamos reached out eagerly and grasped Homer's hand, pumping it up and down. "Glad to meet you, Homer. Tamos Szabó. I understand you are the lad who found my artifact."

At this the old man laughed loudly. "I ain't been called a 'lad' in longer than I can remember, but yeah, we was just boys when we found it. How'd you come across it, anyway?"

"It was at the 1850 House, in town. Joe Crisifulli, the previous owner, had acquired it at some point, and the current owner – A.C. LaFleur – found it in the storage shed in back of the restaurant. Joe had marked it with the date and place he'd originally bought it." The professor indicated the area around the house with a small wave. "Here, almost twenty years ago."

"Yeah, that's right," Harlan said. "We cleared that old barn out, you probably saw it as you drove in, had a big yard sale. My grandfather had been collecting stuff in there for years. I recall that Joe bought quite a bit of stuff for his place."

"Where exactly did you find it, Mr. Saltway?" Tamos asked, directing the question to Homer.

"Just up there a bit, in the lake."

"Yes, but where, exactly?" Tamos repeated. "It's important."

"Well, can't have been too far up, we wasn't allowed to go off a long way. Me and Teddy, that's my brother; we lost him in Korea, you know." Homer said this in the matter-of-fact way people use when relating a tragedy long reconciled, then continued. "Well, I been thinking about it since you called, and as I remember, we was going along the lake, playing soldiers, most likely, when we saw it out in the water. Ted said we should get it – that's my brother; we lost him in Korea." Homer stopped and looked around, then turned and sat back down in his chair and gazed out at the lake.

"Pop?" Harlan said. Homer continued to stare out across the lake. "Sorry, folks," said Harlan, "he gets this way sometimes."

***

It was the summer of nineteen forty-five. Homer and Teddy were on a secret mission.

They broke through the dense scrub bordering Sandy Pond, swatting aimlessly and without much effect at the shifting, incessant clouds of midges and black flies swarming around them. The heat and humidity was sweltering, and would have slowed even older boys, but at eleven and thirteen, Homer and younger brother Ted were filled with the unbounded energy of the pre-adolescent.

They had on ragged khaki shirts and cut-off denim trousers, with oversized military caps slouched on their heads, discards from a rummage sale; with VE-Day only weeks past, there could very well be a sad story behind such quick cast-offs, but if so, the boys were blessedly unaware of it. Armed with wooden rifles and a sheath knife hanging from a rope belt at Homer's waist, they were intent on capturing the Kraut POWs who'd just escaped from Fort Ontario, and who they knew to be holed up in the abandoned cabin down by the shore. They were on a mission, and nothing would slow them down.

Nothing except a deer fly.

"Yow!"

Homer looked back at Ted, who was slapping wildly at the back of his bare calf, arching back and twisting around in his tracks.

"Ow, ow!"

"What is it?" yelled Homer. "Ambush?"

"Ow," yelled Ted again, a little less desperately. "I think was a G.D. deer fly. Man, that hurts!"

Homer put on his exasperated look, breaking character. "Okay, come on. The lake is right over there." He motioned to Ted to follow him through the edge of the scrub and out onto the nearby beach. Homer had intentionally kept them in the brush to heighten the adventure; walking along the beach would have been much too simple.

"Go on," Homer said, pushing aside some branches for Ted. "Go stick your leg in the water. The cold will stop the stinging."

Homer followed his brother down to the edge of the water, planning the next move. *Too bad Ted has taken a hit; it will slow us down. As soon as Ted is released by the Medical Officer, we can continue the mission.*

"Better?" Homer asked, as Ted waded into the lake.

"Yeah."

"Just stand there a second. Then we'll get going." He turned away, reconnoitering.

"Homer?"

"What?"

"C'mere. I see something."

Homer, anxious to continue down the beach to the cabin, turned towards his brother. "What is it?"

"I don't know. Just c'mere!" Ted repeated. "There's something in the lake, some kind of metal sign or something."

Homer walked to the edge of the water.

"I don't see anything."

"You can't see it from there. It's over by that big rock," pointing.

"Jeez, Ted, we got to get going."

"Just come and look, will ya?"

Reluctantly, Homer went into the water and moved over next to Ted, scanning the lake. "I don't see nothing."

"There," said Ted, still pointing, "right under the edge of that rock. See?"

"Oh, yeah. What is it?"

"I don't know. Let's get it. Follow me." Ted inched his way towards the rock.

Homer was not accustomed to taking orders. "Hold on. We're not supposed to go swimming, remember?"

"This isn't swimming. It's right there!"

That was hard to argue against. And the thing did look pretty interesting. It was large, flat, colored red and green, sort of, as near as he could tell through the reflection of the water. "Okay. Hang on to me." He reached out and put his hand on Ted's shoulder, as Ted did the same to him. "It's not very deep."

They edged out towards the rock, slowly and clumsily, stepping on stones embedded in the sand, holding on to one another for balance. The water soon reached their waists – in Ted's case, nearly his armpits – before they realized that differential refraction had played them false. The thing was deeper than it looked, and was still two or three feet away.

"I don't know," said Homer, assuming the role of the cautious squadron leader. "Maybe we shouldn't –"

"Jeez, Homer, it's right there," said Ted, the devil-may-care would-be hero. "Let's just get it."

They stood there, each rehearsing favored parts gleaned from recent combat newsreels, Homer the responsible NCO, only reluctantly consigning his men to certain death, and Ted, though now starting to shiver, drawn to glory and eager to show up his over-protective squad leader.

"Okay," said Homer. "But we do it my way."

Homer's way turned out to be the only way, really, to do it – on "three" they dived down together and grabbed onto it, pulling it up behind them. The water was colder than they had realized, and by the time they frantically grappled it over onto the beach, they were both gasping for breath.

Even after getting it out of the water, they still weren't sure what it was. It was dull green, nearly four feet long and about three feet wide. There were ragged chunks torn out of it along one side; it had apparently been part of a larger structure. In bright red, inside a thin white circle, was a large five-pointed star.

"Jeez, Homer. What d'ya think it is? A part of a submarine, I bet."

"Nah. Submarines are out in the ocean. No way a sub could get into the lake."

"Yeah, I guess not."

"That star isn't an American star," said Homer, knowingly. "This must be some sort of foreign thing."

They stood shivering, pondering.

"Must be Canadian," Homer finally said. "From an airplane, I think." With some difficulty, he stood it up on end. "See how it looks like part of a wing?"

"Yeah, I guess," agreed Ted. "Pretty neat, whatever it is. What are we gonna do with it?"

"Already got that figured out. This is the new roof of our fort." He wasn't squad leader for nothing.

It took a while to get it home. It was awkward and heavy, and hard to hold on to. They took the old fishing road, avoiding the brush, and even then, it was slow going. Once home, they dragged it to the barn, where Homer hammered out the rough edges on an anvil. Installing it over the dug-out they'd made for the fort took only a few minutes. Once they wrestled it into place, they covered it with some burlap and threw a few branches over it. Crawling inside, they lit their carbide lamp.

In the reflected light, the red star shone down on them like the ceiling of the Sistine Chapel.

***

Harlan gave Maggie and the professor an apologetic look and went to his father, shaking his shoulder gently. "But the big metal plate, Pop, with the star on it? Where did you find it?"

Homer looked up, as if surprised to see them all still there. "Oh, that?" He picked up the story where he had left off. "Just up the shore a bit; up past Cranberry Pond, or maybe in that channel at Colwell Pond, it gets kind of rocky up there. Right around there, anyway. Seem to remember it was kind of rocky. That channel used to be bigger. It wasn't too deep; we just dunked under and got it. Pretty sure that's where it was, there at Colwell. Don't really remember what we did with it. Not surprised it ended up in the old man's barn, though. He never threw away a thing."

"When did you find it?"

"Tell you exactly. Summer of '45. June, July. No, June. That water was *cold*!"

"You're sure? June, 1945?"

"Absolutely. I know because Teddy, that's my brother, well, his birthday is in June."

"Do you know how it got there? Had you ever found anything else like it, or seen or heard anything, say, the year before?" Tamos knew he was grasping for straws here.

"How it got there? It floated in, I guess. Maybe from Canada?"

"And you never found anything else like it?"

"No, nothing."

"Okay, Homer. One more question. Do you remember hearing – or seeing anything else – any time earlier? The winter before, maybe. Like an airplane flying over?"

"An airplane? When?"

"In the fall, in November, nineteen forty-four, the year before."

Homer looked thoughtful. "Well, maybe. Ted, my brother, he thought it was from a submarine, but I told him, no. Now you mention it, I think we *did* see an airplane. Yes."

"Thank you, Homer."

Tamos turned back to Harlan. "Is it possible to get down there, to that spot on the lake?" Tamos asked.

"Oh, sure. Just go back out the highway and turn left; Montario Point Road is the next road you come to, just a few hundred yards, maybe – Montario one way, Clark the other – just take a left on Montario and it'll take you right down to the lake. Lot of fancy houses down there now, but I reckon you might be able to walk out to the beach, if you want."

"God, I hate to see that," Tamos said, as Maggie pulled away from the house.

"What's that, Prof?"

"Homer. Hate to see someone so young lose his mind like that."

"Well, he's not exactly young. If they found it in 1945, when he was, what, twelve, thirteen? He's well over eighty now."

"Well, it's a shame, that's all."

They rode in silence down Montario Road, all the way to the end. Maggie turned onto a small road that turned out to be a short loop taking them back out to Montario. At the professor's urging, she drove back around again, stopping at the north end of the loop, next to the lake. They could see the shore just on the other side of a large house, its back yard edged by a large rock breakwater. Maggie went to the front door. She returned a minute later and came around to Tamos's side of the car, which was sitting there still idling, air conditioner running. He rolled down the window.

"She says it's okay, we can walk over to the point from here." Tamos rolled up the window, then reached over and shut off the engine.

They walked to the beach slowly, Tamos picking out each step carefully on the rocky ground. When they got to the channel, he took Maggie's arm and led her as close to the water as he could manage. With one hand on Maggie's arm, shading his eyes with the other, Tamos looked out over the lake, and south along the shoreline. A few terns flew aimlessly by, their shadows flickering across the shining water; a cloud of gnats hovered in the air close enough for the professor to see them as a hazy, shifting blur. Small waves hit the sand with a muted slap.

"So, she's been right here all along," he said, soft as the breeze.

"What was that, Prof?" Maggie asked.

"Oh, nothing," he said. "I'm ready to go now."

They drove back to Oswego in silence, Maggie wondering all the way what it was all about.

Searching for Gertie

ROCHESTER, NEW YORK

The professor got off the bus at Gleason Circle and looked around nervously, blinking in the late afternoon sun like a startled dove; it was an unusually sunny day for Rochester. He reached into his suit coat pocket and pulled out a pair of oversized sunglasses and slipped them on over his heavy, black-rimmed glasses with a sigh, muttering under his breath. He'd come alone, making two changes on the way down from Oswego, and was pleased that he'd made it without missing any connections.

Seeing that artifact at the 1850 House had more than just shocked and surprised him. It had electrified him, energized him. He'd thought about almost nothing else for nearly two weeks. And he had been making plans. But he was not yet willing to subject himself to the close questioning he knew would come from Maggie and A.C., had he asked Maggie to drive him to Rochester. He'd been having a difficult enough time putting them off after the trip to Sandy Pond; he just wasn't ready to get into it yet. Not before he had the plan in place.

Once he could see more clearly, he quickly regained his composure. Orienting himself based on the directions he'd been given, he moved purposefully from the bus stop down a wide sidewalk towards one of the modern red brick buildings that made up the Rochester Institute of Technology campus. He was heading for the Gosnell Building, center of the RIT College of Applied Science and Technology. The director of the graduate program, Dr. Rodney "Red" Aldridge, had agreed to meet with him, based more on Tamos's reputation than on the sketchy proposal Tamos had described over the phone earlier that week.

The professor adjusted his sunglasses and shifted his small briefcase to the other hand, and repositioned the large cardboard tube he was carrying under his arm. Rolled up in the tube was a large NOAA soundings chart of Lake Ontario – a detailed, four-color, polyconic projection of the area from Clayton to False Ducks Island – covering the section of the lake just north of Sandy Pond, including the Duck-Galloo Ridge.

The director didn't know it yet, but he was going to help the professor make some history.

On first meeting, Tamos couldn't help thinking that Dr. Aldridge looked more like a lumberjack than a senior professor of mechanical engineering.

Large and expansive, with a dense crop of unruly red hair and an equally unruly reddish beard, just touched with gray, Red greeted him warmly. Tamos had been told that Dr. Aldridge was a bit of a maverick, and one of the more popular professors at the college. He had been recommended to Tamos by an ex-colleague who had worked with Aldridge a few years earlier on a project not unlike that which Tamos was about to propose. Known for his willingness to stretch divisional boundaries as much as for his technical and academic capabilities, Tamos had been assured that Aldridge would bring in resources from any department necessary, from imaging to electrical engineering to software development, whatever it took.

"I have to say, Professor Szabó, that you were a little vague on the phone," said Aldridge, as Tamos spread his chart across the desk. "Intriguing, but vague."

"Yes, I apologize. And thank you again, by the way, for agreeing to see me without knowing the whole story, and on such short notice. If you will allow me to first provide some background, I believe the rest of what I have to say will go more easily."

"Okay," said Aldridge, gesturing at the chart. "Tell me what we're looking at here."

"Starting here," Tamos said, reaching out and pointing to Stony Point with a pen he had picked up from the desk, "from this point on the east, out across the lake to Stony Island, then to Galloo Island," tapping the map, "out to Main Duck Island and on to Canada, to Prince Edward Point and Point Petre" (tap, tap, tap) "these islands denote the major elements of the Duck-Galloo Ridge. Near Oswego," he said, as he indicated an area off the map, "in what is called the Rochester Basin, the depths can range down to two hundred feet or more. But up here," pointing again to a spot near Galloo Island, "there is a large shelf that gets shallow gradually, up to the shore and the islands, maybe only twenty feet deep in many places along the shore, down to eighty or a hundred just south of the ridge, here. I have been studying this area for years. The major lake currents run generally counterclockwise, due to Coriolis effect – well, that's not important – anyway, counterclockwise. Closer to shore, in shallower water, currents tend to shift somewhat unpredictably, with changes in temperature, wind, seasonal changes, and so forth. But in general," he said, circling his pointer, "counterclockwise. That is very important."

"And you think there's something down there that we can help you find," said Aldridge.

"Not 'think,' Dr. Aldridge, I *know* it is there. Probably no deeper than one hundred, or one hundred and twenty feet. Maybe, if we are lucky, even shallower, eighty, ninety, maybe even over here near Stony Point. In any case, near the ridge."

Aldridge, apparently not missing the inclusive "we" in the professor's pronouncement, raised a bushy eyebrow. "And if *we* are not lucky?" he asked, with a smile.

"That does not matter," Tamos said, with a quick wave of his hand. "I misspoke. Luck won't enter into it. With your expertise and my direction, we cannot fail to find it."

Aldridge leaned back in his chair. "You haven't told me yet what it is we'll be looking for."

"No, no you are right. I haven't." Tamos put the pen down on the map and took a deep breath.

"It's a long story," he said.

Thirty minutes later, Aldridge led Tamos out of the building and down a wide pathway to the Engineering Center, to visit the lab where the majority of the technical work – if the project came off – would actually be done. He had called a few minutes earlier to confirm that the lab's director, Jamila Sayvetz, was available.

The engineering lab took up several open, interconnected rooms, each filled with a jumble of racks, benches, tables, rolling carts, and bookcases, all covered with an eclectic assortment of equipment and materials: electronic meters; hand tools; stacks of papers and books; instrumentation of various kinds; unusual and unidentifiable mechanical devices; multi-colored coils of insulated wire; overflowing plastic in-boxes; yellow and green tanks, acetylene and oxygen, if he remembered correctly; soldering irons; computer monitors; open cardboard boxes, their contents and packing material spilling out; a small drill press; and the occasional Mountain Dew or Red Bull can nestled in amongst everything. He felt suddenly at home.

Rolling stools with red vinyl seats, dilapidated office chairs – cast-offs from administrative offices, most likely – sat next to the crowded tables and benches, or were shoved into corners, where they were piled high with small crates, boxes, and bubble-pack envelopes. Obviously, a working lab. This was exactly the kind of hands-on, trial-and-error, get-the-job-done place he was looking for. Too many modern applied physics labs, in his experience, were stark, sterile, soulless places, computer labs where all the science was done remotely, complex simulations running on a server farm somewhere, teams of graduate students mining huge datasets searching for validation of some adjunct professor's pet theory or a plausible justification for a grant extension. No, this was more like it; something real. And he already had a good feeling about Aldridge, too. Just the man to head up this type of exploratory venture.

Dr. Aldridge paused as Tamos caught up with him, indicating the open door of a corner office at the back of one of the lab areas. "Let me introduce you to someone else you'll need to convince," he said. "Jamila, you busy?" he asked, leaning in through the doorway.

The woman who swiveled in her chair to greet them was about forty years old, small and dark, dressed all in black – trimly cut jacket and pants, black turtleneck – as compact and neat as Aldridge was large and unruly. She had an air about her – an aura, had Tamos believed in such things – that radiated both a professional competence and an easy confidence. Tamos was enthralled, and immediately trusted her completely. He would find over time that she had this effect on everyone she met.

But she gave Tamos a shock when she stood, held out her hand, and said, "Hello, Professor Szabó. I think you knew my mother."

Tamos shook her hand distractedly, drew back a moment, looked at her intently, and then turned to look at the name plate next to the office door. *Jamila Sayvetz.*

"I'm sorry, I can't place anyone by the name of Sayvetz."

"My mother's maiden name was Weismann," Jamila said, smiling now.

Tamos blinked and turned back to her. "My God. *Weismann.* You are Sarah's daughter? No, no, certainly not! What am I saying? You are Sarah's *granddaughter?* Little Golda's daughter?"

"Yes, that's right."

"Ah, Jamila! Of course! I should have known right away!"

Jamila lightly laughed, a sound like a bell rolling on pebbles in a clear stream, a sound that instantly sent Tamos back seventy-some years, to a hot summer day in the camp when he'd walked with Sarah Weismann along the stone walls of the fort, Golda trailing along behind.

Jamila turned to Aldridge. "Red, Professor Szabó met my grandmother during the war, on the refugee ship on the way to Fort Ontario."

"Well, professor, you're just full of surprises. When was that?"

"August fifth, nineteen forty-four," said Tamos, quietly, naming the date when the train had pulled onto the siding at Fort Ontario.

And now here was Sarah's granddaughter, standing in front of him; proof that life, strange life, endures.

Now, certainly now, the project would go forward.

The professor rolled his chart out on top of Jamila's desk, at her invitation – and only after they had quickly and fervently made plans to meet that evening over dinner to reminisce – as he reviewed what he had already told Dr. Aldridge. Which, if not exactly the whole story, was close enough for his purposes at the moment.

"As I was telling Dr. Aldridge –"

“Please, professor; call me Red,” Aldridge interrupted.

“Yes, Red, thank you,” Tamos said, a bit uneasy at the quick familiarity. Strict Eastern European manners had been inculcated soundly by his father during Tamos’s childhood in Hungary, and he sometimes wondered if the reluctance to let that sensibility go was a subconscious effort to hold on to his parents’ memory. His pre-war memories had become increasingly scattered, it seemed – a consequence of extreme aging, he supposed – and yet once triggered were clear and sharp. It was as if those early events had been carefully catalogued, tagged with images and emotions, ready for retrieval. He had a sudden vision of his father correcting him, mildly but firmly, on the proper way to address one of his father’s visitors, after he had used a too familiar form of address.

“Professor?” asked Jamila. “You were saying?”

“Ah. I’m sorry; I lost my… my train of thought there for a moment. Yes. Well, as I was saying, I know this is a bit outside of my area of expertise; but then so many exciting discoveries are made that way, aren’t they? I have been studying this area for many years, and have no doubt that that certain aspects of the problem have been, well, overlooked is perhaps too strong a word. Misinterpreted? In any case, in spite of my admittedly ‘amateur’ status, I’m quite sure my analysis is correct. Everything I have learned over the past twenty years or so. I know, I know, you might think this is just a hobby of no more use than to fill an old man’s retirement years; however, everything I have learned points to one conclusion. All I lack at this point is the technology to bring my work to fruition. And after all, that is why I came to you.” He paused for breath. “Your record in this department,” he said, waving his hands around the office to take in both professors and the surrounding labs, “is superb. The underwater remotely operated vehicle, that is, the ROV, the project you managed, Dr. Aldridge – Red – that was done in just a few months, as a graduate project, am I right?”

Aldridge nodded agreement as Tamos continued. “And what I am proposing, Jamila, is no more difficult than that, in fact perhaps even less so, as much of the additional equipment we need is readily available. ‘Off–the-shelf,’ I think the term is, yes? As I explained to Dr. Aldridge earlier, using side-sonar technology to scan the area of interest, we should be able to quickly find possible targets, and then follow up with the ROV for further identification. I assume there is no shortage of graduate students to perform the hard labor?” Tamos permitted himself a smile. “But perhaps I am once again getting ahead of myself.” He turned back to the chart covering Jamila’s desk. “I have shown you where I want to search. From Sandy Point to the Duck-Galloo Ridge. Here to here,” he said, marking the chart with his index finger. “But I have not yet told you exactly what it is we will be searching for. I am being melodramatic, I know. An indulgence – I have been waiting for this for so long – well, yes, no excuse. You have been very patient. Before we came over to your office to meet you, Jamila, I told Dr. Aldridge that in addition to making a study of the lake over many years, its prevailing currents, temperature gradients, depths and topography, I have also done extensive research on the many airplanes that have been lost in the lake, particularly those lost in the years 1943 and 1944. I have new information related to one of the most famous of those disappearances, the B-24 Liberator bomber known as *Gertie*, or more exactly, *Getaway Gertie*. She vanished into the lake on February 18, 1944."

Jamila and Dr. Aldridge looked at one another, not quite in alarm. "Really?" they said in unison.

"Really," said Tamos.

Well, not really. But close enough.

The next hour went by quickly as the professor alternately explained, cajoled, and charmed his way to a tentative agreement. There had been more questions than answers, at least initially, until questions diminished and his answers, they admitted, gradually made more and more sense. The use of sonar in locating shipwrecks and other underwater objects – including schools of fish – was fairly common. Aldridge saw no difficulties there. And the professor's knowledge of the area of the lake he was proposing to explore was more than adequate, in Aldridge's opinion. Some issues remained.

Dr. Aldridge was at once the most difficult and the easiest to win over, paradoxically for the same reasons. He had managed the ROV project the professor had mentioned, two years earlier, working closely with a well-known underwater explorer who had been attempting to locate the missing B-24 for years. They had proven the utility of the ROV and in the process, had given the grad students on the project valuable practical and resume-building experience, but had succeeded only in locating two small and previously unknown shipwrecks, important in their own right, but no *Gertie*. He knew the odds, as he emphatically explained. On the other hand, he could not resist the opportunity to try again. He grilled the professor on a couple of details.

"But the reports of *Gertie*'s disappearance – I thought the consensus was that it went down much closer to Oswego, near Nine Mile Point. Surely not as far north as Stony Point, or Galloo Island?"

"Those reports were made very shortly after the crash, I believe. Something about a wingtip found floating offshore?"

"That sounds right."

"And there was a considerable amount of ice around the lake, not unusual at the time of the crash – February is not spring on Lake Ontario – that hindered the search. Which was abandoned relatively quickly, as I understand it. Many competing wartime priorities. And so, not surprisingly, searches in both earlier and later years have only determined 'where it isn't,' to quote a spokesman for the Oswego Marine Foundation. That's where my evidence comes in. As I said earlier in your office, Dr. Aldridge – Jamila, this is new information for you – I have located what I am sure is a piece of the wreckage discovered much farther north, north of Sandy Pond. It was found in the spring of 1945." Here Tamos decided to stretch things slightly. "I have talked with the man who found it – he was just a boy at the time, of course – and he has corroborated other reports made at the time. He was never interviewed previously, apparently, but said that the plane was heard flying over the lake as far north as Galloo Island. In fact, my source goes one better." *Okay, this is stretching it quite a bit; and let's not mention Homer's Alzheimer's here.* "He saw it pass by Sandy Pond, going north."

"He's sure, your witness?"

"Yes, absolutely. And don't forget; I have the piece of wreckage."

"It's been verified? It's definitely from a B-24?"

"Well, that's something we can pursue at some point, certainly," hedged the professor. "If we have the time, of course. Time is racing by. And your students are free to work on this only for a few weeks, I think you told me?"

"Yes, I have two grad students who are somewhat at loose ends at the moment; I'm sure they'll be interested. But we only have until fall semester starts, late August."

"Then we need to get started right away."

Aldridge paused, glancing at Jamila. "There's an old saying, professor, 'Beware an old man in a hurry.' Should we be worried?"

The professor squirmed a bit in his chair, scratched an ear, and tried not to sound nervous at the unexpected question. "No, Dr. Aldridge. Not at all. *You*, actually neither of you," he said, pointing at each of them, "have any cause to worry. No, you have absolutely nothing to fear from me. Others, perhaps, but not you." Realizing he had perhaps said too much, he quickly turned the discussion back to the matter at hand. "Assuming we can work out the remaining details, are we in general agreement?"

"Well, I'm assuming the details can be worked out," said Aldridge. "We haven't discussed funding yet; but I'm in. Definitely in. Jamila?"

Jamila was slightly less circumspect, questioning the professor not so much on the technical aspects of the proposal than on his motives. Which was precisely what he didn't want at this point.

"Well, Professor. What is it about this B-24? Why are you so intent on locating it? You're obviously not just another treasure hunter – at least, I don't think so. But –" She left the rest of the thought unspoken.

"That's rather hard to explain, I'm afraid."

"It seems like an important consideration," insisted Jamila.

The professor's faced flushed pink and screwed up, a painful look, like a newborn baby about to cry. "It's personal," he said, at last. "Can we come back to that?"

"I suppose so. I am very curious, however, so don't expect that the subject will not come up again."

"Thank you. I promise you that all will be made clear at the appropriate time."

It was Jamila's turn to screw up her face, though she did not otherwise express her obvious concern.

"I do have another question, professor."

"Please," said Tamos.

"You must be familiar with the tremendous amount of effort put forth by Caplan Exploration," she said. "What makes you think you have any better chance? Caplan is no slouch, you know. He's very active in this area. Famous, practically. Everyone around here knows he's been looking for *Gertie* for years. Why didn't you go to him with your information? Why come to us?"

Tamos had, in fact, thought about this long and hard. He had been greatly tempted to go to Caplan UW Exploration, Ltd.; they were known to have located a large number of shipwrecks, and more than one airplane, the latest fairly recently, a Canadian trainer of some kind, no, a C-45, if he remembered the reports correctly. And yes, it could not be denied that they were the most prominent group involved in the search for *Gertie,* and perhaps Caplan would have been the logical choice. But the way Jamila had prefaced her question gave him a perfect way to answer.

"As you say, Jamila, Caplan is very qualified, and certainly has put a considerable amount of time into locating the wreck. And I did think of contacting him. But there is something of the treasure hunter about him. He lacks a certain *élan*. But it's not just that. Any venture using a large operation like his would generate a lot of advance publicity, which for many reasons I prefer to avoid." He looked around thoughtfully, as if gathering his thoughts, then turned back to them. "I would say that it has more to do with my, well, call it a 'philosophy of effort.' For an entrepreneur like Caplan, and others like him, the work often comes down to a simple measure of profit plus self-aggrandizement against effort expended. Then if things go badly, the tendency is to simply abandon the effort and go on to the next thing. I have a different philosophy. It is important, for me, personally, especially in this case, that the effort is just that – *personal* – and that the effort expended should have –"

Here he paused again, close to the right words. And then he knew. But would she understand? He thought so.

"What I am trying to say is this: it is not just some measurable amount of work that is important. It is not *just* the trying, or even, for that matter, the ultimate reward of success. There must be something more. There must be, in the effort, some measure of –" He reached out and took Jamila's hand.

"Elegance," he said, quietly. "There should be in all important things an elegance of effort."

Tamos and Jamila, in spite of themselves, and in spite of the professor's earlier cautions, became caught up in the romance of treasure hunting, and began chattering like excited kids at a science fair, their eyes sparkling with possibility. It appeared Jamila had fallen for Tamos quickly. Dr. Aldridge looked on, somewhat bemused. At a break in the conversation, he tactfully brought the conversation back to the still unresolved issues; time, money, and legalities.

"It's getting late. Perhaps we should turn to matters of practicality?"

"Ah. Yes, of course. You mentioned funding."

"That is one concern, yes. At this late stage, it will be difficult to requisition –"

"I am not unaware of the financial pressures facing universities," Tamos uncharacteristically interrupted, holding up a hand. "Even in my time at SUNY, twenty – no, thirty – years ago, things that fell outside of what were considered 'normal' channels were considered undoable. Normal channels being the most mundane, and unproductive; but, in any event, I understand the difficulties. I trust you will be pleased to know that I have already spoken with the dean of Engineering – at the risk of overstepping, I admit – and preliminary arrangements have been made for a grant, something of a "pre-memorial" grant in my name. My good friend and lawyer Lawrence Spiegelman, of Oswego, made the arrangements. The terms allow the College of Engineering immediate access to the funds, which have been pre-approved." He glanced down at a document. "Yes, here it is; 'pre-approved for any experimental or developmental use as determined by specified Senior Faculty, said authorized Faculty to be named at the time of the grant application, in accordance with the wishes of the Grantee,' that's me, 'not to exceed –' Well, it goes on from there. So, we should not have any problems covering expenses."

Jamila leaned forward. "Professor, can you, I mean…well, this could cost a lot."

Tamos raised his hand again. "Jamila, please do not worry. I am an old man, to belabor the obvious." He smiled. "I presume you are not unfamiliar with the phrase, 'the miracle of compounding interest?' I have never been one to live extravagantly. In fact, my colleagues always thought that I lived like a hermit. My needs are few, my life comfortable. And now I have the desire to accomplish something that I hope will have some small measure of significance." He realized he had fallen into his old habit of over-formality, and paused for a breath. "Please, at this point in my life, I can afford to be a little extravagant."

"Well, if you say so. I have to say I'm impressed."

Aldridge, shaking his head, said, "Well, it appears that you have that covered." Tamos nodded in satisfaction. "But there are other issues."

Tamos leaned forward expectantly, guessing what was coming.

"What happens if we actually find it?" Aldridge asked.

"I have already made arrangements," the professor replied, "contingent, of course, on locating the wreck, with one of the more reputable salvage companies operating in the Great Lakes area. They have done this sort of thing many times before. As soon as we locate the wreck, they are prepared to have divers on the scene within one or two days to verify the find. A small platform ship, suitably equipped, can be on site quickly, again within days of verification. We expect to be able to use a relatively simple process, using compressed air lift bags, a technique well suited to raising aircraft in particular. We do not anticipate –"

"Whoa, slow down, Professor!" said Aldridge. "You intend to actually raise it?"

"Yes, of course. What did you think?"

"Well, I guess I thought that once it is located – *if* it is located, that is – it would be reported to the appropriate agency, or agencies, I don't know who exactly, and then, well, that's another question, before we go much further. Who has jurisdiction in a case like this? New York State? Or the Feds? What is the procedure here? Is it just a simple salvage operation, or does this fall under the same laws as old Spanish shipwrecks, you know, the ones found by the treasure hunters you read about."

"No, this won't fall under the same laws as sunken treasure. But there is an extensive set of regulations covering cases like this, federal regulations, in fact. It's all governed by the Navy, these days. Special permits may or may not be required, depending on circumstances. But we don't need to cover all the details right now." He bent over and picked up the small briefcase sitting at his feet. "I have a copy of all of the necessary permit applications here; I'll leave them with you." He opened the case and pulled out a sheaf of papers. "You can go through it all – have your administration check everything over – and let me know if you have any questions."

"These permits, professor," said Jamila, looking with some alarm at the pile of paperwork the professor was pushing across the desk, "were they very difficult to obtain?"

"Ah, well," he said, "the permit requirements *are* extensive, one could say almost daunting. But I've been working on this for some time. And please be assured that Mr. Spiegelman now has everything in hand and all necessary arrangements have been made. Or are in progress; he is fast-tracking any additional authorization I'll need once we raise the wreck. And you will see," he went on, gesturing at the permits Jamila was leafing through, "just as in the financial arrangements, that the University is fully indemnified." He looked over his shoulder in the direction of the hallway. "Excuse me, but is there a restroom nearby? At my age…"

"Of course, professor. Down the hall and to the right." Red pointed the way, and Tamos rose, a bit stiffly – it had turned into a long session – and made his way down the hall.

As he walked away, Jamila turned to Red and held up a page from the pile. "Look at this, Red. The original date on this salvage application is August, 1998. Submitted by L.J. Spiegelman, Attorney at Law, with a mailing address of Temple Adath Yeshurun, Syracuse, New York." She handed the page to Red, looking back down at another sheet, "And this one, the same," she said. She flipped the page and looked at a sheet stapled to the back. "Updated just last month." She shook her head slowly. "It's as if he's been setting this up for years, but using his friend the lawyer as some kind of front man, or something. As if he wanted to remain invisible."

"And now he's willing to 'go public,' in a sense?"

"It seems that way."

"What do you think he's up to? You think it's safe for us to get involved in something like this? Just who is this attorney? And look at this stack of documents. It's amazing, the amount of effort he must have put into this."

Jamila looked up suddenly from the document she had been studying.

"Ah, that's it, Red. That's it exactly. The 'elegance of effort.'" She smiled. "How can we possibly turn him down?"

Sleep Over

ROCHESTER, NEW YORK

Jamila had suggested a restaurant close by campus, a little European café she had come to like, small and quiet, with a simple menu she thought the professor would enjoy, reminiscent of the old country; *rahmschnitzel*, roast duck, goulash. Not quite within walking distance, but close to a bus stop so he could get home easily and early.

As they settled into their chairs after being escorted to a corner table, she could not help exclaiming, "I can't believe it! You knew my grandmother!"

"And I knew your mother, too," he said. "She was, what, only five or six when we came to the camp."

"Five. She told me about her sixth birthday party, in the camp, in December; it was held in the mess hall. She said they couldn't believe how much food there was, that they'd never seen anything like it! 'Three different kinds of cake,' she told me, 'and ice cream, cookies.' And not just on birthdays, she said, there was food like that every day. So much food. And she always mentioned white bread! I guess that was a novelty."

"Yes, for someone coming from Europe, in those days, someone who had never been in the United States, it all must have seemed quite unbelievable."

Jamila look at him curiously. "But you came over with all of them, from Italy, on the *Henry Gibbins*, on the troop ship, right? As a refugee?"

"Well, yes," the professor said, "though I had been living in America before the war. Before America got into the war," he amended.

"But if you were already in America – how did you get to –"

"Good evening," said the waiter, an otherwise attractive young man with a large wooden hoop in one earlobe. "May I get you something to drink before dinner?"

Whether it was the lateness of the hour, the ambiance of the restaurant, Jamila's smile, the excitement of finally arranging the salvage project, or the scotch (probably a combination of all of the above), Tamos became quite talkative, as if he had been waiting for years to tell his story. Which in fact was nearly the case, and though he was fairly well known around Oswego, and known to have had something to do with the refugee camp, no one was too sure, anymore, what that was, exactly. He had outlived all of his fellow adult refugees, those few who had stayed in Oswego, and so was one of the few living representatives of his generation. After he'd retired from SUNY, nearly thirty years ago now, his circle of friends had narrowed to a few casual neighborhood acquaintances, his close friends Larry Spiegelman and his wife, Arlene, and – outside of Maggie and A.C. – almost no one else.

The chance meeting with Jamila had triggered an emotion he had thought long dead: sentiment for the past. Not just sentimental nostalgia, however; he had no patience with the shallow reminiscences so common with the extremely aged. No, this was (he sat there telling himself) something real, something he had been missing in his life for a long time; a direct link to his early life. A past that with Jamila's help he would soon – if all went well – resurrect.

As they waited for their dinners to arrive, he began.

"I came to the United States as a young boy with my parents in 1931, when I was eleven years old. My father could see what was happening in Europe, like many Hungarians of his generation and station in life – he was in the film industry – and yes, he did know Béla Lugosi," he said, smiling, deflecting the inevitable question, then continued. "He was determined to get me away from what he saw – correctly, as it turned out – as the disintegration of Europe. It is surprising how many people lived under a false sense of security; but, then again, it is extremely difficult to abandon everything you know to start over again in a strange place.

"Being somewhat precocious, I had done extremely well in school up to that time; I was currently in a somewhat elite technical preparatory school, you see, and so he was certain I could get a position in a similar school in the US, and then go on to university. We settled in Los Angeles, where my father knew some people who could help with his resettlement. But then the unspeakable happened. My parents were killed in a late-night car crash, on Hollywood Boulevard, of all places. Well, it was a much different city in those days, and not the good old days we'd all like to think." He took a deep breath. "We had been in the United States for barely more than six months."

"Oh, my God." Jamila sipped at her wine. "What happened to you then?"

"Well, my Uncle Béla – a prominent lecturer at a university in Budapest – came to Los Angeles to make all the necessary arrangements following the deaths, and then I returned with him to Hungary."

Jamila sat quietly, not knowing what to say.

"Well," the professor went on, "as you can imagine, I was devastated. But I had always been fond of Uncle Béla, and remember having been very sorry to have had to go to America with my parents, leaving the rest of the family behind. Oh, Béla had assured my father that he and his family would follow, but after my parents' death that never happened. Béla became entrenched in his life at the University, and in the city, and heavily involved in politics, something my father had always strictly avoided. And that is how I became part of a new family. I continued to do extremely well in school –

I believe the trauma had strengthened my resolve – and when it was time to enter University, when I was eighteen, Béla assisted me in returning to the United States and getting admitted to the California Institute of Technology. Even though he himself was determined to stay in Hungary and do what he could to resist the gathering storm, he wanted me away somewhere safe, where I could continue my education. The United States at that time was still accepting a small number of foreign Jews."

Before Tamos could continue, dinner was served, by a waitress who lacked earlobe enhancement but had opted instead for a full-length tattoo on her left arm, a colorful if uncertain depiction of what was (as they discussed after she left) a tribute to either Elvis Presley or Justin Bieber; given the age of the waitress, Jamila guessed the latter. Tamos had never heard of him.

While they ate, the conversation veered back to the ROV project, and how the work would be divided between Aldridge's group of grad students, and Jamila herself, who was going to take on the job of image analysis. Tamos tried to follow Jamila's detailed explanation of how the raw data from the scanning sonar would be processed, but realized quickly that technology had left him far behind.

"Well, I have to admit I understood only about twenty percent of that, but that is why I came to you." He leaned forward. "How soon do you think we can get started?"

"That's really up to Red," she replied. "But I'm pretty sure it won't be long, if the funding is in place as you indicated earlier."

"It is."

Then I say, 'full speed ahead!'"

They finished their dinners in relative silence, making general small talk. By the time the waiter had cleared their plates away, Tamos had settled back into his chair and nodded off, breathing heavily, making an occasional squeaking noise in the back of his throat. Jamila paid the check and then gently nudged Tamos awake.

"Ah," he said, sitting up and looking around owlishly. "I need to get the check."

"Already done, professor."

"Oh, no, I cannot let you do that," he complained, arching his neck and searching in vain for the waiter.

"Professor, please," said Jamila. "Don't worry about it. I'll expense it."

He knew she wouldn't – couldn't, she worked for a university, not a tech startup – but he gave in, saying only that he would not allow it ever again. "Well, then, I should be getting home." He held up his watch and tried to see the time. "Is it very late?" he asked.

"I've already decided, professor, that it is too late for you to catch a bus to Oswego. I'm not even sure they are running at this hour. Probably not.

Even if they were running, you'd be getting back to Oswego much too late. No, you will stay over at my house. I have a very nice guest bedroom I hardly ever get to use."

"Oh, no. I will be fine. Let's check the schedule. Isn't there a bus station close by?"

"Professor, no arguments. You're staying with me tonight. Oh, my, Grandmother Sarah must be turning in her grave, me asking a man over!" They both smiled at this; Jamila hugely, Tamos a bit ruefully. "I have everything you'll need in the morning – well, except clean clothes, but I expect you can manage. Besides, we still have a lot to talk about. We can pick up where you left off in the morning."

The fatigue of the day wrapped itself around him like a cheap, woolen blanket, and he nodded his agreement.

Immediately upon opening his eyes in the morning, Tamos knew instantly where he was. He'd never felt that fleeting uncertainty of time and place that everyone else seemed to suffer when waking up in an unfamiliar place. He suspected it was an ability acquired during his sojourn in Europe during the war.

Small clatterings drifted up the stairway from the room below – Jamila preparing coffee, from the sound of it – pleasant sounds. He turned his head from side to side, loosening up the muscles in his neck, then went into his stretching routine: limbering up one leg at a time, flexing first the toes, then the ankle, the calf, finally the entire leg, until he could feel the circulation stirring. Then he did the same with each arm; fingers, wrists, shoulders. It was a routine he'd started at about age eighty, one that got him up each morning. It not only got the blood running, it confirmed the fact that he'd made it, against all odds, one more day without a major physical failure of some kind. While he stretched, he often closed his eyes and imagined himself at an earlier age, when simple things like getting up in the morning took less motivation. His little wakening routine was, though he seldom thought of it in these terms, life affirming.

Tensing his entire body in one last effort before carefully swinging his legs over the side of the bed, he then levered himself up with his elbows. Sitting at the edge of the bed, he could already smell the coffee.

He'd slept in his underclothes; after a quick glance into the hallway to assure himself that Jamila remained busy downstairs, he padded quietly into the hall bath and splashed a bit of water on his face (ah, hot water – forget art, literature, religion, the rule of law – hot water, that was the true mark of civilization). Awakening was quickly followed by other necessities. He then returned to his room, dressed, and carefully made his way downstairs.

Waiting until the professor finished his last bite of scrambled eggs, Jamila repeated her question of the night before.

"You started to tell me, professor; what happened to you after you returned to the States?"

Tamos sipped at his coffee, swallowed carefully, and continued his story.

"I had just entered Caltech, on an immigrant student visa, a situation which was stressful in itself. I was working as a tutor to supplement the little money my parents had left – that was the only way I could stay in school, stay in the United States, as Béla could not provide for my entire welfare – and the program I had entered was extremely taxing. Do you know of Theodore von Kármán?" Tamos asked.

"The aerospace engineer?"

"Yes, exactly. At the time I was at Caltech, he was the Director of the Guggenheim Aeronautical Laboratories. He also founded Aerojet, an early rocket propulsion company, and later helped create the famous Jet Propulsion Laboratory. I'm impressed that you know of him; many people, even engineers, have forgotten his name, even though well aware of the legacy he left behind."

"I have to admit I don't know that much about him."

"No? Well, he is certainly not as famous as Werner von Braun, say, but his work in rocketry was extremely important. Not to mention supersonics – well, that's not really what I wanted to talk about. The thing is that I was almost certainly in line for a position that would have led to working directly with von Kármán – he was a Hungarian Jew; did you know that? From the same sector of Buda, the hilly side, the west side, where I grew up. I'm sorry, I seem to be drifting. Well, as it turned out, I never got to work with von Kármán, but that came not to matter.

"One day I received a telegram, which in those days, for someone of my position, was an extremely rare event. And this, a telegram from Europe – I knew it had to be something out of the ordinary. And it was: my family in Hungary had been forced to abandon everything and flee to Spain.

"But the worst part of it was that my uncle Béla had gone missing, right after the rest of the family escaped."

"My God, that sounds awful," Jamila said, in a tone that Tamos had heard many times before, when relating this story; a tone of nervous empathy, an awkward note of attempted understanding. This even from someone like Jamila, who had heard many stories like this, he was sure, many times.

"And that leads me to Harry Zook," Tamos continued. "He made the rest of my life possible." Tamos was looking down at the table, his voice a fraction lower, causing Jamila to lean forward to hear. "From the time of my parents' death to this moment, much that I have accomplished I owe to Mr. Harry Zook. He created for me a new life in California. A new beginning.

There are many things – some I cannot talk about –" He glanced up, lowered his head again. "Not yet, in any case." Tamos straightened up in his chair, placed his hands palm down on the table. "Harry Zook was, after Béla, the most remarkable man I have ever known. He was also a Jew, by the way; his parents came to this country in the early twenties. Somewhere along the line their name was Americanized from 'Z-h-u-k' to 'Z-o-o-k.' In any event, he saved the life of my uncle. Well, indirectly, perhaps, but that is a trivial distinction. He made it possible for me to go to Hungary, as a civilian, and in wartime, no less, to find my uncle. Which I did."

Tamos looked up at the clock on the wall. "I have kept you too long, Jamila, after all of the kindness you have shown me. I should go. Can you take me to the bus?"

Jamila looked at him with a slightly shocked look on her face, open mouthed, and asked, in quizzical disbelief, "Are you serious?"

"What do you mean? My dear, you have done more than enough. It is time for me to go."

"But, professor! How did you know Harry Zook?" asks Jamila. "And how did he – how did you – I mean, it sounds fantastic."

"Yes, well, so it was. Fantastic." Tamos looked around Jamila's kitchen, gesturing here and there, as if conjuring up their surroundings on the spot. "Here, for example. How did you end up here, in this lovely house, so comfortable, so settled, so successful? And from virtually nothing; there was nothing in your grandmother's day, as you know, no home, no prospects, no country – no, no, please I understand, I assure you, I am not being facetious when I say this. We, both of us, we come from the most fantastic of beginnings, the most unlikely of circumstances. When I think of how your grandmother, and your mother, how they came to this country – and believe me, they had a much harder time than I had – I sometimes wonder how any of us made it.

"There is something I have come to call 'the chain of chance.' That series of seemingly unrelated, random events that somehow defines everyone's life; every decision, every chance meeting, every accidental encounter, every external influence, the summation of an endless series of such events, each influencing the next. Each day, each moment, leading to the next, and, if you are paying attention, every day, every moment either fulfilling or negating expectations; and if you are not paying attention, each moment sliding imperceptibly into the next. Either way, it all leads here, to a moment, this moment." He paused for a deep breath.

"But what is chance? How random is the universe, really? How do events become forged in the chain, how maintained, how broken? As a scientist, I believe you can appreciate what I see as certain quantum mechanical elements at the heart of our existence." He raised a hand as Jamila seemed about to interrupt. “Oh, I know there have been many ‘new age’ interpretations of quantum theory as related to large scale physical systems. But that’s not exactly what I am talking about here. I see the chain of chance as an algorithmic system, unable to be created by either human or computational means, but something more basic, more elemental. In my more fanciful moments I think of it as the ‘God algorithm.’ Or perhaps from a secular humanist perspective, the ‘algorithm of life.’ A universal, quantum mechanical algorithm that operates at a level far above our understanding; an algorithm comprising all the elements of free will, choice, and chance, perhaps based in quantum entanglement, or some other universal force of which we are currently unaware.”

At this the professor stopped with a sheepish smile. “I let myself get carried away at times.”

“Oh, Professor, not at all. I’m fascinated! It is a little overwhelming, though, all at once.”

“Well, I hope we get the opportunity to discuss these ideas again, soon. In any event, back to what prompted my philosophical outburst. Regarding the project we are embarking on, you and I, and as for my relationship with Harry Zook, well, these are all links in the series of fantastic and wonderful and sometimes terrifying circumstances that led me here. Here to you, and to what I am sure is the final chapter of my life. But that is for another time.”

Jamila could only stare as the professor carefully folded his napkin, pushed back his chair, and stood up, ready to go.

There’s more to this, she thought. Much more.

Aces Up

1850 HOUSE

Oswego, New York, with its admittedly upstate parochialism – considered a mere backwater by many sophisticates in places like New York City or Boston, for example, or even Albany – makes few social demands on its residents, including its professional classes. Most professors make do with one dark suit, one light suit, and two or three differently patterned ties for each, which they wear on alternate days, if they wear a suit at all, or more usually, the standard issue, elbow-patched corduroy sport coat. The only tuxedos in town are owned by the doctors, dentists, lawyers, and bankers who wear them to fund raisers, New Year's Eve parties, and the weddings of one another's sons, daughters, nieces, and nephews.

But neither the blue collar/white collar nature of Oswego, host to many a "town and gown" conflict, nor the equally informal environment at SUNY, Oswego (considered by the aforementioned sophisticates to be a poor relation to the otherwise prestigious State University of New York system) had dimmed Tamos's memories of his father's immaculate formal dress and his mother's no less stunning gowns, when as a young boy he'd seen them off to a ball, or to the splendidly ornate Vígszínház theater – one of the finest in Europe – or to important cinema functions. The Budapest of the nineteen-thirties was a vibrant, cosmopolitan city, and had made a lasting impression.

As a result, Tamos out-dressed nearly everyone in town on a regular basis. Especially on the second Friday of the month: poker night at the 1850 House. This was his theater night, his special event, and he never failed to impress. LaFleur often wondered where the professor kept such a large wardrobe – the professor's house, he knew, was rather small – but hadn't had the temerity to ask.

Tonight, Tamos looked as if he'd just stepped out of an advertisement in a 1938 issue of *Gentlemen's Gazette*: trimly cut black jacket with wide satin lapels, beautifully starched white shirt, with studs and cufflinks, no less, black bow tie, tan vest, black stovepipe pants, and patent leather shoes. The only thing missing was the top hat; even the professor had to draw the line somewhere, if reluctantly. And he never allowed himself to fall out of character while he played. He was like Howard "The Man" Lancey in *The Cincinnati Kid*; he never took off his jacket, never even loosened his collar. The formal persona he put on did not prevent him, however, from telling the occasional joke, sometimes dry and acerbic, as befitted his reserved character, but at other times outrageously corny, the contrast only heightening the effect. He enjoyed it immensely.

LaFleur's poker games were becoming legendary. He'd started them on his houseboat a few years ago, and since he never took a rake, or promoted them for profit, there was never anything illegal about them; at least not according to New York state law, though he had profited from the games significantly over the years, simply by being an extremely proficient poker player. Tamos had learned early on that having a strong hand against A.C. was often a disadvantage. He had never, he often said, seen anyone play a weak hand better than A.C.

The professor had arrived a bit early on this Friday night, around eight-fifteen. Alberto was tending bar – LaFleur brought him in on poker nights and special occasions – and greeted the professor in his Spanglish and heavy, Salvadoran accent.

"Hola, professor, como esta? You win big esta noche, si?"

"Hola, Alberto. How are you? Yes, I'm going to try to win tonight, but you know who we are up against."

"Yes. Señor A.C., he is very hard to beat."

Tamos passed by the bar, tipping his hat to the photo above the jukebox, and made his way to his seat at the table. The table was eight-sided, oak trimmed, covered with dark putting-green felt, with a built-in tray for chips and drinks at each position. LaFleur had had it custom made to replace the old pasteboard card table he'd lost when the houseboat caught fire and sank; this was a definite improvement.

Alberto brought over the only drink the professor would have that night, a scotch "floater" – Frontenac Crystal Springs water over ice, with a shot of Famous Grouse carefully poured on top. Tamos would nurse this for the first hour or so, and then switch to plain water until he left the game at eleven.

By eight-thirty, all of the regular players had arrived.

Michael Fuentes had previously been only an occasional player, attending as often as his hospital schedule allowed. Which given the way his career at the hospital was going lately, was becoming more and more often. Never one to suffer fools gladly (a trait he shared with Tamos), the higher-ups in hospital administration were somewhat intimidated by Michael, if not actually threatened, by his both his work ethic and his competence. The fact that Michael was not in return intimidated by them made him even more dangerous in their eyes. There had been more than a few confrontations during the past year over a variety of issues – policy, pay, equal treatment of staff, medical issues (not to mention his involvement in the publication of a mystery novel that put the hospital in a bad light) – to the extent that Michael often wondered how he had kept his job this long.

Larry Spiegelman made every game without fail. Larry was a slightly built, exceeding good-natured man, always ready with a joke and an invitation to a barbeque on his patio. Larry's history had always intrigued LaFleur. Though they had both grown up lower middle-class in Oswego, they hadn't known one another; Larry was four years older, they'd gone to different schools, and Larry went off to college after graduating. With SAT scores near sixteen hundred, he'd received a full scholarship to Stanford. After getting a degree in English, he went on to Stanford law school, making many contributions to the Stanford Law Review, and graduating top in his class. From there he went into legal aid, which gave him experience in a wide variety of cases, and over time, more and more exposure to local and state agencies. He never lost an appeal. His career ultimately led to a professorship back at Stanford. Reputation growing, he began receiving requests from both governmental and corporate offices to provide opinions in complex and sensitive cases. He also married Arlene along the way. Then Larry had abruptly resigned from teaching, he and Arlene moving back to Oswego. Just needed a change of pace, he'd told LaFleur once. Once back home, he opened a consulting practice. Still quite well connected to powerful figures in all the right places, his services were in high demand, but he took on only those cases that highly interested him.

"Big Frank" Ivanovich turned over the kitchen to his assistants on poker nights; regular customers could tell the difference and stayed away on those occasions. "Big Frank" was called that for a reason; six feet tall and pushing two hundred and thirty pounds, no one messed with Frank. He'd served as a medic in Vietnam, and on his return, had completed a pre-med degree in chemistry on the GI Bill, before changing his mind and going back into government service. He claimed to be ex-CIA – LaFleur suspected NSA, but Frank wasn't saying – and LaFleur had lately come to believe it. Based on Frank's services on past cases, he was sure that Frank's expertise stemmed from one or both agencies, on top of his military experience. LaFleur had come to trust him implicitly, and relied on him for much more than coming up with next week's menu.

Doug Freese, typically the first to show up for every game, was a long-time friend, a retired dentist, famous among those in-the-know for hosting "standing shots" at his home bar, while deer grazed outside the picture window and wife Diane served pretzels. Doug was also one of LaFleur's regular golf partners, proud of the fact that he'd never bought a new ball in his life. Why buy something that everyone just leaves lying around in the weeds waiting to be picked up? he said.

Father Thomas Manetti was the last of the regulars to come in. Known as "Father Tommy" to everyone in Oswego, now retired, was yet another lifesaver, having prevented St. Mary's church from burning down with both him and LaFleur in it. He'd been extremely close to Maggie over the years, and was a frequent dinner guest at the 1850 House upstairs apartment.

As the regulars chatted, catching up on personal circumstances and reviewing the latest breaking news from the Palladium-Times – a car crash in Pulaski, the ups and downs of the local mayoral race, a police slush fund uncovered – LaFleur came in, carrying a small, black case, looking like a cross between an undertaker and a CPA. He took his poker seriously. The case contained a set of professional chips, antique clay composite, beautiful to look at, but even better to hold; heavy and smooth, and perfect to manipulate while pondering a next move. LaFleur had mastered several hand tricks involving flipping, shuffling, and rolling chips, as an aid in concentration, and not coincidentally, a distraction to an opponent.

"Let the games begin," said LaFleur, placing the heavy case on the table, flipping the latches open, and finishing with his traditional opening, "and may the best – or luckiest – man win."

When the professor got home that night, around eleven-fifteen, he placed his winnings, forty-five dollars, in the small drawer in his desk, the one dedicated to his poker fund. He estimated that with this deposit, he was up overall, around two-hundred, he guessed. He didn't keep a close tally; with the stakes they played, no one could win or lose more than fifty or so on any given night, and he kept the fund separate more for convenience than anything else. He was proud of the fact that he hadn't had to replenish the fund for about six months now. Maybe he was finally learning something from LaFleur about playing a weak hand.

Just as he was about to make his way from his office down the narrow hallway to his bedroom, he noticed the message light on the phone blinking. *Never postpone, etc.*, he thought, with some annoyance, as he picked up the phone and punched in the access code.

"Hello, Professor? This is Jamila. I'm going to be in the area tomorrow. Would you mind if I stopped by for a visit? Maybe around noon? I have some papers we need to go over, and some additional information concerning our plans. Please call me back before nine tomorrow morning if that's okay. So, um, hope to hear from you in the morning. Oh, call me at the university, extension 4005. Thanks. Bye."

Ah, good news. The project must be going forward, more quickly than he had hoped.

And besides, he liked Jamila quite a lot.

Tiny House

E. SEVENTH STREET, OSWEGO

Jamila arrived at the professor's house at around twelve-thirty, pulling up in front, perplexed at where to park. The house on E. Seventh St., close to Fort Ontario Park, was tiny – one room wide and maybe four rooms deep, she guessed as she drove by – and fronted the old railroad tunnel that went under Schuyler Street and directly into the park.

The homes in this section of Oswego had been more or less continuously occupied since the mid-eighteen hundreds, many built at the same time as the Fort. The professor's house was one of the more unusual on the block. It was long and narrow, built in 1868, not more than twenty feet wide, about forty feet long, on a stone foundation, wedged in between two larger turn-of-the-century houses. Being alone for so many years, the professor had never had the inclination to move into anything larger. It suited him perfectly; in fact, he liked to boast about having the skinniest house in Oswego.

Jamila turned right onto Schuyler, looking for an alley. No, nothing there, so she went around the block on Eighth, back to Seventh, and passed the house again. Then she noticed the small parking area across Schuyler, on an area directly over the tunnel, which must be for the houses on the other side of Seventh. She pulled in and parked, grabbed her briefcase, got out and walked over to the house.

The professor was, Jamila saw this immediately, ebullient (a word she had never used, but which instantly sprang to her mind) at her arrival. She was, of course, glad to get an enthusiastic reception, but at the same time somewhat overwhelmed.

"Jamila! Please come in!" Tamos held open the storm door and ushered her onto the small airlock entrance – a necessity in upstate New York – then followed her into the living room, the first room in the house. "I'm so glad you are here," he said, gesturing for her to continue through a small arched doorway, "Please, come into my office."

The office was a small room – in this house, it had to be small – just to the right, across from what Jamila could see was a small bathroom. She glanced down the hallway and saw a door leading into another room – the bedroom? – and a narrow kitchen at the back.

The office was just large enough for a desk – an unusually large desk, given the size of the room – and two filing cabinets in one corner. The desk was ornamented with stacks of books, collections of papers, piles of magazines, sheaves of bills and receipts bundled or clipped together, mostly, some scattered about, and, of course, the chart.

"I would ask you to sit, but, well, obviously I have only the single chair – wait, I have a small stool in the kitchen. Excuse me one moment." The professor hurried out of the room and was back with the stool before Jamila had a chance to demur. He placed the stool at the corner of the desk, carefully made his way around it and Jamila to the front of the desk, shuffling and side-stepping in a way that reminded Jamila of Buster Keaton and she had to laugh.

"Oh, professor," she said, "What a marvelous little place you have here!" As he finally made it to his chair and sat down, she put her hand to her mouth in sudden consternation. *Was that rude*?

Tamos beamed, obviously not offended. "Thank you! You know, I read the other day about this new movement, the 'tiny house' movement, or something like that, people living in very small, yet very cleverly designed houses, some not more than three or four hundred square feet. Well, this house is bigger than that, almost six hundred, and of course there is the basement, but in any case, it is all I need. I have lived here for over sixty years now; can you believe that?"

Lowering herself onto the stool, Jamila could not help exclaiming. "That is remarkable! I have been in my house nearly twenty, and I thought *that* was a long time."

"Well, you know, when you get to my age, twenty years is nothing. It goes by like that." He snapped his fingers, or at least made the motion, but papery skin and arthritic fingers don't make much of a snapping noise. "I am sorry I missed you when I called this morning and left my return message. What brings you to Oswego, if I may ask?"

"A visit to a colleague, Dr. Prakesh in the physics department. After our meeting at RIT last week, I started thinking about possible directions we might go – in addition to sonar – and thought of him. He specializes in magnetometry. That sounds like something that could be useful when searching for a large metallic object. Actually, as it turns out, his work uses something called a vibrating sample magnetometer, used primarily in the lab for thin-film research. Still, he was very helpful; he said there are magnetometers that can be used for large scale archeological use, and, specifically, in *marine* archeology. He gave me some names to follow up on in case we need something more than the sonar."

She paused. "Actually, there is more to it than that. My friend is thinking of creating a new program in the department, and has asked if I would be interested in heading it up. Nothing definite, yet, of course, but it looks promising." She smiled and cocked her head. "But it was also an excuse to come here to see you."

"Ah, now, don't make me blush," he said.

"No, actually," she said, "I do have some news from Red concerning the project. I thought it would be good to discuss the next steps in person. And besides," she said, giving him a deliberately provocative look, "you never finished telling me about Harry Zook."

"An ulterior motive!" said Tamos. "I like that."

At this, Jamila actually did blush, but countered, "Can you blame me?"

Tamos smiled. "Of course not. I did set you up, I admit. But first, the project. Then I will bore you with my personal history."

At this, Jamila reached down and brought up her briefcase, which she had propped against the legs of the stool. "Okay. Bureaucratic necessities first, she said, opening the case and pulling out a handful of documents. "Administrative authorizations, academic credit approvals – these are just copies for your records – can't expect the students to do anything that doesn't inch them toward graduation. Uh, let's see, insurance waivers, mandatory University privacy and diversity guidelines – you'll need to sign those – yes, I know, things have changed," she said, noticing his inquisitive look.

Tamos reached out and took the documents, nodding in approval. "Marvelous, Jamila. We can get all of this taken care of this afternoon. I want to be out on that boat as soon as the ink is dry. Or sooner."

Jamila graced the professor with another of her bell-like laughs. "I hope we can keep up with you."

"You will manage," Tamos said. "But don't think I'm going to be easy on you."

"Oh, don't worry. We're used to dealing with graduate students, remember. That should prepare us for anything. Well, almost anything; that generation seems to be a lot more casual about things then we are, so they can be a bit unpredictable at times."

"I suppose so. Well," he said, laying the documents down on the desk, "what else do you have for me?" he asked. "You said earlier – implied, rather – that you have additional information? Perhaps regarding technical aspects of the project?"

"Yes, certainly. But, professor, before we get into that, please: what about your life in California, during the war?" She was determined not to let him get away this time without telling her the story he had started at her breakfast table the week before.

Tamos glanced at his watch.

"Are you hungry?" he asked.

Jamila blinked at the sudden diversion. "Um, sure, I guess so. What do you have in mind?"

"Follow me," he said, pushing himself up off of the desk. "It's time you met my friend A.C. LaFleur."

"Oh?" she said, following as instructed, as he walked to the front door.

"Yes," he said, holding open the door for her. "He doesn't know it yet, but A.C. is going to be helping us out with our little venture." He closed the door behind them and walked purposefully down the steps to the street. "This way," gesturing to his left.

"Shall I go get my car?" Jamila asked.

"Oh, no, that is not necessary. It is only a few blocks. Right next to Kim's, where I send my laundry. We can easily walk. The restaurant is called the 1850 House. The chef there, Frank, makes a tomato-basil bisque that is – to use a word that has completely lost its original sense of wonder – awesome."

The bisque was as good as promised, thick and spicy, complimented with a lump of Maytag blue cheese floating in the center, and a small *bruschetta pomodoro* on the side. Frank knew his stuff.

A.C. had waved hello from across the room as the professor and Jamila sat down, busy with another customer. One of the reasons – aside from the food – that people came to the 1850 House was the near certainty of getting personal attention from A.C.; or if not A.C., then Maggie. It was an open question as to which of the two hosts was the more popular, a question often discussed good-naturedly over a late-night Limoncello. Maggie claimed to regard this private competition as pointless and infantile, but was secretly determined to lay claim to the title; she was devising a small leaflet, to be distributed to guests along with the check – much like the surveys so popular in chain restaurants – but with a twist: it was essentially going to be a ballot, the questions cleverly phrased so as to not give away the true intent, which she planned to use as proof that she was indisputably the main draw, and A.C. a mere hanger-on. She expected that this would enliven bedtime conversations, with the additional expectation that this could also stimulate post-debate activities.

As it happened, Tamos and Jamila hit the exacta (first and second place still undetermined), as both A.C. and Maggie were on duty today, and came over to their table just as Imogen was taking their orders.

"Professor," said A.C., reaching out to shake Tamos's hand, "Welcome."

"Hello, Prof," said Maggie, with a slight bow. "May we join you and your guest?"

"Of course!" said Tamos, turning to Jamila with a flourish. "Please meet Dr. Jamila Sayvetz, a colleague of mine from the physics department at RIT. Well, a new colleague, to be sure, but already a collaborator, shall we say?" He smiled as Jamila looked down with some embarrassment, still not quite sure of how to take the professor's formal, if exuberant, ways. "Jamila," he said as A.C. and Maggie seated themselves, "may I introduce you to the owners of this fine establishment, Mr. A.C. LaFleur and Ms. Maggie Malone. Oswego fine dining has not been the same since they took over the operation of the 1850 House."

Maggie and A.C. both managed to look at once gratified and dismissive of the compliment, murmuring thanks.

"What brings you to Oswego, Dr. Sayvetz?" asked Maggie.

"Call me Jamila, please," she replied. "And hasn't the professor told you about the wreck?"

The lunch crowd at the 1850 House had been slow in clearing, and LaFleur and Maggie had been busy alternately excusing themselves to tend to customers, and so the story of the professor's project came to them in bits and pieces, one hearing one aspect, the other picking up another detail, giving them only a vague idea of what the professor was planning.

Jamila, for her part, realized on the walk back to his house that the professor had once more eluded her concerning the legendary, life-saving Harry Zook. She'd been hesitant to bring it up earlier, on the walk to the restaurant, and they hadn't talked much on the way back to the professor's house. He seemed distracted, and she didn't want to press him too hard. Still, she thought, it can't hurt to bring it up again.

In the event, the professor beat her to it.

"Well, Jamila," he said, "you have been anxious to hear my life story."

"Not exactly anxious, Professor," replied Jamila. "Just, well, perplexed, I guess. You did sort of leave me hanging."

By this time, they had reached the house. The professor led her up the stairs and opened the door. "Yes," he said, "and I apologize. It is not something I talk about much anymore, you see. Until now, there has been no need. I've not even told A.C. very much. Oh, he knows some of my history, generally, but nothing really, well, significant. How I came to Oswego. Why I stayed."

Tamos paused as the door closed behind them, a sigh expressing a willingness, but mixed with resignation – no, not resignation – resolve. It was time. He motioned her to a couch near the front window, while he made his way to a large overstuffed chair.

"It has to do with airplanes." He settled deeply into the chair. "Speaking of airplanes, what else do you have for me from Dr. Aldridge?"

Jamila gave an inward shrug and reached for her briefcase, wondering why the sudden shift. "He's put together an outline describing the ROV and side-scanning sonar – actually, his grad students have put this information together – so you'll be familiar with both the capabilities and the limitations of the particular equipment we'll be using. Red, of course, realizes you are pretty well-versed in the general aspects of what we'll be doing, but wanted to make sure you know exactly what we have available for this project. They've included spec sheets, process descriptions, and a general timeline.

"One of the students is working on a project management track, so we have a detailed schedule. With any luck, we won't need as much time as has been allocated, but you never know. I'm a big fan of pessimistic budgeting, and we want to try to bring this in as cheaply as possible, certainly." Tamos waved his hand dismissively. "Well, we are also under some time constraints; we only have our student labor force for a few weeks. Along with the technical and project information, I've provided an overview of the data processing side of things. You can read through it and call me with any questions."

Jamila waited expectantly for him to get back to his story. *Airplanes?* When nothing more was immediately forthcoming, she closed her briefcase and placed it on her lap.

"Well, do you have anything more? You said it had to do with airplanes?" she asked, trying not to sound plaintive.

"Oh, you mean, Europe? All that? Well, it gets very involved. Are you sure you have time?"

"Professor, right now I have nothing but time." She lowered her head, suddenly contrite. "I mean, if you are up to it, that is."

"Of course. Well, to begin with, I had to get to Europe in order to find Béla. Portugal was nominally neutral, so the path to Europe lay through Lisbon. From Lisbon, I was to be guided, as it were, by contacts made for me through the American Jewish Joint Distribution Committee, more commonly known as 'JDC,' which was headquartered in Lisbon at that time. My first stop after Lisbon was Barcelona, where I met with my aunt briefly before making my way to Hungary. That took nearly two weeks, constantly on the move. Then once in Hungary –"

"But, professor," Jamila interrupted, "how did you get to Lisbon in the first place? That must not have been easy."

"Well, again it was Harry Zook who made it possible. He was an entertainment lawyer, with many famous clients in New York and Hollywood, and managed somehow to get me attached to a USO troupe going to Europe via Lisbon, Portugal, on the Pan Am Clipper.

"And that's a story in itself."

***

On a fine spring day in nineteen forty-four, Tamos, after three days on the train, arrived in New York to a strange vision: huge yellow flying fish leapt between tall, pointy blue waves, one after the other. Wrapped completely around the top of the building, they formed a long unbroken stream. A bit disconcerting this early in the morning. On reflection, Tamos had to admit it was an enchanting, and appropriate, tile decoration for the new LaGuardia Marine Air Terminal.

The second thing that caught his eye was the large, black-rimmed clock sitting above the entrance: OFFICIAL AIRPORT TIME, it announced authoritatively. Tamos glanced at his watch, chagrined to find it four minutes slow. An equally commanding designation bounded the clock on both sides, in tall, black letters: ALL AIRPORT OPERATIONS.

Trying to shake off the jitters, he turned and walked quickly through two large, brightly polished, stainless steel doors into the terminal, only to be overwhelmed yet again. The room, an expansive rotunda, was lit by a huge, multi-tiered skylight, now glowing in the morning sunlight. Brightly colored murals lined the outer walls. The service desk encircled a series of desks and cabinets, with a magnificent globe, perched high on a wooden pedestal in the center of the room.

As Tamos stood there looking around, semi-dazed, still getting his bearings, a uniformed Pan Am representative approached him.

"May I be of help, sir?" she asked.

"Oh, yes, please," Tamos said, relief obvious in his voice. "My name is Tamos Szabó. I'm here to meet Miss Jo Norman. I am accompanying her, to, to..."

"To Lisbon," the agent completed for him. "Yes, of course. Your party has gathered in the restaurant. You have some time yet before boarding. Please come to over to the desk; we'll take your bag and get your paperwork out of the way. Your colleague, a Mr. Zook, I believe...?" Tamos nodded. "...has taken care of nearly everything. Just a few remaining details. Once that's done, I'll show you to the lounge."

"Mr. Szabó! Welcome! I'm Jo Norman."

The warmth of the famous band singer's greeting succeeded in putting Tamos at ease for the first time since he'd left Los Angeles. That, along with a cup of hot, black coffee and a large doughnut, made him begin to feel this might work out after all.

Jo was seated at a small table, alone, to his surprise; the agent had said his "group" was waiting in the lounge. She was very pretty, of course; he'd expected that, but the way she was dressed! She looked like she was on her way to a fancy-dress ball, not about to embark on a long overseas journey.

Dark brunette hair coiled out from under a large, black velvet hat, a big bow on top. Her gown was also black, probably not velvet, but something soft – Tamos knew nothing about fashion – draped with a thin cape of dark fur, matching the color of her hair, all accented by a large striped bow at her neck, and an immense red corsage covering one lapel.

"Harry was *so* mysterious when I met with him in Los Angeles," Jo gushed. "I had to practically swear an oath on my mother's grave that I would not give away any details of your little plan. Not that I actually *know* any details," she added, probing.

He was spared a clumsy answer by a call from someone across the room, another classily dressed woman, another performer, he guessed. "Jo! We're ready for the photos!"

"Please excuse me, Mr. Szabó," Jo said, standing quickly. "Publicity photos. Everyone is excited about this tour – Pan Am, the Army, radio sponsors, everyone wants some promotional material. Be right back." As she made her way to the back of the room, Tamos allowed himself a very theatrical sigh of relief. *This might even be fun.*

As soon as the photo session concluded, everyone gathered in the lounge, where Tamos was duly introduced to the rest of the troupe as "Miss Norman's personal assistant," a job description just coming into vogue. He did his best to act the part. Even though Harry had coached him before he'd left for New York, he was still uncertain about what, exactly, would be expected of him. Since he was leaving the group soon after arriving in Lisbon, he supposed he shouldn't worry too much about it. Jo took him to one side and assured him (discretely) that she would take care of everything while they were *en route*, and that she considered shepherding him to Europe to be just another small, patriotic act on her part.

Nothing had prepared him for the scale of the Clipper. Emerging out of the shadows of the short tunnel leading from the main terminal to the dock, blinking in the sunlight, he nearly bumped into Jo.

"Wow," she said. "Look at that, will ya?"

He stopped next to her and shaded his eyes, peering out to the end of the long floating pier that led to the ship. They'd had a brief look at it earlier, of course, from the terminal windows. But approaching it, out here in the open air, it appeared much larger. It loomed, a floating fortress, displaying a true military bearing in its new camouflage paint and large American flag, painted on the nose. Tamos felt a sudden, gripping certainty that something that big could never get into the air. Glancing back for perspective, he saw that its wingspan stretched nearly as wide as the terminal building itself; one hundred and fifty-two feet, he'd be informed later. Almost fifty percent longer than its length. The tenders plying along the sides, and the men loading cargo and supplies, looked like toys. The four engines embedded in the leading edge of the wings appeared ridiculously small, certainly too small to carry a behemoth like this. As he got nearer, he could see the sharp, knifelike bow, an echo of the sea-going clipper ships of the previous century.

"Come on, Tamos," Jo urged. "Let's get onboard!" She turned and headed down the dock.

Trying not to be overwhelmed, Tamos marched boldly alongside the rest of the group, who were now laughing and joking, still dressed in their publicity finest, on parade. They all must be giddy with fear to carry on like this, Tamos thought, then immediately regretted the uncharitable thought. They are all embarking on a journey no less dangerous than mine, he reminded himself.

An attendant took his elbow. Tamos unconsciously shied away from too close a physical contact; the money belt Harry had provided felt as if it were two feet thick. Tamos had been reluctant to take it at first, but Harry quickly convinced him that, especially in this situation, money does indeed talk and would more than likely save his life more than once. Engirdled with US dollars, Portuguese escudos, Spanish pesetas, Hungarian pengős (where on earth had he procured those?), and three varieties of gold coin, he moved to the ramp, and without another glance back, walked onto the flying boat and into an uncertain future.

The flight had been the marvel of technology and luxury that Harry had promised. The interior of the plane was more like an oversized train carriage, with a series of large compartments on either side, a large companionway running down the center. Each compartment converted at night into a two-berth sleeping room. Near the front was a large, formal dining area which also served as a lounge. It was like traveling in a private railway car, somehow transported into the air.

And now the lights of Lisbon shimmered dimly in the twilit haze as the Clipper crossed the narrow mouth of the Targus River leading to the sea. The weather was calm, the river smooth and shining. The larger harbor, actually just a widening of the river, opened up below them. A hostess passing by Tamos's seat pointed out the string of lights marking the landing site just off Cabo Ruivo, on the west bank, a dark red lamp at the northern end. As the plane began to bank down and to the left, Tamos rehearsed in his mind the next steps, the crucial steps that would get him from Portugal to Barcelona.

The plane banked steeply – more steeply than Tamos remembered from the last landing at the island of Horta. He glanced around nervously, but no one else seemed to be alarmed. At least, not until a cry was heard from the other side of the aisle: "We're on fire!"

As sounds of general alarm echoed throughout cabin, the huge craft leveled, then tilted again. Out of his window Tamos could see the wing dipping quickly towards the water. For the briefest of moments, he marveled at the beauty of the flume suddenly emanating from the wingtip as it grazed the silver surface of the river.

A shudder went through the entire airplane as the wing dug deeper into the river, and then Tamos was jerked violently forward. His seat belt held him dangling in the air, looking down and out at the passageway. His flying companion in the row across from Tamos, the band leader, had not had his seat belt buckled and was thrown from his seat, his body crashing into the wall now beneath them. The hostess he had seen pass by so calmly only moments before flew through the air, screaming. Her head hit the side of the compartment divider with a hollow thud, splattering Tamos with blood. As the plane lurched, she crashed into the bulkhead of the compartment, crumpled, broken. His mind reflexively, perversely, brought forward the image of the rag doll that his younger niece had played with on the stairway of the family home in Budapest, sliding it down the oaken banister, letting it fall to the floor, laughing.

Then the plane shook again, even more violently than before, the noise deafening. Tamos was thrown sideways as his seat broke away from its mounting and he slammed into the compartment wall, still slick with the blood of the hostess, whose name he could not at that instant recall.

He would never quite know how he got out of the airplane. Later, all he could recall of the minutes immediately following the crash were vague impressions of water, smoke, and an eerie silence punctuated by strange, unidentifiable noises.

Barely conscious, he floated in the dark water, clinging to some bit of debris, until he lost his grip. He floundered, somehow found another bit to grasp onto, a bigger chunk, part of a seat, he dimly thought. *My seat.*

He wiped something wet from his eyes, water, or oil, or blood. He slowly began to understand what had happened. The wingtip – he'd seen it graze the water. Then time had slowed. When the wing dug deep into the water, he had been wrenched violently forward in his seat, doubled over, held back by his seatbelt. He hadn't screamed (at least he thought not). Others did scream as they were thrown from their seats, or were wrenched crookedly in their seats as he had been, twisted, battered by objects hurtling through the cabin as the ship cart-wheeled on the river.

Sounds of the airplane tearing itself apart.

Screams, certainly. His among them, he now recalled.

The hostess, when she hit his compartment wall, had not screamed. Her name was Dorothy, he remembered now. He had tried to call her name out then but could not.

Now he was here, alone in the water.

He pulled himself a few inches above the surface of the river. Documents were scattered about on the water and floated serenely by, limp paper boats. Lumps of unidentifiable stuff bobbed all around.

There, to his left. A hulking shape. The great flying boat, half submerged. He dragged a wrist across his face, across his eyes, clearing his vision.

The Clipper disappeared in a rush of boiling water. A few black eddies whirled to mark its passage. The river flattened once more into slate.

He heard cries. Cries for help. *I should call for help.* "Help" eked out of his throat, more like a murmur than a cry, and he tried again, tried to make it louder, gagged and sank back into the oily water.

A boat appeared. A small speedboat, teakwood hull gleaming in the fading light. There were two men on the boat, fishing things out of the water with long poles. He watched in dumb incomprehension as one of the men gaffed a leather mailbag and pulled it up into the boat, while the person floating next to it sank beneath the water.

"Help," he managed to cry, this time loudly enough for one of the boatmen to turn to him. He looked oddly foreign, not the Portuguese look Tamos expected to see. Small, with sallow brown skin, squinting eyes. He heard him speak to the other man on the boat. Definitely not Portuguese. Tamos listened intently as the men chattered in a high sing-song as the boat approached.

"Help me," he managed again.

The men looked down, turned away. Then the boat began to move away, slowly. *They are not going to save me.*

Recognition burst like a bright flame. *Japanese.*

He called out one of the few Japanese words he knew. He could not have said where or when he had learned it.

"Kudasai!"

Please.

Perhaps it was the shock of hearing one's own language, in such a lonesome place so far from the homeland, that sparked the men in the boat to action. Perhaps that one word had kindled some small measure of compassion. It was a momentary lapse, as it happened, for they rescued no other passenger that night.

One of the men reached down.

Tamos felt himself rise from the water.

"Kudasai," he mumbled. "Kudasai, kudasai."

Dazed and bleeding, Tamos had been left on the Cabo Ruivo pier, alone, as his mysterious saviors fled in a long, black car. One of the Lisbon-based Pan Am ground crew assigned to the rescue operation had found him there, sitting on a dock post.

He was taken initially to a local hospital. There, he was treated for shock, his minor cuts and scrapes bandaged, and after a visit with a Red Cross nurse, released to the care of a Pan Am representative.

A radiotelephone link had been set up with the State Department in Washington, as well as with Pan Am headquarters in New York City, but it was seemingly a matter of pure chance whether or not a connection was made, and chancier yet if that connection would hold up long enough to connect with someone else. By this time, it was almost dawn in Lisbon, therefore eleven P.M. in New York, so of course it was impossible to contact anyone. After two hours of futile attempts to reach anyone, Tamos had to settle for leaving a message with both the State Department and Pan American.

Now without papers (but money belt still intact), and with ill-fitting, donated clothes, Tamos was delivered by the Army Air Corps to the office of the American Jewish Joint Distribution Committee. This had all happened not quite as Harry Zook had envisioned it, but here he was all the same.

The aide-de-camp who had taken charge of Tamos filled him in on what he knew on the way to the JDC offices. Many people had died in the crash, at least twenty, he thought. Jo Norman had been severely injured, rescued from the wreck by either the co-pilot or another passenger, it was not clear. The pilot was still missing and presumed dead. That's about all the aide knew. The fate of the others he'd traveled with Tamos would not learn for many months.

"Who rescued me?" he asked, when no more information from the driver appeared to be forthcoming.

"From what you told me? I'd guess goddamn Jap spies."

Tamos looked at the aide blankly, suspecting some sort of sick joke.

"No, really. What happened to me?"

"Listen. The Japs have been operating here for about two years. No doubt they were trying to intercept classified documents."

Tamos could only shake his head, barely understanding.

"Yep. Jap spies. It's a fucking wonder they pulled you in."

The Jeep rounded a corner and the driver slammed on the brakes. "Whoa! Here we are." He backed up to the curb in front of an exceedingly unprepossessing office block. "This is the JDC office."

Tamos sat and looked around, unmoving, not quite ready to continue on.

Things had been moving around him at a terrific rate, and he was still quite unsteady.

"I was told they're expecting you," the officer said as he came around to help Tamos out of the Jeep. "Good luck and Godspeed."

Tamos shook the aide's outstretched hand. "And to you," he managed.

The Jeep pulled away as Tamos stood on the sidewalk, marveling at his deliverance.

A broken link in the long chain of chance, reforged.

***

He had talked nonstop for nearly twenty minutes, editing some details along the way, Jamila all the while enthralled and afraid to interrupt for even a moment.

"So, that is part of the story I had promised you earlier," the professor said. "But now, please forgive me. I'm a bit tired." Tamos's voice trailed off sharply, as if the shock and fatigue of that remote day in the past had resurfaced.

Jamila sat quietly, eyes a bit wide, not quite sure of what to say. This was all so...astounding.

"Professor," she finally managed. "How...how harrowing."

"Well, yes, yes it was. Certainly, um, well, yes, harrowing."

Jamila broke the awkward silence by gathering up her papers and briefcase. "I'll go," she said, standing. "I apologize for overstaying my welcome –"

Tamos waved this away. "I won't get up, if you don't mind," he said, reaching out to shake her hand. "Thank you so much for coming."

"Oh, no, thank you!" She leaned over and gently took his hand in hers. "Thank you so much!"

As she turned towards the door, Tamos leaned forward suddenly and said, "Oh, Jamila?"

"Yes?"

"Let's keep all this to ourselves for now, shall we?"

With a perplexed look, Jamila agreed, forcing herself not to ask why. "Well, certainly, Professor, if that's what you want."

"Thank you, Jamila, and good afternoon."

Tamos sat quietly for a few minutes and listened as Jamila let herself out. The door closed behind her with a soft click, and he heard the drumming sound of her feet on the wooden steps, tapping a soft rhythm as she descended to the walk. The sharper noise of her heels on the cement sidewalk faded quickly as she walked down the street.

As soon as he was sure she was gone, he pushed himself purposefully up out of his chair and walked to the back of the house, taking a screwdriver out of a kitchen drawer on his way. He switched on a light at the top of the small stairwell leading into the basement and carefully made his way down the stairs, gripping the handrail tightly as he went with one hand, screwdriver in the other. A fall was his second-most dreaded occurrence. The first was something he was on his way to address.

Once downstairs, he flipped a switch to turn on the two bare bulbs, which hung from a twisted black wire that ran along the center of the low ceiling. The bulbs were low wattage, sixty, or maybe even forty watts – the professor conserved when he could, in sometimes slightly irrational ways – and they floated eerily in the dank, stone-walled basement, like oversized fireflies, swaying slightly in the light breeze that flowed down the open stairway behind him.

He stopped in the center of the nearly barren, cement-floored room. There was no furniture of any kind down here, just a small furnace in one corner, previously coal-fired, now converted to oil, and a small water heater next to it. An old porcelain laundry sink was attached to one wall, yellow with age; the plumbing for it had been stripped away years ago, and now it just hung there, forlorn and faucetless, a small monument to the industrious housekeeper of forty or fifty years ago who had kept house for him. Now volunteers from the local senior service organizations picked up and delivered his laundry, swept up, and kept the house in order. They never went into the basement.

He looked slowly from one side of the room to the other. Which was it? Left, or right?

He nodded decisively. Left. It had been the front left corner the last time. He went over to a spot in the wall just in front of the furnace. With the tip of the screwdriver, he carefully pried out one of the smaller stones in the wall, being careful not to make a mark on the front of the stone. Once that stone had been removed, he was able to grab the larger stone next to it, pull it out of the wall, place it on the floor, and then the stone next to that, revealing a small chamber. That stone went on the floor next to the other two.

He reached into a hole in the wall and pulled out a small leather case, held closed by two straps with brass buckles in the center. He placed it on the floor as well, then picked up and carefully replaced the stones, again noting closely that he had left no visible scars.

He bent down and picked up the case, glancing around the room as he did so. *So, from left front, now it goes right rear.*

He carried the case back to the back of the room, under the small window, and after locating the correct position, repeated in reverse order the steps he had just completed. Once the case was safely tucked into its new location in the wall, he carefully cleaned the area surrounding both depositories with a soft cloth.

He stood back and wiped his hands with the cloth. The documents were again safe, for now, in their new location. The two basement chambers were actually relatively new hiding spots. The case had been stashed in various other locations throughout the small house over the years. He'd been using the basement for only a short time; a year, maybe two. He would move it again in six months. Maybe back upstairs. It was getting more and more difficult, climbing these narrow stairs. Yes, time to move it upstairs.

While moving the case he was reminded of another set of important documents in his possession, which he might need very soon, and mentally congratulated himself on the foresight he had shown, several weeks earlier, when he had traveled to New York and cleared out the small safe located in Harry Zook's old office. He still had access to it, thanks to a thoughtful provision made in Harry's will. He'd left the safe empty, but had asked the firm currently occupying the office to keep the arrangement intact; who knew when he might need it again? The new firm had been quite accommodating. The legacy firm created at Mr. Yerkes Sr.'s death had remained in business as Penrod, Penner, Yerkes & Zook. A Yerkes grandson was now a senior partner, Harry being only honorary, as the founder of the original "XYZ" partnership. (Poor Mr. Xerxes had, like Harry, also left no heirs, but it was not deemed necessary at the time to carry his name forward, though it saddened the now very elderly Yerkes somewhat.) The previous contents of the now empty office safe were stored away from the house in what Tamos thought an extremely appropriate location. A very "safe" location, indeed, he thought. But he still liked the option of moving it back to the New York office, if necessary. And the key was cleverly hidden, as well.

Ah, well, enough of that. He turned out the lights and began the weary climb back up.

Moving the letters around, he knew, was unnecessary. Perhaps even hiding them at all was unnecessary. But it was all a part of the process by which he had kept himself sane for many years.

A way of keeping a memory alive.

A way of ensuring that the effort did not die.

As she drove back to Rochester, Jamila, still marveling at the story of the professor's daring wartime flight, tried to imagine what it must have been like; not just the almost unbelievable flight to Portugal, but simply living through that era, that war. She had no frame of reference, no emotional gauge to use to measure the depth of that experience, in spite of all the stories she'd heard from her mother, her grandmother, all the books she'd read, the movies, the documentaries she'd seen. Nothing could flesh out the intellectual framework, the skeleton of understanding acquired merely second-hand.

Until now. As she sat in that small house, on that hard stool, listening to the professor as he regaled her – for she could see that he had, now that he had finally begun, truly enjoyed the telling of it – she felt for the first time as if she really got it, really felt it, felt some of the anguish, the passion, even the pride. Yes, she could also sense that he was proud – justifiably proud, she would soon learn – of what he had done.

And she could also sense, though dimly, the high price he had paid.

Pillow Talk

1850 HOUSE

Long after the restaurant had closed that night, lying in bed, Maggie and LaFleur were still trying to piece together a coherent picture of the professor's mysterious project, sorting out what little each of them had heard as they had rotated separately in and out of the lunch table.

Maggie laughed softly, shaking the bed.

"What?" asked LaFleur.

"Oh, I was just thinking of something the professor did the other day. In the bar. Old Charlie Case was there. The professor was in rare form, standing at the bar, waving his hands the way he does, very animated, telling this long, involved story. Something about disguising himself in order to 'sneak out' somewhere. I came in part way through the story, so I don't quite know what it was all about, except it had something to do with going out to that roadhouse, the one on the highway up near Sandy Pond. Remember, the one he was so anxious about spotting on our trip up there. He said something about it that day as we passed by, you know, like, 'Boy, could I tell you stories about that place.' Well, anyway, Charlie C. was really cracking up over this story, but as soon the Prof noticed that I had come in, he stopped and said, 'Well, those were the days.' Then he waved that little wave of his, and said, 'Don't pay any attention to me, Maggie,' and sat back down at the bar.

"When I tried to ask him what 'sneaking out' meant, he just shook his head and told me not to worry about it, it was just a silly story. Obviously, Charlie knew exactly what he was talking about, but I could tell the professor didn't like being questioned by me. Just like at lunch today. He kept dropping hints, talking about looking for some kind of World War II airplane." She raised herself up slightly and looked at him. "You know him better than I do, A.C. What's he up to?"

LaFleur blinked and let out a long breath. "Damned if I know."

That answer was not going to wash, not for a second, and they both knew it, even as the words left his mouth. The look he got from Maggie as he said it was totally unnecessary. Their conversations had, over time, taken on the character of Japanese Noh drama, without the music and the dancing but definitely using masks, which changed constantly. Maggie's masks were typically a bit more transparent than LaFleur's; given her more open and forthright manner, and her nursing sensibilities, this was only natural. LaFleur's masks were opaque, reflecting years of caution, suspicion, the habits of investigative process and procedure.

"It's got to have something to do with that damned piece of painted metal," LaFleur finally said.

"That's obvious," replied Maggie. She rolled off of her back to face him, doing her best Cheshire cat impression.

"Humph. Well, what else is obvious is that this has been coming for a long time. Though he's been trying to play that down."

"He did seem to be protesting too much at a couple of your more pointed queries as to what he's doing."

"Yes."

There was a short silence as they adjusted their masks.

"You seem to be rather enamored of the professor," said LaFleur, suggestively.

"Enamored?"

"You can't deny it; I've seen you two together. I'm pretty sure you wouldn't throw me over, or anything –" That thought was interrupted by a mild slap on the shoulder. "You do like him, though," he finished.

"Like him? I adore him! He's so charming! So romantic."

"Ah. The truth comes out. Romantic, is he?"

"Oh, you know what I mean. He's so Old World. His European background makes him very attractive, compared to your average Joe. And he's maintained that romantic aura, even after living here for, what, sixty years?" She paused. "When did he come to Oswego?"

"In the forties, I think. Late forties? He doesn't talk about it much; all I know is that it was near the end of the war. Maybe after. And don't think you can get away with changing the subject. I believe we were discussing your predilection for older men."

"Yes, well, I was attracted to *you*, after all. You being so much older."

"Careful. I've seen your driver's license. But back to Tamos. You 'adore' him?" Raised eyebrows.

"Absolutely. I can't think of anyone else I know who has such a presence. The way he talks, his mannerisms – so cultured. And, well, romantic! But there's something serious about him, as well, a kind of hidden determination, maybe. I saw that on our trip up north; he was so intent, so focused."

"He has that kind of focus at the poker table."

"I can imagine. But there is something else, under the determination, under the reserve. A tenderness. An adorable tenderness."

They shifted positions, Maggie spooning against LaFleur's back, her arm draped possessively across his chest. After a long quiet time, it was LaFleur who spoke first. "I didn't mention it earlier. He called right after dinner tonight. Very excited. He wants me to meet him at the marina in Rochester next week."

"The yacht club?"

"No, Malone's. The big one, out on Lake Road." He sighed. "He's being so damned mysterious. I'm not sure I want to get involved."

"You did promise at lunch to help him with – well, with whatever it is."

"I know."

"I'm a little worried about him."

"Yeah."

Maggie gave him a light squeeze. "So, what do you think he wants?"

"Damned if I know."

ROAMER

LAKE ONTARIO

The professor stepped carefully from the dock to the deck of the hired dive boat, looking rather like a praying mantis climbing over a large crack in the sidewalk; arms akimbo, neck craning, his oversized sunglasses reflecting the early morning glare glinting off of the lake. A.C. could hardly hold back his laughter.

LaFleur, who had come down early to help load equipment and set up, reached out for him. "Here, take my arm," he said, as Tamos waved his hand around, trying to maintain his balance. With one foot on the boat and the other on the tiny gangplank that had been laid out, the professor grabbed LaFleur's wrist and pulled himself the rest of the way onto the deck, while Maggie fluttered around helplessly behind him, unable to reach out far enough to steady him.

As soon as the professor was safely on board, Maggie gave them a wave and headed back to her car. She and LaFleur had agreed to take turns shepherding Tamos to and from Rochester on search days. While they were out on the boat, she was going to spend a few hours at the George Eastman photographic museum; there were a couple of special exhibitions currently running that she was interested in, one on the history of photography, the other, which she knew nothing about, intriguingly titled "Collecting Shadows." Which is also how she had been feeling about the professor recently, when trying to pin him down. Just when she and LaFleur thought they knew what was going on, he shifted the focus away from himself, away from what she had started to think of as the "shadows" of his past, and on to the current adventure – a treasure hunt, inexplicably out of character – but what else could it be?

Tamos straightened up, smoothed his coat, and after thanking LaFleur absentmindedly, looked balefully around at what he had hoped would have been a slightly larger, and newer, marine platform.

A tug which had been long ago converted to a scuba charter boat, the *Diving Duck* had perhaps seen better days. Chipped white paint, yellowing with age; gray, weathered wood railings; and what Tamos took to be ominous rust stains running in large ochre streaks down the side of the small forward cabin; it all created a first impression of dereliction, not to say decay. Before sinking too far into despair, however, he reminded himself that he should not have expected a luxury liner.

His thoughts were interrupted by a cheerful "Hullo!" coming from just inside the door to the cabin. Turning at the sound, he stepped back in amazement as the largest person he had ever seen stepped out on to the deck. "Welcome aboard, professor! I'm Captain Dave." Still unwinding himself from the low crouch that had been required to exit through the cabin door, and now towering over Tamos by at least a foot, Captain Dave smiled, then reached out to the professor and offered a hand as large as a Smithfield ham.

Tamos automatically put out his own hand, which was immediately engulfed in Captain Dave's, and stammered out a reply. "Pleased, I am sure...to meet...that is, I –" Words failed him at this point, and he withdrew his hand, stepping back a couple of feet in trepidation. LaFleur put his arm on the professor's shoulder, finally unable to hold back a laugh.

"Don't worry, Prof, Dave won't hurt you."

"No, no, of course not, it's just, I mean – well!" He stepped forward a bit, now taking in fully Dave's full stature. He was at least six-feet-four, Tamos estimated, and, well, substantial was the only word that came to mind. Looking up, Tamos saw that Dave was still smiling, obviously enjoying the effect he'd had; this was something that must happen often. But it was such a friendly smile, and Dave's face so ordinary – tanned to leather, but smooth-featured, open, and pleasant – that Tamos instantly relaxed. "Please accept my apologies," he said, taking another step toward Dave, reaching out. "Pleased to make your acquaintance," he said forcibly, taking Dave's hand in his and shaking it vigorously.

"Don't apologize, professor. I shouldn't have startled you like that. It's a bad habit of mine. One of many, I'll admit, but all harmless." He glanced over the professor's head and winked at LaFleur. "Right, A.C.?"

LaFleur nodded in agreement. "We've known one another for years; I'll vouch for him. But I was as surprised as you were, Prof, to see him when I stepped on board this morning. I thought you had gone to the Pacific Northwest, Dave, maybe Vancouver?"

"For a time, yes," Dave replied, "but it wasn't the same. Had to come back to Ontario."

"Well, we're lucky to have you. Dave's one of the best," LaFleur said, turning to Tamos. "A good start, Prof."

"Let me show you around, Professor," said Dave, motioning him forward. "Right through there."

Tamos stepped gingerly over the rim of the door – it was actually a large, oval hatch – and into the cabin. Captain Dave followed him in, nearly filling the space up. "Welcome to the bridge."

Tamos looked around in amazement. The contrast with the exterior of the boat couldn't have been any more dramatic. The small cockpit was immaculate, well-organized, and fitted out with what appeared to be the latest in navigational, communications, and operational equipment. "Quite impressive!" he said. "Not what I had expected given the somewhat dilapidated condition of, well –"

Dave laughed. "The old girl looks a little rough around the edges, I'll admit, but only on the outside. I'm only halfway through a refit. I started with the engine; there's a brand-new Perkins marine diesel down below, and as you can see, the latest technology here in the control room. We've already got everything set up in the forward cabin," he said, directing the professor to a stairwell.

Once below, after a very careful descent down the stairwell, the professor was greeted by Red Aldridge.

"Hello, Professor," said Red warmly. "Welcome aboard. Let me introduce you to our two grad students – they'll be doing most of the hard pulling – Aaron and Erin."

"Glad to meet you," said Aaron, stepping forward and shaking the professor's hand. "I'm Aaron." Tall and thin, with a thick mop of dark hair – a Beatles cut, the professor would have called it – he backed away shyly as Erin stepped up. "Pleased, Professor. We are *so* excited about this project, I can't tell you!" In contrast to Aaron, Erin was short and slight. Her bright green eyes, pale complexion, and auburn hair, along with a low, contralto voice completely out of character with her size, charmed the professor right off of his feet.

"Pleased to meet you both," he said, beaming at Erin, while Aaron looked on, a bit bemused.

"We call them "A" and "E," said Dr. Aldridge, "to avoid confusion."

"Ah," said Tamos. "I see how it could be confusing if simply calling out to one or the other." He opened his arms expansively. "Well, you can all call me 'Tamos.' No need for formalities out on the bounding main, eh?"

LaFleur had come in to the cabin at just this moment. "Bounding main? Prof, I swear that sometimes I think you just stepped out of an old nineteen-forties radio series."

Tamos turned to LaFleur with a thoughtful look.

"As do I, A.C. As do I."

The tour of the "nerve center," as Aaron called it, took about ten minutes. Monitors were set up on a low table at the far forward end of the cabin, with myriad cables running between various laptops and other electronic equipment. Here, Erin explained, is where she and Aaron would be spending most of their time while they were out on the lake, primarily watching the sonar monitor.

Sitting near the back of the deck were two large instruments, one bright yellow, the other a big, square contraption of silver and gold anodized aluminum, both connected to large spools of cable. The yellow unit, the side sonar module, the "sonde," Red called it, sleek and torpedo-shaped, had been purchased by the professor (at no small expense). He had not seen it until now. The boxy unit – the ROV that had been designed and built by RIT students the year before – sat next to it like an ungainly relative. A small crane-like mechanism attached to the deck near the main cabin would be used to deploy both. Red steered Tamos over to the ROV.

"Let me introduce you to ROAMER, our Remotely Operated Aquatic Motorized ExploRer. Even though we won't be using this as our primary search vehicle, once we locate a possible wreck, this thing is going to be invaluable. Without a close look at what we've imaged with the sonar, we'd have no idea if it's worth sending a diver down for a closer look." He bent over and carefully turned the ROV around to show the professor the front end, where the lights and cameras were positioned. "We've got three video cameras, each one on a separate feed, and although we can only view one feed at a time, the operator can switch between cameras at any time, which are positioned at slightly different angles. Four powerful HID lights – high intensity discharge lamps – two on each side, here and here, provide illumination. It gets dark fast underwater, so these are very bright, very efficient, and draw low power; everything we need in an application like this." He motioned to the rear of the ROV. "It's propelled by four high output thrusters – off the shelf technology, in this case – and everything is battery powered. Communications are linked through a standard RS-232 serial cable. The microcontroller programming and all of the related software was developed by the students. The whole thing is controlled through a custom graphical interface, using a joystick."

"Very impressive," said Tamos, shaking his head in wonder. "It looks like a commercially produced piece of equipment, not a senior project."

"It's every bit as good as anything you can get on the market currently, for its size and depth rating."

"How deep can it go?" asked Tamos, showing his first signs of anxiety.

"It's rated at four hundred feet," replied Red, "but hasn't been tested that deep. But from what I understand, you expect to find our wreck much shallower than that."

"Yes, that is right. Between one and two hundred, I should think. Maybe shallower, but that is not very likely, as it would have been found by now in that case."

"Yeah, that's what we thought," said Red. "And you're pretty sure you know about where this B-24 is located? We're going to be starting our search much farther north than what is generally accepted as the last known position."

"Exactly." Tamos looked over, a wry smile on his face. "Perhaps that is why it's never been found." He turned away and pointed at the bright yellow torpedo unit lying alongside the ROV. "Now, tell me all about my side sonar."

An hour later, the sonar unit was gliding through the depths of Lake Ontario behind its tow cable, about a hundred feet deep, its fan-shaped acoustic beam playing across the lake bed like fingers stroking the face of a long-lost love. Ghostly images appeared on the monitors above: creases, whirls, and folds, rocks and clefts and sandbars re-imagined in false color and enhanced contrast, a lakescape of ever-changing and yet unvarying expanse, seemingly never-ending, barren, dark, and empty. But it was a large lake, and it was only the first day – the first hours – so Tamos was unperturbed.

Side scanning sonar was a wonderful invention, and like many wonderful, technological marvels, it had been invented by a German scientist brought to the United States after World War II; one of those scientists with whom Tamos might have worked, had Germany not lost its senses. A scientist like von Kármán, who with uncanny foresight had departed a failing Europe in good time, and who, by the unkindest of fates, Tamos had missed meeting and working with in California, at Caltech.

It was a remarkable irony, thought Tamos, that German engineering should be responsible for ultimately locating the wreck of an airplane which had been produced solely for the purpose of defeating the German war machine, the maws from which the Szabó family had only narrowly escaped. And from which, in the incarnation of the infamous Hungarian Nazi offshoot, the Arrow Cross, Tamos and his uncle Béla had even more narrowly escaped. And, more remarkably, it was the almost unbelievably massive production capabilities of the American war effort that had created by its sheer power – along with thousands of tanks, LSTs, minesweepers, merchant vessels, armored personnel carriers, Jeeps, destroyers, battleships, cruisers, fighters, and bombers – the one airplane he hoped to find.

While he sat and looked out over the lake – placid, calm, shining, sliding slowly by as the sonar mapped that which was hidden from sight – he felt a similar calm, a certainty, and a wonderment, too, that he, Tamos Szabó, had lived long enough, and now had the opportunity to put right an ancient injustice. No matter how long after the fact, no matter the stakes involved, no matter the effort, the expense, the difficulty, it was something that had to be done, and he was doing it.

If the wreck was down there – and he knew it was – he would find it. After all, he understood something which the others did not.

He understood the elegance of effort.

"How are you doing, Prof?" LaFleur asked, as he pulled up another deck chair next to Tamos. Tamos looked up in surprise, as if drawn back from a long distance, or a dream.

"Ah, A.C., hello. I was wondering where you were."

"Getting initiated into the arcane world of computer graphics. I had no idea."

"I cannot say I know anything about it."

"The display graphics they've created for the ROV are amazing. Aaron showed me some footage of a test run, and how they control the unit. Really impressive."

"Yes, they appear to be very competent. I was just thinking about how lucky I am to have them – to have RIT – involved in this project."

"From what I hear, it's your project all the way. Red is 'just along for the ride,' he says."

"Yes, that sounds like him. Somewhat self-effacing. Obviously very good at what he does, and very good at shepherding his students through complex projects, mentoring them. He has a very good reputation. I wonder why he hasn't gone on to a larger institution."

"I could ask the same question of you, Tamos. Why did you stay at SUNY all those years? Couldn't you have been at a more prestigious college, or in the private sector, aerospace, or something along those lines? I got the impression from Jamila that at one time you were destined for much greater things, as they say. Didn't you start out at Caltech working with a famous rocket scientist?"

There was a long pause.

"Jamila has somewhat overstated the case, I am afraid. It is true that I was at Caltech. My college career was unfortunately interrupted by the war."

"What happened?"

"Family. There was a crisis. Most of my family escaped from Hungary, to Spain, just as things were getting very bad in Budapest. But my uncle Béla, my father's brother, went missing. Béla was my second father, in a very real sense. My parents died in an auto accident in California soon after we emigrated here – oh, I have never mentioned that? In any case, it was Béla who came to the U.S. at that time and made sure that I was well taken care of, taking me with him back to Hungary. After I finished what you would call high school, Béla helped me return to the United States to attend Caltech. It was not long after that time that he disappeared. And that forced me to leave school for a time." He paused. "How much of this has Jamila told you?"

"Only that you were going to school in California, but got called away.

She didn't go into any detail."

"No, I would not expect her to have said too much, for fear of speaking out of turn."

"Am *I* prying too much, Prof?"

"No, not at all. I have been perhaps, well, excessively circumspect, shall we say, when it comes to my past. But at this point, there is really no reason to remain so close-mouthed concerning certain aspects of my early life. Many details of which you will shortly learn, assuming all goes according to plan."

"That's another thing. Just what do you intend to do, once you've found this thing? And as you just said, assuming you find it, of course."

"Oh, we will find it. I have to find it. I have waited so long." He sighed, looked away. "Maybe too long."

LaFleur edged his chair around to face Tamos. "Prof, I've never seen you so downbeat, so…so, I don't know what. Just not yourself. Ever since you saw the chunk of metal in the restaurant, you've been a different person – quiet, withdrawn – brooding, almost. I thought this was supposed to be something exciting, an adventure. But you act like the whole world is riding on it." Tamos had looked up at this, and pulled off his sunglasses. Squinting in the bright light, he reached out and laid his hand on LaFleur's knee.

"It is, A.C. My whole world. Everything I have left to live for is lying somewhere on that lakebed. It's been lying down there in the dark, in the cold, just lying there – dark and alone – for these seventy-odd years. I never thought I would ever get the chance, ever again see –" He put his dark glasses back on, fearing that he was exposing too much through his eyes: "windows to the soul," isn't that what the ancients had called them, glassy portals to the innermost secrets of being? What had LaFleur seen there? How much had he just revealed to him, and how much should he *now* reveal, now that he was so close to finding what he knew was down there, what he needed to believe was down there?

"Prof – Tamos – what is it? What are you really looking for? It's not the B-24, is it?"

"Not the B-24? What do you mean?"

"C'mon, Prof. What possible interest could you have in an old legend? There's no way of knowing if *Gertie* is even in the lake. It was during a blizzard, no one could have seen it. And I read the other day that it could have stayed in the air for five more hours before running out of fuel. May have even ended up in the Adirondacks."

"No, the plane almost certainly went down in Lake Ontario. Witnesses heard it circling, even as far out as Galloo Island. The left wing was found floating in the lake, a few days later, just east of Oswego. It could have floated for miles. I've studied the prevailing currents for years; there is also something that forms in the lake called a seiche, a standing wave, that could have –"

"Hold it," LaFleur interrupted. "Even if all that's true, can you tell me what the bloody hell any of it has to do with the piece of painted metal you found hanging on the wall at the 1850 House?"

Tamos ducked his head in abject defeat, giving out a small groan. LaFleur waited patiently as Tamos regained his composure. "Well done, A.C.," Tamos finally said. "You're seeing farther and farther ahead. I'm glad we're not at the poker table; you've just called my 'all in.' Because you're right, I've been bluffing." LaFleur began to exclaim at this, but was immediately quieted by Tamos, holding up his hands. "This can't go beyond us." He waited for LaFleur to acknowledge the need for secrecy, which he did with a nod and a quick "of course." Tamos continued. "I'm not looking for the B-24, for *Getaway Gertie*. I'm looking for a fighter plane, a P-39. A *particular* P-39." He looked at LaFleur, hesitated a moment, then went on, his voice low and intent. "And when I find it, all hell will break loose."

LaFleur could only stare in bewilderment. "But what about –"

Before LaFleur could finish his question, they were interrupted by Aaron, who had been standing nearby, behind the cockpit door.

"Professor. We've found something!" he called over to them.

Tamos waved, called out "Thanks," and began to push himself up out of the deck chair. "Don't worry, A.C., it will all become clear," he said, starting towards the door. "But now let's get below and see what they've found."

What they'd found turned out to be a scattering of old logs that had settled at about eighty feet into a more or less geometric configuration. Unmistakably artificial in the sonar image, standing out clearly from the loops and whorls of sand and rock ridges, it had immediately caught their attention. In this case, though obviously not a wreck of any kind, and certainly not an airplane, it was interesting enough to take a closer look at, even if just for practice. They needed some time with the ROV in actual lake conditions; when the time came to look at something more promising, Red didn't want to be floundering around. After letting everyone take a quick turn at maneuvering the ROV around, they loaded up the equipment and moved a bit farther north.

They spent the next couple of hours towing the sonar module in a small grid pattern near Stony Point. As the afternoon light softened the calm surface of the lake into scatterlings of light, they passed by the old Stony Point lighthouse on one of their turns at the north end of the pattern.

"I remember when that lighthouse was operational," said the professor. "Privately owned, now. Can you imagine that, living in a lighthouse?"

Red glanced down at his watch. "Time to head back in. It's almost an hour back." He stretched and turned toward Tamos. "You're sure we need to be this far north, Professor?"

"Oh, yes, absolutely. Those are the Galloo Islands just over there, aren't they?" he asked, pointing to the northwest.

"Well, that's Stony Island, closest to us," said Red. "Little Galloo and Galloo are just to the west. Duck Island's a little past that, just across the Canadian line."

"That's where we need to be," said the professor. "Duck-Galloo Ridge."

"Then that's where we'll go," said Red.

Tamos nodded. "Excellent. What time tomorrow? Early, I trust."

Elegance of Effort

LAKE ONTARIO

There had been day after day of tedium, days when nothing at all appeared on the monitors except for the occasional school of fish. Nothing that could not be immediately dismissed as too small, too irregular, too indistinct, or much too deep to allow easy investigation. There had been a couple of sightings of what may have been boats, but these were also quickly dismissed as objects of disinterest. These lakes were littered with the carcasses of small fishing trawlers and pleasure boats. They'd already spotted a half dozen, close to shore.

Michael had a rare day off, and he'd offered to take the Professor out that day, giving a break to Maggie and LaFleur. It would be his last chance to spend time with the professor for a while; in a couple of weeks, he'd be on a three-week leave of absence, two weeks of which were to be spent in El Salvador on a medical mission, doing anesthesia for cleft palate surgeries.

"Isn't it dangerous there?" Tamos asked. They had settled into their deck chairs behind the boat's cockpit.

"Oh, not really," Michael said. "No more so than, oh, Chicago, say. Or Budapest in nineteen forty-four."

Tamos glanced slyly over at Michael. "Oh, so you heard about that?"

"Maggie gave me the overview. I'd love to hear more about it."

Tamos looked away. "Perhaps another time."

"Tamos, you are always so mysterious. What else is there about you we don't know?"

"Oh, not that much, Michael. Not that much."

They gazed out at the lake for a while, flat and calm today, its serene face hiding whatever it was the professor was searching for, which had become the topic of some debate between A.C., Maggie, and Michael. A.C. had hinted broadly a couple of days earlier that Tamos was concealing something, but when pressed, played it down. Probably just my imagination, LaFleur had said.

"What are we looking for out here, Tamos?"

"Just as I've said, Michael. The famous *Gertie*."

"But you've been acting – we've all noticed it – well, almost paranoid lately. Or maybe not paranoid, but certainly evasive." Michael studied the professor's face, looking for a clue. The professor's milky blue eyes stared back. "There's been an aura of, oh, I don't know, uncertainty about you."

"Everything is uncertain, Michael."

They both turned back to the face the lake, an uncomfortable silence descending over them.

Tamos suddenly clasped the arms of his deck chair and straightened up, still staring out past the stern.

"We are all of us in this world linked together by a chain of chance, like charms on a bracelet. Links break, are reforged, the chain is constantly altered. Those to whom I was linked with in the past are gone, to be replaced by others. You – and A.C., and Maggie, and also now Jamila – have entered this chain. A chain of chance."

"Were does the chain lead? Somewhere good, I hope?"

"I cannot say. No one can. But I truly hope that one day you can look back on this and remember it as an adventure."

"Ah, Tamos. You told me once that no true adventure can promise safe return."

"That I did. And it is sadly so. But that does not mean safe return is impossible. Michael, I see the chain of chance as life's algorithm, the outcome determined by all of the various inputs, the actions, the happenstances, the decisions, all of the parameters that specify how and when the chain gets altered, extended. Or broken. And you share a chain with only a few others, and then only shortly."

"Shortly? Your chain has endured a remarkably long time. And should continue for some time to come."

"There is no denying that my time is growing short, Michael. Oh, I know I am in exceptionally good health for someone my age. But I also see what time has done to the people I sometimes visit at the nursing home in Oswego, people much younger than I am who can barely function. No, Michael, if I am to complete my mission here, I must hurry. And I am afraid that if this goes on too long – if I am unable to hurry it along somehow – it will be left to you, to A.C., to Maggie to solve the mystery."

"So, there *is* a mystery! Well, if it's a mystery that needs solving, of the three of us A.C. is best suited for it."

"Yes, I agree. Especially as it may be a very weak hand I leave behind. A.C. plays a weak hand like no one else."

"That's true." Michael looked over at Tamos. "Does he see farther down the chain than most of us? Is that part of his unique ability?"

"Yes, I believe so. Very perceptive, Michael."

"And the way he narrows down the elements of chance, his Occam's Razor approach – the simplest answer is often the best – that must be a big part of it, too."

"Indeed."

Michael looked thoughtful, going back to something he'd heard Tamos propound late one night at the 1850 House. "And this 'elegance of effort' you sometimes talk about, how does that come into play?"

"In my view, it is the elegance of individual effort that allows us some measure of control in our lives. It has to do with the elemental properties of matter."

"What, like atomic weight or something? I'm not following you."

"I am talking here, in very loose terms, about certain quantum mechanical effects and how they may relate to human effort. Certain atomic particles, photons, for example, can become what is called 'entangled,' wherein there is an instantaneous interaction between them, even when separated by a huge distance."

"Like gravity?"

"Much more profound than gravity, although you are close. It's what Einstein famously called 'spooky action at a distance.' That in quantum mechanical systems, there can be a kind of spooky communication between elemental particles. It is fanciful, I know, and perhaps not a very good analogy, but that is what I think of – though again, I am being outrageously imprecise in my use of quantum theory – as a property of the elegance of effort.

"Now, particles, of course," Tamos continued, "do not choose how to behave; they expend no effort, per se, when it comes to this action at a distance. But even though I am a physicist, and tend to think in those terms, I am also, I think, something of a humanist. You may have heard another famous statement by Einstein, that 'God does not play dice with the universe.'" Michael nodded. "I take this to mean that despite the uncertainty, the seeming randomness of the universe, at a human level we can impose order, to whatever small effect. Through the elegance of our effort."

"And this effort somehow gives direction to what would otherwise be pure chance?"

"I truly hope so. I must believe that the effort one invests in the daily forging of the chain, the connections one makes; that these can make all the difference. For me, it is everything. It is what I am doing here, today, and always."

As they were nearing the dock, Michael slipped down to the salon and motioned to Jamila, who was seated next to Aaron at one of the monitors. She furrowed her eyebrows in an implicit "what?" and then shrugged as Michael motioned again, more urgently this time. She stood and made her way over to him.

"What is it, Michael?"

"What are we doing out here, Jamila?" He kept his voice low, and she unconsciously matched his tone in answering.

"Well…looking for *Gertie,* right?"

"Jamila, do you believe that?"

"Michael, what are you getting at?"

"You've talked a lot with Tamos, right? About this 'project' of his?" She nodded. "You probably know more about his motives than anyone, with the possible exception of A.C., and he is being as tight-lipped as the professor. Jamila, do you really believe he's looking for *Gertie*? An airplane he apparently has no real connection with?"

"Well, he's said repeatedly that he wants to be the first to find her."

"Yes, I know. But, really, how likely do you think that is? Haven't you noticed how evasive he has been on certain points? And a little while ago, I had the most perplexing conversation with him. I asked him about this nebulous 'elegance of effort' thing he talks about sometimes, and he got almost mystical. Talked about a 'chain of chance' that everyone is connected to, and the connections between everyone associated with a particular chain, or something. And how important individual effort can be in, well, in somehow influencing events."

"Yeah, he's said something along those lines to me. And how he might not have enough time left to finish the chain. Or influence it in the right way, bring it to some sort of completion. Something like that. That he is 'in a hurry.'"

"Exactly! He keeps saying that he's 'an old man in a hurry.' I think there is something a lot more profound going on than a simple treasure hunt for an old bomber, one that doesn't even have a history in the war. It was just a bomber on a practice run, and the crew had some bad luck, as far as I know. Sure, sort of a mystery, I guess, but what possible interest could Tamos have in it?"

Jamila glanced around, as if to make sure no one was eavesdropping. "Okay, Michael, I'll level. I've wondered the same thing myself, especially lately. You're right, Professor Szabó has told me something about his experiences in the war; not a lot of detail, granted, but the big picture I get is that he had some rather prolonged, and somewhat traumatic, experiences. None of which appear to relate to *Gertie* in any way whatsoever. So, yes, I have started to wonder what is really going on."

At this point, Captain Dave hollered down the stairwell, "Everyone please take your seats! We're getting ready to dock."

"I'd better get back to the professor," Michael said. "Let's talk again, soon."

Jamila nodded solemnly.

"And Jamila," said Michael, "let's not mention our discussion to Tamos?"

Jamila smiled, and nodded again. "I think we'll soon know what's really going on," she said.

"You're probably right," he replied. "And I have the feeling it's going to surprise us all."

Burning Fences

OSWEGO COUNTRY CLUB

On the morning of the Eighth Annual Oswego Hospital Benefit Nine-Hole Golf Tournament, the previous year's 1850 House team gathered in the clubhouse prior to the eight A.M. "shotgun" start. They'd paired off the same as before: Michael and LaFleur, Frank and Doug, Maggie and the professor following in their own cart, Tamos serving as the team's "swing coach," and on call for clutch putts as well. Their last place showing the year before was not a topic of conversation.

"So, I don't know how this arthritis is going to affect my swing," said Doug, holding up his wrist in a pathetic attempt to preempt any poor performance on his part.

"Arthritis? I doubt you have arthritis," said Michael. "Probably just tendonitis. Here, let me take a look. Hold up your hand." He grabbed Doug's arm and hand. "This is called the Finkelstein test." He quickly manipulated Doug's thumb, fingers, and wrist. "Feel any pain?"

"Well, no."

"Okay, no tendonitis, and no arthritis either. No special allowances."

"Well, I don't care. And this year I'm drinking a beer for every hole."

"In that case, I'm driving the damn cart," said Frank.

Frank's abrupt start in Cart One caused Doug to spill his first beer down the front of his shirt. The cursing could be heard for some distance as they drove away.

Michael and LaFleur made a more leisurely start, Maggie and Tamos right behind. "Michael, I noticed last week you're trying out a new stance," said LaFleur.

"Yeah. Mo Norman style. Wide, sweeping swing, called 'single-plane.' Very unconventional, but I think it's helping. Speaking of changes, what's with your new clubs?"

"The professor's suggestion. They're all the same length, so your swing plane stays constant. Sort of like what you're doing, I guess, but with club design. I'm still adapting to it."

"Where did Tamos get that idea?"

"Apparently, he invented it. Years ago, for a friend; can't think of his name at the moment. He said this friend built the clubs – had them built – by a contact at Grumman Aircraft. Guess he had connections there. It's all based on physics. Tamos calculated that the resulting distance difference between various irons was eighty-five percent due to loft angle and fifteen percent due to differing length. Tamos did this in the nineteen forties. It's only been since the eighties that it's been commercialized. Tamos said that even though he wrote it up for a small journal, he never had any commercial rights to the theory. Guess he was still in his twenties then." He glanced back at Tamos in the cart behind them. "Michael, how does he stay in such good condition? What is he now, ninety-two?"

"Ninety-four. Well, some of it is genetics, of course. But the professor has been doing all the right things for years to keep himself fit. Low-fat diet, B-complex vitamins, and plenty of exercise. And socialization plays an important part. Along with a feeling of purpose."

"Socialization?"

"Sure. And at his age, it's something he has to consciously work at. All of his friends and colleagues are dead. He never married. The 1850 House gang has been his whole world for quite some time, and keeps him going."

"And a sense of purpose; where does that come in?"

"That's why he's our swing coach!" said Michael, laughing.

The conversation between Maggie and Tamos in Cart Three was animated as well.

"Maybe I can manage to get these poor souls out of last place this year," he said, nudging Maggie in the ribs.

Maggie nudged back, gently. "Oh, Doug has a plan for that," she said. "He claims to have filled all of the nurses' carts water bottles with Cosmos."

"Ah, yes, that sounds like our Doug. In any case, I hope they do better this year."

"Oh, I don't think they care that much about it. It's more a way to support Michael. Maybe help him relax a little. He's been having a hard time at the hospital lately."

"How so?"

"There seems to be a lot of resentment directed at him; people think he's too critical of their work, and that no one puts enough effort into it. Well, nobody likes to hear that, even if it's true."

"Sounds like what A.C. was always up against on the force."

As they approached the next tee, the professor leaned out and hollered at Michael and A.C.

"Let's see a little effort out there!"

While driving the cart from hole seven to hole eight, a circuitous route around a large grove of trees and a pond, Michael turned to LaFleur and asked, "Has Prof ever told you about his experiences in Spain, during the war?"

"Spain? No, not a word." LaFleur shook his head. "He never talks about the war. What in hell was he doing in Spain?"

Michael laughed. "Don't know. That was never explained."

"Seems like sort of an important detail."

"Well, you know how closed-mouthed he is about his past. I was surprised he was talking about it at all. He told me this story out on the boat the other day. Don't know what prompted it."

"What was the story?"

"It was about a wood-fired car or truck, something that had been converted from a regular car into a sort of truck, actually, and the fuel tank replaced by a wood-fired device of some kind."

"A gasifier," said LaFleur. "They were used during in the war, due to fuel shortages. Used coal, too, I think."

"Right, that's what he called it, a gasifier. You burned wood in this thing attached to the back of the car, and through a distillation process it provided fuel for the engine. So, he was apparently helping drive one of these wood-fired vehicles, with one other guy, his 'guide,' he said, in Spain of all places. Actually, he said they started out in Lisbon. They were going to Barcelona. He explained that Spain was neutral during the war, which made this trip possible in the first place." Michael raised his hand, anticipating a question from A.C. "No, I don't know how he got there or what he was doing. Like I said, that didn't come up."

They pulled up to the eighth tee, the other two carts close behind. Michael looked back over his shoulder as Maggie and Tamos rolled to a stop. "To be continued," he said.

LaFleur sliced into the rough. Tamos had stayed in the cart, but leaned out to call to LaFleur, "Keep your head down!" Michael drove to the right as well. Frank and Doug ended up about ten yards from one another, far to the left, but still on the fairway.

After they had all finished on the green – LaFleur after a great pitch from the rough and a one-putt to make par – and were on their way to the final hole, Michael resumed the story.

"Well, the description of how they had to keep running back to the unit to refuel it – he said it looked like a big garbage can hanging off the back bumper – had me laughing out loud. Not that it was that funny in itself, but it was the way he told it. We were stopped, and the lake was calm, so he got up from his deck chair and demonstrated, running back and forth like Buster Keaton, with funny little shuffling steps, miming the way they stoked the fire, then drove for a while, then ran to the back of the car to stoke the fire again. Well, they were in a desolate area, very arid, no trees, not much around, but not that far from Barcelona. And they ran out of wood. Oh, the man he was with spoke no English, in fact spoke a Catalan dialect, and Tamos had very little Spanish, and they had to communicate through sign language, practically. Anyway, they knew they didn't need much fuel, just enough to fire the thing up and get them twenty or thirty more miles. These things were apparently very efficient, so just a handful of wood would get them there, they thought. And they were out in the road, looking around –"

"Is this going to take you as long to tell as it did for the professor to actually do it?" LaFleur interrupted.

"Quiet. I'm giving you the short version. As short as I can make it and still get across the way the Prof was telling it. It's important; otherwise you won't get the point."

"Okay, sorry. Go ahead."

"They were out in the road. Middle of the night, pitch dark. And he's imitating walking around in the dark, searching for a scrap of wood, anything. They try to pull up a bush at the side of the road. No good. Then they see a light, off in the distance. Not too far. They head for it. On the way – well, I'll skip ahead, for your benefit – I can't do it justice, anyway."

LaFleur nodded. "That's okay. Go on."

"Oops, here we are," Michael said as they pulled up to the last tee box.

LaFleur had to wait to hear the rest of the story. There was to be a small ceremony in the clubhouse to present the trophy to the winners, none of whom were among the 1850 House group. Maggie left to take Tamos home, and Frank and Doug begged off the post-tournament celebrations, Frank to get back to the restaurant, Doug to get back to Diane. A.C. and Michael found a quiet table in back.

"So, Michael," A.C. said, after the waitress brought their beers, "Finish your story. Prof's story."

Michael took a long draught of beer. "Okay. After making their way through the scrub, they find themselves at a small casita surrounded by an adobe wall, with some ramshackle pens off to one side, very primitive. His partner motions to the pens, says, 'cabra,' and shakes his head, then says 'cabra, no mas.' Tamos recognizes this as 'no more goats,' and for some reason he thinks this is a good sign."

"And?"

"It *is* a good sign, because the guide is able to make some sort of deal with the farmer. Apparently, since the goats are all gone, he doesn't need the pens. At least not for now. A small amount of cash changes hands, and Tamos and his *compadre* become the proud owners of about thirty feet of old goat pen fencing. Which they have to break down and haul about half a mile. And that's what got them to Barcelona."

"And what happened then?"

"Damned if I know," said Michael, taking another swig of beer.

"So, what's the point? You said there'd be a point."

"It has to do with the sense of purpose we were talking about earlier. After telling this story – and all the way through it he'd been very animated, enjoying himself, obviously – he sat back down, looked at me, the way he does, you know, as if trying to look right into you, and said, 'That was the beginning of one of the supreme efforts of my life.' Then he leaned back, pointed out at the lake, and said, 'And this is the other.' It gave me chills, I'll tell you."

LaFleur nodded, looked out the window. "I've said it before. Wish I knew what he was up to," he said.

"Well, hopefully we'll find out soon."

"I hope so. I truly do." LaFleur tipped his bottle up and drained it. "But I doubt that it will come easy."

Duck-Galloo Ridge

LAKE ONTARIO

The water darkened from pale blue to steel gray over the trench separating Galloo and Main Duck islands, lightened again to reflect the pastel sky overhead as the water shallowed near one or the other island, darkened again after the grid turn. It was here that they'd spent the last two days, at the professor's insistence, combing the ledges and banks along, beside and between the two islands, turning only at the Canadian line, or as close as their GPS could pinpoint it. Tamos wasn't sure what standing he would have with the Dominion (as he still thought of that government) if they'd found something on that side of the border. He was (fairly) sure he was in a strong position regarding any discovery made in U.S. waters (thanks to Larry Spiegelman).

"Professor?" It was a call from Aaron. Maggie and Tamos turned to see him bound out of the cockpit, breathless. This had not happened before.

"We've got something. I mean, we've *really* got something." He turned and ran back down below without waiting for a response, footsteps clattering on the metal steps.

"Well," said Tamos, "it is certainly about time." Maggie laughed and helped him to his feet.

"Okay, come on, then. Let's get down there and see what Aaron's so excited about."

Even from the stairway they could see something on the monitors. As they got closer, they could make out more, but the images were fuzzy and indistinct. It took some imagination to see anything other than wavy blotches, blank patches, and a collection of brighter and darker lines. But it was markedly different than anything they had seen so far. Geometric. Regular. Man made.

The professor craned over Maggie's shoulder, trying to get a better look.

"Prof, come over to this monitor," said Aaron, getting up from his seat. As the professor sat down, Aaron leaned over and pointed out a central area on the screen. "This is an image captured a few minutes ago, as we passed over Duck-Galloo Ridge."

"We're coming around now to make another pass," said Red.

"Right," confirmed Aaron. "We want to get several angles on it. Then we can analyze the images back in the lab, enhance details. But we can already see, even without any image enhancement, what looks like a fairly large, and, um, interestingly configured...artifact." He reached over the professor's shoulder and tapped a command on the keyboard, causing the previous screen to disappear, replaced by a moving image.

He could see only more wavy lines, brighter and darker patches flowing across the screen. And then, an outline shining brightly in the monitors, briefly but clearly: a definite *shape*.

The professor's breath caught in his throat.

"That's it," he squeaked.

The shape that so excited the professor was distinctively cross-shaped, slightly bulbous at one end, narrowing at the other, and in his mind, unmistakable. He had spent too many years studying the various configurations of World War II-era fighter planes to be anything but positive in his identification. It was all he could do to restrain himself from jumping up from his seat, running up the ladder, and diving over the edge to get a good look.

"Where's my mask and snorkel?" Tamos cried, twisting in his chair. "How deep is she sitting?"

Captain Dave, who had come down at hearing the commotion, laughed and pointed out figures displayed alongside one of the images. "Looks like she's at about eighty feet, maybe a bit deeper," he said. "Do you free dive that deep, Professor?"

"Ahhhh! The ROV! Red, how quickly can you get that thing in the water?"

Red, who had been standing behind Aaron at the other end of the salon, smiled and shook his head. "Sorry, professor, but we're about out of daylight. It'd take at least an hour to get set up. Then once we got it into the water, it would take about two hours to do an initial survey. So right now, all we can do is log our exact location. It'll be easy to get back to this exact spot first thing tomorrow."

Dave held up his hands. "Don't want to rain on anyone's parade," he said, "but weather's moving in later tonight, so no guarantees on tomorrow. After we get a last set of sonar images, we'll head in. Once we get back to shore, we can talk about next moves."

At Dave's words, LaFleur looked over and saw Tamos's face fall at the news. He got up and walked over to him and laid his hand on the professor's shoulder. "Don't fret, Prof. It'll still be there tomorrow."

Tamos looked up.

"I suppose you're right. It's been a long wait. One more day won't kill me, right?"

1850 HOUSE APARTMENT

Weather, as Captain Dave had predicted, did move in that night, with an unwelcome vengeance. Rain slashed at the windows of the upstairs apartment, short gusts making it slap loudly against the panes between longer periods of a lighter staccato. A comforting ambience, in spite of the occasional violence. A bit like life in general, LaFleur thought, lying in bed waiting for Maggie to finish her nightly rituals; ease punctuated by various levels of distress, but ultimately bearable, even enjoyable.

He waited until Maggie turned off the water at the sink, then called out, "You never finished telling me about Prof's trip to Europe during the war."

"Just a minute," she called back. "There's not much more to tell."

She came back into the bedroom and sat at the edge of the bed. "So, like I told you on the way home, after he returned to the States to go to school, he was helped out by a friend of his father's, someone named Harry Zook. 'Taken under his wing,' as he put it. And you said he told you about his uncle, that he disappeared right after, or before, the invasion of Budapest?" LaFleur nodded as Maggie switched off the bedside lamp and got into bed.

"Yeah, that's where you left off. By the way, how on earth did he manage to get to Hungary at all, during the war? Somehow, we never got into that, when he told me about his uncle."

"I asked him that. He put me off, like he so often does lately, with the 'long story' excuse. All he would say is that it was Harry Zook who arranged everything."

"Harry Zook. He's the guy who had the golf clubs made."

"What? Golf clubs?"

"Yeah. I was telling Michael about it the other day. I'd forgotten the name, but that's it, the friend Tamos designed some golf clubs for, back in the forties. Harry Zook."

"Well, in any case, that's also who got him to Europe. The short version, which is all I got, is that he somehow managed to find his uncle, barely saved him from being deported to who knows where, the camps, whatever, and together they got back to the States."

After nothing more appeared to be forthcoming, LaFleur turned to her. "That's it? That's all he told you? How did they –"

"He was just getting into that when Aaron came up saying they'd located what looked like a wreck," Maggie said. "And so that was that. I tried to bring it up again on the way in to the dock, but he was so excited about finding something that looked like a real possibility that he didn't want to talk about anything else. Well, you were there when we got in, you heard him going on about it."

"Yeah. Well." LaFleur was glad she couldn't see his face in the dark; he was sure the regretfully abject look that he could feel contorting his features would have distressed her. As he was suddenly distressed at the thought that he hadn't yet told her. "About that."

Maggie shifted around to look at him. Streetlight, flickering and distorted from the rain flowing down the front windows, creased his face. She saw him grimace slightly, adjusting the mask he was about to take off.

"I'm waiting."

"It was couple of weeks ago. Tamos let something slip, or maybe he did it intentionally. I didn't tell you earlier because I wasn't sure – oh, hell, I don't know why I didn't tell you. He told me that he was not looking for the B-24, *Getaway Gertie*; had never been interested in it. That was just a cover."

"Cover? For what?"

"He's actually looking for a P-39. Or as he put it, a *particular* P-39."

"And?"

"That's it. That's all we had time for. We were interrupted by something. That may have been the day they found the logs."

"Logs."

"Yeah, just some big logs. Well preserved, I'll bet. I think that old sunken hardwood is worth a lot of money these days. I wonder if they logged the location –"

"You're drifting, A.C.; what about the airplane?"

"That's all he said. A particular P-39."

"And you haven't asked him about it since then?"

"Hasn't ever seemed like the right time. Talking with him lately…I don't know, it's almost like the interrogations I used to do, you know, feeling your way, trying to gauge the suspect's attitude. Is he scared? Over-confident? On edge? Clueless? There's an art to it, something most of the guys I used to work with never had a feel for. They just bludgeoned their way through an interrogation like they were *owed* an answer. All intimidation, no finesse. And for the past few weeks, talking with Tamos, I catch myself thinking in terms of doing an interrogation.

"Feeling my way to the truth."

Zebra Mussels

DUCK-GALLOO RIDGE

It was three days before they got back to the Duck-Galloo ridge. By this time, Tamos was frantic to get the ROV into the water. But simply to verify the find, he said. Not that there was any doubt in his mind. It was all LaFleur could do to keep him out of the way as Aaron and Red lowered the unit into the water.

"My God, A.C., look at that!" The professor was leaning over the rail, staring down into the lake. "You can see it from here!"

LaFleur leaned over the rail next to Tamos. "I don't see anything."

Tamos looked over at him in exasperation. "Take off those polarized glasses," he said. "Look. Right down there, just to the left of where they are dropping the ROV."

"I'll be damned," LaFleur said, raising the sunglasses with one hand, shading his eyes with the other. "I can see it. Not like what we saw on the sonar; just sort of an odd shaped blob. But definitely not natural." He slipped the sunglasses back down. "Why hasn't someone seen it before now?"

"The water is clearer now than it has ever been," answered Tamos immediately. "In recent years there has been an infestation of Zebra and quagga mussels, which are voracious filter feeders. The mussels have cleaned up the water. It used to look like old bathwater."

"Hmm. I knew about the mussels, but didn't know there was anything good about them."

"Oh, it is not all good. Clearer water means more light, which leads to increased algae growth. That is likely what is covering the wreck now."

They looked up as Red called out to them. "Okay, Professor, there it goes," he said, pointing at the ROV, now sinking into the unnaturally clear water. "Let's get below to the monitors."

The professor was right about the wreck being covered with algae, growing on top of a thin layer of silt. The outline, however, was clearly defined. Unmistakable. Definitely an airplane.

Tamos sat at one of the monitors watching with the intensity of a tennis line judge, immobile, head tilted forward, unblinking. As the ROV got closer, the outline visible from above came into clearer focus.

The wreck was lying on a small shelf – exactly eighty-eight feet deep at the nose, as reported by the telemetry from the ROV – with the tail angling downward at about a sixty-degree angle. The ROV approached the wreck from one side, closing to within about twenty feet. Even at close range, in the crystal water, the level of detail was sparse, yet evocative. An obvious bulge near the front had to be the cockpit. In front of that, at the nose, unmistakably, one arm of a bent propeller. The broad outline of a wing, edges softened by the overlaying sediment, stretched away from the fuselage.

The ROV lifted slightly as Erin maneuvered it across the top of the wreck, spinning it around once it got to the other side. Looking back across the wreck they saw that the wing on this side was incomplete, the wingtip torn off. A ragged hole was just visible on the underside, ahead of what looked like a partially raised flap. To the professor's mind it looked like a foreshortened arm reaching out in desperation, clinging to the shelf to prevent the whole thing from sliding down into dark oblivion two hundred and twenty feet below. The sigh that he allowed himself was almost a prayer of thankfulness.

The ROV drifted slowly alongside, inching closer, but revealing no more detail. Erin moved down to the tail section, which appeared to be intact, and protruded above the rest of the wreck in a truncated arc. Although somewhat corroded, it was relative clean. Faint traces of what appeared to be numbers drifted across the screen as Erin piloted the ROV in a close pass past the damaged tail section.

Tamos gripped the edge of the table. "That's it," he said quietly. "That's got to be it."

The ROV swung around to begin another circuit. Aaron was the first to mention the fact that it did not look anything like what they had been led to expect. "Professor? Um, it looks pretty small for a B-24."

LaFleur looked over at the professor, expecting a visible reaction. But if Tamos was at all nonplussed by this, LaFleur didn't see any indication of it.

"Let's just finish our initial exploration and see where that takes us, shall we?" the professor said, with just a glance in LaFleur's direction. "Jamila has not finished her image analysis yet. There is no way to know what that might tell us."

"But, professor –" began Aaron, only to be cut off by LaFleur.

"The professor is right, Aaron. Let's not jump to any conclusions. Stuff underwater looks a lot different than if it were sitting on dry land. We need to get some divers down there to take a closer look. The ROV can tell us only so much."

The professor's look back over his shoulder this time was one of grateful relief.

E. SEVENTH STREET, OSWEGO

The sonar image analysis had taken only a day; Jamila brought the results directly to Tamos at his house the next morning. He had spread the pages of the report out over his small desk, shuffling through them over and over.

He could hardly believe it.

"Jamila, these images are excellent. Just what I'd hoped for. This is it, there's no doubt." His eyes were lit up like a kid finding his first Easter egg.

Jamila didn't quite know how to broach the subject. "But, Professor," she said hesitantly, "this is not the B-24 that you said you were looking for. It's a P-39."

"Yes, yes, exactly. A P-39."

"But, Professor," Jamila repeated, stumbling for something to say, "it's a P-39. Why were you searching for a P-39?"

"Would you be surprised if I told you it was a long story?" answered Tamos.

Jamila laughed. "I've got time," she said.

He motioned to the office door. "Shall we go into the living room?" He pushed himself up from his desk chair. "I'll tell you everything."

Once settled into his chair in the living room, with Jamila on the small sofa across from him, Tamos began.

"You recall the crash at Lisbon," he said, as Jamila nodded, "but the real story has nothing to do with that. That was just an unfortunate bump in the road, as they say. I was very lucky to have survived, certainly. And fortunately, it did not delay me significantly. I was able to make contact with the JDC almost immediately after the crash.

"The trip to Barcelona was relatively uneventful. Once there, I was able to locate my Aunt Eva after just a few hours. She unfortunately had had no word from Béla.

"Two days later, I was on a fishing boat to Sicily, hidden in one of the holds. Though it took only about twenty-three hours to cross, it seemed like an eternity. It was dark, dank, and the reek of rotted fish was overpowering. I have never eaten fish since.

"My next rendezvous point was Dubrovnik, in what was then Croatia, later part of Yugoslavia, recently occupied by Yugoslav partisans. Passed off to a new cadre of JDC operatives, I worked my way north, at first earning my keep doing various menial jobs, gathering firewood, carrying ammunition or radios, that kind of thing. There were episodes along the way that are hard to talk about even now. I was very young, and forced to do things I had never imagined. I am despite it all somewhat proud to say that I earned my keep."

Tamos sighed heavily, looking around the room as if slightly disoriented.

"May I bother you to fetch me a glass of water?" he asked Jamila.
"Of course, Professor," she replied quickly, rising.
"Glasses are in the cupboard to the left of the refrigerator. Tap water is fine, no ice," he said. "Oh, please help yourself to anything in the refrigerator; I believe there are some sodas there, or water, whatever you prefer."
"Thanks," she said, on her way to the kitchen. "Be right back."
Tamos leaned back in his chair and closed his eyes.

***

He had been working his way north for almost three weeks, traveling with several different groups of partisans. As he became known to each partisan faction, he was quickly incorporated into the group as a working member, and given more and more responsibility.
He was now traveling with just four members of a large Croatian partisan group known as the 1st Sisak Partisan Detachment. They were not far from the Hungarian border. Typically moving only by night, they had been forced by circumstances to continue through an occupied area during the day. It was in mid-morning that they emerged from the woods near a tiny village that they smelled the smoke.
It was a favorite Nazi tactic – herd unsuspecting prisoners into a church, creating a false sense of security, and then murder them. It appeared to have some symbolic value, doing it in a church, rather than just killing them in a field or out on the road (which, of course, was also done, if it were more convenient.) Sometimes it was done methodically, several soldiers working their way through the group – who had been forced to lie prostrate with hands behind backs – shooting them in the head. The younger ones were usually killed first. Occasionally, as in this case, the Nazis simply chained the church doors closed and set the church on fire.
From where they now were standing, they could see both the center of the village, a collection of just fifteen or so small houses and a couple of dilapidated two-story buildings, and the small church, which stood some distance away to their right, situated on the road leading away from the town and just on the other side of a stream. There were only remnants of the building still standing – a stone alter, some unevenly burned portions of two walls, and one large section of roof near the back. The rest was smoldering embers, some still flaming, wavering in the soft breeze.
"Milan, Drago." The leader of the partisans, a rough-looking man named Radovan, summoned two of the group to his side. "Check the village, make

sure no one is still there."

The two partisans ran down the road, returning after about twenty minutes.

"It seems empty," reported Drago.

Radovan motioned them towards the church. As they approached, still about fifty feet away, Radovan turned to Tamos.

"You should not go closer," he said, waving Tamos back. "We will look. Wait here."

Tamos shook his head. "No, I will come," answered Tamos.

"As you wish," said Radovan.

It was apparent that as the fire had built up inside the church, everyone locked inside – it looked like the entire population of the village – had gathered at the front doors, scrabbling to get out. The bodies were piled up in a mass, some blackened and burned, others remarkably untouched by flames. At the rear of the building there was a small door, barricaded from the outside, where they found three more bodies.

Radovan called for everyone to gather at the rear of the church. "Well, we must go on," he said. "There is nothing we can do here."

"No burials?" asked Tamos. "Not even a mass grave?"

"No time," said Radovan, brusquely. "It is daylight. We are not safe here. We must return to the forest. We must move."

It was just as they were walking away that Tamos heard it. A muffled cry, off in the woods, not too far away.

"Did you hear that, Radovan?"

"I heard nothing," he said. "We must go now."

There was another cry, unmistakable, louder.

"Radovan," Tamos said, "there is someone out there."

Before Radovan could object further, Tamos had started down a heavily wooded ravine in the direction of the sounds. He stopped after a few steps and turned around. "I'll be back shortly."

Radovan shook his head. "Okay, Tamos, okay. We'll come with you." He motioned to the others and they followed Tamos down the hill.

The ravine made a sharp turn to the right after about one hundred yards, opening on to a tiny clearing. Four women – just girls, really – were lying face down on the ground, hands tied behind them, clothes in disarray, shoes scattered on the grass around them. Two were naked, bleeding from several cuts on their backs and legs. Three Nazi soldiers, helmets off, shirts open, stood over them, passing a wine bottle back and forth, making loud comments and laughing. Their rifles were lying on the ground a few feet away. They still wore their side arms.

Tamos held up his hand in a signal to stop the others as they came up behind him. At this point, they remained well hidden by thick undergrowth, about one hundred feet from the soldiers. Radovan edged up closer to Tamos, leaving Drago, Milan, and Mirko slightly farther back.

"Tamos," he whispered, "this is not our fight."

"We have to act. Should these girls have been saved from the slaughter at the church, only to die this way, horribly, now? How can we let that happen?"

Radovan looked at the ground, then back up at Tamos. "What do you propose?"

Tamos indicated that they should pull back a bit farther into the ravine. When they were all together again, he quickly explained to them what he had in mind. Turning back towards the clearing, he pointed to his left. "This brush extends nearly to the edge of the open space, very close to the soldiers. On the right, there is less cover, but only a short space to cross once we are near. It appears that they will soon be," he said, "well, let us say, busy. We will move into position and wait for the right moment. I will take the right side, with Mirko and Milan. Radovan, you and Drago go to the left. Watch for me to move first; the three of us will be closest to them. Once they are distracted by their business, we all rush them. We cannot risk gunfire, as there are surely others nearby. Use your clubs to subdue them."

"Then what?" Radovan asked.

"Then we will see," said Tamos.

After removing their heavy packs and laying their rifles down, Tamos led them back to the clearing.

Tamos could see the other three across the clearing from him and Mirko as the two of them crawled carefully through the underbrush. The soldiers had become louder and rowdier, drowning out any noise the partisans made. Two of the Nazis had pulled one of the girls up off of the ground and were ripping at her dress, while the third soldier hung back watching, opening another bottle of wine, perhaps to embolden himself. When they had gotten as close as they dared, Tamos moved into a low crouch, as did Mirko. On the other side, he could see the others, also crouched and waiting.

Tamos looked over at his companions. "Now!"

The three of them jumped through the brush, angling towards the two soldiers holding the girl. Tamos brought his cudgel down hard on the head of the first soldier, who collapsed with a loud grunt and remained on the ground, unconscious. Mirko and Milan grabbed the second from behind, and Milan, a huge bear of a man, put his arm around the soldier's throat and took him to his knees and held him there, choking, while Mirko pulled the gun from the soldier's holster. Radovan and Drago had reached the third soldier by now, Radovan tackling him with a flying leap. As he went down, Drago jumped on the soldier's back and was trying to tie his arms behind his back with a piece of rope. The soldier made a violent thrust upward, throwing Drago off onto the ground, then jumped up and made a lunge for Radovan.

Tamos ran over and plunged his knife into the soldier's thigh. With a scream, the soldier fell to the ground, grabbing frantically at his leg. Radovan took this opportunity to kick him squarely in the balls.

The three Nazi soldiers were quickly bound and gagged; they had been completely surprised by the attack, and had been given no opportunity to fight back. Tamos and Radovan untied the women – two quite young, two somewhat older – then stepped back while the two older ones helped the other two back into what was left of their clothing as best as they could. Once that was done, Tamos led them into the shade of a tall tree at the edge of the clearing. They were quaking with fear and adrenaline, sobbing and gasping.

One of the women, perhaps the oldest of the four, looked up at Tamos. "You will kill them now?" she asked in Croatian. Tamos looked to Radovan, his raised eyebrows asking for a translation.

"She says, we should kill them," Radovan said.

Tamos looked over at the three German soldiers. They weren't much older than the girls they had been raping, only seventeen or eighteen, Tamos guessed. The one Tamos had cudgeled had not yet regained consciousness.

"Help me with them," Tamos said, walking towards the soldiers. "Drago, please get the roll of heavy wire from my pack."

While Drago ran up the hill to fetch the wire, Tamos and the others dragged the soldiers to the base of a large pine on the opposite side of the clearing. As soon as he had the wire, Tamos directed the others to stand the two conscious prisoners up against the tree, leaving the third on the ground for the moment.

First, they tied their hands and feet tightly with wire, doing the same for the one lying on the ground. Then, as Milan and Mirko held the third one up against the trunk of the tree, Tamos and Drago pushed the others next to him as Radovan bound them all to the trunk with several wrappings of the wire, under their arms and around their legs just below the knees. When they had finished, they stood back for a moment, ensuring that the three were securely bound. As they finished, the unconscious soldier awakened and looked around dazedly, fear in his eyes.

"I slit their throats," offered Drago. Milan and Mirko assented, offering to help. As they moved for their knives, the three soldiers struggled against the wire in panic.

"No," said Tamos. He walked to the tree and faced the soldiers. "We will not kill you," he said, in German. "We will leave you here, like this." He turned away. "Radovan, please help me talk with the women." They went back to the shade where the women were waiting.

"Radovan, please tell them that we will not kill the soldiers. We will leave them here to their fate." He paused as Radovan related this to the women. The one who had spoken earlier looked up in fury, speaking in a low voice.

"She cannot believe you are so weak as to not kill them right now," Radovan translated.

"Tell her I do not wish to add to their sorrow. They have witnessed family and friends burned alive and themselves terrified and molested in the worst way. They need not add murder by their own hands to their burden. They will bear enough in whatever the future holds for them."

Radovan relayed this to the woman, who replied, still somewhat angrily. "But what will happen to these dogs, she asks?"

Tamos spoke directly to the women. "You can see that the soldiers are tightly tied to the trees with thick wire. Other partisans will find them, if they don't die of exposure first. They will be brutally questioned for intelligence and probably left to die, or killed outright. And we would do the interrogation ourselves, but we cannot stay here, during daylight hours. We have lost much time and must go now. We will take you with us to a safe place. You cannot stay here." Radovan again translated, a short version this time, it seemed to Tamos.

The woman turned and said something to the others sitting beside her, then shrugged. She then said something to Radovan. He did not translate either of her statements for Tamos, but simply said, "Yes, we must go now, Tamos, you are right."

They helped the women to their feet, assisting them in finding their shoes and giving two of the girls some better clothes to wear.

Then they went back up the ravine the way they had come, not looking back. They could hear the Nazis' stifled screams for some time after they slipped back into the deep woods.

They traveled for only forty-five minutes, just far enough to be relatively sure they were out of range of any Nazi encampment that may have been near the village. The women kept up without complaint, but were obviously relieved when Radovan signaled a halt in the middle of a dense thicket of trees.

"We will stop here until nightfall," he said, throwing off his pack.

It took only a few minutes for the men to establish a temporary camp and settle in for a much-needed rest. Secure in the deep woods, they arranged themselves on the ground as comfortably as possible, and in a short time all but Radovan, who had taken first watch, were asleep.

Tamos was awakened just before dark by a noise out in the forest. He jerked upright, seeing that Drago had taken over the watch. Oddly, Drago showed no signs of alarm at the commotion off in the trees.

A moment later, Radovan appeared, followed by the older woman from the village. While Radovan avoided Tamos's gaze, the woman gave him a defiant look as she sat down with her companions, speaking to them softly. Then she turned her face away.

In that one, brief look, Tamos had learned the truth of war.

***

When Jamila returned from the kitchen, the professor was sitting back upright, and reached anxiously for the glass of water.

"Thank you, Jamila." He drank the water down almost desperately, as if suffering great thirst.

"Certainly, no trouble," said Jamila, watching him drain the glass in one long gulp. "I grabbed a soda, thanks." She paused. "Would you like more water?"

"Oh, no, thank you. Well," Tamos continued briskly, "where was I? Oh, yes, it was a little over six weeks later that I was delivered by my partisan colleagues to a safe house in Budapest.

"That is when I met Raoul Wallenberg."

***

Budapest, when Tamos finally reached it, was quiet.

The streets of Buda, on the west side of the river, were deserted, forlorn. A few furtive pedestrians shuffled along the sidewalks, passed by an occasional government or military car. All of the color seemed to have been washed out of the grandiose government buildings lining the banks of the equally drab and decidedly un-blue Danube. Even the trees lining the great boulevards, once so brilliantly green, seemed muted, as if only painted a dull leaf-green. The opposite side of the river was even worse, the steep lanes and alleys of his boyhood were no longer a symbol of the strength and vitality of Pest, but now merely impediments to travel.

Tamos had by this time heard many stories of the mad Swede of Budapest but had not really believed them. But when he saw the blue-and-yellow

Swedish flag displayed prominently above the entrance to a large apartment house in the old Jewish quarter of Pest, which was to be his new temporary home, and then more flags, adorning house after house in the old Jewish quarter, he began to revise his opinion. And when he arrived at the Swedish legation annex, the location of Wallenberg's office, in order to receive his *Schutzpass*, his Swedish "passport," he learned the true extent of Wallenberg's activities.

"My name is Reszö Müller," the dark-haired young man said breezily, taking Tamos's hand firmly. "I've been told you have a mathematical background?"

"Mathematics and physics, yes," answered Tamos. He'd been waiting patiently in the cramped and crowded hallways of the main legation on Benzcûr Street for several days, trying to get in to see anyone who could help him in his search for Béla. That morning he had been sent to another building a few blocks away, and told to report to "C Section." After a wait of more than two hours, he had been ushered in to Müller's office.

"Good, very good," said Müller. "How are you at mental calculations? I'm afraid we don't have any mechanical adding machines to spare."

"Well, I'm tolerably good at it, I suppose, but what I came to see you about –"

"Yes, yes, your uncle, Béla Szabó. We've been working on that; we hope to have definite news any day now. We'll get to all that very soon, I promise. In the meantime, however, I need your help with some rather tedious economic projections. It's important work, creating a relief plan to help rebuild the Jewish community in Hungary after the war. Raoul has been assured by the War Refugee Board and the JDC that they will provide funds to implement such a plan."

Tamos couldn't help but be somewhat taken aback by this. "But isn't that overly optimistic? The current situation is, surely, quite dire."

"You have yet to meet Raoul, who is the soul of optimism. By the way, he is anxious to meet you. He's heard of some of your recent partisan exploits and thinks there may also be a place for you in his field organization. But not until you perform some mathematical wizardry for me." He moved to the door and motioned to Tamos. "Follow me."

Béla, Tamos soon learned, had indeed been taken by the Arrow Cross. Wallenberg's private intelligence network had also learned of his exact whereabouts. The problem was that there were rumors that Béla, along with almost one hundred other captives, were scheduled to be transported by train to the West, presumably to one of the camps, within weeks.

It was during those three short weeks that Wallenberg brought Tamos into his organization, quickly learning that he could rely on Tamos to suggest the least hazardous but optimally effective methods of diverting Jews out of German and Arrow Cross hands and into Swedish-controlled enclaves. Tamos in turn was astounded at the energy and nearly boundless optimism of Wallenberg; his inventiveness, his courage, and his passion combined to make him one of the most impressive persons Tamos had ever encountered.

Wallenberg was to be soon equally impressed with Tamos.

At two o'clock one afternoon a few days later, a report came in to the office that a train was to leave Józsefarós Railway Station at two p.m., bound for Auschwitz. Béla was among those to be taken.

Wallenberg called his driver. With Tamos and two other agents, they were immediately driven to the station, followed by a large number of cars flying the Swedish flag. The prisoners had been boarded, but the carriage doors and windows remained open. There were both German SS and Arrow Cross lined up along the platform. A young SS officer seemed to be in command.

As Wallenberg got out of the car and saw the situation, Tamos saw a flash of doubt in his eyes. It was the briefest of moments, but it was the first time Tamos had seen Wallenberg hesitate.

Wallenberg stood almost motionless, staring at the train and its guards.

"Mr. Wallenberg?" Tamos asked softly.

Wallenberg turned almost imperceptibly towards Tamos. "Yes?"

"Something must be done, sir." Tamos was trembling with the audacity he had just shown, momentarily unsure of himself.

"Have you any ideas, Mr. Szabó?" asked Wallenberg, quietly and without much enthusiasm.

Tamos lifted the attaché case he was carrying. He had a sudden inspiration. "We have over one hundred Swedish passes. In the past three weeks, I have seen you perform what a religious person would call 'miracles,' sir. Many times. Against all odds. I believe now is the time for yet another miracle. Force them to release the prisoners."

Wallenberg continued to stare at the train, as if calculating his odds.

"There is no good outcome without action, sir," said Tamos forcefully. "We don't have much time."

Wallenberg turned slowly now, looking Tamos in the face. "Well, as you have proven many times in the recent past, you truly are a young man in a hurry, aren't you? So, we will do as you suggest. Back me up if necessary," he added, knowing full well that he could rely on Tamos to do whatever was required of him.

With that, he took the briefcase from Tamos and stalked to the platform, his long leather coat trailing in the wind, waving the briefcase over his head as he walked. "These are my people," he shouted. "These are their passes. Issued by the sovereign state of Sweden."

To the amazement of everyone there, German, Arrow Cross, and the Jews on the train, Wallenberg then did a most remarkable thing. He climbed to the top of the first railcar, and bending precariously over the side as he walked along the roof of the car, handed out passes to outstretched hands.

At a signal from the commanding SS officer, several Arrow Cross soldiers raised their rifles and fired into the air, over the top of Wallenberg's head. The SS officer screamed at Wallenberg. "Stop what you are doing!"

Wallenberg, scarcely noticing the gunfire, ignored the officer's threats and calmly continued along the car, handing out passes the whole way. Several more shots were fired.

Tamos quickly pulled a yellow-and blue placard embossed with the Swedish diplomatic seal from his coat pocket and ran to the platform. He thrust the card into the air, practically into the faces of the men firing at Wallenberg. "Cease firing!" he shouted in German and Hungarian. "By authority of the Royal Swedish legation, I order you to cease firing immediately!" He moved down the line of soldiers, card held high, shouting at each of the men in turn, until he reached the German officer commanding the troops. "You! Are you in charge here?"

The officer nodded dumbly, cowed by the fury in Tamos's voice, the authority in his stance.

"These people are under the protection of the Royal Swedish legation," shouted Tamos. "Order your men to stop firing immediately!"

The officer, not much older than Tamos, was completely intimidated by the force of Tamos's demands. He raised his hand and made a short chopping motion. The soldiers stopped firing.

Wallenberg continued down the line, until he had distributed passes to all three train cars at the platform, then climbed down and ordered everyone off of the train. As the passengers hesitantly disembarked and milled around on the platform, Wallenberg walked to where Tamos was standing, now a few feet from the Nazi officer.

"Tamos," he said, loudly, "please escort our citizens to the cars."

Tamos moved quickly to the door of the first carriage, and motioning the other two aides to the platform, instructed them to assist at the other two cars.

Abruptly, standing in front of him, was Béla.

Tamos enveloped Béla in a strong embrace, but could find no words. Béla, tears streaming down his face, was unable to speak as well. Then there was time for only a few, short instructions, as Tamos continued to herd the disembarking passengers to the waiting cars, Béla among them.

"You are being taken to a Swedish legation house." Tamos explained quickly as they walked. "It is essentially Swedish territory, no one can touch you there. I will find you, whatever house you end up at, as soon as we have everyone resettled." Béla started to be pulled away by the anxious crowd around him, and he reached for Tamos. "Don't worry!" Tamos called as their fingers brushed. "I will see you soon!"

Tamos turned his head and saw an old man stumble next to him. He caught him in his arms, helped him steady himself, and sent him on his way to the cars. When he turned back, Béla was already gone.

The chain of chance had been once again extended.

Or broken, depending on perspective.

***

It was fairly late by the time he finished the story and Jamila left for home. Reliving those two episodes of his life, one kept private, the other related to Jamila, had exhausted him. Tamos drank another large glass of water, stretched out on his bed without undressing, and fell asleep instantly. Fortunately, he did not dream; all of his dreams these days were waking dreams, out on the placid water of Lake Ontario.

Stop the Presses!

1850 HOUSE

LaFleur was behind the bar, slowly leafing through a four-day-old Palladium-Times someone had left behind, while sipping a Famous Grouse (this early in the afternoon, just a floater).

"The timing is almost perfect," Tamos was saying. "I talked with Hamilton UWS this morning; they are just finishing up a job for the Toronto Police, and only one other obligation scheduled at the start of next week, so they should be free in about five days. Seven at the most."

The company Tamos had contracted with operated out of Hamilton, Ontario; not ideal, being some distance away, but the smaller company he'd contacted in near-by Kingston had not given him a good feeling, and the large, Toronto-based outfit he'd checked with earlier was now completely booked until the fall. "Hamilton's divers can get started on the preliminaries in a day or two." Tamos raised his glass (mineral water) and nodded in the direction of the Wurlitzer. "Not long now," he said, as the first bars of *In the Mood* bugled out.

LaFleur tilted his head up from the newspaper and pulled his glasses down off the bridge of his nose, looking over at the professor. "Um, Prof? Do you read the Times?"

Tamos put down his drink and shifted his chair in LaFleur's direction. "The New York Times? 'All the news that fits, we print?' That Times?"

"I've heard that joke before. No, the Palladium-Times, the Oswego paper."

"Oh, I subscribe, an old habit, but I rarely do more than skim through it occasionally. There is not much there that interests me anymore. I stopped reading obituaries long ago."

"Well, there's something here I think you need to see," said LaFleur, coming around the bar. He folded the paper into quarters and put the resulting page on the table in front of Tamos. "This is from a few days ago. There, in the corner."

The small headline might as well have been a foot tall: *WWII P-39 Fighter Plane Found in Lake Ontario*. Tamos didn't even read the article before jerking his head up. "What is this, A.C.?" he said, his voice weak. "How did that get there?"

"Not sure. There's a byline." He spun the paper around and took a closer look. "Tiffany Peet. That name sounds familiar, for some reason."

Tamos looked up in alarm. "That's Aaron's girlfriend. He told me about her a few weeks ago, oh, what was it, how they do not get to see one another very often. Since she is majoring in Journalism at SUNY Oswego, and has a summer internship at the paper." He shook his head. "I am afraid I wasn't very sympathetic."

"But had you even told Aaron this?"

"No, of course not." Tamos scowled, his face wrinkling up in distress. LaFleur had never seen him quite this unsettled. Then Tamos's face cleared. "Ah. He must have overheard us on the boat that day, when I told you I wasn't really looking for *Gertie*. I remember him standing there, while we were talking, now that I think of it." He reached out and pulled the paper back in front of him and read the article, two short paragraphs. "No details. That is something, anyway. Well, of course, there are no details, we had only just discovered it, and there is after all no guarantee that it –" He held a hand to his forehead, as if in pain. "In any case, Aaron has let out the cat."

LaFleur smiled. "I'll talk to Aaron, make sure he doesn't say anything more to this girl," he reassured Tamos. "And no real harm done, right?"

"I suppose not," a still glum Tamos replied. "I know it will be impossible to keep this quiet, after we actually raise the airplane. In fact, I do not plan to even try to keep it quiet at that point. Just the opposite. But for now, I want as little publicity as possible. The time is not right."

"Well, once the wreck comes up, it's going to be sensational. If it is what you say it is."

"Oh, it is that, A.C., it is that. And it will be at *least* sensational." He pushed the paper away and took another sip of his drink. "Well, as you say, no harm done."

A few days later, Michael had a visitor.

"Dr. Fuentes?"

Michael looked up from the journal he was reading. Brandi, one of the new girls from reception, stood in the doorway of his office.

"Um, yes, what is it?"

"There's an elderly gentleman in the lobby who would like to talk to you."

Michael sighed. Brandi surely could have just called from the reception desk. But this was the third – no, fourth – time that she'd found some excuse to visit his office in the last week.

Michael pushed his chair back and sighed again. He'd just heard from one of the orderlies that there was a sort of contest going on between a few of the single female staff – who would be the first to get a date with Dr. Fuentes. There were no bets placed, as would have been the case had this been male staff angling for a date with a new nurse, but according to the orderly the competition was heating up.

“Did he give you a name?” Michael asked as he stood up and started for the door. Tall and athletic – and according to some of the nurses, so good-looking as to be nearly unapproachable – Michael’s approach seemed to fluster Brandi, and she stuttered, “Uh, “Say-bow?”

“Professor Szabó?” *Tsah-bō.*

“Yes, that’s it,” she said, obviously relieved that she’d gotten it almost right. Michael could be impatient with staff at times, but so far, she hadn’t done anything to annoy him. She backed into the hallway.

“I’ll walk you down,” she said.

“That’s not really necessary, Brandi.”

“Oh, I don’t mind at all, Dr. Fuentes,” she said brightly, stepping to his side.

Michael was afraid for a moment that she was going to try to take his hand, but by the time they got to the elevator, she’d calmed down, and they rode down together in silence.

The professor was sitting off to one side in a waiting area.

“Hello, professor,” said Michael as he sat down across from Tamos. “How are you?”

“Fine, fine. I need some advice, Michael. I hope I am not intruding?”

“No, it’s okay. I have a few minutes.”

“It is not a big issue, just a slight disagreement I’m having with my GP.”

“Remind me, who are you seeing?”

“Linnabarger, at Port City Medical Clinic.”

“Oh, yes. Across from Fort Ontario, just down the street from your house. I don’t know him that well personally, but I hear he’s good.”

“He is doing a fair job, so far, I guess. But I’ve learned from you, that as an anesthesiologist, you cannot focus on just one aspect of a person’s health. You need to look for anything that could conceivably cause a problem during anesthesia. Things that might be out of the ordinary. That’s why I came asking for your advice.”

“Well, yes, it’s true that I try to look at a person’s entire history. And I spend a lot of time on observation. But, anyway, what’s the issue? Not related to too much excitement out on the lake, I hope?”

“Oh, no. I have no trouble keeping up. No, my question concerns diet. Dr. Linnabarger tells me I am drinking too much milk.”

Michael cocked his head, repressing a smile. “How much are you drinking? And what does he think is too much?”

“Oh, no more than two quarts a day, most days.”

“Why do you think you need to drink that much? That is quite a bit.”

“Ever since I fell and cracked my hip, seven or eight years ago, I’ve been drinking a lot of milk. To stave off osteoporosis. And I love milk. Sentimental reasons, you could say. I guess it goes back to the early days, when I first came to the Fort."

"You developed a love of drinking milk at the Fort? How did that come about?"

"Oh, never mind. That is not important. In any event, is it all right for me to drink a lot of milk?"

"Well, I always go back to the Greeks: 'all things in moderation.' But you're probably okay drinking that much. Certainly, a great source of easy protein, as well. No signs of any lactose intolerance, no gastrointestinal issues?"

"No."

"Then I'd say, enjoy your milk. Linnabarger may be trying to micromanage a bit too much. Don't tell him I said that."

"No, certainly not. In any case, that is what I wanted to hear."

"There's nothing else?"

"No. Michael, that's it. Thank you."

"Any time, professor."

Bot

WASHINGTON, D.C., FOUR DAYS EARLIER

In a dimly lit computer room in the lower levels of a huge but otherwise unremarkable office tower, a warning bell chimed on a computer monitor.

The operator, a youngish man with a full, dark beard and tinted glasses, read the message that popped up. An Internet bot had just flagged two small newspaper articles, one in the Syracuse Post-Standard and one in the Oswego Palladium-Times. A WWII-era aircraft, a P-39, had been located in Lake Ontario.

The operator typed a quick command. A notification went out, and the message disappeared.

That's No B-24

DUCK-GALLOO RIDGE

The aircraft emerged from its obscurity slowly. Soft edges hardened into sleek, hard lines. Colors, though extremely muted and dull at this depth, began to display themselves. Details quickened almost magically as the divers siphoned off the overlaying sediment. By three in the afternoon, after an hour-and-a-half surface interval, they had also finished their survey of the underlying ledge and surrounding topography, in preparation for setting the lift bags. It was now obvious to everyone what was lying beneath them, and the ROV video dramatically confirmed what the final sonar imaging had shown it to be: a Bell Aircraft P-39 Airacobra.

The professor had been busy for the past couple of days, apologetically explaining his subterfuge, trying to convince everyone that it had been necessary, for reasons that would become clear, and that the true object of his search had never been the B-24, *Getaway Gertie*, but had all along been a P-39. *This* P-39. Beyond admitting to that, however, he remained as evasive as ever. The necessity of the ruse, however, even if accepted by the rest of the crew, was not at all clear to A.C., not by a long shot. But given the current level of excitement, and the activity surrounding the salvage operation now in progress, his doubts would have to wait.

The professor had been staring intently at the ROV monitor as the divers worked. He had been sitting at the monitor all morning, in fact, and into the afternoon, not daring to move. A.C. finally managed to get him up on deck, but not until the divers had surfaced and were climbing back up onto the boat. Even then, Tamos would not sit still. He edged to the back of the boat to the dive deck, hauling himself carefully along the side railing. The first diver was still standing at the dive ladder in full gear when the professor began questioning him.

"How does it look?" he asked anxiously. "Is it damaged? It looks very solid on the ROV images. What did it look like to you?"

The diver, Danny Mack, one of the owners of Hamilton Under Water Salvage, slipped off his neoprene hood, and shook out his long, curly hair, laughing. "Hold on a minute, Professor! Let me get settled." He moved to the side and sat down heavily on the dive bench while the other diver – the professor couldn't remember his name at the moment – came up the ladder, then sat down next to Danny. As they both stripped off their scuba gear, Captain Dave came over to carry it to the rinse tank at the back of the deck.

"It looks very solid, Professor," Danny said, pulling the top half of his wetsuit down and toweling off. “Surprisingly solid. Of course, we can’t say for sure, but I don’t see any problems with bringing it up.”

“What about the cockpit? Any broken glass?”

“Nope, looks intact. Can’t tell too much, though, about the condition inside. Can’t see through the glass. It’s still covered with scum.”

“But the cockpit, it is not damaged? From the ROV, it does not look like it had been opened. Could you see any evidence of that? As if it had been opened, I mean?”

“Not that I could see. And it looks like it has a solid roof…is that normal? I thought those old fighter cockpits were all glass canopies or something.”

“No, the P-39 had a solid roof. And swinging side doors. Sort of like car doors.”

The other diver – Buddy, Tamos now remembered – was now standing and pulling off his wetsuit. “Yeah, looks real solid, the doors looked closed tight.”

A.C. came back over to them – he’d been helping Dave with the dive gear – and stood by Tamos. “What’s the next step, guys?” he asked. “Is it ready to come up?”

Danny reached up and ran his hands through his hair. “Don’t see why not,” he said.

A.C. put his hand on Tamos’s shoulder. “So, Prof, are you ready to bring ‘er up?”

Tamos jerked his head towards LaFleur. “What did you say?”

“I said, are you ready to bring up the wreck?”

Tamos reached up and put his hand on LaFleur’s, which was still resting on his shoulder. “Ah, yes, A.C., I am ready.” Tamos turned away and closed his eyes.

Captain Dave walked up behind them and clapped his hands. “Okay. Time to get back.”

“What, now?” asked Tamos, incredulously.

“Yeah, it’s getting late. What do you think, guys, leave the dock at eight sharp tomorrow? How long will it take to load your salvage gear?”

“Let’s make it nine, Dave,” said Danny. We’ll see you the dock at about seven?”

“That works.” Dave went forward. Danny and Buddy began to stow their gear.

“Help me over to a deck chair, A.C.?” Tamos asked.

“Sure. Hang on to my arm.”

As Tamos settled into his chair, LaFleur taking a chair at his side, they heard the engines start up. A few minutes later Dave turned the boat and headed back to shore.

Tamos didn’t speak all the way in.

Red Star

DUCK-GALLOO RIDGE

The cockpit emerged first, like a miniature whale breaking the surface, shedding water in silent sheets. A tiny spot of light flashed brightly – reflected perhaps from a sliver of exposed metal or glass – as the canopy bobbed and floated in the sun, as if signaling its unlikely arrival into the future. A bare moment later, with a rushing sound of flowing air and water, the entire wreck surfaced, like a submarine in an old war movie. There was dead silence on the deck of the *Diving Duck* for that brief moment as the waters parted, and then: pandemonium.

Oblivious to all of the shouting, whistling, and hollering, Tamos gripped the rail tightly, supported by LaFleur on one side and Maggie on the other. The rest of the crew crowded along the side rail along with them, fore and aft, Aaron up top, Dave at the rear dive deck, watching for the divers to come back to the boat.

"My God, A.C.," Tamos finally managed to say. "Look at that. Look at that."

Held up by several large, black inflatable bags, some of them visible in front of the wings, the wreck swung slowly back and forth, tethered by a long cable that stretched out from a winch at the stern. One arm of the propeller stood straight up, its tip bent as if in salute. In the back, just in front of the tail section, more black pods hovered just below the surface of the water, attached by a wide belt wrapping the rear fuselage. Other inflatable pods, Tamos knew, clung to the underside of each wing, but were not visible.

"Congratulations, Prof!" yelled Maggie and LaFleur, nearly in unison. Tamos looked from one to the other, beaming. As they shook hands and patted one another on the back, Jamila came up behind them, followed closely by Red.

"Can we crash this party?" she asked, with a broad smile.

"Jamila!" cried Tamos, turning to gather her in his arms. "Jamila, thank you, thank you!"

"Oh, Professor, no thanks, please! This is your doing. I was just glad to come along for the ride."

"Ah, but Jamila, without RIT this never could have happened." Tamos turned to Aldridge. "And you, Dr. Aldridge, you also deserve a great deal of credit."

"Don't worry, we'll take credit where it is due."

"Tamos," Jamila said, waving her hand out across the water towards the wreck, "this is your victory!"

Tamos turned back to the railing and looked out at the object floating out on the lake, about forty or fifty feet away. Tamos strained to take in every detail. Olive drab, streaked and blotchy from its long rest under water, the plane drifted serenely in the afternoon sun, defying time and nature and circumstance. Numbers were painted on the side, some indistinct, others clearly visible, white on the fuselage in front of the cockpit and yellow on the rear tail section. Also, plainly visible, on the fuselage just ahead of the tail, a star: a five-pointed star on a white background.

A red star.

LaFleur left Tamos standing at the railing and walked aft, where Captain Dave was helping one of the divers up from the rear dive platform – Mark, LaFleur remembered. "Great job, guys!" LaFleur said, taking the diver's elbow to help support him as he turned to remove his scuba gear.

"Thanks!" Mark slipped out of his gear as a crew member stepped up to carry it off to the side. "What an amazing find, huh?" he said. "Incredible!"

"That it is," agreed LaFleur.

"Is it a Russian fighter?" Mark asked.

LaFleur glanced out in the direction of the wreck. "Russian? No, it's American, a P-39. Why do you ask that?"

"The star on the side. Isn't that a Russian insignia?"

LaFleur rubbed the back of his neck as he considered the question. The scrap of metal that had been found off of Sandy Point – the one the professor had seen hanging on the wall of the 1850 House – had the same star on it, and LaFleur had always been vaguely troubled by it. It had never looked quite right. And now that the diver had questioned it, LaFleur suddenly realized the diver was right. It *was* Russian. Soviet, actually. A Communist star. *What the hell?*

Before they could continue the conversation, they heard someone yelling. Danny had surfaced and stripped off his tank and buoyancy compensator, which were now floating next to the airplane, and had climbed up onto the wing of the wreck. Waving, arms outstretched and rotating above his head, he called over to the boat. LaFleur made his way back to Tamos's side at the railing.

"What's he saying?" asked Tamos.

"Can't quite make it out," said LaFleur.

Danny cupped his hands around his mouth and hollered again, his voice reaching the boat more clearly this time: "I've found something!" He leaned over and pointed emphatically to the cockpit, then reached out and wiped his hand over a small, clear patch of glass. He stood up and megaphoned his mouth again. “The pilot!” He pointed once again at the cockpit. “The pilot! The pilot is still in here!’

Before anyone had a chance to respond, Tamos reached over to LaFleur, taking him by the elbow and leaning in close. “That’s not just any pilot, A.C.,” he said quietly.

“She’s my wife.”

BOOK III: WARTIME

Flying with Amelia

1928: CANASTOTA, NEW YORK

When Amelia Earhart landed her new Airster biplane at Canastota airport for the dedication ceremony, Jeri Jillette was ready with the wheel chocks. It was not even two months after Earhart's famous flight across the Atlantic, and just two days before Jeri's tenth birthday.

The opening of Canastota Airfield was a minor triumph for George Jillette, who had been promoting it for years. Now it was a reality: two perfectly graded, two-thousand-foot sod runways, on-site gas, a new Airway Beacon, and a red course light continuously flashing the airport code "H" in Morse – *di-di-di-dit, di-di-di-dit.*

As soon as it stopped rolling, Jeri ran to the ship with her father, dragging one heavy chock block behind her, her father pulling the other. She was a slim girl, though tall for her age, but very strong, and so a bit awkward. There were very few jobs at the field she didn't help with, except pumping av gas. Dad and Natty, her older brother, handled that.

Jeri had her chock in place quickly, and as soon as the prop had stopped turning, they ran around to the left side of the plane. Together they waited as the pilot stepped off of the wing down to the ground. Wearing black jodhpurs, a white blouse with a short black tie, and a long, leather flying jacket, Amelia Earhart was the epitome of the new era of women's aviation. As she pulled her goggles up onto the top of her flying cap, she suddenly saw Jeri standing there, hanging on to her father's arm.

"My goodness! Look at you!"

Jeri just gaped, shrinking a bit behind her father, who stepped forward and offered his hand.

"Miss Earhart, welcome to Canastota Airfield!" He reached out and shook Earhart's hand, as Jeri continued to gape. "Let me introduce you to my daughter, Jeri," he said, pushing her into view from behind his back.

"Well, hello, Miss Jillette," Earhart said brightly. "Was that you I saw blocking the wheels?" Jeri nodded, peering out from under her long, dark bangs. "Well, that's marvelous. I'll bet you are pretty excited about your father's new airfield!"

"Yes'm," Jeri managed to croak, in a voice low and tremulous.

"Interested in flying?"

“Oh, yes, ma’am!” Jeri couldn’t believe her ears. Amelia Earhart was offering to take her flying!

“We’ll see what we can do about that.” Earhart turned to Jeri’s father, George Jillette, who at six-feet-one, towered over the slight Earhart, who was all of five-eight and one hundred and eighteen pounds. “Has the Kinner sales rep arrived yet?” she asked George. Earhart was in the middle of a mini-barnstorming tour across the east, promoting the latest model from the Kinner Airplane and Motor Corporation, a three-seater with a new, more powerful K-2 engine.

“Yes, yes, he’s over at the diner,” George replied, pointing across Route 5, which ran along the airstrip to the south. “Mother’s been taking good care of him while we were waiting for your arrival.”

“Wonderful. Oh, what time is the ceremony?”

“Two o’clock,” said George. “Plenty of time to get you a bite to eat before the festivities.”

The three of them marched off to the diner, George and Amelia side-by-side, Jeri running circles around them, hair flying, arms spread out like wings.

Sportwing

1933: CANASTOTA, NEW YORK

Harry had flown solo around the world in a single-engine airplane, one short jump after another, seeing sights most people couldn't even imagine. He flew almost daily from Lloyd Harbor, Long Island, near Oyster Bay, to the marine terminal on the East River in the city, commuting from his estate to his law office on Fifth Avenue, passing over some of the most scenic bays on the east coast. He'd even helped design a new model seaplane for Grumman Aircraft, now one of the most popular ships in its fleet.

But given all that, it was flying around upstate New York that enthralled him. Soaring over the lakes and fields and forests, landing at small grass strips or short gravel runways, a paved runway a real treat in a "larger" town. Grabbing a bite to eat in a small-town luncheonette, a roadside diner, or a lakeside tavern. And the lakes: Saranac Lakes in the Adirondacks, spread out like inkblots on billiard table felt; the Finger Lakes, huge bear claw marks groping their way south from Lake Ontario; Lake Champlain, hanging like a dark silk shawl down from Canada. He loved the small towns, founded not long after the revolution, towns with hopeful, patriotic names recalling the great generals and statesmen of the Golden Age, all but forgotten by the local townspeople of the current day, but great heroes to the founders: Cincinattus, Hannibal, Scipio, Sempronious.

Most of all he loved the unpretentiousness, the simplicity of those townspeople. A welcome relief from the scrabbling, voracious world of entertainment law. Yes, law afforded him the estate, the Packard automobiles, the townhouse on Park Avenue, and most important, the airplanes; but – and he knew this to be a cliché, but nonetheless true for all that – at what real cost?

So, for no reason other than that it was a bright, fall day, and the landscape below him looked particularly inviting, Harry Zook touched down at the tiny Canastota Airfield, just east of Syracuse at the southeastern tip of Oneida Lake (the name "Canastota" derived, he was later told, from the Oneida words for pine and still waters, a prefect description).

And so it was that Harry first met Jeri.

She was sitting on a bench in front of the hanger with a large drawing pad balanced on her knees, sketching the old Stearman biplane that was sitting out in the field, when the Kinner Sportwing came barreling in. She had her Oshkosh overall pant legs pulled up to just below her knees, shirt sleeves rolled halfway to her elbows so they didn't smudge the dark pencil. She'd just bobbed her hair the week before. Mother said it made her look like a tomboy, which Jeri didn't mind; she was off boys this season. At fourteen, going on fifteen, she had started to "fill out," as it was said, and that sort of attention just made her anxious. She'd never been one to primp and preen, always thinking herself a bit plain.

She did not, in her mind, at fourteen going on fifteen, have the sort of features that inspired comparisons to movie starlets. Her chin was too sharp, her forehead too wide, her nose too small, her mouth too thin, her ears too low, and her hair mousy brown. In truth, her chin was well-formed and in correct proportion to her somewhat narrow face, her forehead high and intelligent, her nose pert, her lips unassuming, her ears just right, and her hair – well, yes, it was mousey brown. Still, if comparisons were to be made, she looked a bit like Mary Astor. All in all, not bad.

The Sportwing made one pass, low and loud, then angled up and away to make another approach. *Judging the length of the runway*, Jeri thought to herself. *Smart*. The second time around, the Sportwing touched down at the east end of the runway, its streamlined wheel skirts thrust out in front of it like stubby little arms. The tail wheel dropped quickly, and the pilot wasted no time in bringing the sleek little ship to a stop, doing a one-eighty at the far end of the runway, then taxiing back towards the hanger.

As the noise of the engine died, Jeri ran out to greet the visitor, who was just pulling up his goggles and looking around. She'd taken over some of the airport operations, now that she was older, to give Dad a break once in a while.

The pilot looked very small sitting in the one-seat, open cockpit; his head barely reached the level of the windscreen. At seeing Jeri, he raised a hand. "Hello, there!" he called. "Where am I?"

This stopped Jeri in her tracks. *Where am I? Was he lost?* "Canastota!" she hollered. After a moment's hesitation, she added, "New York!"

At this, the pilot climbed out onto the wing, holding on to one of the struts. "New York!" he said. "Thank goodness! I thought I might have missed a turn and ended up in some far-off, exotic land, like Pennsylvania, or maybe Vermont." He said this with such good nature in his voice that Jeri immediately caught on to the joke.

"Oh, no," she replied, solemnly. "This is New York, all right. Either that, or my parents have been lying to me all these years."

With a laugh, the pilot jumped down to the grass. He was short, as Jeri had expected, and a bit bow-legged, though she could see through his flight suit that he was stocky, a little bull. He pulled off his flying helmet and goggles to reveal a large head of shortly cropped, graying hair above a finely formed face. Jeri immediately thought of a picture of a Roman bust she had seen in her history book, and the phrase 'chiseled features' popped into her head.

"Well, Miss, now that we have determined *where* I am, I should tell you *who* I am." He offered his hand. "Harry Zook, at your service."

Jeri took his hand with a slight curtsey. "Jeri Jillette, sir. Pleased to meet you." She gestured toward a small building at the edge of the airfield. "Please follow me to the operations office," she said. "You can wait there while I run across the road and get my father. He's the manager."

After lunch and gassing up, Harry came back from the diner and got ready to leave. "Best apple pie I've ever had," he had assured Jeri's mother.

"This has been great, kiddo," he told Jeri as he pulled on his helmet. "Next time I'm here, it will be in a two-seater, I promise."

Jeri just nodded, already counting the days. Two weeks, he'd said. She suddenly looked over toward the hanger. "Oh, my sketchbook," she said. "I don't want to leave it lying there while you power up; just a second." She ran to the bench and grabbed her pad, then ran back.

"What have you got there?" Harry asked.

"Oh, just my drawing book. I like to draw airplanes."

"May I see?"

"Sure, I guess so," she said, shyly, handing it over. "There's only a few."

He flipped through the pages carefully, pausing at each one. "These are wonderful!" he said, handing it back. "Do you want to be a professional artist someday?"

"Oh, no," she said. "This is just something I do for fun."

"Well," Harry asked, and this was a question, being without children of his own, he was always anxious to ask, "what do you want to do?"

"Fly," she said.

Harry dropped in to visit Canastota pretty regularly the rest of that fall, until the weather turned, and always in a two-seater, or bigger, just as he'd said he would, taking Jeri up more than once. She had a glorious time, especially since Harry didn't treat her like a kid, and was not afraid to show her some pretty radical maneuvers. They never let on to Dad, though he suspected she was getting the thrill of her life. Mother, Jeri knew, didn't like the thought of her flying at all, but she kept it to herself, mostly.

At Christmastime, Jeri packed up four of her favorite artworks – wrapped in tissue paper, sandwiched between layers of cardboard, with a handmade Christmas card laid on top, placed in a very sturdy box, marked "Very

Fragile" and "DO NOT BEND" in four places – and sent them to Harry in New York.

Arvin, the old postman, seeing the address, teased her unmercifully: "Oh, a rich boyfriend in New York City? Park Avenue! Ooh, la la!"

Ears burning, Jeri pushed the package across the scarred wooden counter. She'd had a hard time finding Harry's address. She knew he had a big estate out on Long Island somewhere, but also had a townhouse in the city. She'd finally gotten his Park Avenue address from the long-distance operator.

"Your stupid Post Office better get this there in one piece!" she blurted. It was the best she could come up with on short notice.

Arvin laughed and picked up the package gingerly. "Oh, don't worry, Miss Jillette, it will get there fine."

"Well, see that it does," she said in her best adult voice. "It's very important."

Arvin nodded, abashed. "Sorry, Jeri. You know we'll take good care."

With a quick nod in return, Jeri whirled and marched to the front door, throwing a sharp glance back over her shoulder as emphasis. Out on the steps, she stopped and looked down at her feet.

I hope he likes them.

Harry had invited a few friends over to the townhouse for an impromptu Christmas Eve party. Since everyone he'd invited had already arrived, the call from the doorman was unexpected.

"Late mail delivery, Mr. Zook."

"Alright, send it up, please."

After taking the package from the bellman, Harry started to put it on the foyer table, intending to deal with it later. Then he saw the return address. He peered back at the living room where his guests were gathered, four of the most prominent men in New York – one a partner in Harry's firm, one a member of the Exchange, the other two well-known financiers and partners in his aviation venture – and saw that they were deep in conversation and conviviality. He rummaged in the small drawer under the table top, found a penknife, and carefully slit the package open. He saw immediately that the table was too small. Carrying the package into the other room, he laid it on a large sofa table, pushing a small sculpture to one side.

"Excuse me, gentlemen," he said, "but I've just received something from a friend of mine, and I'm anxious to see what it is." He looked quickly at the card on top, smiled, and set it aside. Pulling the first sheet from the box, he unwrapped it and laid it on the table. His friends had gathered around by this time, drinks in hand, peering curiously at the drawing.

"Some new art acquisitions, Harry?" one asked. "Something from

Widenstein, perhaps?" he said, naming a prominent art gallery close by. He took a closer look. "No, surely not."

"No, no. Something from a friend," Harry said, as he looked down at a pencil drawing of an old Stearman biplane sitting in a field. *The picture she was making when I landed there the first time*, he realized. "A girl I met at a small airfield out west, Canastota," he said as he pulled the next picture from the box. "She could be a great artist, but she –" His voice caught in his throat as he unwrapped the picture and saw what it was. The Sportwing. Not just a pencil drawing, it was a finely executed watercolor, every detail correct, the red Sportwing logo practically glowing on the side of the gleaming, white fuselage, the laminated wooden prop shining, every rivet and strut portrayed perfectly. It was exquisite. He glanced at the two remaining drawings. They looked equally fine. *She must have spent hours and hours on these.* He felt a pang at the thought of his comparatively uninspired gift to her, a set of hair clips. Well, yes, Tiffany, and gold, but picked out by his secretary. His eyes burned.

He cleared his throat, carefully rewrapped the drawings, and said, a little brusquely to cover the tremor in his voice, "Well, you fellows are not interested in these little things." He motioned them back to the living room.

As they made their way back to their seats, Harry stopped suddenly and looked around. He must soon decide which of the Old Masters to take down off the wall to make room for his newly acquired, and already treasured, masterpieces.

Coast to Coast

BOSTON TO NEW YORK

From the journal of Jeri Jillette, twenty years old, aboard an American Airlines Douglas Sleeper Transport, recording her experiences on her first coast-to-coast commercial flight, from Boston to Los Angeles, via New York.

She is on her way to a new job at Douglas Aircraft in Long Beach, California.

5:30 PM - Close to Newark

We are above the clouds over Connecticut - twenty-five minutes from Newark. It's not like being in a glider, or a small airplane - we are at a much higher altitude. Things look a lot different from this high up. The clouds stretch out as far as I can see, making it look like a separate world up here. It isn't as unreal as I expected, though. The clouds look just the same as they do from below, except that in the spaces between the clouds, instead of blue sky, I see winding roads, miniature houses, fields, woods, and lakes. A light mist fills the spaces between the cloud billows.

A few minutes ago, the hostess passed out slips of paper giving our current altitude, airspeed, ground speed, temperature, and weather conditions. It said, "The head wind is steadily increasing as we near Newark." I wonder if that will make us slow down at all, or if they will just increase the power?

We are right inside the clouds now, and they are blowing by the windows like a heavy fog. The hostess just passed some gum around to the passengers - Wrigley's spearmint. Now we are crossing the Hudson.

The air is bumpier now and the ride feels just like a rough road. The up-and-down motion is about like that of an automobile, but there is very little sway from side to side.

6:30 PM - New York

By the looks of a river and the city below, I gather that we are just over Trenton and the Delaware River. A few minutes after crossing the Hudson, we started down and got a good view of the skyscrapers and the George Washington Bridge.

My pen is leaking badly - it just made a big blob on the paper, and is about to make another one. They gave us Kleenex on the other plane to catch the ink, but none has turned up yet here. There must be a big difference in air pressure, because I had it only half full in the first place, and now it is running over. Ah. The hostess just came by and gave me some more Kleenex, so all is well.

As we came down for our landing in Newark, the hostess sat down on a little seat in the rear of the plane and fastened a safety belt around her. Just a precaution, evidently, because it would have been easy to keep one's feet during the landing, it was that smooth.

The next time I fly from Boston to New York, I'm going to sit on the left side, because we passed west of New York, and in order to see the skyline I had to sit on up the arm of my chair and look out the window across the aisle.

6:45 PM - Ready for Take-Off

When I first got to the American Airlines office at the New York airport, I found myself being paged - "Miss Jillette, on the plane to Los Angeles." I rushed to the desk thinking I might have a friend there, but found it was just a man wanting my ticket and making sure I had everything I needed for the night. I could say, yes, very definitely, having my little travel case with my nightie, etc.

They just called boarding for my flight over the loud speaker.

Fancy Meeting You Here

NEW YORK TO LOS ANGELES

She climbed the stairs to the aircraft door carefully. She was not used to these heels. And the new suit she was wearing was a bit tight across the bust, making it hard to twist around to get a last glimpse of the skyline as she reached the top of the stairs. She reached up with her free hand to adjust her hat, wondering when she'd ever be back in New York, then turned and walked quickly into the plane.

Looking at her ticket, she saw she had a compartment on the right side. There were three compartments running down each side of the plane, separated by partitions, with two seats in each compartment, face-to-face, separated by a small table. *Just like the train*, she thought.

When she reached her seat, there was already a middle-aged man sitting in the first seat, facing to the rear of the aircraft. She stowed her travel case in the compartment above, then slipped into her seat.

Her traveling companion was looking down, intently studying a magazine. She took a quick look while she settled in, and saw it was open to a page with several pictures of airplanes. *Oh, if he's interested in flying, this could be an entertaining trip.* She turned to the window, craning her neck to try to see if her luggage was being loaded, but couldn't see the baggage handlers.

As the man in the other seat flipped the page of the magazine, he glanced up briefly, then went back to his reading. A split second later, he raised his head again, and with an incredulous tone, said, "Jeri?"

Startled, Jeri jerked her head around at his voice. She couldn't believe it.

"Oh, my gosh! Harry?!" She slapped the table with both hands. "What are you doing here?"

"What am *I* doing here? Why, I take this flight nearly once a month! What are *you* doing here?"

"Oh, Harry, I can hardly believe it. It's so good to see you! It's been so long!"

"Yes, I know, and I apologize, I've been so busy –"

"Oh, don't be silly. How are you? Are you going to Los Angeles? Oh, of course you are. How silly of me. Oh, I'm just so excited to see you!"

"Me too! And you haven't changed a bit. No, that's not true. You are more beautiful than ever."

"Oh, Harry. Always the flatterer."

Harry held up his hands. "No, it's true! And just think, you were just a kid the last time we flew together – that was just after your graduation party, as I recall…"

"A kid! I was seventeen!"

"Yeah, that's what I said. Quite a grown-up kid, I have to admit."

"Well, you look wonderful, too," she said forcefully. "How are you?"

"Oh, well. Can't complain. And even if I did…"

"…what good would it do," she finished for him.

He laughed. "But you still haven't told me why you're going to California."

"I have a job! My brother's friend, John, he's at Douglas Aircraft. An engineer, very smart. I won't be surprised if he's running the place in a few years. He's my brother's best friend – my brother is in the Navy now, a pilot – and he put me back in touch with John a few months ago, because I'd told Natty, that's my brother, oh, of course, you know him, anyway, I told him that I wanted to get out of New York – Buffalo is dismal, I can't believe my father moved there, but he had to give up the airport – oh, you didn't know that, did you? Anyway, he wrote to John, and John helped me get a job as a technical illustrator, at Douglas. And he's arranged an apartment for me, and everything. Oh, but I'm rattling on like a schoolgirl."

"It sounds like we have a lot to catch up on," Harry replied. "Fortunately, between here and California, we'll have plenty of time."

"Oh, this will be grand. I'm so glad we ended up together!" She pointed at the magazine he had been leafing through. "What are you reading, a flight magazine?"

He held it up, showing her the cover. "*The Sportsman Pilot*," he said, and then flipped the magazine open to the page he had been reading and put it down in front of her. "Here, look at this. Can you believe it? I didn't know this was going to be in here."

It was a picture of Harry and three other men, standing in front of a Grumann G-21, a new eight-seater float plane known as "The Goose." The caption described how the ship had been commissioned by Mr. Harry Zook, prominent New York lawyer, and several associates, who commuted regularly from Long Island to the city.

"That's your ship?" she asked, eyes wide.

"Yes. Well, one of them."

"Harry, when I grow up, I want to be just like you."

"Now, don't get too carried away."

"Oh, you know what I mean. Flying. Did I tell you I'm planning to get my private pilot's license?"

"No, but I'm not surprised. But living at your father's airfield, I thought you might have it by now."

"School interfered, and I never got the chance. And then Dad had to give up the field – bad back, arthritis – he just couldn't manage it anymore. That's when we had to move back to the city, to Buffalo. And now, of course, with the war starting up in Europe and all – well, everything is pretty unsettled. I did get to take glider lessons at the University of Michigan, though."

"Gliders! I've never tried that. Don't like the idea of being up there without a power plant. What got you started in gliders?"

"Well, they have a glider club there, and a friend asked me to a glider meet one Saturday. He told me that flying gliders was sort of dangerous. That appealed to me."

"Yes, you've always been a bit of a daredevil."

"I know. It drives my mother crazy. You should see how they get the gliders up on the air! They use a big winch run by a Model T engine mounted on an old truck chassis. Other places they just tow them behind a car; I was at a launch site once when they asked a sightseer to tow us down the runway. It can be a bit scary at times."

"As I gather. But I interrupted your story, about getting your pilot's license."

"Well, just as soon as I'm settled in Los Angeles, I'll sign up with the Civilian Pilot Training office, and I can start my flying lessons right away." She reached out and took Harry's hands. "Remember, Harry, when you promised to come back that time and take me up? After I told you how Amelia Earhart had promised me, and then didn't do it?"

"Yes, I remember."

"By then, of course, I'd already had my *first* ride, from a barnstormer passing through, a year or so after the airfield opened, although Dad was furious. When that old guy landed, Dad didn't think he'd ever get that 'crate,' as he called it, back in the air again. Then when he came back from the diner and saw the plane circling the field, and me nowhere in sight, well, he about had a fit. And then, later, after we'd been flying together a few times, there was that emergency landing I never told him about."

"That was exciting, wasn't it? As I recall, that field wasn't much longer than this airplane."

"Oh, Harry, it was a *bit* longer. Anyway," she said, squeezing his hands, "I'll be forever grateful to you for taking me up all those times, and showing me how glorious it is. Thank you."

"C'mon now, it was always a pleasure," he said, giving her hands a quick squeeze in response. "And now you have a lifetime of flying ahead of you. Let's just hope you never have to land in corn field."

The hostess came by and tapped Harry on the shoulder. "Excuse me, sir. We're about to take off. Please fasten your safety belt."

"Certainly, dear," said Harry. "Can't be too careful."

8:40 PM - Over Roanoke

Mr. Zook and I had a very chummy dinner just after we flew over Washington. My appetite didn't suffer a bit from the flight, and although I was hungry the dinner was so large I couldn't eat it all. Here is the menu:

tomato juice
vegetable salad
cheese and crackers
string beans
boiled potatoes
chicken, dressing, and gravy
strawberry ice cream
cookies

When we went over Washington, I could pick out all the important buildings plainly - the Monument, the Lincoln Memorial, the Capital, Hains Point, and the Potomac with its bridges. However, we were too far to the side to recognize the streets, and try as I would I couldn't find Massachusetts Ave. If we had gone straight over I could have found it, but being off to the side, most of the streets were hidden by trees and houses.

As we went into Virginia I looked down and saw some clouds far below which looked as if they were sitting right on the ground. When I asked about them, thinking that fog on the ground might look like that from the air, Harry told me they were just ordinary clouds, probably several thousand feet above the ground. Our altitude was about 7,000 feet.

9 PM - Somewhere west of Virginia

It is dark now, but it doesn't look it, what with the moon lighting up the sky and reflecting on the plane and on the clouds below. We are just coming to a level field of clouds, quite different from the tall billowy ones I saw over New York. Now there are several open spaces where I can see city lights twinkling 8,000 feet below, but soon I will be able to see nothing but the clouds below us. It looks like a broad, flat sea with a thick blanket of cotton batting floating on it. Above us the sky is perfectly clear, with a few stars visible, as well as the moon.

The droning of the engine is making me so sleepy that I don't even have the energy to turn the pages of the magazine the hostess gave me. Anyway, she just came through and said they will be reconfiguring the seats into the sleeping berths shortly. The sleeper is fixed as comfortably, if not more so, than a Pullman train, upper berths and all.

The lower bunks are formed by folding the seat backs down, and the upper berth drops down out of the ceiling. There are two dressing rooms on the plane, one for men and one for women, with running water. The berths are very nice, and come complete with reading lights, linens, and blankets. Time for bed!

(later, in my berth) I went to bed at 10 o'clock but didn't go to sleep right away, because I wanted to be sure to be awake for the landing at Nashville, which turned out to be uneventful. Well, I guess you should hope that every landing is uneventful!

After taking off from Nashville (taking off is always a thrill), I dozed off and on, but was awakened by a peculiar pain in my right eye. I couldn't figure it out, but when I looked out of the window I saw we were just about to land at Dallas. I figured out the pain must be from the great decrease in altitude, which affected my sinuses, because it went away as soon as we had been down a few minutes. I went back to sleep right away.

9:30 AM - Arizona!

About 8 o'clock in the morning, I woke up and out the window could see the sun rising over some beautiful mountains in Arizona. The stewards reconfigured the berths, and we had a nice breakfast. We landed in Tucson, and I watched the sun finish rising over the mountains. The airport was on a huge flat plain surrounded on all sides by mountains.

The building was a nice looking little Spanish type with a red tile roof and palm trees in the front yard. In a few minutes, they will call boarding for California. Almost there!

7 AM - over Palm Springs (10 AM Eastern)

We just came through a mountain pass. It was very impressive. Palm Springs looks like a little oasis in the desert, which I guess it is. I'd like to go there someday.

I mentioned to Harry that the Sierra Nevadas we just went through were very impressive, but he corrected me - we had actually gone through San Gorgonio Pass, between the Santa Rosa and the San

Jacinto Mountains. He flies out here all the time and really knows his way around. It won't be long and I'll know my way around in the air, too.

For five hours, we have been going over the desert with mountains here and there - no foliage except for scattered green dots which are desert shrubs. There were farms sprinkled here and there, forming patterns in the sand. Now there is a field below which looks like Swiss cheese. I imagine it is a grain field of some kind, with rows of stacks.

We're getting closer to Los Angeles now. The land isn't quite so bare. Most of the ground between the mountains is marked off into squares. It is like a patchwork quilt with not only color, but a geographical design as well. The fields which aren't colored still have beautiful patterns, caused by the different ways in which they are ploughed. Some are dotted, some just sprinkled with dots, some with straight rows, some in squares, and some with paths going in all directions.

Now we're going over miles and miles of orange groves, all marked into squares and thick with straight rows of trees. From this height, it looks just like the bumpy rubber pads used at cash registers to put the money on.

Van Nuys, California (written later)

As we got off of the plane, Harry and I exchanged hugs (tearful, on my part) and he gave me his business card and promised to take me to dinner some night while he is here. He said he had to go back to New York on Friday, but he should be free one night before then. He said he can get us into any restaurant in Los Angeles - he winked and said he has "connections." In return, I gave him the phone number at the apartment, and said of course I would love to go out with him, but it didn't have to be anything too fancy.

My friend John met me at the airport and took me to my apartment in Inglewood. He is now back at work until 5 o'clock. Later, after he gets home from work, John is going to take me to see the Pacific. Then I can say I saw the Atlantic one day and the Pacific the next.

I just found oranges, figs, grapefruit, and lemons growing in the back yard, my first experience of seeing citrus fruit actually on the tree! I picked a ripe orange and was as thrilled as a kid over a piece of candy.
This is nothing like Buffalo.

Tomorrow I start my new job at Douglas Aircraft.

In Technicolor

LOS ANGELES

For Jeri and the thousands of California émigrés like her, her arrival in California had been like stepping from Kansas into Oz, from black and white into Technicolor; or in her case, from 'back east' into 'out west.' She'd traveled from the faded red-brick, burnt-orange bulk of Buffalo, New York – draped in industrial gray, pinned in by the cold slate blue of Ontario and Erie, swaddled in the mists of Niagara – to the shining white towers and bright red tiled domes of Los Angeles, surrounded by acres of almost unseemly green groves of lemon, orange, and lime trees, crisscrossed by wide, palm-girded boulevards, all bordered by the sparkling Pacific and its breathlessly blue skies.

It was exhilarating.

On top of everything else, she'd been flying! Not just riding along with her friend John in his Cub. Jeri had enrolled in the CPTP flight training program at Pomona Junior College as soon as she'd gotten settled, along with her new best friend from the office, Francey. They'd quickly finished ground school – seventy-two hours on nights and weekends – and were now more than thirty hours into their flight training. In a few weeks, they'd both have their civilian pilot's licenses.

Jeri had never dreamed it could all happen so fast. It was true that most of the students were men – although a pretty significant number of women also signed up – and they were all being pushed through training in record time and numbers. The government was intent on expanding the country's pool of qualified pilots.

No one knew how quickly they would become desperately needed.

A Brilliant Idea

LONG BEACH

She banked steeply out over the ocean, crossed back over the beach, spiraled down over Long Beach and began her approach. The flashing of the water, the bright band of shallow breakers on the sand, the port jutting out like a huge crab into the harbor, it was all laid out beneath her like a sideshow panorama. Craning her neck, she could see the amusement park. As she made the deep turn that would take her home, she glimpsed the black "trees" lining Signal Hill, old oil derricks sticking up into the skyline. Even after scores of flights, the view always took her breath away, just for a moment, a breath of exhilaration that was always followed by a sort of sigh of resignation, an expression of her reluctance to return to two-dimensional earth. Nothing she had ever done gave her the feeling of liberation she got by flying. And it just got better every time. Ever since her first flight back in Canastota, she'd known that this was what she wanted to do.

On final, Jeri saw what looked like her friend Francey's Piper Cub taxiing to take off. They'd been assigned to the same sector along the coast, patrolling the shoreline with the Civil Air Patrol. Since the panic over the largely ineffective Japanese sub attack up north at Santa Barbara – the "Bombardment of Ellwood," as it was known in the press – shore patrols had been dramatically increased. They'd been getting more hours in the air than they ever expected. So many hours, in fact, that after filling out her log book one afternoon, Jeri had a brilliant idea.

"You can't be serious."

"Why not? Look, Francey, we've got enough hours to qualify."

"You said it was a hundred minimum. I've only got something over eighty. Do you have a hundred?"

"Well, no, not quite, but –"

"And you want to drive all the way to Texas and apply to a program, for which we do not have the required hours, and for which we will be paid miserably, and – oh, gosh, do I need to go on?"

Jeri looked exasperated. "Things just seem to be dragging on, and I don't feel like I'm really contributing anything. Well, not as much as I'd like."

"I thought you liked being in the CAP."

"Sure, I do, I guess, but it just doesn't seem like enough. And we hear every day that they are running out of pilots to do the ferry jobs. The current women's ferrying squadrons just aren't up to it. Not enough women have the hours. I heard Nancy Love on the radio the other day; she sounded desperate. She's forming a new organization with Jackie Cochran. They're calling it WASP, Women Airforce Service Pilots."

"But Jeri, it's such a big jump, from the CAP to something like that. I just don't know."

"So, you just want to sit out the war in some office at Douglas doing menial secretarial work? The only flying to be had is what we've been doing in the Coastal Patrol week after week, up and down the same miserable stretch of coast, flying little Piper J-3s, when we could be flying all over the country, flying all kinds of – oh, I don't know all what we'd be flying, but it wouldn't be a J-3!"

"Jeri, be reasonable. How can we just up and leave?"

"I've got no commitments here. Same as you. Paying month-to-month rent, on an apartment I don't really like, riding the bus to work, to the airfield, walking to the market on Friday, dragging laundry down to the Wash-a-teria on Saturday. What's to leave? Oh, sure, Harry comes out once in a while, and that's always grand, but really, Francey, what do we have to keep us here?"

Five days later, with a handful of saved gas rationing coupons, the back seat packed to the windowsills, and a map laid out on the front seat with a red circle drawn around Houston, Texas, they drove away in Francey's 1933 Chevrolet Eagle sedan, nothing behind them but the quiet streets of Long Beach, and nothing in front of them but the open sky.

The Army Hour

HOUSTON, TEXAS

A group of WASP trainees were huddled around a tiny speaker in the radio room, waiting to hear the program that was going to be broadcast live from the other side of the hanger, where all the big brass had gathered with the crew from NBC. A tinny trumpet fanfare blared from the speaker, and then they heard the announcer's authoritative voice: "*This is the Army Hour.*"

"Oh, boy, here we go," said someone, only to be shushed. "Be quiet." "Pipe down!" They all pushed a little closer to the speaker.

The announcer went on, his dramatic baritone cutting through the ambient noise.

"*For the thirty-ninth consecutive week in wartime, the War Department, through the cooperation of the National Broadcasting Company, invites you to accompany the Army of the United States on a military operation.*"

This was followed by another long fanfare, and a longer introduction.

"*Today, on this 385th day since Pearl Harbor, on this 1211th day of the war forced upon the world by the Axis Nations, The Army Hour brings you news from the front. The Chief of Ordnance of the United States Army, who has recently returned from the North African theatre of operations, will report from various posts and stations throughout the United States; and then we will hear first-hand word-and-sound pictures of the part women are officially playing in the operation of the Army.*"

The introduction was followed by yet more music, a military march this time.

"What is this, a news show or a band concert?"

"Sheesh, get on with it! We want WASPs!" Laughter.

Before any WASP segments were aired, however, the group was treated to reports and interviews from several other NBC remotes: from Fort Huachuca, Arizona, Colonel Edwin Hardy interviewed members of the first all-Negro division of WACs; at Aberdeen Proving Ground, Maryland, two Ordnance women were interviewed; at Maxwell Field, Alabama, Captain Glen Miller talked with several women aircraft machinists at a manufacturing facility.

The girls had been chattering through all of these reports. One or two of the women had bent down closer to the speaker to listen, and one of them suddenly raised her hand.

"Here it is!"

Everyone quieted down, unconsciously leaning toward the speaker as the announcer said: *"We switch you now to our studio in Hollywood, California."*

After being in Texas for several weeks in training, Jeri felt a twinge at hearing "California," but it passed quickly. She was having too much fun to miss California that much, and besides, she had Francey here for company. She'd never had a sister. Her brothers, Nathan – known as "Natty," which he hated – and Matthew ("Matty," which he also hated) had always treated her like one of the boys, which had not hurt in some ways, making her very self-reliant and independent-minded. Stubborn, Dad said. But Francey was better than a sister. There was none of the usual cross-current of familial conflict weighing them down. Their relationship was close and easy, each one relying on the other for whatever was lacking. Jeri, for example, was quite adventurous, often pushing Francey to excel where she might have just settled, while Francey was typically more cautious and methodical, which helped keep Jeri on the rails.

Jeri looked around, wondering where Francey had wandered off to. She wouldn't want to miss this.

"From Hollywood, California, which is the nearest pickup point to the field at which she is working, we will hear briefly from Miss Jacqueline Cochran, famous woman flyer and head of the training section of the Women Airforce Service Pilots, or WASPs."

After a slight pause, the interviewer came on the air.

"Miss Cochran, can you tell us something about the WASP training program of which you are the head?"

"Certainly. Last September I was appointed by General Hap Arnold to help organize advanced training for women pilots. Our initial base for advanced training is in Houston, Texas at the Municipal Airport. Our first two classes are already in training. We are adding about seventy girls per month."

"How will these girls be used after training?"

"They will be available for any non-combat flying duties assigned to them by the Army Air Forces."

"Are these women members of the military?"

"No, they are Civil Service employees, but they are answerable in every way to the Army Command and subject to military discipline. In short, we consider ourselves a part of the Army Air Forces. Though we are just at the starting point, we hope to be a part – an important part – of the Air Forces which are so surely moving on toward victory."

"Thank you, Miss Cochran."

Jeri looked over just as Francey walked up.

"Oh, there you are! The broadcast has already started."

"I was trying to get closer to the action over in the training room. No such luck."

"You haven't missed much. They were just talking to Jackie for a minute. We should be up soon."

The broadcast had switched again, from California to Niagara Falls, New York.

"Here at the edge of the field at the Bell Aircraft Company at Niagara Falls airport, airplanes are lined up in quantities that would make a good Nazi – if there is such a thing – gasp with alarm. Familiar figures in flying suits putter about these ships just as pilots have always puttered about the ships they're taking off...but here these pilots are women. I can see one... three...seven...eight – a good many pilots out there among the planes – and every one is a woman.

"Mrs. Nancy Harkness Love, one of the leaders of this organization of women ferrying pilots, has just come out of the operations office – she, too, is dressed for flying – and we're going to have her speak to you briefly of her work and the work of the women in the WASPs.

"Here is Mrs. Love."

Nancy Love's rich contralto filled the room.

"The idea behind the WASPs is easy to understand. Planes must be ferried from factories to the places where they are going to be used. We need ferrying pilots badly. As it was before we were organized, men pilots were flying all of the planes. Now, the WASPs ferry many of the planes, and the men can be assigned to other duties, including combat operations. We earn our way, you see."

"What do you do with the women when they come into the WASPs, Mrs. Love?"

"First they go to flight school to learn flying Army style. Then they go to work. We don't waste much time in preliminaries. Now, we have a moment or two; I'd suggest we step over here to the plane that Miss Marie Garabaldi is checking out. She's going to take off in just a minute or two. Hello, Marie. How have you been?"

"Fine, thanks, Nancy."

"Last time I saw you was in San Antonio."

"That's right. We sure get around, don't we?"

"We certainly do. Well, good luck! Leave the door open so we can hear you check with the tower, will you?"

"Yes, I will."

As the sound of an airplane powering up blared out of the small speaker, they heard a short conversation between the pilot and tower, and Nancy Love hollering "*Good Bye, Marie!*"

"There she goes," said Love, as the sound died down. *"And now they are bringing my plane over. That's our job: getting them from here to there in a hurry. And thank you all for listening. The WASP organization still needs women pilots – if you can qualify, let us hear from you! Good bye and good luck!"*

"Oh, brother," said Francey. "They really know how to schmaltz it up, don't they?"

Airplane sounds filled the radio room as the announcer did a voice-over, switching to the next segment.

"We take you now to the Municipal Airport in Houston, Texas."

"We're on, girls!" one woman shouted, drawing a few more stragglers into the room, jostling and bumping. "Quiet" "Move over!" Excuse me!" More laughter, gradually dying down while the interviewer introduced one of the WASP trainees, who had been selected earlier and was now over in a training room near the hanger, script in hand.

"Good afternoon, Army Hour Listeners. I am Tom Lambert, a wandering and wondering Air Corps Lieutenant here today to inspect something entirely new to military flying and to tell you about it. But as a matter of fact, I am almost as perplexed as you are. I am armed only with this information – that our "something new" is called the 319th Army Air Detachment or Women Airforce Service Pilots – WASPs – and that, having been organized only a few months ago, it's the first of its kind anywhere. The girls here are not feminine GIs. They have a Civil Service status; most of them have given up good jobs for a purpose. They are fine pilots – they have to be because after graduation they are going into the air transport command and that is a tough job. Here is one of them, Mary Lou Colbert. Mary Lou, how about an interview for our Army Hour listeners?"

"All right, but I am due for a flight in the LINK trainer. Give me a minute to climb in, Lieutenant, and please give me my course once I am inside."

"Will do. While Mary Lou is getting onto the trainer," said the announcer, suddenly an expert, *"let me explain just what it is. The LINK trainer is a miniature airplane cockpit, on a special platform, and maneuverable like the real McCoy, built to teach students the elements of blind flying – the instrument work. Okay, she's in. Mary Lou, can you hear me?"*

"Yes, Lieutenant."

"Okay... Fly to Galveston...That's approximately forty miles away... make a 180 degree turn and come back. How's that?"

"Fine, Lieutenant."

"You know, ladies and gentlemen, this LINK trainer will take care of more details than you think. When Miss Colbert returns you'll be able to see how fast the ship was traveling, her actual course, and whether or not she

overshot her mark. Now, while she's en route to Galveston, here's another young lady I'd like for you to meet. She is Mrs. Dottie Kalani of Hawaii. Hello, Dottie. How did you happen to join the WASPs?

"It all started the day Pearl Harbor was attacked. My family has a home on a hill overlooking the bay and we could see the whole thing right from our front porch. My husband's ship was blown from under him in that battle. Believe me, it was no fun just sitting and watching. I already had my private pilot's license and 225 hours in the air, and I wanted to put that training to work. As soon as my husband and I got back to the states and I learned about the WASPs, I joined."

"That's the old fighting spirit. Tell me, Dottie, what did you find when you arrived?"

"Work, Tom, and lots of it...but the kind of work we all love – flying, mostly, and all the things that go with it. We have a twelve-hour day that includes calisthenics, drill, ground school – you know, math, navigation meteorology, theory of flight, and so on – and then flight instruction. It takes four months to complete the training in the transport command."

"Sounds like a pretty stiff schedule to me."

"Right you are."

"Well, Dottie, what about the planes?"

"We fly everything from sixty up to six hundred horse power planes, single and multi-engine. We'll be ready for anything we are called upon to fly, from trainers to pursuit fighters."

"With girls like you ready to lend a capable, experienced and helping hand to us Army men, how could we lose?"

The announcer broke in.

"We now return you to The Army Hour in New York."

After a brief musical interlude, the announcer set up the next segment. *"In a few moments, the Army Hour brings you a first-hand picture of the Army Nurse Corps at work; but we pause now for a tribute to the nurses of another of the Armies of the United Nations: the Russian War Nurses Song."*

As a wavering choir of Russian women's voices swelled up out of the radio speaker, one of the girls cried, "Hey, what about Mary Lou? Did she ever make it to Galveston?"

"Oh. Yeah!"

"Yoo, hoo, Mary Lou!"

"If she gets lost as often as Jeri, she'll be lucky she's not in Omaha by now!" yelled Francey, digging Jeri in the ribs for good measure.

"Yeah, but that wasn't in the LINK," Jeri retorted. "I was actually flying an AT-6."

"Oh, that's *much* better!" laughed Francey, joined by several other women. They could all laugh, Jeri included, because almost every one of them had been lost at one time or another, landing at the wrong field, or in one case (Jeri again) on the playing field of an Indian boy's school in New Mexico.

"Okay, now that we're all famous, let's get back to work, girls," said the squad leader. "And let's go get May Lou out of that LINK!"

Dinner at The Breakers

LOS ANGELES

January 19, 1944

Tonight, Harry Zook is taking me out to dinner, and bringing someone to meet me. And - this is just like Harry - we are meeting at the Sky Room. In the Breakers Hotel. Only the most exclusive restaurant in Los Angeles. Why does Harry insist on doing these things to me? I always have to scramble to find something to wear, usually borrowing from one of the girls.

But Harry seems very excited about our dinner date tonight. I hope I don't make a fool of myself.

Jeri had wanted a change, and she'd gotten it. She was flying more than ever, in ships that made the CAP and training craft seem like toys. Full time ferry duty had started only days after the graduation ceremonies at Avenger Field in Sweetwater, Texas, a never-ending series of long flights in often unfamiliar ships, interspersed with the constant training required in order to be checked out in the new aircraft. (She was already qualified to fly nine different types of airplane.) It was made more difficult by being separated from Francey. She'd been assigned to Romulus Air Base, in Michigan, while Jeri had been posted back to California – not to Douglas at Long Beach, where they were building larger planes, C-47s, B-17s – but to North American Aviation, in Inglewood, where they were building the P-51 fighter. Qualifying for P-51s had required three weeks of pursuit training in Palm Springs. During flight training, she'd often thought of the first time she'd seen Palm Springs, from the comfortable seat of the American Airlines cross-country liner. The cockpit of a P-51 was anything but comfortable. Thrilling, yes; comfortable, not so much.

There was one advantage to being stationed in Los Angeles, and that was the luxury of being squired around by Harry Zook during his visits to L.A. He never failed to let her know when he was coming, and never failed to impress her on their outings, which invariably included some of the most exclusive, expensive, and celebrity-infested (his term) venues in the city. Last week it had been Ciro's nightclub, on Sunset Strip, where Harry had introduced her to Lana Turner. This week it was to be the Breakers Hotel, Conrad Hilton's latest venture, and considered one of the best hotels in California. Harry had not told her much about his mystery guest, other than that he was also a California émigré, but from someplace more exotic than Buffalo. *Well, what isn't?* He was the son of an old friend of his, now deceased, from Budapest, Hungary. Harry pronounced the third syllable "pesht," not "pest," as Jeri had always heard. At least she knew now not to make that mistake, if it happened that she was required to say "Budapest" at some point in the evening. (Harry pronounced "Los Angeles" with a hard "g" and a long "e," "Los Anga-leese." She'd learned quickly that this signaled a non-native, and she took great care in pronouncing it like a local.) Thinking herself a not very erudite conversationalist, she always made a conscious effort to listen carefully to everything that was said to her in order to improve her social skills. One never knew what unexpected topic would turn out to be significant. Also thinking herself not particularly attractive (an unfortunate misconception fostered by an inattentive mother), Jeri took extra care with her appearance. And when being escorted by Harry Zook, she thought this was of crucial importance.

Jeri stood in the lobby of The Breakers (Harry had sent a car for her, of course), nervously awaiting their arrival. Earlier that day, after having her hair waved, she had spent two hours preparing her for her night out. The dress was borrowed, an older semi-formal gown that she'd hemmed up to mid-calf to be more in style. It was a deep crimson, with short sleeves, a shallow V-neck, and a gather at the waist that created an exotic look. She had also altered the sharp padding in the shoulders for a more rounded look, and added a small round hat (no veil) and gloves that nearly matched. She borrowed a large handbag from Doreen at the barracks – her own bag was much too small to be fashionable. At the last minute, Jeri got out her mother's faux pearl necklace. Too much? she had asked. Oh, not at all, Doreen had said: *très chic*. All-in-all, she was happy with the result; the color of the dress light enough for early spring, dark enough for evening, the length at least acceptable, and with a small touch of glamour. It was, Jeri had told Doreen, about the most glamorous thing she'd ever worn, being from a small town, and all.

Jeri walked over to a large mirror on the wall in one corner of the lobby to make a final assessment. As she bent down to smooth out a crease below one knee, she felt a stocking give way.

"Oh, no." She turned and looked around quickly to see if anyone was watching. An elderly couple walked by arm-in-arm and nodded a good evening.

"Hello," Jeri said, as she carefully backed over near a potted plant, a ficus, a kind of fig, she thought. The stocking began to slip to her knee.

"Oh, dear." It was her last good pair of stockings, and she couldn't bear to have them ruined, much less walk around with one stocking bagging around her ankle. Some of the girls she knew were wearing leg makeup in place of stockings – even going so far as to draw seams up the back of the leg with an eyebrow pencil – but Jeri had thought that a bit odd. Now it suddenly seemed like a brilliant idea.

She backed a little closer to the plant, crouched down a little to one side, and felt behind her, under the dress. Yes. It was a garter strap in back. She tried reattaching it with one hand, but it was immediately obvious that was not going to work. She bent over and reached back with her other hand, lifting the back of her dress up far enough to reach the garter, and snapped the top of the stocking back into the clip. As she straightened up, she saw Harry and his friend walking briskly across the lobby toward her. With one quick brush to the back of her skirt, and a large sigh of relief, she stepped forward to greet them.

Harry was, as usual, dressed to the nines, as they say: he could be mistaken for Cary Grant, if only he were not quite so short, old, and tending to flab, and wearing his (rather shabby, she thinks) fedora.

His young friend impressed her immediately, and she felt herself blush, even before they were introduced. Not too tall, but nicely built, he was dressed rather more haphazardly than Harry, in what Jeri took to be a gallant attempt at savoir faire, which nearly succeeded; brown pants a little too baggy at the knees, and a trifle low at the waist; a jacket alluding to padded zoot suit shoulders but without the requisite length, and of an off color, a dark tan; a tie that looked European, though she didn't know why she thought this, probably just pre-judging based on what little Harry had told her. And unlike Harry, he was not wearing a hat, his thick, black hair brushed back and glistening in the subdued light.

This could be nice.

"Jeri! You look wonderful!" Harry walked up, leaned over and kissed her on the cheek, then stood back. "Let me introduce you to my good friend Tamos Szabó. Tamos, Jeri Jillette. Jeri, Tamos." With a sweeping gesture, he ushered Tamos forward.

Tamos tipped his head ever so slightly and held out his hand. "Miss Jillette. I am pleased to make your acquaintance."

As she took his hand lightly in hers, she thought she saw something flash in his eyes, a look of quiet confidence quite at odds with his somewhat awkward appearance. She found out later that like her, his evening clothes had been borrowed from a colleague at the university, and he had been just as anxious to make a good impression as she had been. Over the coming weeks and months, they would discover they had much in common. But tonight, under Harry's good graces, the evening remained light and cheery.

"Well, kids, let's go up, shall we?" Harry said, leading them to the elevator. When they reached the restaurant, located on the top floor, the maitre d' greeted Harry like a long-lost friend.

"Monsieur 'arry! ZO good to zee you! And zeese mus' be your eh-zspez'al guests!" He bowed low to Jeri and Tamos, hand at his waist. Jeri covered her mouth to hide a smile; it was all too perfect, right out of a Hollywood film. She looked over at Tamos and was pleased to see that he, too, appeared to be amused by the flamboyant performance.

The maitre d' led them through the restaurant, past large neoclassical white columns and smoothly curved white walls to a table at the window. Long Beach Harbor glittered below them in the fading light, and she could almost hear the breakers for which the hotel was named. Tamos moved in quickly in front of the maitre d' to seat Jeri, to the maitre d's consternation and Jeri's delight. It was immediately endearing, and not the last unconventional act he would perform for her.

"Why, thank you, Mr. Szabó."

"Certainly, Miss Jillette."

Harry made a face as they settled into their chairs. "So formal, you two? I thought everything in California was supposed to be relaxed, easy going. Not like the stiff-necks back East. Of which I am obviously not one. C'mon! Loosen up, kiddos!"

Tamos smiled, cautiously, it seemed to her. "You're absolutely right, Harry. But you know how difficult it has been for me to adapt to such a strange culture." He turned to Jeri. "I'm not actually from here, you know."

He'd said it with such a solemn look and grave tone that Jeri was quite taken aback, and involuntarily gave a little laugh. She immediately threw her hands in front of her face. "Oh, dear, I'm sorry. I didn't mean to –"

At this, both Tamos and Harry burst into laughter. Jeri looked at both in turn, flustered, and then looked down at the table. When she looked back up, she wore a knowing grin. "Oh, so that's how it's going to be, is it? A tag team." She shook her head. "I should have known."

The tide went out, the moon came up, and the night rushed by outside the dark glass.

Harry had said almost nothing the whole evening, enthralled by the almost instant rapport he saw developing between his two young companions. Drinks, hors d'oeuvres, and meals came and went almost unnoticed, and the evening grew late.

And after Harry had dropped her off at her apartment, very late, Jeri knew something important had happened that night. And when Harry let Tamos off at his rented room, Tamos knew as well.

The depth of the attraction had taken them both by surprise. Especially given how little time they had to spare, and how little experience they'd each had in this sort of thing.

Harry was ecstatic, of course, shepherding them around L.A. whenever possible, and treating them as if they were his own children. When he wasn't treating them like royalty, that is. Surprisingly enough, the socialite in Harry appeared to be mainly a business thing; he had very few close friends in Los Angeles, or New York, for that matter. Jeri got the impression that she and Tamos were Harry's closest companions, even though they were seldom together.

He could be a bit overbearing at times, and a bit of a showman – his job required it – but they both loved it, though it took some time away from their opportunities to be alone with one another. And in spite of the war and everything that went with it – the privations, the grueling schedules, the uncertainties – they all managed to enjoy themselves.

But chance, ever on the lookout, soon presented itself in a way none of them had imagined.

A Crazy Idea

PASADENA, CALIFORNIA

The knock on the door was unexpected, at this time of day. Tamos lowered his book, stood up, and moved to the door. He peered through the small window, and there stood Mrs. Kastapopoulos. He was taken aback. Mrs. Kastapopoulos had never come down the hill to the back of the house – never once in all the time he had lived here in the basement apartment, not in the past two years.

He opened the door to find Mrs. Kastapopoulos looking more haggard than usual. Which is saying something. Although not an old woman – Tamos thought she was perhaps forty – the stress of war combined with the warmth of the California sun had not been kind, adding to her face the weathering of at least ten years. She was dressed as usual in a loose, flowered smock, unflattering to say the least, but she no longer cared that much. She had no one to dress for, at least not until her husband came home.

"Hello, Mrs. Kastapopoulos. Is there something wrong?"

Wordlessly – her English was still marginal, even after fifteen years in the States – she handed Tamos a telegram. Even Mrs. Kastapopoulos understood that telegrams often bring bad news. A husband in the Army, who knew where; family in Greece, still getting by day-to-day, as far as she knew. The next telegram could be for her.

Tamos took it from her, and she nodded and turned away, heading back up the side hill, weaving through the stand of lemon trees, now in blossom, up to the front of the house, gone before he could thank her. He turned the telegram over in his hands, curiously; it was not the standard Western Union envelope, with its "Money in a Hurry" logo on the back flap, but rather a flimsy, yellowish piece of paper, folded over and sealed raggedly along one side. It looked foreign, but like nothing he had seen before. Looking closer, he saw "Barcelona, España" printed at one corner, along with some other indecipherable markings.

He carefully tore it open. It was, in the manner of most telegrams, short and to the point.

WE ARE SAFE. BELA STILL MISSING. COME QUICKLY. EVA.

Tamos closed the door and sat back down at his desk to reread the telegram. The words did not change. As he read, he relived, with each short phrase, his first reactions: "We are safe." Relief. "Béla still missing." Anguish. "Come quickly." Helplessness. He read it over. Relief, again. Then shock, mixed with disbelief. Finally, uncertainty. *What am I supposed to do?* And Béla missing – no, *still* missing.

He set the telegram aside.

There had been only the scantest communications from the family in Hungary as the war progressed. With the German occupation in March, the exodus had begun in earnest. The Szabó family, six in all, had arrived in Spain just a few weeks earlier, via southern France, where they had first spent an additional two months. And not a moment too soon; Spain was neutral, to a point, and was still taking in Jews. This would not last forever, they knew, and some of those coming to Spain even now did not get papers, and were sent back, or taken to prison. And back in Hungary, the Germans and the Arrow Cross, the Hungarian arm of the Nazi party, were becoming more ruthless by the day.

But now, according to this telegram from his Aunt Eva, Béla had disappeared. Béla had last written from Hungary before their attempt to get to Barcelona, so it was with real relief that Tamos read of their safety. As for Béla, whether targeted by the Arrow Cross, or by some other, equally rabid Hungarian political faction, no one knew. Politics in Hungary had become a convoluted, twisting affair, loyalties changing daily as the few remaining uncorrupted Party members attempted to maintain some semblance of independence. Béla had been active in a nationalistic, though moderate, opposition group; but moderation counted for very little in these times. He had been missing now for over seven weeks.

And Eva, poor Eva. Doesn't she know he cannot just go to Spain? And even if he could get there, somehow, by some miracle, what then? Go to Hungary?! Impossible.

Tamos caught himself wringing his hands in his anxiety. He stopped, took a deep breath, and looked at the telegram one more time. There he saw another clue, a small, handwritten notation: *JDC*.

An hour later, after much thought, he made his way up the hill to see Mrs. Kastapopoulos.

"Please, may I use your phone?"

"Long distance? she asked, suspiciously.

"Yes."

"Collect," she said.

"Yes, of course."

"Alright."

It took several minutes for the operator to make the connection, while Tamos rehearsed his proposal. He was not at all sure this was a good idea; but what choice did he have? Harry Zook finally came on the line.

"Harry?"
"Tamos?"
"Harry, can we meet? Right away."
"Tamos, what's the matter? You sound distraught."
"It's my uncle Béla –" He paused.
"Yes, I remember Béla, of course." Harry was well aware of the close relationship Tamos had with his Uncle Béla. It had been Béla who had taken young Tamos in those many years ago, and who had made it possible – with Harry's help – for Tamos to return to the U.S. "Is he here? In the States?"
"No, no. That's the problem. I just received a telegram, that Béla, he is – he has – disappeared."
"Disappeared. You mean, missing?"
"Yes, exactly. That is exactly what Eva tells me," Tamos said, his proper, nearly unaccented English suddenly failing him. "Béla, still missing, she says, and come quickly. Harry, how can I? In Barcelona, Eva says they are safe, but, Béla, he is not there. He is still missing, she says, and I must come."
"Tamos, you keep saying 'still missing.'"
"Yes. Still missing."
"Tamos. What does that mean, exactly? 'Still missing.' How long has he been missing?"
"Weeks. Seven, maybe eight weeks."
"Tamos. What do you want?"
"I want to save my uncle."
"Tamos, given the current situation, that seems impossible."
"But, Harry, it is you who taught me that nothing – nothing that does not violate the laws of physics, in any case – is impossible. Look what you have done. Many so-called impossible things."
"But, Tamos –"
"Please, can we meet right away? I can explain everything. I'm sure you will know what to do."

When Mrs. Kastapopoulos saw the long, black car pull up in front of the house and stop, she gave out a small cry of shock. She hadn't heard from her husband for over six weeks. It didn't *look* like a military car, but then again...

Feeling a little lightheaded, she moved closer to the window and watched as someone got out of the driver's side door. She gave another little gasp, this time of relief, as she saw that the person walking towards the house was a chauffeur. The government didn't send chauffeurs in tidy grey uniforms and smart caps to visit widows. Did they?

Mrs. Kastapopoulos hurried to the door just as the bell rang, now more curious than alarmed.

"Yes?"

"Is Mr. Szabó in?"

"Ah. You want the apartment at the back." The chauffeur looked around. "Just down there," Mrs. Kastapopoulos said, pointing to the right. "Past the lemon trees."

"Thank you." A quick tip of the hat.

"My pleasure," she said.

She went to the kitchen, got a glass of water, and sat down, still flustered.

"These foreigners!" she said.

The car, a 1940 Packard 120 club sedan, stood out glaringly against the other cars straggling along the small street; old boxy Fords, rusted-out Chevrolets, one Buick. The Packard was classy but mid-priced, Harry had told Tamos one night on their way to dinner. Certainly, he could have afforded something much grander – a Cadillac, Lincoln, even a Delahaye – but quality, not ostentation, was the goal. And his California clients – all of whom drove much more exotic automobiles than Harry – liked to think they had one up on him. Harry's New York City car, a Lincoln, spent most of its time in the garage; his New York clients rarely saw it, since Harry commuted by float-plane from his estate on the North Shore of Long Island to the city. The Packard was still a very impressive looking car, and Tamos always felt somewhat self-conscious climbing into the back seat as the chauffeur held the door for him.

The ride from Pasadena to the prestigious Hollywood Melrose Hotel took about fifty-five minutes. Harry had sent the car for him since he knew that it would have taken at least two hours for Tamos to take the trolley-bus, changing several times, walking the last half-mile. Harry saw no need for that.

The lobby was glowing in the yellow light of a huge chandelier, reflected from the large round mirror above the fireplace. The walls gleamed dark red, the subtlety patterned carpet a soft camel beige. Tamos found Harry sitting in a French-style chair in the corner, papers piled high on the small table in front of him. Harry glanced up and waved Tamos over with a quick, one-fingered wave, and turned back to his papers. Tamos nodded and walked across the room, dodging a couple in evening dress, which made him feel even more out of place in his brown, European suit.

In the boardrooms, backrooms, and barrooms where lawyers tend to congregate, the name Harrison Zook was widely known. More than that, admired, and respected, even a bit feared. For Harry was that most unlikely of characters: an honest lawyer.

Honesty had not come easily to Harry. The son of a prominent New York banker, he'd worked hard and long to overcome the handicap of too much wealth at a too early age. In spite of growing up in an area remarkably similar to the famous (fictional) West Egg, Long Island, Harry determined early on that he would never become Jay Gatsby. It seemed to be more a matter of pure willfulness on his part, rather than a conscious, philosophical choice. The real determination to leave behind his father's Gilded Age sensibilities came with his graduation from Harvard Law (a benefit of privilege he was wise enough not to forego).

After turning down positions at several prestigious firms with close connections to his father's banking legacy, positions that would have meant years of drudgery involving financial and corporate law – boring – Harry drifted around New York aimlessly for several months. Then a chance meeting with George Gershwin (at a New Year's Eve party) led him in an unexpected direction. Perhaps a bit pretentiously, and with the cushion of a large bank account, which he understood and appreciated, he threw himself into the world of entertainment – actors, musicians, directors, writers – artistically temperamental and financially inept, all notoriously in need of counseling. His client dossier could have been mistaken for a *Variety* subscription list. New York theatrical connections led him to the Los Angeles film industry. Which is how Harry met (as Tamos subconsciously reviewed Harry's history as he made his way over to the corner) and became close friends with Tamos's father. Part of the Hungarian and Eastern European film industry diaspora in the thirties, Tamos's father had engaged Harry regarding a contract dispute. This simple business transaction became a link in the chain of chance that would lead Tamos, via a long series of unlikely events, to Oswego, New York.

"Tamos!" Harry said, standing and reaching out his hand. "How was the ride over?"

"Oh, fine, Harry. Really fine," Tamos said, taking Harry's hand deliberately. "Thank you for sending the car."

"Certainly. Now, please, sit down," Harry said, gesturing to the other chair at the table. He then sat and gathered his papers together, slipping them into a thin attaché. "I have some good news." He paused theatrically, a habit he'd picked up from his clients, naturally a very expressive group. "I've found a way to get you to Europe."

Only someone of Harry's status could have arranged it, especially on such short notice. It had been only a few days since Tamos had called with his plea for help. The plan was as audacious as it was simple. It took him all of about five minutes to explain it to Tamos.

"You know who Jo Norman is?" Harry asked.

"Yes, the big band singer. She is extremely popular."

"She happens to be a client."

"Yes? I am not surprised. But what does that –"

"I'm getting to that. Like I said, she's a client; in fact, that's why I'm here at the Melrose. I just met with her concerning the very thing I'm about to tell you." He looked around the room. "I don't stay here when I'm in Los Angeles – too stuffy, too ornate. I stay down the street, at a much smaller place." As Harry continued to study the elaborately filigreed wallpaper, Tamos began to fidget.

"Ah, yes, Tamos. As I was saying," Harry said, sitting up and straightening his tie. "I just met with Miss Norman, and she is in complete agreement."

"Agreement about what?"

"About the tour."

"What tour?" Tamos said, twisting in his chair again.

"Oh, yes, we haven't gotten to that yet, have we? I'm sorry. I'm trying to rush through this. I'll slow down." He put his hands on the table and leaned forward. "Okay. You need to get to Europe, right?"

Tamos nodded, a bit uncertainly.

"It's impossible for a civilian to travel to Europe at the moment, right?" Harry continued.

Tamos nodded again, still wondering where this was leading.

"Well. When I say impossible, I mean *almost* impossible," Harry went on, waving his hands in the air. "After all, there's a war on. Which brings me back to Miss Norman. She is headlining the next European USO tour. The entire company leaves for Lisbon on the Pan Am *Yankee Clipper* next week. And Miss Norman, at my suggestion, has just hired a new personal assistant to accompany her." Harry sat back with a satisfied look, pointing his finger at Tamos. "You!"

Tamos looked at him in disbelief.

"Harry, you are crazy."

"*I'm* crazy?" Harry cried, in mock distress. "Hell's bells, Tamos! *You're* the one who's going!"

Over the drinks he'd ordered for both of them, Harry laid out the plan in more detail.

"The military has commandeered the whole Pan Am fleet," he explained, "although all the routes are still flown by Pan Am pilots. They ferry mail – some to Europe, some to South America, classified stuff, mostly – and carry big wigs back and forth across the Atlantic. Military cargo all over the world; Liberia, Cairo, even Tehran. They also transport USO companies, of course, to our great advantage. There's currently no other way for non-military personnel to get to Europe other than through neutral Portugal.

"And the Clipper, Tamos! Boeing B-314, to be exact. You'll be amazed!

One of the wonders of the modern world. It's a veritable flying hotel. Dining room, white linen tablecloths. Lavatories. Full-size sleeping quarters – well, you'll be in a shared berth, of course, only the VIPs get their own quarters – but still, amazing. I've never flown on one myself – can't afford it." (Tamos raised his eyebrows at this. Harry? Can't afford it?) "You'll be making a couple of stops: Bermuda, Horta – that's an island in the Azores – then on to Lisbon. You land in the harbor there, actually the Targus River. Quite the adventure you have in front of you, lad. Oh, on the way back – assuming we can arrange it, you'll have to make it back to Lisbon at the right time, of course, and who knows how we'll explain your uncle – anyway, you'll stop off in Foynes, Ireland, on the Shannon River. Oh, it's a grand airplane, Tamos. And a grand plan."

Tamos sipped at his drink. It was Scotch, something he'd never tasted, with a strange name: *The Famous Grouse*. It was very good, he decided. "And once I get to Lisbon?" he asked, trying to steer Harry back on track.

"I've arranged for you to leave the USO troop at Lisbon. Jo will provide cover for you on the way over, but I'm still working on a story to explain your sudden disappearance after you land. In any case, I'm going to put you in touch with a colleague who is active in the JDC, and he'll be able to –"

"JDC," Tamos interrupted. "That's the mark on the telegram I received!" Tamos exclaimed.

"Exactly. The American Jewish Joint Distribution Committee. They were headquartered in Paris, but relocated to Lisbon after the fall of France. With their help, I believe we can get you as far as Barcelona without any major problems. That's where the rest of the family is now, right?" Tamos nodded. "Spain is technically neutral, even though Franco has been hedging his bets. But travel along the coast is relatively safe. JDC has been crucial in providing support to Jewish refugees in Spain. And even though Jews fleeing into Spain from France were not turned back, things are not exactly great there. But I'm confident JDC can provide everything you need to get to Barcelona."

"And then?"

"I've been assured that parties in Barcelona can get you to the coast of Yugoslavia, perhaps through Sicily, or Sardinia; they have been liberated. From there to Dubrovnik, where more JDC operatives will be waiting. They say they can even get you all the way to Budapest."

"Harry, this sounds impossible. How…who…I mean –"

"I have many friends in very high places, Tamos."

"And they can get me to Budapest?"

"Probably. Most likely. But after that, well, Tamos, after that, you're on your own." Harry looked at Tamos with an intensity Tamos had never seen in him before. "Tamos, this is not something I have done lightly. And now that I have it arranged, I'm not sure it was the right thing to do. Had you not been so insistent...Well, I have to say I'm already starting to regret it. Tamos, this will be dangerous; very dangerous. There is a good chance you will not make it to Budapest. And even if you do, there is an even better chance that you will not get out. There are rumors, Tamos, of camps. Your uncle may already have been sent to one. You, Tamos, you yourself, God forbid, may end up in one of those camps."

Tamos had known in advance that whatever plan Harry might come up with to get him to Europe, it would be difficult, uncertain of success, and dangerous. What Harry had just outlined was more preposterous, however, than he had imagined. How could he possibly go through with this? Regardless of the dangers. He had found stability, a chance for a life, a career. The past few months had brought huge changes. Things were not so simple now; how could he just run off to Europe? What about Jeri, what would she think? How could he take the chance of losing it all, now that it was so close? Losing her?

"I believe I have to make an effort, Harry. No matter the cost."

"My God, Tamos. You are an unusual man." He straightened in his chair and took a sip of his drink. "Okay. With luck, you can be back here in two or three months. While you're away, I'll prearrange passage back from Lisbon. It'll be much easier to get you back than to get you there." Harry leaned forward. "You're sure about this?"

Tamos looked long and hard at his drink, then longer and harder at Harry.

"When do I leave?" he finally asked.

Picnic on the Beach

LOS ANGELES

"Tonight, Harry?" Jeri was standing in the flight room at Mines Field, near North American Aviation, the early morning light streaming in through the tall windows. It had taken the operator over thirty minutes to track her down. "Gosh, Tamos and I were just going to –" She twisted slowly back and forth, listening, phone to her ear, head down. "Well, okay, Harry, just a short ride. You'll talk to Tamos? Okay. See you tonight. Bye."

Harry had seemed anxious to get them together tonight. He was going to drive them out to a spot on the Pacific Coast Highway he loved, Westward Beach, close to a famous movie star's vacation home. He had nothing special planned, he'd said. Just a picnic.

Jeri lifted her gear bag over her shoulder and walked outside, heading for the flight office, trying to shake off a feeling of dread. She'd just been told to expect new orders. She couldn't bear the thought.

It will be nice to get away tonight.

When she heard the big Packard pull up in front of her apartment, Jeri looked out and was surprised to see Harry in the driver's seat. He rarely drove himself. He almost never drove in New York, as flying into the city was easier than driving from his estate, and once in the city, well, no one drove themselves; not in his circle.

While she watched through the window, Tamos got out of the passenger side and started up the walk, past the hydrangeas and jacarandas that lined the path. Part way up the walk, he paused and glanced nervously over his shoulder. Harry waved him on. Jeri looked on, now somewhat anxious. It was not like Tamos to act hesitantly under any circumstance.

"Ah, Jeri," Tamos said, as Jeri came out, closing the door behind her. He took her arm at the front porch and steered her towards the car. "Let's go, shall we?"

"Of course, Tamos." She turned to him halfway down the walk. "Is anything the matter?"

"No, of course not. We're just running a little late. I apologize."

"But you said six, and it's just going on six now."

"Oh, so it is," Tamos said, pulling out his pocket watch. "I must have looked at the time wrong." He ushered her to the back door of the car, opened it, and helped her into the back seat. After closing her door, he hurried around to the other side and slid in beside her.

Harry craned back to look at Jeri as she settled into the seat. "I'm your guide tonight," he said. "Chauffeur, caterer, tour guide. You're getting the all-inclusive package."

"It sounds wonderful, Harry." She reached over and took Tamos's hand, then leaned over and gave him a peck on the cheek. "Hi, sweetheart."

Tamos pulled her close, pressing his cheek to hers. "Sweetheart," he replied softly. He held her this way for a long moment, and then straightened up. "How are you?"

Jeri, still somewhat perplexed at his manner, started to answer, but Harry, already pulling away from the curb, interrupted her. "How did your day go, Jeri?" he asked.

"Um. All right, I guess," she managed.

"Good, good. Well, I think we'll have a grand time tonight. Right, Tamos?"

"Of course, Harry." Tamos squeezed Jeri's hand, then reached over with his free hand and covered their hands with his. "Grand."

Harry tried to keep the conversation going as they made their way out to the new Highway 1, but once they got to the coast, talk died down and they rode the rest of the way to Harry's picnic spot in relative silence, gazing out at the view.

"Here we are, kids," Harry said, pulling off onto a small dirt road that ended at Westward Beach. A large beach house sat a few hundred yards away; other than that, they were secluded, as if on a private island.

"Oh, it's beautiful," said Jeri, as Tamos helped her out of the car. "Just lovely."

Harry walked around to the back of the car to retrieve the picnic gear from the Packard's huge trunk. They made their way across the small dune separating the beach from the road and located a spot near the rocks that bordered the south edge of the sand. He and Jeri laid out a checkered blanket while Tamos looked on, holding the picnic basket that Harry had handed to him. Once the blanket was in place, Tamos put the basket down, Harry sat with a thump next to it, and then motioned the two of them to do the same.

"Let's eat before it gets dark," said Harry.

After chicken salad, fresh rolls, fruit, and shortbread, all washed down with champagne, Tamos suddenly stood up and walked a few paces towards the beach.

"Jeri, please come with me. We must talk," he said. She stood and joined him and he led her away, towards the beach. Harry said nothing as he watched them go.

The light was fading fast as the sun lowered itself into the ocean behind thin clouds. When they reached the hard sand at the water's edge, Tamos stopped. They stood there silently, arms around one another, small waves slapping a few feet away.

"Jeri, I have to tell you something." He tightened his grip on Jeri's side. "There has been a crisis building in Hungary for some time, as you know, but now something has happened." He faltered for a moment. "I am sorry to sound so formal. This is something I've been wanting to talk to you about."

"What is it, Tamos?"

"My uncle Béla, while facilitating the escape of the rest of the family to Spain, has disappeared. There is recently, well, some weeks ago now, some information – sketchy information – that he may still be in Budapest. However, the fear is that he is in the hands of the Arrow Cross, the fascist arm of the Nazi party in Hungary. He had many political enemies."

"Oh, my."

"Yes. Definitely, oh, my," Tamos agreed.

"Why didn't you tell me before now?"

"I did not want to worry you, before I knew what…what I must do."

"What you must do? What do you mean?"

He did not answer immediately, but turned and led them along the beach for a few yards, before stopping and turning to her.

"I am so sorry, Jeri. I must go."

"Go?" She broke away from his arm and moved to face him. The setting sun lit his face with a dark glow. "Go?" she repeated. "Go where?

"To Budapest, of course."

The glow was fading fast. "But, Tamos – when?"

"In three weeks."

It took her several moments to process this revelation, struggling to understand what he had just said.

"How?" she finally managed. "How is it even possible?"

"I'll explain everything. Harry has it all arranged."

"Harry?" she cried. "Harry has arranged this, this…lunatic mission? God damn it, Tamos. How could he?"

"I asked him for help, Jeri."

Jeri leaned back to look into his face, now hidden in shadow. She shrugged a small shrug, as if suddenly resigned. "So, what I have to tell you is nothing, now. I've dreaded telling you all week."

"Tell me what?"

"I'm being transferred. Back east. To Romulus Field in Michigan."

Tamos reached out and pulled her close. "Oh, is that all?" he said.

Jeri clasped her arms around him, as if to keep him from ever leaving. As aggrieved as she was, and as selfish as she yearned to be, she understood. Could not help, in spite of the yearning, but pull back a few inches to gaze at him in admiration.

"Tamos," she said, a mixture of awe and regret in her voice, "you are an uncommon man. *My* uncommon man." She put her head back down on his shoulder. "Come back to me."

On the way back to town, the murmurings from the couple in the back seat stayed just out of Harry's range of hearing. When he pulled up to the curb at Jeri's apartment, they leaned forward.

"Harry?" said Tamos.

"Yes?"

"Will you be best man?"

"I thought you'd never ask."

It was a small wedding – particularly small by Harry's standards – at the Breakers. Tamos and Jeri both wore their borrowed clothes, the clothes they had been wearing the night they first met.

Jeri's friends John and Jack attended, along with a handful of girls from the office. One of Tamos's professors and two classmates were there – not friends, exactly, but they ate lunch together occasionally – and Harry's chauffeur.

Francey had managed to come out from Romulus and was radiant as the bridesmaid. Harry was equally radiant as best man, giving away the bride in the place of Jeri's father. Wartime weddings seldom had the whole family gathered. Jeri's mother had sent her wedding veil.

Jeri was flustered when she tried to put the ring on Tamos's ring finger – on his left hand, as usual – but Tamos insisted it go on his right hand. "An old Hungarian custom," he whispered.

It had been a frantic honeymoon, again at the Breakers (where else?), all paid for by Harry, and the first and last time either one of them would experience such luxury.

Three days later, Jeri was sitting in a P-39 at the Bell factory airfield in Niagara Falls, New York, preparing to fly to Bismarck, North Dakota. Tamos had just arrived at the New York City marine air terminal.

Tamos had called her from his hotel the night before to say goodbye, but it had been less a conversation than a series of long silences broken by awkward murmurs.

"Are you still there?"

"Yes."

Long silence.

"When will you get to Lisbon?"

"Two days."

Again, silence.

"Will you be able to call me?"

"I do not know. I will try."

The final goodbyes dragged on for a minute or two, until neither could stand it any longer. They hung up at the same time, on the count of three, each wondering when they would next speak to one another.

Or if they would ever speak to one another again.

BOOK IV: EVIDENCE

Property Record Number:

OSWEGO POLICE DEPARTMENT
EVIDENCE CHAIN OF CUSTODY TRACKING FORM

Case Number: ____________ Offense: ____________
Submitting Officer: (Name/ID#) ____________
Victim: ____________
Suspect: ____________
Date/Time Seized: ____________ Location of Seizure: ____________

Description of Evidence

Item #	Quantity	Description of Item (Model, Serial #, Condition, Marks, Scratches)
1	1	Mechanical Device

Chain of Custody

Item #	Date/Time	Released by (Signature & ID#)	Received by (Signature & ID#)	Comments/Location

Patience Is a Virtue

HENDERSON, NEW YORK

Floating at the dock at Henderson, New York, after its seventy-year rest at the bottom of Lake Ontario, the wreck waited patiently through the night, under guard, until the next morning.

LaFleur stood by while Tamos paced anxiously awaiting a last set of authorizations. The P-39 floated there next to them as if tied up at a marine terminal. Tamos had a flash memory of the first and last time he had flown on a seaplane, the *Yankee Clipper*. That flight, more than seventy years ago, had also ended under water. The P-39, or course, was never meant for a water landing, but based on the relatively undamaged condition of the wreck, it appeared that she'd made a damned fine attempt.

Official vehicles had been coming and going all morning, as the various agencies interested in Tamos's find reviewed his permits and signed off on the various requirements that must be met before the plane could be brought on shore. It had taken a series of somewhat frantic cell phone calls from the *Diving Duck* to Larry Spiegelman – once it had been determined that there actually was someone in the cockpit, something Tamos had both hoped and feared – to make the necessary arrangements.

All of the rest of it – the marine archeological permits, government waivers, transportation – had been prearranged by Tamos months earlier with meticulous care. A logistics team gathered at the harbor ready to pull the plane out of the water and onto a set of trailers specially prepared to transport the wreck to a temporary storage facility, before taking it on to National WASP Museum in Texas for restoration. The only thing holding them up was the wait for the coroner to appear with Larry Spiegelman.

They had to arrange for the disposition of the body.

At a brief lull in the activity surrounding Tamos, Jamila and Red edged their way through the group surrounding him, not quite sure of what to think about the astonishing find.

"Professor," asked Jamila, tentatively, "did you have any idea that, well, you know, she was going to be there?"

"I knew only that the aircraft had to be in Lake Ontario, most likely at or near Duck-Galloo Ridge. But, no, I had not dared hope for such a successful recovery."

"But you seem to be very well prepared to handle the logistics involved.

I mean, you've got all these agencies practically falling all over themselves to get this thing wrapped up and on its way. How did you ever –"

"Prof?" It was LaFleur, who had just walked up behind them. "Sorry to interrupt, but I've got Larry on the phone." He handed the phone to Tamos.

"Hello, Larry. Any word?" He nodded absently while listening to what Larry had to say, turning to LaFleur at one point and giving an "okay" sign. "Thank you, Larry."

He handed the phone back to LaFleur. "One step closer." He looked down at the ground, then softly repeated, "One step closer."

After a moment he raised his head, turned to Jamila and said, "Oh, Jamila, I anticipate having some additional technical work for you, once I have everything from the cockpit secured."

At this, he nodded quickly, then turned and walked quickly back down to the dock, LaFleur following behind.

"Well," said Jamila, "he certainly is an old man in a hurry."

Red laughed. "Yes, indeed."

Jamila motioned for Red to move away from the group. "Should we be worried?" she asked in a low voice.

"Worried? How do you mean?"

"It all seems sort of, well, sinister, I guess. All this mystery, keeping the real target from us. And now that we've brought the plane up, the urgency to get it out of here and on to the museum. And the mad rush to get the coroner over here. We're pretty deeply involved in this thing, you know. So, yeah, is there something we should be worried about? Any unforeseen liability?"

"I've never known you to be a conspiracy theorist."

"You know what I mean."

Red looked over at the professor, who was now conferring with LaFleur down at the dock. "Yes, I do. And no," he said, reluctantly, it seemed, "I don't think we need to be worried. I think we're safe here."

Jamila followed his gaze. "Maybe. But even if *we* are 'safe,' as you say, is there anyone else who could be worried about this?"

Red frowned. "I'm not sure I follow you."

"I just have a feeling that finding this wreck could have serious repercussions."

"Who would be worried, and why?"

"I don't know."

They stood there watching the professor as he talked with LaFleur, gesticulating, nodding, acting exactly like an old man in a hurry.

"I wonder what he meant by additional work?" said Red.

"You've got me. Now that the plane is going to Texas, I don't know what else he could have in mind. I guess we'll find out soon enough." She looked back over at the professor. "I also hope he's not going to do something crazy," Jamila said.

"Like?"

"Oh, I don't know, Red. I just don't know." She turned and walked back up the hill, where a car was waiting, looking back over her shoulder at Tamos, who was walking quickly down the pier.

"Oh, Tamos," she said, to no one.

The promised ten minutes had turned into two hours, to no one's surprise. Finally, Tamos saw a dilapidated, black Ford Taurus veer into the Henderson boat ramp parking lot, trailing dust. A stenciled sign on the side of the front door read "Oswego County District Attorney." Two men got out, the driver being Cecil M. Groenik, D.A. and County Coroner, a dual position that saved Oswego County a considerable sum each year, as the duties of the job more often than not overlapped, particularly when it came to drug overdoses. The man climbing out of the passenger side was Larry Spiegelman. He hurried over to Tamos and LaFleur.

"Tamos, I can't believe it. I just can't believe you actually found it."

"I know. I know. But you know, Larry, I never doubted it." He gripped Spiegelman's hand. "Thanks for doing this."

Larry clapped Tamos lightly on the shoulder. "Of course. We've been preparing for this for a long time."

"Well, 'patience is a virtue,' as I believe it says in the Torah?"

Spiegelman chuckled. "Ah, well, Tamos, it is one of the thirteen attributes of God, but usually not regarded as one of the greatest of Jewish strengths. But you've had good reason to keep the faith all these years. And it's paid off today." He paused. "She's coming home, Tamos." Tamos's hand, still clasping his, tightened for a brief moment, then released.

Groenik, while still keeping one ear on the conversation between Tamos and Larry, had been pumping LaFleur for information. "How is it even possible, after so long at the bottom of the lake?" he was asking.

Tamos, glad for the chance to get back to the business at hand, broke in. "That's *exactly* why it's possible. Cold and at ninety feet, relatively dark. And somewhat anaerobic, they tell me. Natural cold storage. In fact, a P-39 was recovered in a Siberian lake about three years ago. The pilot's body along with all of his gear had survived; even the log books still legible. Perfectly preserved tins of food were found in the door hatch. So, yes, it is extremely likely that we have the same situation here. Not unexpected, actually. We've left the cockpit totally intact," Tamos went on. "I didn't want there to be any chance of anything compromising the legal…well, anything, that is, interfering with the extrication of the pilot and her effects."

"But still, still, how on earth…? And you claim it's your wife? I, really, I –" Groenik began to stammer.

"Mr. Groenik," Tamos interrupted, "we've been waiting here for hours. And I'm an old man. I don't have the luxury of time on my side. Can we please get on with it?"

Groenik tried unsuccessfully to put on the officious look he'd perfected in the course of his career. "Very well, though I have to say this entire operation has all the appearances of being very well stage-managed. Melodramatic, one might say. I hope I will find nothing compromising?" Eyebrows still arched, he turned to Spiegelman. "May we proceed?"

"You have all the documentation, Cecil. As Tamos says, let's get on with it. Is the morgue ambulance on the way?" he asked, as an afterthought.

"Yes, yes," said Groenik, impatiently. "All arranged. They should be here any minute."

"Fine," Larry replied. "Tamos, lead the way," he said, sweeping his arm out toward the airplane.

Tamos started deliberately down the dock, gesturing to a couple of the salvage crew members to follow them. They'd be the ones opening the cockpit door to allow the coroner to make an initial determination of the status of the body. Tamos would have preferred it to be a private moment; this was unfortunately as private as the legalities allowed.

Just as they approached the airplane, Tamos suddenly slowed, stumbling slightly.

A.C. quickly moved up closer to his side. "All right, Prof?" he said quietly, taking the professor's arm.

"Soon, A.C.," Tamos said, regaining his composure. Together they took a final few steps and stood at the side of the wreck. Tamos motioned to the salvage crew. "We're ready." He stood back, still partially supported by LaFleur.

"Yes," he said. "Very soon everything is going to be all right."

Secret Mission

HENDERSON, NEW YORK

From where the plane was moored, floating serenely on its inflatable bags, the wingtip barely reached the dock. Groenik had been forced to climb up onto it from a small step ladder and go the rest of the way on hands and knees. The salvage crew had prepared the doors, which opened, as Tamos had explained to Groenik earlier, almost exactly like car doors, so it was a simple matter to give him access to the cockpit, though he did have to hang over the door frame. After only about fifteen minutes, Groenik crawled his way back to the dock.

Tamos felt his heart literally skip a beat as Groenik got down off of the wing and walked over to him. *Calm down. Just a palpitation; doc says your heart is fine.*

"Mr. Szabó? With your permission, I believe we are ready to remove the remains. May I summon the EMTs?" Groenik's manner had changed markedly after his examination. Brusque and condescending when he'd arrived, his voice now had a subdued, almost reverential, tone. When Tamos did not respond immediately, he took a step back, cocked his head, and said again, "Mr. Szabó?"

Tamos arched his back, took a deep breath. "Yes, of course, Mr. Groenik, let's proceed." As he motioned the coroner to move closer, he called out to A.C., who had been standing well off to the side having a discussion with the museum representative. "A.C.? Please come over here. I would like you to hear this."

LaFleur broke off his conversation and went to the professor's side.

"I believe the coroner here is finished," Tamos said as A.C. approached. "Mr. Groenik, what did you find?"

"Well, sir, first let me say in all my experience, over thirty years, now, I have never seen a case like this. It's just so – I'm sorry. Of course, I have never seen a case like this. Let me begin again." He held up his tablet. "You will get the full report as soon as it's been filed. But briefly, I can tell you that in all probability it was a sudden death. In my opinion, she did not drown. I hope that is some comfort."

"Please explain."

"Well, it looks as if the seat belt, that is, the safety harness, was loose, maybe even unbuckled. Perhaps in preparation for the water landing, in order to avoid being trapped in the cockpit? Those look like heavy doors; it would certainly not have been easy to manage an exit under the circumstances."

"Yes, that is correct," Tamos agreed. "The entire canopy cannot be jettisoned, as was common in other craft. Although the doors themselves *can* be jettisoned. I wonder…" He shook his head. "Ah, never mind. Please continue."

"Yes. Without a postmortem, I can't be one hundred percent on this, but –" He interrupted himself. "Are you going to request a postmortem?" Tamos shook his head. "Well, in any case, it appears that at impact, she was thrown forward violently, hitting her head on the instrument panel. There are indications of a skull fracture. I believe she died instantly."

Not trusting himself to speak, Tamos reached out to shake Groenik's hand, simply nodding his thanks. After shaking hands, Groenik began to walk back up the dock in order to bring down the EMT team, but then stopped and turned awkwardly. "Uh, Professor?" Tamos looked up. "I'm very sorry."

"Thank you, Mr. Groenik. I appreciate that. And Mr. Groenik?"

"Yes?"

"Don't let them touch anything else."

"Of course."

Tamos clapped A.C. on the shoulder. "Let's get out of the way and let them do their job, yes?"

As the late afternoon deepened, the sky clouded over and drew the light from the lake, leaving it flat and grey. The professor stared out past the dock in a sort of daze, his eyes reflecting the dull water. He began speaking softly, under his breath.

"What's that, Tamos?" LaFleur asked.

Tamos looked up, as if surprised to see LaFleur standing there. "Ah, I was just recalling a poem, A.C., Jeri's favorite. 'My candle burns at both ends; It will not last the night; But ah, my foes, and oh, my friends – It gives a lovely light.' She often –"

He was startled by a loud rumbling noise off to their left. A gurney rolled up the ramp. The black body bag, held down with orange straps, looked pathetically small. Tamos watched as the body was transferred to the ambulance. A moment later, it pulled away.

Tamos turned to LaFleur. "Time to go!"

Together they hurried down the dock. "You'll have to crawl out on the wing," Tamos was explaining, for the second or third time.

"Yes, I know, no problem," answered LaFleur.

"You know what we're looking for, yes?"

"Log book, personal effects, and some sort of travel bag, right?" They had been over all of this only minutes before.

"Exactly."

A short time later, LaFleur was back on the dock, having carefully dragged back a small overnight case, a large leather-bound log book, and a bulky, oilcloth satchel, yellowed and water-stained. LaFleur stopped at the edge of the wing and held the bag out toward Tamos. "This what you were looking for?"

"Yes, that's it, I'm sure," said Tamos excitedly, as he took it from LaFleur. He set it down carefully, then took the other two items, setting them on the dock as well. He stood back as LaFleur slowly made his way off of the wingtip and back down to the dock.

"What now?" asked LaFleur.

"We're to meet Larry at the funeral home," replied Tamos. "He has the evidence bag ready for me."

This took LaFleur a bit off guard. "Evidence bag? What kind of evidence? And evidence for what?"

"We don't have time to go into that now. Larry will be waiting."

LaFleur shook his head. "Okay, I guess. Here, let me help you with that," he said, bending to take the satchel.

"No!" Tamos reached down and grabbed the bag out of LaFleur's hand. "I'll take it. You carry those, please," he said, pointing to the log book and overnight case.

"Sure thing, Tamos," said LaFleur.

As they approached the parking lot, a television reporter and his cameraman rushed up to them. The cameraman's ball cap read "WSYR 9 NEWS" in large red letters, embroidered across the front.

"Professor Szabó?"

"Yes, I am Szabó," Tamos replied.

"Professor, we understand that there has been quite a discovery here this afternoon. A World War II-era airplane?"

"Well, the discovery was actually made yesterday. We have located a missing fighter plane; a P-39, to be exact, which was then raised and towed to this bay late yesterday afternoon." He pointed down to the lake. "It is right down there," he said.

"We'd like to get a few words with you, down at the airplane, if we could," the reporter said, already moving that direction.

"Well, yes, I suppose," replied Tamos, "but it will have to be brief."

"Of course."

Tamos glance nervously over his shoulder as the doors to the ambulance closed. "Very brief," he repeated.

"Absolutely," said the reporter. "Please, lead the way."

The reporter positioned Tamos at the wing tip and had the cameraman move down to the edge of the dock. "Okay, Jason?" The cameraman nodded and turned on a bright video light. The reporter moved in next to Tamos, held up his microphone, and addressed the camera. "We're here with Professor Tamos Szabó," he began, "who is the latest in a long series of treasure hunters to have had success in finding a lost –"

"No, no!" interrupted Tamos. "I am not a treasure hunter!"

The reported signaled the cameraman to shut down. "Okay, Professor. Sorry. This is more of a, shall I say, historical find?"

"Archeological."

"All right, archeological, good, I'll go with that." He signaled the cameraman again, the light flared and he began again: we are here to speak with, recently discovered, etc.

"And this airplane, it was lost during World War II?"

"Yes, in late 1944."

"And the pilot, Professor. It is rumored that the pilot is actually your wife, is that correct?"

"Yes, that is correct." *How did they get that information, so soon?*

"That is simply amazing, Professor. How did she come to crash in Lake Ontario, of all places, and in a fighter plane? And even more amazing, a woman pilot?" He looked incredulous.

"Yes, a woman pilot. As a WASP – that is, as a member of the Women Airforce Service Pilots – she flew many different aircraft, all over the country."

"And this particular aircraft, what was its destination?"

Tamos shifted his gaze around, reluctant to answer. "All I am prepared to say at this time is that this P-39 is one of merely a handful of surviving examples, out of more than nine thousand built during the war.

"I will be releasing detailed information concerning the aircraft and its mission at the appropriate time. I will only add that this find has ramifications that go far beyond that of the discovery itself, far beyond my personal interest, in fact."

As he turned away, the reporter attempted to get a clarification. "But, Professor! What do you mean by 'ramifications?' Where was she going? Was it a secret mission of some kind?"

Tamos turned and shook his head. "Secret mission?" The professor's eyes gleamed for a brief moment. "Yes, yes, I suppose you could call it a 'secret mission.' There have been, well, certain 'artifacts,' let us say, recovered from the wreck that relate to that mission, evidence of great wrongdoing, the details of which will be forthcoming." He paused, but becoming caught up in the moment could not help but to continue, his voice strenuous, almost breaking. "The truth will come out. There will be consequences. Serious consequences, and in high places." He blinked into the camera lights, regaining his composure. "But I repeat, that is all I prepared to say at this time."

The reporter thanked Tamos and turned to the camera. "As you've just heard, much more on this story to come. We'll be right there to keep you up to date." As Tamos and LaFleur walked away, the reporter wrapped up the report with a teaser concerning tomorrow's weather report – rain? And if so, how much?

"Professor Szabó?" A man in a dark suit approached as the ambulance pulled away. "A moment, please?"

Tamos turned at the question, "I'm sorry, I can't talk just now," Tamos said abruptly. "I've already spoken to the press."

"Only a minute," the man persisted, moving in between the professor and LaFleur.

LaFleur was forced back a step, giving him a good overall look at the intruder. Black suit, plain black tie, carefully groomed hair, a back-room office pallor lying just under the surface of a quick artificial tan. LaFleur moved to one side in order to hear the conversation.

"Just a couple of questions, Professor. It's important."

Tamos scowled and nodded a "go ahead."

"The P-39 you've just found, do you know which factory it originally came from? Were there ever any alterations done to it?"

Another scowl, and a shake of the head. "What reason do you have for your questions?"

"Oh, we're just interested in the history of the aircraft, that's all. So, you don't know where the plane was manufactured?"

"I believe it came out of Buffalo, New York," Tamos replied. "But why do you want to know?"

"Historical interest, as I said before. Do you have any documentation concerning the origin of the aircraft? Flight history, maintenance records, anything like that?"

"I really don't see –"

"What will happen to the wreck now?"

"It's going to be restored for the WASP Museum in Texas. Now, I really must be going."

As Tamos tried to turn away, the man stepped closer. "Were there any other items recovered?" He looked down at the satchel in the professor's hand.

LaFleur suddenly stepped in, facing the questioner. "That's enough."

The man didn't flinch at the interruption, saying, "Hey, just trying to establish the facts. You know, historical –"

"Interest, yeah, so you said."

Tamos turned away, muttering, "I really do not have time right now." LaFleur followed close by. They had only gotten a few feet away when the man called out to him. "The red star, professor. Why does it have a red star painted on it?"

Tamos simply waved his hand impatiently behind his back, and walked on.

LaFleur took Maggie aside. "I think this is going to take a while," he said. "You should go on home."

"What's going on?"

"I'm not sure. We have to go to the mortuary. Larry will be waiting."

"You know, I really should have known."

"Known what?"

"That Prof was married."

"Huh?"

"I should have realized it earlier."

"I'm still not following you."

"The ring he wore. On his right hand."

"Yeah, a plain, gold band?" LaFleur had seen it but not really paid much attention to it. "So?"

"In Eastern Europe, it was very common in those days to wear the wedding ring on the right hand."

"It was, huh?"

"Yes. A clue we both missed."

"Well, I seem to be missing a lot of clues these days."

"Oh, stop it. Anyway, it doesn't matter now." She leaned over and kissed him quickly. "Call me when you're on your way home."

Tamos carefully placed the oilcloth bag on the floor of the back seat. LaFleur put the log book and the other small valise – both now wrapped in plastic bags obtained from one of the crew – on the seat, and closed the door. He then helped Tamos into the passenger side of car. As Tamos settled into his seat, LaFleur leaned in and said, "I didn't like the looks of that guy, did you?"

"What do you mean?"

"Well, he never said who he was, and he seemed to be trying awfully hard to make us believe he had a legitimate interest in the wreck. And he was trying to look the part, like he had some official reason for being there. But I just didn't buy it. Did you notice his shoes?"

"Shoes?"

"Crepe-soled shoes with waxed laces. Thought at first he might be a Fed, but not with those shoes." He closed the door, walked around to the driver's side and got in the car. As he buckled his seatbelt, he turned to Tamos.

"But I have to say, Prof; that was a very good question. Something I've been wondering about myself." He paused. "Why *is* there a Soviet star painted on it?"

Chain of Evidence

OSWEGO, NEW YORK

"Do you have the evidence bag?"

At the query, Larry Spiegelman motioned in the direction of a small office at the back of Abruzzo's funeral home.

"Ready to go, as we discussed."

"And the police, they are agreeable?"

"Chief Boyko said as long as I record the chain of custody, and seal it properly, it will be considered official."

"Excellent. Thank you."

Tamos and LaFleur followed Larry to the office, Tamos still carrying his satchel – he hadn't let go of it since they arrived – where they saw a large, yellow plastic bag sitting on a desk, imprinted on the front with two multi-line forms. Larry picked up the bag and turned to Tamos.

"Here's the evidence bag. Do you have your items ready to go?"

"Evidence of what?" interrupted LaFleur. There was no answer.

LaFleur tried to ask again, but was drowned out by Tamos loudly exclaiming, "A plastic bag? That's it?"

"Don't worry, Tamos. I have everything we need," Larry replied. He opened the briefcase lying next to the bag and brought out a roll of bright yellow tape, showing Tamos the large black print – EVIDENCE SEAL – running across the tape. "Once we place the article in the bag, I seal it with this tape. The bureaucratic details on the bag itself – case number, et cetera – we'll fill in later."

Tamos picked up the bag and peered closely at the form printed on the front. "Description," he said. "How specific does that have to be?"

"Well, anything to be entered into evidence – at whatever time that may happen – has to be properly identified."

"I cannot make that sort of declaration at this time."

"But, Tamos," Spiegelman protested, "there must be a detailed, accurate description of the evidence. Otherwise, how could it ever be admitted?"

LaFleur, who had been standing at the doorway, interjected. "Can someone please tell me what's going on here?"

Tamos looked over at LaFleur, then, ignoring his question, he turned back to Larry, a look of intense consternation filling his face. "Please," he pleaded. "If this were to get out –"

"Tamos, don't worry. It will go directly to the evidence room at police headquarters."

"In Oswego? No, I simply cannot allow that."

Larry shook his head. "What? But it has to be entered into evidence through the department."

"No."

"I still don't know what's going on here," said LaFleur, more perplexed than annoyed. "But, Tamos, assuming you have something here that's going to be used in any sort of legal proceeding, it should go through the department. It's just S.O.P."

"I'm sorry?"

"Standard Operating Procedure, Tamos," Larry explained. "Once the evidence is sealed, it's logged in to the evidence room. For safekeeping; it's required."

"I'm sorry, I cannot allow it," he repeated. "It's much too risky."

"But it's required," Spiegelman repeated. "And it will be perfectly safe. Right, A.C.?"

LaFleur rubbed the bridge of his nose. "Well. Yes. Theoretically."

Larry made an exasperated noise. "What do you mean by that?"

"Nothing is perfect, Larry. Weekends, holidays, some nights, if there's no clerk available to process the evidence, for example, it might sit in a locked vehicle, or a desk drawer, until there's someone on duty who can check it in to the evidence locker. And there have been cases – not often, but it has happened – where there have been locker break-ins, and evidence tampered with, even stolen."

Tamos looked at Larry in vindication. "There, you see? Exactly my point."

"But, Tamos, surely the risks are small. A.C. just said as much. Not worth worrying about. Wouldn't it be better to have it stored away safely?"

"I believe I can manage that much better than 'the authorities.' It's just those 'authorities' who allowed –" Tamos paused. "What I have in this satchel," he went on passionately, "I have waited seventy years to recover. Seventy years! It is the only proof I have. Do you understand what that means? No, of course not, you cannot. Forgive me." He bowed his head. "A.C., Larry," he said, staring at the floor. "You have no reason to believe this, I know. But what I have in this bag –" He held it up at arm's length, obviously straining at the weight before dropping it back to his side. "I do not wish to sound melodramatic, gentlemen, but what I have here could conceivably be the culmination of a decades-long search for justice. Justice well-deserved and long overdue. Justice denied, justice subverted, from that time to this." He took a deep breath. "And you want me to trust that to the Oswego Police Department, after what we've just heard? No, thank you.

"Now, can we please get on with it?"

Conceding Tamos's greater need, Larry taped closed the top of the evidence bag, which now contained a single, heavy object wrapped in oilskin. Still having no idea what he had just sealed away, Larry had added a description that read simply, "Mechanical Device."

Tamos placed the evidence bag in his oilskin case. "Now, to the next order of business," he said briskly. "Larry, please direct us to the director's office."

Phil Abruzzo saw Tamos coming down the hall through the side window of his office. A member of the third generation to operate the mortuary, Abruzzo was imbued with the gravid formality common to morticians, at least in his professional persona; rumor had it that he could be quite a cut-up at parties. Abruzzo stood and walked around to the front of his desk as Tamos approached. "Professor Szabo, please come in. Mr. Spiegelman, Detective LaFleur. Everyone, please come in. Plenty of room." He slid a chair from the corner closer to the desk to make three in a row, and they all sat down.

"Professor," Abruzzo said as he sat back down, "my sincere condolences. This must all be a bit overwhelming." Tamos nodded. "First," Abruzzo continued, "let me assure you that the remains are already in our custody and are being prepared."

"Thank you."

"Mr. Spiegelman tells me that the services will be held immediately, and that those arrangements have already been made? I understand there is somewhat of an historic aspect to the proceedings, regarding the internment."

"Yes, that's true," said Tamos. "It's taken a bit longer than we had hoped, but still, I don't know how Mr. Spiegelman got everything in place on such short notice –"

"Friends in high places," interjected Larry

"Very high, apparently," said Tamos. "In any case, Mr. Abruzzo, yes, she is to be buried at the Fort Ontario Post Cemetery, five days from now, on Saturday. The first such burial there since nineteen-forty-three."

"Excellent, excellent. We are ready to facilitate in any way necessary."

"I believe the only thing remaining is the transportation on the day of the service," said Larry. "Other than that, it's all being handled by the military and the park service."

"I understand." He turned to Tamos. "Professor, just your signature on two or three documents, and we're finished. Oh, our services are being provided *gratis*, of course."

"I appreciate that."

Tamos handed the papers Abruzzo had passed over the desk to him to

Larry. "Larry? Anything here I need to look at in detail?"

"No, Tamos. We prepared everything while waiting for you; just the standard agreements, oh, and a waiver of fees; that's it. Here, I'll show where you need to sign."

Paperwork completed, Tamos picked up his satchel and stood to go, followed by the other two. Abruzzo stood as well, offering his hand. "Again, Professor, anything at all, just let me know."

"Yes, well, thank you again, Mr. Abruzzo. We'll see you on Saturday."

As the three men made their way down the hall toward the parking lot, LaFleur leaned close to Tamos. "You've got a lot of explaining to do," he said, in a low voice.

"Yes, yes, A.C., all in good time. With the appropriate confirmation of the evidence – an effort now urgently required – all will become clear." He waved his free hand in that way he had, dismissive yet friendly. "All in good time."

Wake

1850 HOUSE

The restaurant was overflowing; people were even lined up out on the sidewalk, the first time that had ever happened. Word of the discovery of Tamos's deceased wife had spread with remarkable speed through the Oswego rumor mill, which in effect meant that everyone in Oswego who wanted to know about it, did, very quickly. And they all knew that there was to be a gathering at the restaurant that evening, and they all wanted to be in on it. Frank soon realized he was in danger of being swamped, and took the expedient way out; he gathered up all of the standard menus, had Maggie quickly print out fifty single page menus with a simple "prix fixe" meal, and raided the freezers.

In the back bar, what had been planned by A.C. as a simple celebration of the recovery soon turned into an impromptu wake. Fortunately, Frank also had had the forethought to prominently post a "Private Party" sign at the entrance to the bar, which didn't stop people from congregating there, waving to various members of the group in back, but it did provide a small measure of calm.

Tamos and LaFleur sat at Tamos's regular table. The satchel, bulky and awkward, which Tamos had carried with some difficulty through the crowd in front, sat at his feet.

"It's all been quite overwhelming, A.C.," he said. "And when you suggested we all come here tonight, well, I wasn't sure I was ready to do something like this."

"I guess I felt it would be a bit anticlimactic to just take you home to bed. I hope we're not rushing you too much."

"Oh, not at all. Once I got here, I realized that this is just what I need, to be surrounded by friends. We do have something to celebrate, after all. And it's a perfect distraction from what lies ahead. I expect the next few days to be, well, somewhat difficult. But tonight, I'm just going to try to relax and not think about things for a while."

Just then, Jamila and Maggie came over. "Mind if we intrude?" Jamila asked. LaFleur stood up and offered his chair to her. "Why, thank you, sir," she said, sitting down next to Tamos. Maggie took an empty chair across from him.

Tamos raised his drink in Jamila's direction. "To the brains behind the project," he said. He then leaned forward, raising his glass to Red Aldridge at the next table, and getting his attention, called out, "And to the brawn!"

Red smiled, raised his glass, and gave a little shrug. "Ah, he couldn't hear me," said Tamos, shrugging back. "Ah, well, no matter. I will congratulate Red later."

As Tamos turned back to Jamila, he felt a tap on his shoulder. "Professor?"

Tamos looked up to find Aaron and Erin behind him. "Ah! A and E! I didn't get a chance to talk to you at the Henderson dock. I'm glad to see you!" He looked around. "Where are you sitting?"

"Oh, no, professor, we can't stay," replied Erin. "I have a family thing, and Aaron has a date with Tiffany. But we just had to stop by to congratulate you. This is, like, the biggest thing to hit Lake Ontario in years! We are *so* glad you let us work on it with you."

"It was a great experience, Professor," added Aaron. "I can't believe I'm getting credit toward graduation, on top of everything. Thank you so much!"

"Well, you two performed admirably, both of you; you are very accomplished young people. I was very lucky to have you there to handle the search. It must have been very tedious at times"

"Oh, no, professor, we loved it," said Aaron. "Every minute. And like Erin said, we are grateful to have met you, and worked with you. It was all very exciting. And from what I hear, the story is just beginning."

Tamos looked as if he had just remembered something important. "Ah. That reminds me. Erin said you were seeing Tiffany tonight? That is Tiffany Peet, from the Palladium-Times?"

"Yeah. She's still working there. Just got promoted!"

"Wonderful. There is something you can do for me, Aaron."

"Sure, Professor, anything."

Tamos reached into his inside jacket pocket and pulled out an envelope. "Will you please deliver this to Miss Peet for me?"

"Yeah, I'm on my way to pick her up now." Aaron took the envelope and slipped it into his back pocket. "What is it?"

"Well, let's just say it is a lead up to 'the rest of the story.' Oh, you don't get that reference, do you? In any case, please tell Miss Peet that I would like to get it published prominently, right away; tomorrow, if possible. I believe her editor will agree that it is newsworthy."

"Sure, Professor, no problem."

"And can she get it into the Syracuse papers as well?"

"Probably. Hey, can she post it to her blog?"

"Absolutely, Aaron. Tell her to get it out however she can. It is very important."

"Will do. And thanks again for everything."

"Yes, thanks," echoed Erin. "I hope we can work together again someday!"

As Aaron and Erin made their way out of the bar, Maggie turned to Tamos and asked, "What was that all about, Tamos? Something related to finding the plane?"

"Yes, precisely."

Maggie cocked her head quizzically. "Care to let us in on it?"

Tamos shifted in his chair, fidgeted with his drink, took a sip, looked around. "Now is not the best time or place," he said. "Let's just forget it for the time being, and I promise you everything will be made clear very soon. Now, please, let's just continue with our little memorial celebration."

A few minutes later, Maggie excused herself to visit the restroom. As she exited into the narrow hallway a few minutes later, she nearly ran into the professor, who was just exiting from the Men's room next door.

"Ow," she cried.

The professor stopped and looked over in alarm. "Oh, my. What's the matter?"

"Oh, it's nothing; sorry to startle you. I just bumped my knee on your bag."

Tamos shifted the bulky satchel to the other hand. "I am sorry. I shouldn't be carrying it around; I'll get it out of the way."

"Oh, don't worry about it. Here," she said, seeing that Tamos was having a hard time with the heavy bag, "let me help."

"Of course, thank you," he said, unable to politely refuse this time.

"What do you have in here, rocks?" she said, hefting it with some difficulty.

"Oh, no, just an item for the WASP museum," he extemporized. "I'll take it home tonight."

Tamos followed Maggie closely back out into the room, stopping her when she began to carry the satchel over behind the bar. "Here, at the table, where I had it before," he instructed. "This will be fine." He took the bag from her and placed it back under the table where he'd had it earlier. Newton, who had been lounging by the bar, jumped down and ran over to the bag, sniffing it with obvious interest. The professor laughed and looked down at him. "You know it's been in the water, don't you, Newton? Well, no fish in it for you." Newton took one more sniff before heading back to his perch behind the bar.

"There! That's fine." He sat down. "Now, may I buy you two lovely ladies another drink?"

"Buy?!" said Maggie. "Prof, this is your party! It's all on the 1850 House."

"Well, in that case," he said, "make it the best you've got!"

Eulogy

FORT ONTARIO MILITARY CEMETERY

The lowering sun etched the edges of the simple tombstones in a reddish, late-afternoon glow. Long shadows stretched in irregular patterns from the stones, many of which tilted at odd angles, or were partially broken, scattering the shadow and light through the trees and neatly mown grass.

A simple paved path led from just below the parking lot to the graveyard, past twin flagpoles, left and right, through a break in the split rail fence; the original "Post Cemetery" arch marking the entrance had been removed years before. A small dais had been erected at the edge of the cemetery, near an open gravesite. A color guard of local reserve officers from each of the four services flanked the dais, two on each side. A formal portrait of Jeri in her dress blues – dark jacket, matching cap, WASP wings on the lapel – was displayed next to the podium.

A small audience – Tamos had severely limited the number of attendees – stood by, silently expectant. LaFleur, Maggie, Michael, and Larry and Arlene Spiegelman sat quietly in a row of chairs arranged in front of the grave. A video camera had been placed unobtrusively near a large tree off to one side to record the event, manned by the WSYR television news crew, the same crew that had interviewed Tamos at the dock only days earlier.

A representative from the New York State Historic Sites department, a Mrs. Podhertz, and Lt. Colonel MaryAnne Dembrowski, an Air Force pilot, both scheduled to speak at the service, stood to one side talking in low tones. Mrs. Podhertz, dressed in a conservative dark suit, was at least a foot smaller than the colonel, and was unconsciously leaning backward in order not to look only at the colonel's chin. Colonel Dembrowski, tall and impressive in her dress uniform, was describing the Congressional Medal of Honor ceremony that had been held in Washington a few years earlier, presenting all WASPs with the gold medal.

"Oh, yes," said Mrs. Podhertz, "I heard about that. And every one of them got a real gold medal?" she asked, a tone of slight disbelief in her voice.

"Well, each WASP received a bronze replica, or their family did, if the WASP was no longer alive. The original gold medal is now in the Smithsonian."

"Ah. That makes sense," said Mrs. Podhertz, a definite sound of relief in her voice, leaving the distinct impression that giving out so many gold medals would not have been fiscally responsible.

LaFleur leaned to one side, nudged Maggie, and gestured toward Tamos, who was standing at the dais, head down, hands clasped, waiting on the hearse.

"You think he's okay?" he whispered.

Maggie glanced over at the professor, and then turned back to A.C. "Just tired, I think. This week has been very hard on him, waiting for this all to be over."

LaFleur craned his neck back in the direction of the parking lot. "Weren't they supposed to be there by now?"

Maggie held up her watch. "Only a few minutes late."

"Yeah, well, hope they don't take too much longer."

Maggie patted his knee. "Over soon."

LaFleur looked back to the podium. Tamos had stepped back and was gazing around at the crowd. He noticed LaFleur looking at him, raised his hand, and made an exaggerated swipe across his forehead, as if wiping away sweat, then shrugged his shoulders. LaFleur laughed. *Prof. Can't keep him down for long.*

It was an unusual time for a funeral, this late in the afternoon, but Tamos had been insistent. It was to be done at this time of day, as close to the actual time of the crash as he could determine. He had been there, after all, even if unknowingly; that late afternoon was as thoroughly etched in his memory as the names and dates on the stones lined up in front of him. *No, not a good analogy, he thought.* Many of the tombstone inscriptions were eroded to imperceptibility. Most of what was known about the seventy-odd people buried here – military officers, their wives and children – had come not from the faded lettering on the stones but from old military records. *Then again, perhaps my memory is not as sharp as I think.* He silently thanked Larry for arranging this most unusual of honors for his wife.

The hearse arrived. The pall bearers quietly assembled – LaFleur, Michael, Larry, Big Frank, Red Aldridge, and Colonel Dembrowski (a last-minute replacement for Jamila, who couldn't bear the thought) – and carried the coffin, draped in the American flag, to the bier.

In deference to both the darkening sky and the professor's age, the speakers kept their remarks to a minimum. Mrs. Podhertz commented briefly on the history of the cemetery and the privilege of now having another unsung hero gracing its "population," as she called it.

Lt. Colonel Dembrowski was next to speak.

"Today we are honoring not only Jeri Jillette Szabó," she began, "but all of the truly heroic women who served during the war in so many ways, in all services, and in civilian roles as well. As an Air Force pilot, myself, I am particularly grateful for their contribution, which has made it possible for the women pilots who followed to serve in all capacities, flying everything from Apache helicopters to transport ships to fighter planes, even in combat.

"It is perhaps not well known that Jeri and her colleagues, along with the thirty-eight WASP pilots who gave their lives in service to their country, were not officially recognized as veterans until 1977. This meant that WASP funerals were often paid for out of their own funds, and sometimes held without military honors, as even draping the coffin with the American flag was at that time 'against regulations.' In many cases, these prohibitions were rightfully ignored by both sides.

"Another honor was recently bestowed on all WASP members, living or dead, when they were awarded *en masse* the Congressional Medal of Honor in March of 2010. I have arranged for Professor Szabó, as Jeri's only remaining relative, to receive his bronze replica of the medal.

"I will end with a brief tribute to Professor Szabó. It is through his remarkable efforts that we now have this opportunity to provide Jeri the honor she is due. We lay her to rest, after so many years, in this historic place, a place close to the professor's heart. It is here that Professor Szabó was returned to this country as a war refugee, to be reunited with Jeri for only the briefest of times before losing her to the war. This is a loss he has carried with him for these many, many years, a loss that can never be requited, but a loss that also carries with it the knowledge of a life of courage, integrity, and strength. And may that knowledge inspire and strengthen us. We can only hope, and aspire, and acknowledge our debt to those who have gone before." At this she seemed to break off, as if she was not quite finished but could not go on. But she'd said everything that needed to be said.

As the colonel moved away from the podium, two members of the color guard, an Air Force reservist and a Navy pilot, removed the flag from the casket and folded it into the traditional tight, triangular packet. The pilot presented it to Tamos, saluting, then stepped back into formation with the others. From the hillside behind them, near the lake, a bugler played "Taps." As the last note faded along with the light, Tamos suddenly lurched to one side.

LaFleur, Maggie, and Michael all started out of their chairs, but Tamos recovered quickly, and a nod and a small wave reassured them that he was all right.

As the ushers began shepherding the attendees to the path out of the cemetery, Maggie leaned over to LaFleur. "War refugee?" she asked, in a low voice.

LaFleur lifted his eyebrows and tilted his head in the direction of the professor, who was still at the grave site, flag clutched under his arm. "I think there may be a few things we don't know about the Prof," he said.

"Or Jeri," said Maggie.

"Definitely," said LaFleur. "Or Jeri." He looked back over at Tamos. "Well, time to get him home, I think."

As LaFleur helped Tamos navigate his way out of cemetery, he turned and said, "You know, Tamos, that's the first picture we've ever seen of Jeri. She was beautiful!"

"Oh, well, she never thought so. She was not glamorous, by nineteen-forties movie star standards, that is, but then again, who was? Not even the pin-up girls of those days were as glamorous in real life as they were depicted. But, oh, yes, she was a beautiful girl. A beautiful girl." At this he shuffled slightly and leaned against LaFleur's shoulder.

"Tamos, are you feeling okay?" LaFleur asked. "You gave us start there earlier, you know, during the service."

"A bit fatigued, A.C. That's all."

"Well, not surprising, given everything that's happened recently. Nothing else bothering you?"

"To be honest, I was hoping I could see Dr. Linnabarger tomorrow. Some recurring nausea; I think that is what is dragging me down. I don't know what could be causing it."

"You let me know when you get an appointment; one of us will take you over."

"Thank you, A.C., that would be very helpful."

Just as they got to the parking lot, LaFleur spotted Jamila a few spaces away, just getting into her car.

"Maggie, would you go ahead and take the professor home? I'd like to stay for a few minutes." He waved at Jamila, indicating he wanted her to wait.

"Sure." She walked to the other side of the car, where LaFleur had been holding the door open for the professor. "Ready, Prof?"

"Yes, thank you."

Maggie went around to the driver's side. "Is he okay, do you think?" she asked LaFleur, before getting into the car. "Maybe I should just get him over to the urgent care clinic for a quick once over."

"Not a bad idea, if you can get him there. He just told me he's been experiencing some stomach problems, and was thinking about seeing Dr. Linnabarger."

"Okay, that clinches it. I'll take him over now."

LaFleur leaned down to the professor's window. "Maggie wants to take you over the clinic for a quick exam."

"That is not necessary, A.C.; I am just fine."

"Well, humor her for me, will you? You know how nurses are."

"Oh, all right."

LaFleur tapped the roof of the car. "All set. See you later."

As Maggie drove off with the professor, LaFleur hurried over to Jamila's car.

"Jamila? Thanks for waiting."

"Sure, Mr. LaFleur."

"Oh, call me A.C., please. You know the old joke."

She laughed. "Okay, 'A.C.' it is."

"Sorry to hold you up, but I wanted to ask you something. "

"Of course. What is it?"

"The Air Force Colonel who spoke at the service, Colonel Dembrowski?"

"Yes, I think that was the name."

"Well, she made reference to the professor as being a 'war refugee.' We weren't quite sure what to make of that. We knew he'd been in Europe at some point during the war, but that's all. I thought you might know something more; he once mentioned that you have some sort of family connection?"

"Yes, as a matter of fact, I do. The professor knew my grandmother, and my mother when she was a small girl, in the camp."

"Camp?"

"Yes, Safe Haven."

"The Jewish refugee camp? Here in Fort Ontario?"

"Yes, exactly. When we first met, he told me he'd met my grandmother on the troop ship, the refugee ship, on the way over from Italy." She looked at LaFleur quizzically. "You didn't know this?"

"No; as odd as it may sound, and as long as I've known Tamos, no, we didn't know he'd been at the Fort." LaFleur scratched the back of his neck absently. "But how on earth did he happen to be there? He lived in California before the war, right? How did he get from California, to Europe, to Fort Ontario?"

"Well, that's a very interesting story. Do you have some time?"

Safe Haven

FORT ONTARIO

LaFleur had always had a hard time understanding a particular image in Dylan Thomas's poem *Fern Hill*, a phrase in the third stanza: "fire green as grass." But as he and Maggie walked across the lawn bordering Fort Ontario Park, under a bright-hot, broiling sun, he finally got a feel for it. Even the green grass looked hot, felt hot.

Crossing around the back of the Oswego Players theatre, housed in one of the original barracks buildings, they cut over to the small structure around the corner, the Safe Haven Holocaust Refugee Shelter Museum. The museum had once been the camp's administrative office. They'd both been to the museum before, of course, but not in a very long time; recent revelations had prompted a new visit.

Anyone who had lived in Oswego for more than a few years had been to the museum, either on their own or when escorting out-of-town visitors. The refugee camp had long been a point of pride for a city with more than its share of past moral bankruptcy. Schools, health care, law enforcement, city government – over the years, all had been plagued with the triple threat of corruption, incompetence, and under-financing. What sustained Oswego in spite of the failures of the city fathers was the innate goodness of neighborhood life. Residents watched out for one another, and for the best interests of the community; neighbor helping neighbor was the lifeblood of Oswego, not the actions of the mayor and his crony aldermen. The Safe Haven museum honored not just the refugees who had been sheltered at the Fort, it also mirrored the generous community spirit that had sustained the inmates during their time at the Fort, and which lived on in the surrounding neighborhoods.

The small room just inside the entrance of the museum was deserted. As they looked around, a diminutive woman in a black and grey striped dress suddenly appeared from a side office. Her short, wavy hair matched her dress – grey streaked with black – and her old-style black heels rapped the worn wooden floor in a staccato beat. No more than five feet tall, she projected an authoritative stature well above her physical size.

"Welcome to Safe Haven!" she said, sharply. "I'm Mrs. Rothstein. Our entrance fee is five dollars, which I will collect from you before you leave. Your entrance fee includes a historical overview of the camp, as well as a brochure describing the exhibits. If you will please step over here to the small diorama of the camp as it appeared in 1944, we'll get started."

Slightly taken aback by this abrupt introduction, LaFleur began to explain, "Well, we've been here before and know something of the camp, so I don't think –"

"I'm sorry, but I believe in delivering full value for your money. You've paid your five dollars – that is, you will be paying five dollars – *each* – and so are entitled to the complete service we provide. Now," she motioned to them again, "please walk this way."

Abashed, LaFleur and Maggie followed her to the display.

"Now, here you can see the camp layout as it was when the refugees arrived." She pointed out the various sections of the camp: barracks, dining hall, clinic, administrative offices, and so on. "Fort Ontario was closed as an active Army facility in March, 1944, but left intact, so it was an ideal location to house the refugees.

"Of course, as you may be aware," she said, pointedly referring to LaFleur's earlier comment, "there had been considerable dissention at high levels of government regarding the establishment of the camp, the one and only Jewish refugee center ever created in the United States during the war. It was through the efforts of a remarkable woman named Ruth Gruber – then a low-level State Department official – that the camp was established. She also had the foresight, and temerity, to enlist Eleanor Roosevelt's assistance, which proved crucial. There were some officials in the State Department who held – let's be frank – anti-Semitic opinions and who were adamantly opposed to the establishment of the camp. It wasn't until June of 1944 that FDR, at Eleanor's urging, designated Fort Ontario as a so-called 'free port' in order to allow refugees into the country as undocumented 'guests' of the United States. The refugees had no legal immigration status, a fact that became significant later on."

Maggie bravely interrupted this narration with a question. "How many Jews were brought here?"

"I was just coming to that. However, an interesting question, as they were not, in fact, all Jews. The same State Department officials who opposed the creation of the camp in the first place insisted that some number of non-Jewish refugees were brought over, to avoid the appearance of showing too much sympathy towards Jews. But to answer your question: out of the one thousand refuges originally specified as the maximum number allowed, nine hundred and eighty-two ultimately made the trip; of these, eight hundred and seventy-four were Jewish."

"Thank you. Sorry for interrupting," she added.

"Not at all," the museum guide said, her tone clearly signaling *please don't interrupt again*. "The nine hundred and eighty-two refugees were selected from a pool of over three thousand applicants. The selection process was completed in liberated Italy in the early summer of 1944. Each applicant selected then got a berth on the troopship *Henry Gibbins*, along with over a thousand wounded soldiers, mostly from Anzio and Cassino, who were being returned home. That ship left Naples in July of 1944, shadowed by German U-boats the entire way, but arrived safely at Pier 84, New York Harbor, on August 3. They disembarked and were processed at a warehouse nearby, and by 'processed,' I mean, stripped, sprayed with DDT, clothes steam-cleaned, and registered. From there they were taken the next day by train to Fort Ontario. Here, to the Emergency Refugee Center, now also known as Safe Haven. Now, any questions?"

Maggie shook her head, remembering her last attempt. LaFleur, only slightly intimidated, raised his hand, feeling like he was still in the fourth grade.

"How long were they here? That is, when did they get out?"

"In order to qualify for admittance, each applicant had been required to sign an affidavit declaring that they would return to Europe at the end of the war. Since they now had no legal status, it took some time for the State Department to determine how they could possibly let them stay here, as most of them had gone back on their word, so to speak, and opted not to return to Europe. After all, what had they to return to? In any case, it was not until early in 1946 that a scheme was concocted to provide them the legal status they needed. They were all put on buses, taken across the Rainbow Bridge at Niagara Falls into Canada, given visas, and then returned to the United States. The camp was closed in February of that year."

"Niagara Falls," said LaFleur, quietly. "Appropriate."

The docent continued. "You may now visit the exhibits. Stop by my office on your way out and I'll collect your admission fees."

They stood there quietly, looking at the wall of names.

LaFleur was the first to speak.

"There it is. Tamos Szabó."

"I never saw it before," said Maggie.

"Me either."

"Why would he keep this a secret?"

"I don't think it was exactly that; not a secret, not something intentional. And apparently Jamila knew."

"She told me he wanted to keep it quiet."

"It was so long ago. A different lifetime."

"Yes. It was."

"I can't imagine."

"No."

"It explains a lot."

"Some. Not everything."

"No. Not everything."

They stood there a few minutes longer, holding hands, not speaking.

"Let's go talk to him."

"Yes."

They didn't bother Mrs. Rothstein as they left. They just put a twenty-dollar bill on top of the diorama case, tucked under their brochure, and slipped out quietly through the front door.

Important Business

WASHINGTON, D.C. / NEW YORK CITY

In a nondescript basement office in an anonymous office block somewhere in Washington, D.C., a computer alarm sounded discretely. There was no name on the door, but a privileged few knew the building to be owned by Wharton General Industries.

The operator reached for the phone.

In a large, ostentatious office on an upper floor of WGI headquarters in Manhattan, a cell phone rang, the sound muffled by the heavy oak drawer in which it sat. A frail, age-spotted hand pulled open the drawer and answered the phone with a curt "Yes."

After listening intently to the caller for a few moments, a clarification was requested. "This is regarding the P-39 in Lake Ontario, is that correct? Recovered by Professor Tamos Szabó? What did he say, exactly?"

Nodding at the response given by the caller, the old man ended that call, then speed-dialed another.

Instructions were given.

"That's right. Permanently."

Moments later, the phone was returned to the drawer.

"Thought I'd taken care of those Jew bastards in nineteen forty-four," the old man mumbled. "How did this guy live so long?"

And the important business of WGI moved forward.

BOOK V: AIRPLANES

It's Raining Airplanes

LONG BEACH, CALIFORNIA

Bless 'em all! Bless 'em all!
The strong and the short and the tall;
They'll be no promotions
This side of the oceans,
The P-39 gets 'em all!
– *WASP Song*

"A P-39 in the drink."
"Where?"
"Out off of Santa Rosa. Three-fifty-sixth fighter squadron."
"Pilot okay?"
"Didn't make it."
"Oh, God."
"Engine failure?"
"Mechanical failure's all I heard."
"Okay, girls, that's enough. Get over to Ops for your flight assignments."

"Did you hear? A P-39 fatality."
"A WASP?"
"No, Army flyer. In Palmdale."
"Know what caused it?"
"Engine failure."
"At least it wasn't pilot error."
"Small comfort."
"Still."

"Another P-39 crashed. A WASP. On takeoff. At Long Beach."
"Bad?"
"Bad enough. But she made it out okay."
"What was it?"
"Sabotage."
"Where did you hear that?"
"Out at Long Beach."
"Who told you?"
"Oh, I don't remember. It's common knowledge."
"What was it?"
"Sugar in the tank, I heard."

Airplanes were falling out of the air.

Covert conversations at mess tables, rumors up and down on the flight line, hushed revelations secreted between the newsreel and the main feature, speculations whispered in the barracks after lights out. And bar talk. All this talk, dominated by one topic: airplanes were falling out of the air, and there didn't seem to be anything anyone could do about it.

Some of these airplanes had gone from spec to tarmac in less than two years. Of course, there would be problems. Design problems, manufacturing defects, rushed production schedules, condensed flight test programs. Problems were to be expected. Mechanical failures, some due to poor maintenance, were daily occurrences; some required a quick fix, some a major overhaul, and too many went undetected until it was too late.

Accident reports circulated almost like an underground newspaper. Not for public consumption, of course. Pilot error was not uncommon, again given the rushed training schedules, the high pressure, and the proclivity for some pilots to push the boundaries. Mid-air collisions, bail-outs, ground collisions, ground loops, short landings, long landings. There was even a "friendly-fire" fatality, occurring during live target towing. Not the WASP who was towing the target, but the Army pilot stunting in the wrong place at the wrong time. He hadn't paid enough attention to that day's activity roster, was not even authorized to be up that day. But things happen. Not all accidents were fatal, but the number of fatalities in relation to more mundane accidents was becoming alarming. May, 1943, was a particularly bad month, with fifteen fatalities in P-39s alone.

The women were getting edgy. Which led to a lot of bar talk. They were spending more time in the bar, in fact, than they had ever thought possible; some had never even had a drink before coming to Avenger Field. Not that they drank as much as the men; not possible. And never to excess, just enough to take the edge off. And the edge was getting sharper day by day. Too many unexplained accidents.

The rumors spread. Sugar in the tank. Grass, pulled up from the edge of the field, put in the tank. Tires partially cut through, to blow out on landing. Bolts loosened, even removed, from crucial structural points. Even parachutes were sabotaged, in one case a slowly leaking bottle of acid folded into the shroud.

And it was not just stories of sabotage that were putting everyone on edge. There were cases of intentional manufacturing subversions. War profiteering. Yes, the women were getting edgy.

March 12, 1944

A ship came in late this afternoon, making a forced landing after the engine overheated. The pilot had ignored orders from the tower to circle and await instructions. She landed as the engine seized. Two days later she learned from the mechanics why the engine failed - the coolant and oil lines had been crossed. At the factory. Not a rumor.

Operator?

GREAT FALLS, MONTANA

The P-39 fighters were lined up, bullet-nosed, round-tailed, shining in the sun, the Soviet red star freshly painted on wings and fuselage. The ships had been flown from the Bell factory in Niagara Falls to Bismarck, North Dakota, and then on to Great Falls, Montana, their last U.S. stop. From there the planes would be taken on to Alaska and ultimately Russia, on Lend-Lease. It was an exotic route Jeri and many other WASPs desperately yearned to fly, the first part, anyway – Great Falls to Fairbanks, then on to Galena, Moses Point, and Nome – but the WASPs weren't allowed to ferry past Great Falls. The planes were taken to Alaska by male pilots, or Russian pilots brought in specifically for the purpose; women, ironically enough, most of them. From Nome, it was across the strait to Yakutsk, Kirensk, Krasnoyarsk, Novosibirsk.

Jeri had met some of the Russian women pilots – given them lipstick and nylons – and was a bit afraid of them. One of their nicknames for the P-39 Airacobra was *Kobrastochka*, "Dear Little Cobra." And the Russian women also flew combat, not just ferry missions. They were fearless, fierce warriors. *Nachthexen*, "Night Witches," the Nazis called them. Those godless Russians, one of the WASPs said in the mess one night. Godless or not, Jeri retorted, they are winning the goldarn war in Russia.

Jeri was sitting in the officer's mess at Great Falls (WASPs had some privileges, not many), when someone passing by dropped a newspaper next to her. She automatically glanced over as the paper hit the table, then turned back to her ham and cheese sandwich. It was several minutes before she turned back to the paper. No one she knew had come in to the mess hall, so she decided she might as well pass the time with the news.

Picking it up, she was startled by words just visible below the fold: "BODIES OF 20 LOST ON YANKEE CLIPPER."

Another plane crash?

Then a sudden chill. Sudden recognition. A momentary flash of bright light distorted her vision. She looked back down at the paper, now unfolding in her hands, trying to focus.

"LISBON HARBOR POLICE SEARCH FOR –" And then the rest. It began to register.

YANKEE CLIPPER.

She read the article, numbly, barely comprehending.

Oh, God, no.

She read the headline again, reread the whole article. There was no question.

Tamos.

The base personal use telephone – FOR ATHZD USE ONLY, the sign on the window in the door said – was sequestered in a small office near Lt. Blage's corner of the Operations Center.

"Please, try again. Zook. Harry Zook. He's a lawyer in New York."

"I'm sorry, I don't find a 'Harry Zook' listed."

"In New York City!"

"I'm sorry."

"But you've got to have listing. Zook. Z-O-O-K."

"I am sorry, I just –"

"But he's well-known. Famous, practically."

"Do you have any other number, any other way I might reach him?"

"Oh, I don't know. Oh, try Long Island. I think he has a house there."

"Please hold on."

"Operator? Operator?"

Several minutes later, the operator came back on the line. "Ma'am? I did find a Long Island number, but I'm sorry, I can't raise anyone there."

Jeri bowed her head. What was she forgetting? "Wait. His law practice. It's called the XYZ firm. Um, Xerxes, Yerkes, and Zook. XYZ! New York City. Look for that!"

"One minute, please."

Another several minutes later, the operator came back on the line.

"Yes, we do have that number, but I'm afraid I cannot connect you. There is no answer."

"Okay, okay. Let me think, Long Island. XYZ. Oh, God, Harry."

After a long pause, the operator spoke up. "Ma'am?"

"Yes?"

"Is there anything else I can help you with?"

"Zook! Harry Zook!"

"Yes, ma'am, I understand. I have been unable to reach –"

"Fifth Avenue! He has an apartment on Fifth Avenue!'

"Yes, ma'am. Do you have an address?"

"Yes! I mean, no, I have it, just not with me, here. Please, just look for Zook on Fifth Avenue. There can't be that many of them, right?"

"Please hold on."

An eternity later, she heard the operator.

"Ma'am?"

"Yes, yes!"

"I'm sorry, ma'am, I was able to locate a Zook on Fifth Avenue, but I am unable to reach anyone at that number."

"Can you try the New York law office again? There must be someone there."

"Please hold."

After something slightly less than an eternity, she heard the operator back on the line.

"Ma'am?"

"Yes, go ahead."

"I have Mr. Yerkes on the line."

"Hello? Hello?"

"Mrs. Szabó?"

"Who? I mean, what?"

"Mrs. Szabó? Mrs. Tamos Szabó?"

"Oh, yes. Yes! This is Mrs. Szabó. Have you heard from Tamos? Where is he? Is he all right?"

"Mrs. Szabó, we've been trying frantically to reach you. The commander at Romulus wasn't able to –"

"I'm in Great Falls, Montana. They should have known that!"

"Yes, they did know you were on the way to Great Falls, but we've had just a terrible time getting through."

"Well, there was weather. But where is Tamos? Is he all right?"

"Mrs. Szabó, please be assured that we are doing all we can –"

"But, Tamos! Is he all right?"

"Mr. Zook is doing everything he can to contact the authorities in Lisbon, Mrs. Szabó. But at this particular moment, I'm sorry to say that we just don't know."

There was a long pause as Jeri tried to understand. She put the receiver down on the desk, still grasping it tightly. Yerkes' voice, tinny and thin, finally regained her attention.

"Mrs. Szabó? Are you there? Mrs. Szabó?"

Jeri raised the handset slowly back to her ear.

"Yes, I'm here."

"Mrs. Szabó, Harry will call you back as soon as knows anything. It should not be much longer."

Marge passed by the telephone room later that afternoon and looked in through the window. Jeri was face down on the desk, sobbing patiently and low.

The call finally came late that afternoon.

"Harry! Oh, Harry, oh, my God, Harry, what…I mean…is it – oh, Harry, how could you let him –"

"Jeri. It's okay. Everything is okay."

"Okay? He's all right?"

"Yes, Jeri. I've spoken with Pan American in Lisbon, as well as the Red Cross nurse who treated Tamos, and –"

"Oh, my God, Harry, was he hurt?"

"Jeri, let me finish. Tamos is fine, just bruises and a few minor cuts. He spent some time in the water, but was rescued fairly soon after the crash, by a couple of local fishermen, it seems. He was very lucky, they tell me."

"Can I talk to him? Where is he?"

"He's still in Lisbon, at the offices of the Jewish Distribution Committee, the JDC. Remember, they're going to help him get to Barcelona."

"Yes, yes, I remember. But he's still going? Why can't he come home? Can I talk to him? Can he call here, or can I call him somehow? Harry, I've got to talk to him!"

"Jeri, you'll be able to talk with him tonight. I've arranged a radiotelephone call for seven A.M. Lisbon time, that's eleven o'clock tonight, Montana time. It will be relayed through the Signal Corps office in Lisbon, to your base commander's office in Great Falls. He's probably looking for you right now to let you know; we finalized these arrangements just minutes ago."

"Tonight? Eleven o'clock?"

"Yes, eleven. Go see your commander; he'll make sure you are there for the call."

"Okay. Eleven. Oh, my God, Harry."

"Jeri, it will be alright. You'll talk to him soon."

She didn't remember hanging up the phone; she hoped she'd thanked Harry.

Alright, she thought. Things will not be alright, not until this war is over.

Not until Tamos is home.

Long Distance Call

11:00 PM GREAT FALLS, MONTANA
7:00 AM LISBON, PORTUGAL

"Tamos!"

"Jeri!"

"Tamos, are you okay, are you hurt? Harry said he talked to a Red Cross nurse, that you had been injured."

"I'm fine! Just a small cut on my forehead."

"Tamos, don't lie to me!"

"Oh, you know me better than that!"

"Tamos, please come home."

The connection had been good, surprisingly clear, in fact, just some crackling and a loud hum, so Jeri was not prepared for the sudden silence; she thought they'd been cut off.

"Tamos!?"

"Jeri, I can't. Not yet. I've come this far already, and now –"

"You were almost killed! And you are going into a very dangerous place!"

After another silence, filled this time with louder crackling noises and several sharp clicks, Tamos replied, cautiously.

"Jeri, you risk your life every day you fly. Do you think I do not worry over you in the same way? Every time you leave the apartment, go on a mission, I think it might be the last time I ever see you. Jeri, I love you so much, but I…I can't –"

So like Tamos to be so direct, and so right, she thought. It took her breath away. She gasped, fighting for an answer. She closed her eyes.

"Oh, Tamos. Tamos, I lo–"

There was a very loud popping noise, followed by dead air.

"Tamos?"

Again, silence.

"Tamos?"

Eyes still closed, holding the handset in both hands next to her cheek like a doll, her little porcelain doll, the doll she'd left behind years ago in the bottom drawer of her little dresser in her parents' house, she spoke into the receiver, knowing she was speaking into the void; whispered, *I love you*, and carefully placed the telephone back in its cradle.

Death Hath No Terrors

BISMARCK, NORTH DAKOTA

A day like no other, like many other days, like every day: a perfect day to fly.

The northern plain stretched out in all directions, horizon to horizon, sunning itself in the warm April air. A light breeze ruffled the long prairie grasses at the edge of the runway, laid flat during takeoffs, but quickly stretching defiantly back towards the sky, beaten down but never defeated.

Women in baggy flight suits sprawled on the rough wooden benches that ran along the side of the operations building, watching as the first squadron maneuvered their P-39s over the rough taxiway. The noise on the flight line was tremendous, and the women loved it.

As the fighters turned, the prop wash mixed with the roar of the engines, sending out a dense wave of wind and sound, the embodiment of power. The women reveled in it, each anxious for their turn to be sitting in the cockpit, eager to feel the shuddering pulse of the engine behind them, the propeller shaft running directly under the seat, shaking their bones. The noise of the huge V-12 engine, muffled by headphones, more physical than audible, at once terrified and soothed, massaged their bodies and their egos, fueled their ambitions, drove them into the air.

They loved it, loved it all; the thrill, the danger, the exhilaration. The sense of purpose. But most of all, they loved floating like angels at ten thousand feet, looking down at God's green Earth, entranced, serene, immortal.

Jeri was hanging out with some guys from a Romulus ferrying squadron at the officer's club when Francey came in.

Interrupting one of the officers in the middle of a joke, Francey said, "Jeri, come to church with me."

"What? Church? Really?" This was unexpected.

A couple of the guys laughed cautiously.

"Yes. It's Easter."

"Well, gosh, Francey. I don't know. I haven't been in years. And I didn't know you were a churchgoer."

"Well, I'm going. Are you coming with me or not?" Francey turned and started to leave.

"Hey!" Jeri called after her. "Okay, wait a sec." She turned to the officer whose joke had been so rudely cut off. "Save the punch line for me, Bill?"

"Sure thing."

They both enjoyed the service, feeling like young girls at church with their parents, singing along comfortably with the standard Easter hymns, hesitantly with two that were unfamiliar: "Death Hath No Terrors," which Francey later said she liked. Jeri had gasped. "Oh. My God, no," she'd said, laughing a little to lighten the mood; Francey had become strangely somber after the service. Fortunately, another hymn, "On the Wings of Living Light!" had been almost uplifting.

That afternoon, Jeri was on the flight line, watching anxiously as the first wave of P-39s left for Great Falls, Montana, waiting for her squadron's turn to go. The next scene would run in her head like a Movietone newsreel for weeks afterward, over and over again:

A ship pulls over to the run-up pad before turning onto the active runway. Jeri listens to the engines rev, hears the sound of the pilot switching between magnetos, nods approvingly as the revs drop as expected, and then blinks in alarm as the engine backfires loudly. Several of the other WASPs look over. The pilot powers down, and Jeri thinks she must be aborting.

The engine revs and drops again as the pilot runs through the magneto check once more. It sounds normal. P-39s are notorious for overheating, for fouling the plugs, therefore the less time spent on run-up, the better. The ship turns onto the runway and goes to full power immediately. Jeri stands up and leans forward, listening intently to the engine. It cuts out, for just a fraction of a second, then surges back to full power, and the plane begins to move. But it still sounds wrong to her, rough, and as the plane begins to gather speed, there is another loud backfire. Jeri jerks her head up at the sound. Abort, abort, she silently prays.

The ship rolls on. The nose wheel lifts and the plane leaps into the air, thirty or forty feet above the runway now, running strong. The women all along the flight line collectively hold their breath.

The engine backfires sharply, once, before it dies.

The plane glides back towards the runway; there is still enough room for a forced landing. Then the left wing drops suddenly, and when the wingtip hits the ground it silently blossoms into a brilliant ball of orange, red, and white. The sound of the explosion reaches them only as the plane cartwheels and lands heavily on its back, now completely aflame. A tower of black smoke coils madly into the air. The fire and the smoke and the remains of the ship seem to collapse in upon themselves, and the prairie, once just large, becomes immense.

Jeri drops to her knees.

The fire brigade extinguished the flames in minutes. Horrifyingly large at first, the flames had actually covered only the surface of the fuselage, and pieces of fuel tank and wing lying behind the wreck.

Jeri, still kneeling next to the flight line bench, stared in shock, unable to move, barely able to breathe.

She had recognized the pilot during the takeoff roll.

Francey. Francey, the cautious one.

Why didn't she abort?

Jeri managed to rise, and started running towards the crash. By now, only white smoke billowed up from the plane, which, with the exception of the left wing, remained intact.

"Jeri!" she heard someone call behind her, the voice muddled as if across the mess hall, or on a long-distance telephone call, tinny and indistinct. She suddenly felt an arm on her shoulder, hard, pulling her part way around, and heard more plainly, "Jeri. Stop." She stopped and turned her head to see one of the other girls standing behind her, Marie, felt again a tug on her shoulder, tender this time. "Jeri, come back. You can't go out there."

Marie led her back to the operations hut. Jeri looked around at the women who had come back into the building after the fire was out, standing in small groups, talking in low tones. Light from the high, narrow windows slashed though the dusty, dim interior of the building like stage lights, illuminating a khaki shoulder here, a mess table bench there. She turned to Marie and started to say something, stopped, turned away.

The movie was already running.

Late that night, Lt. Blage called her into his office. What he told her was intended to ease her mind, and in some way inconceivable to her, it had the desired effect. Jittery and distracted as she was when she entered the office, after hearing what Blage had to say, she calmed.

"Francine died instantly," Blage said. "She hit her head on the stick as the plane cart-wheeled. She never felt the flames."

Jeri nodded, and expressed her gratitude. Blage looked distraught. Jeri suddenly felt she must try to put him at ease, an impulse that had the added advantage of momentarily deflecting her own grief.

"She was doing what she loved."

Blage stared at her blankly for a moment, and then hunched his shoulders, rocking a bit back and forth. He looked down.

"Yes, that is a comfort."

There was a short silence.

"Do they know yet what, what…do they know the cause?" Jeri finally asked.

"No, not definitely. Engine failure, of course, but –"

"You know there have been a lot of reports of sabotage –" Jeri stopped herself before she went on; she didn't want to give Blage the impression that she was reacting hysterically. The brass had been recently discounting the sabotage rumors, trying to keep morale up. "Anyway, Francey told me the other day that there had been some work done on her ship. And you must know there have been rumors going around about substandard spare parts. Could that have been a factor?"

"Well, we won't know until the investigation is complete."

"Did that ship have a replacement carburetor?"

"Carburetor?" Blage looked nonplussed. "I'd have to check. Is it important?"

"I'm pretty sure Francey told me it was a replacement carburetor. Could you make sure they look at that? And let me know what they find?"

"Yes, yes, of course. I'm sure the investigation will be thorough."

"And please let me know if they uncover anything…anything unusual."

"Of course."

"Okay then, um, well, is that all?"

"Yes, that will be all for now. Goodnight."

"Goodnight."

Jeri went back to her barracks, changed into her nightclothes, and crawled into her bunk. Hearing the strains of wavering congregation voices and a slightly clumsy organ attempting "Death Hath No Terrors," she stared into the black, waiting for night to end.

Special Orders

BISMARCK, NORTH DAKOTA

The call to Blage's office to receive her new orders came soon after first light. Blage did not say anything to her as she stood at his desk. He just averted his eyes and handed the thin, brown paper to her.

RESTRICTED

HEADQUARTERS
576TH AAF BASE UNIT
7TH FERRYING SERVICE STATION
FERRYING DIVISION AIR TRANSPORT COMMAND
MUNICIPAL AIRPORT, BISMARK, NORTH DAKOTA

(SPECIAL ORDERS)

There followed a mind-numbingly convoluted description of Army Air Force authorizations, base identifiers, unit designations, and division specifications, acronyms scattered like leaves, held together with seemingly random punctuation, all of which Jeri's eyes flew over with the skill of a speed reader; she'd seen this kind of thing a hundred times:

"Under AUTH: SW, 21 Nov 41; CC AAF 21 Feb 44; and TWX No 4212-G, CG 550th AAF Base Unit, (Hq Ferrying Div, ATC), Cincinnati, Ohio, dated 9 April 44; Jeraldine Jillette, WASP, (Airman Certificate No 64339), 553rd AAF Base Unit (3rd Fer Gp), Ferry Div, ATC, Romulus, Mich, WP, o/a 9 April 44, from 576th AAF Base Unit, (8th Fer 3v Sta), per Div, ATC Municipal Airport, Bismarck, N Dak, to Long Beach, Calif..."

Then came the part she'd never seen before, in jarring AAF bureaucratese:

"...in charge of and accompanying, as Escort and

Attendant, the remains of the late Francine R. McCarthy, (Airman Certificate No 10112), delivering said remains to Fordyce & Fordyce Funeral Home upon arrival and will remain thereat on temp duty to attend funeral services, and, upon completion thereof, will proceed to 556th AAF Base Unit, (6th Fer Gp), Fer Div, ATC, Long Beach, Calif, reporting to the CO for further orders."

Further orders. Further orders. What an odd word, "further." That can't be right, can it? It looks so...odd. "Further." The longer she looked at it, the stranger it appeared. Someone at HQ must have intentionally inserted a fictitious word into the orders, as some sort of inane practical joke. It could not even be pronounced without twisting your mouth into an uncomfortable pout, like a foreign word tried out for the first time, just guessing at how it goes. It began to look suspiciously German. Further. Führer. Further. Führer. She closed her eyes for a moment, and then read on, skimming now:

Travel will be performed by rail. In lieu of subsistence a flat per diem of $6.00 is athzd for travel and temp dy not to exceed...

She had already taken up the barracks collection to cover the cost of her own rail ticket for this "temporary duty;" only Francey's fare was paid for by the AAF. She skipped down.

The above named civ emp is designated competent administrative auth for the purpose of issuing T/R's...

– "civ emp" – civilian employee! Oh, yes, I nearly forgot, I am not really *in* the military, I am just *of* the military, and only when it suits them –

She did not finish reading the orders.

The train left at six that night. Just before she left for the station, she was told by another WASP that her P-39, the one she had been scheduled to take on to Great Falls, had crashed on takeoff that afternoon. Engine failure. The male Army pilot was unhurt.

The funeral was as grim as she'd expected. A large contingent of WASPs in their dress blues formed both an honor guard and served as pallbearers. WASP Commanders Jacqueline Cochran and Nancy Love both attended. No mention was made of the flagrant disobedience of Army regulations prohibiting the American flag that draped the coffin. In fact, the funeral was later reported in the local newspapers as a "military" service – and a bit melodramatically, Jeri thought, as the deceased pilot's "Last Journey."

April 11

As I turned away from the gravesite, I chanced to brush shoulders with Mrs. Cochran. To my surprise - and somewhat guilty gratification, I have to admit - her cheeks were shining wet with tears.

Jeri's mourning period lasted all of about fifteen hours. A P-51 had to go from Long Beach to Newark, New Jersey. On the way, the movie in her head gradually faded into black and white, then to a gray blur, details momentarily lost. The diversion of wrestling a four-ton, fifteen-hundred horsepower, flying artillery machine on and off the ground twice a day for nearly a week blanked the screen occasionally. But the movie replayed itself every night, not in Movietone black and white, but in color, and she had to wait it out again the next day, wait for it to fade.

The rain in Newark when she landed, at twilight, turned all around her into gray, a perfect, monotonous gray.

How to Fly a P-39

ROMULUS AIR BASE, MICHIGAN

"Back so soon?" The WASP, Dorothy, was surprised to see Jeri at the op center.

"Yeah, managed to get a SNAFU flight."

"*Army Airlines*, if you please," said Dorothy. "They are getting very prickly about being called 'SNAFU,' you know."

"Then they'd better start doing a better job." She'd had only about two hours sleep, sitting on the hard, cold, aluminum bucket seat of a B-17 for hours in the middle of the night, relieved only by lying on the equally cold, hard floor, parachute for a pillow, shivering the whole time. And she'd been lucky to get that flight. Air Transport Command was responsible for moving pilots around the country, from base to base or from drop-off points back to ferry command bases. But they had no real schedule, simply waiting for a flight to fill up and then just taking off, at all hours. Many nights Jeri had been roused out of her hotel room at three A.M. to catch a SNAFU flight. As she had been last night. All too often, a RON – Remain Over Night – was cut short in the mad rush to get airplanes delivered.

After dropping off the P-51 in Newark – she'd gotten that assignment only because she'd been in Los Angeles for the funeral – it was back to the regular grind at Romulus: Niagara Falls to Great Falls, via South Bend, Indiana; Rochester, Minnesota; Bismarck, North Dakota (Fargo if there was weather); and Billings, Montana. Again, and again.

BELL AIRCRAFT FACTORY, NIAGARA FALLS

"Damn it all. A goldarn belly tank." She was talking to herself, standing next to the P-39 she'd be taking to Great Falls. The external tank, a big, bulbous thing, hung from the bomb rack under the center of the plane, and, she'd been told, turned the normally agile P-39 into a pig. This was to be her first experience with the tank slung under the cockpit, and she wasn't looking forward to it. "It skids and slips around and loses altitude," Marge Kline had told her, "and the ball plasters itself first in one end of the tube and then the other. Be prepared for a wild ride."

Oh, well.

She tossed her parachute and travel bag up onto the wing, grabbed the hand grip, and pulled herself up. Standing on the wing, she slipped on the parachute, opened the cockpit door, and stuffed her travel bag inside, behind the seat. She always took a few extra items along with her basic travel clothes – sweater, skirt, nylons, makeup – just in case there was a chance to go out during a RON.

Once settled into the hard bucket seat, she began her routine, silently reciting each step as she went. Adjust rudder pedals. Check rudders, elevators and ailerons. Set brakes. Fasten shoulder straps of harness to seat belt quick-release.

She reached down next to the seat and twisted the shoulder harness lock release. This allowed her to lean forward at any time during flight in order to reach a control or look more closely at a gauge. She rocked forward in the harness a couple of times and then relocked it.

The door latches were above her head. She stretched up and secured them, then checked the door handle – fully closed. She subconsciously noted the location of the emergency release, the lever that would eject the door in an emergency. She'd actually only used it once, on her initial checkout, with the instructor there to hold on to the door. It had been hard to operate, but once engaged the door did just fall out to the wing.

She slipped the headset on, attached the cables, selected "voice" on the transmitter, and went back to her silent check off recital. *Landing gear switch* down. *Gun controls* off. *Propeller auto* on. *Test the flaps. Check fuel. Turn on battery.*

She took a deep breath and stretched her arms over her head, working the tightness out of her shoulders. *Okay. Now for takeoff.*

Below her and to the left was the fuel selector. She turned this to "reserve," then sat back up and set her mixture control – *idle cutoff* – and prop governor – *low pitch.* She checked again that the battery switch was on, then switched on the generator. A quick glance out both sides of the cockpit to make sure she was in the clear. Cranking the primer knob open with one hand, she flipped on the booster pump with the other; pulled out the primer; turned off the pump; then pushed the primer back in, locking it. She turned the ignition switch to "both on," reached out with her right foot and pulled the starter pedal back, turned the booster pump back on, then pressed the starter pedal forward. The whirr of the starter filled the cockpit; the engine coughed once and started with a roar.

She quickly moved the mixture control to "automatic rich" and turned off the booster pump.

Oil pressure okay. Temp okay. Open cooling shutters. One more check of the door latches. Set trim tabs. Release brakes.

First stretching up and making sure she was still clear on both sides, she opened up the throttle part way and began her taxi to the runway. Had to be quick with these things or they overheated. She keyed the mike button on the stick. "Tower, P-39, Jillette, final warm up and check-off."

"Roger, P-39."

At the edge of the runway she set the brakes for her rev up and advanced the throttle to 2300 RPM. *Temps and pressures still okay.*

She switched the magnetos, first to the right – *a drop off of 80 RPM* – then to the left – *a drop off of 60 RPM* – then back to both, all the time listening intently to the reassuring shifts in sound. *Back to 2300, good.* She pulled back on the prop governor, heard the RPMs fall off, then pushed it back full forward. *Ammeter okay.*

She reached over and grabbed the laminated checklist hanging off of the control panel to run through everything yet again. Not for a second did she think this was unnecessary; there were too many stories of pilots – WASPs and Army both – taking shortcuts that ended in some sort of disaster.

Fuel tank levels good; selector valve on reserve; prop governor full forward; mixture on automatic rich; fuel pressure 14-15 pounds; oil pressure up; oil temp okay; coolant temp okay; suction up; gear box oil pressure okay.

She released the brakes and keyed the mike. "Tower, P-39, this fuse is lit."

"Roger, P-39, clear to takeoff."

She pushed the throttle up to 3000 RPM – *45 ½ inches of manifold, good* – felt the push back into her seat, gave it right full rudder as she headed down the runway, watching her speed…*those Russian women pilots know only two throttle positions – idle and full on…*

At one hundred miles per hour she pulled back on the stick and the P-39 jumped into the air.

Retract landing gear, check indicators. Okay, landing gear switch to neutral. Ammeter back to normal. Throttle to 37 ½ inches of manifold; prop to 2600 RPM. Adjust trim tabs. Switch fuel to main tank. Open cooling shutters. Level off. 30 inches of manifold, 2280 RPM.

She reached down and cranked on the cooling shutter control, adjusting it down a bit. It was early and the morning temperature was mild. One more run through the checklist. *Temps okay; pressures okay.*

The ship was handling okay, considering; a little logy with that belly tank, a bit of "slipping and sliding" but nothing she couldn't handle. *What was all the fuss?* She'd even seen one of the other P-39 pilots drop *his* tank before takeoff. Sure, it was a little more challenging, but what of it? She wanted all the experience she could get; it made her a better flyer. And she didn't understand why many of the girls were so oddly uninterested in the mechanical details of the ships. They learned just enough to fly them competently, but didn't care to understand the technical details, the mechanical complexity, or the expertise required to get these unwieldy things in the air and keep them there. Learning all she could about what she was flying was just second nature to her; it also made her a better pilot.

She relaxed into her seat and looked out the window.

God, I love it up here.

Burnin' That Candle

BISMARCK, NORTH DAKOTA

Back in Bismarck a week later, Jeri walked through the maintenance hangar looking for Sgt. Mike Zebrowski, the mechanic who had done Francey's post-crash investigation. By this time, the movie in her head had nearly played itself out, and in its place, she had begun to make a plan.

"Mike?" Her voice echoed eerily in the semi-dark space.

She walked around a partially dismantled P-39 and found Sgt. Zebrowski up to his elbows in a Bendix-Stromberg carburetor.

"Hey, beautiful," Mike said, looking up and wiping a brow with his wrist.

"Hey, Mike. Been looking for you."

"Well, here I am." Mike leaned back and wiped his hands with a rag. "I was hoping to see you today."

"Oh?"

"Yeah, see, I got these tickets to a dance over in town, thought maybe you'd like a night out."

"Oh, Mike, I can't. I'm married."

"Yeah, sure, but I know you, you're burning that candle. 'This fuse is lit.' I heard that you girls always say that, taking off. Burning that candle, livin' big, right?"

"Sure, but, flying, well, that's different."

"Hey, it doesn't have to be serious, right? C'mon, just for laughs. Dance, drinks, from there who knows?"

"Mike, I just don't..."

"You know, a lot of girls – even married girls – get around quite a bit, you know what I mean?"

Jeri closed her eyes for just a second, hearing Tamos's voice on the phone, distant and ghostly. "My husband was almost killed in a plane crash the other day. So, I guess I'm not really 'in the mood,' you might say."

"Geez, I'm sorry, sorry as hell. You know I don't mean anything by it. I'll lay off."

"Thanks, Mike."

"Hell, if my ex had been more like you, maybe I'd still be married, huh? Anyway, seriously, I think I've got something for you."

"You've got something?"

"Yeah. Here, take a look." He swiveled a large black, oblong component around on the workbench. "See this? This is the throttle body off of the carburetor." He picked up the throttle body, tilting it into the dim light of an overhead bulb. "There's what's called a throttle plate in there," he said, pointing into a cavity in the center of the mechanism, "but the plate broke up. The missing piece went into in the manifold. That would wreak bloody hell in the engine."

"And that's what caused the crash? Caused the engine failure?"

"No doubt about it. The throttle body is the heart of the carburetor. It controls all of the airflow into the engine, through bores in the throttle plate, and here, here's a venturi –"

He picked up a piece of metal from the bench and held it out to her. "It's all tied to the fuel regulators and other components," he said, pointing out other pieces of the disassembled carburetor, "controlling the flow of fuel. On takeoff, you set your mix to auto rich, right? The control jets regulate the fuel pressures for those conditions, then you set it to auto lean for cruising, and so on. And it all depends on the operation of the throttle body, right? Anyway, if that goes, it all goes. And down *you* go." He saw Jeri flinch at this and smacked his forehead. "Jeez, Jeri, sorry. What a dope I am." He tossed the venturi back on the bench.

She shook her head and bent back down to the carburetor. "That's okay, Mike. Don't worry. So, what was it? Sabotage?"

"Doubtful. Yeah, I've heard the stories, sand in the carb, that kind of stuff. But, no, there's no evidence of that. This thing just failed for some reason."

"But it looks intact." She pointed to the assembly sitting on the bench.

Mike picked up a piece of intricately machined aluminum. "What failed is the throttle plate, here. Cracked right along this line."

"A stress fracture?"

"Exactly! It's weakest at this point here, near the center, where the metal gets thin." He nodded in admiration. "You know your stuff!"

"Well, I grew up on an airfield. Worked on a lot of old crates. Dismantled a Lycoming engine when I was seventeen. See the grease under my fingernails?" She held up her hands.

"All I see is sexy red fingernail polish. Say, how about that dance?"

"Mike, I'm warning you –"

He laughed.

"Back to business," Jeri said. "Is this a factory carb?"

"A replacement. But shouldn't make any difference. Still a Stromberg."

"Why was the original carb replaced?"

"Can't say for sure, but probably didn't even need it. This ship came in last week, the pilot complained of misfiring. Likely that the plugs were fouled, something like that, and someone misdiagnosed it. Got some guys around here, well, I don't like to say it, but –"

"I understand." She looked down at the bench, at the carburetor, the throttle body, at the pieces scattered around it, hearing the backfire, seeing the flames, the movie crowding her vision. “What caused it to fail?”

“Damned if I know, Jeri. But fail it did.”

“Can you get me a copy of your report when you’re done? Oh, and can this carb be traced back to the factory?”

“Should be a paper trail. I’ll give you everything I find.”

“Thanks a lot, Mike.” She smiled. “Might even earn you a dance.”

Mike clapped his hands. “Oh, baby!”

“*Just* a dance!” she said, red fingernail waving. “*If* you get me what I need.”

“You got it.”

Jeri stood back, ran her fingers through her hair, took a deep breath. It was too late to save Francey, but maybe she could save the rest.

The mood was desultory. The rain wouldn’t quit, there was nothing new from Tamos, nothing to do but stare out the windows. There had been a few bridge games, and plenty of bull sessions, but those quickly became wearisome; gossip, and complaining, and more gossip.

The one time she went out, Jeri *had* danced with Mike, once, and they’d had a laugh over drinks. He was seeing his ex-wife again, so no more hitting on her, a relief. She liked Mike. After that one night out, even the nightlife in town had stalled out, as if a switch had been thrown – no more good times to be had here, move along. Everything seemed to be going to hell.

And then Mike came into the mess hall.

“Something to show you,” he said, pointing over his shoulder. “Come over to the hanger bay?”

“What have you got?” she said, swinging her legs over the bench.

“You’ll see.”

“Let me grab my raincoat.”

They made their way across the compound, Mike gallantly guiding her around the deepest puddles, and into the hanger.

“Over here,” Mike said, leading her back to his workbench.

She saw it immediately. “A throttle body plate. Broken in half.”

“Yep. Just like the other one. And I’ve been asking around. We’re not the only ones who’ve seen this, not by a long shot.”

“All…crashes?”

“No, thank God. This particular one failed during run up, about a week ago. The pilot was one of yours, I think. Marge?”

“Yes, she’s based in Romulus with me. We shared a barrack for a while. Oh, my gosh, she was that close to taking off?”

“Damned lucky she didn’t. The other two throttle bodies that have been recovered, the two I know about, anyway, did come from crashes. Not fatalities," he said hurriedly. "One bail out, not much left of the ship, but the engine got thrown wide when it hit the ground. The other one happened on takeoff, like your friend. Fortunately, the ship glided a bit and smashed into some little trees, and the guy walked away from it.

"But that's not all. All of the failed carbs, this one and those other two – some of the parts came from the same plant."

There was a quiet moment while this registered. "So, there's a common thread, these failures might be linked?"

"Yeah. Scary, huh?"

"And do we have – do you have – any documentation?"

"Yeah. A buddy back at the Niagara plant sent me some inside dope. I've got everything for you right here." He pulled a large canvas mail bag out from under the bench and handed it to her. "My reports. Serial numbers of the failed carbs. Engine specifications. Some other stuff." He paused. "Jeri, be careful with this. The brass don't like waves. My buddy, he could get into some pretty hot water over what he sent me."

Jeri hesitated for the barest moment before forging ahead. "Can I also have the broken plate?"

"Geez, Jeri, I don't know…"

"Well, the investigation is complete, isn't it?"

"Yeah, but everything is supposed to be packed up and stored away."

"So, who's going to miss it? No one's going to be looking through this stuff now, are they?"

"No, I guess not. But, listen, if I do this, you're going to owe me, big time!"

"All the dances you want, Mike!"

He picked up the broken pieces and handed them to her. "What are you going to do with it, anyway?"

"I'm not sure yet." She leaned over and gave him a quick kiss on his grizzled jaw – *why can't these guys shave more often?* – and turned to go. "And Mike, thank you. Thanks a lot."

"No sweat, beautiful."

She tucked the mailbag under her coat and went back out into the rain, mindless of the deepening puddles.

2:35 AM

Tamos is in Hungary!!! His telegram came in this morning at just after two A.M., and the duty officer knew not to wait to wake me. The information was very sketchy, but he was able to tell me quite a lot in a short message. He apparently got passage on a fishing boat from Barcelona to Sicily (Sicily has been liberated for several months now,) and from there he went on to Croatia. I checked, and Croatia is still in the hands of the Nazis, but Tamos was able to connect with the resistance there, and passed through Yugoslavia to Budapest under the care of the Yugoslav Partisans.

He hasn't found Béla yet, but is very optimistic. There is a Swedish diplomat there - Wallenberg - that is helping him.

Harry reminded me again last week that all of this is being arranged, as much as anything can be arranged these days, by the Jewish Distribution Committee. I think of them as our special angels. I hope after the war there will be some way to repay them for everything they have done.

SNAFU to Niagara leaves at seven. I know I won't go back to sleep.

The way I feel right now, I'll never sleep again.

Refugee

BUDAPEST / CROATIA / ITALY

"Our best chance is through liberated southern Italy," Tamos was explaining enthusiastically. They were sitting on the edge of a small bed, in a very small room, at the top of a large house on Benzcůr, near the large City Park. "I still have contact with the Sisak partisans in Croatia. I'm sure they can get us to Split, and from there I can get passage to Bari, on the coast of Italy. From there it is just a few days walk to Naples. But I'm sure we can probably get some sort of transport, at least for part of the journey."

Béla's lined face remained set in a grimace. Tamos flinched slightly as he looked over at Béla, for the first time registering the profound change that had come over him since he had seen him last. Once rather portly and full-faced, Béla's jowls now hung like tobacco pouches, grey and leathery. He was sitting forward, his back hunched, his arms – how thin they were! – draped listlessly across his knees.

"Once in Naples, I'm sure we can procure passage on the refugee ship," Tamos continued.

"But Tamos," said Béla without looking up, "are you sure there really is a ship? You know how rumors spread at a time like this."

"Oh, I'm positive. We cannot wait too long, of course. I've been told that there are many applicants. You are certain to get a place, after what you have been through. And as for me, well, I'll take my chances. The main thing is that we get you –"

"Tamos," Béla interrupted, looking at Tamos imploringly, "you know I cannot go to America. Eva, the rest of the family, they are waiting for me in Barcelona."

After a moment, Tamos placed his hands on Béla's, feeling the bones through the thin skin. It was some time before he trusted himself to speak.

"Yes, I know," he said, finally. "Forgive me. I let myself get caught up in the idea. I was so joyful to find you alive, so intent on keeping you near me."

Béla took Tamos's hands in his. "You also must rejoin your family. Come with me to Barcelona."

Tamos, his hands trembling in Béla's, shook his head. "Ah, Béla, no. I must go to America."

"But why? You belong with us. We are your only family, Tamos."

"No, not any longer. I will soon have my own family in America, Béla." He took a breath. "I am married."

Although Wallenberg had been reluctant to let him go, he gave his blessing, along with several variations of official documentation, some to be used with incredulous Germans, if necessary, and some to hopefully facilitate passage on the Henry Simmons, which was quickly becoming a topic of conversation around the city.

The trip to Split with his former comrades was uneventful. Tamos fit back in quickly, this time limiting his duties to cooking, gathering wood and water, and man-hauling supplies. Béla was both astounded and at the same time unsurprised at Tamos's almost revered status with the partisans. He knew Tamos very well, and took no small measure of pride in the knowledge that he had had a part in his upbringing.

In Split, it took several long, anxiety-filled days to get a boat to Bari, but once again, the JDC proved themselves to be near magicians where it came to making things happen. Not to mention Harry's money. They were able to sit above decks – no rotting fish to contend with – and made the crossing quickly and without incident.

Getting to Naples from Bari proved to be slightly more difficult than Tamos had predicted so confidently back in Budapest, and they ended up walking nearly the entire one hundred and seventy miles. It gave them ample opportunity to relate their recent histories to one another.

They arrived in Naples after a hot, dusty, four-and-a-half-day walk, only to find they weren't there yet. "There" was a staging point for applications about twelve miles away from the center of Naples, at an abandoned mental institution in the small village of Aversa. When they finally arrived, very late that afternoon, the line to the application office stretched two blocks. They did not get in to the office that day.

After sleeping in a small park not far from the collection center, they awoke early and made their way to the center. This time they were close to the head of the line.

In talking to others waiting for their turn, Tamos was not surprised to learn that the JDC was playing a role in screening for refugees. But he was somewhat alarmed at some of the things he was hearing the people in line say about the screening process.

"They are taking only families," one man said. "Only those who have escaped from the camps," said another. "And you can't be sick," a woman said from behind them. "No 'loathsome diseases,' they said. If you're sick, you go to an Army hospital. Who knows from then?"

"Just wait until you can talk with them, Tamos," Béla said. "You never know."

"At least we're not ill," said Tamos. "Though I can't help thinking how appropriate it is that this process is taking place in an insane asylum. I must be crazy to think I'll get a berth on this ship."

It was nearly eleven before Tamos, with Béla alongside for moral support, was ushered into a small, stifling hot room at the back of the building. Tamos thought it an especially good omen that his interviewer was in fact a JDC representative. They had performed miracles for him ever since the night he'd arrived, wet and bleeding, at the JDC office in Lisbon. He hoped his luck would hold.

"My name is Max Perlman," said the small, wiry man behind the desk. He glanced at the application form Tamos had filled out. "From Hungary, I see. And you are…Tamos Szabó?" he asked, turning to Béla.

"Actually, no," replied Béla. "I am Béla Szabó, uncle to Tamos." He nodded in Tamos's direction. "Tamos was orphaned many years ago," Béla continued. "I raised him as my son."

"Ah, I see," said Perlman. "But why then are you not listed on the application?"

"It's a long story," Tamos answered for Béla.

Perlman turned to him. "Well, the *Henry Gibbins* does not sail for several days yet," said Perlman amicably. "Not until July 21st. We have time."

The story was, Perlman had to admit, a good one. In the course of relating his efforts to reach Béla, Perlman exclaimed several times, "How extraordinary." It was when Tamos related his account of how he had been working with Raoul Wallenberg, however, that Perlman became quite animated.

"Wallenberg, my God. You were working with Wallenberg!"

"Yes." Tamos reached into a pocket and pulled out a wrinkled, folded up document. "Here is my *Schutzpass*."

Béla quickly produced his pass, as well. "Wallenberg gave this to me the day I was put on a train bound for Auschwitz," he said. "Tell him what you and Wallenberg did that day, Tamos."

Béla was forced to interrupt several times as Tamos tried to play down his part in the day's action. When he finished, Perlman turned to Béla. "But you are not applying for refugee status? You certainly qualify."

"I must go to my family," Béla said. "They escaped to Barcelona earlier this year. I never made it out of Hungary, once they were settled there."

"And Tamos? Why are you applying for refugee status? Can you not just go with your uncle to Spain?"

"Well –" said Tamos, searching for words.

Perlman held up a hand. "Don't tell me," he said. "It's a long story."

There was a fourth criterion for selection, as it turned out. While normally a young (and assumed unmarried) man would be denied passage, unless part of a family, there was a need for many special skills in the future camp; for primarily political reasons, it was supposed to be self-sustaining. Tamos had convinced Perlman that he certainly had skills. So, by what Tamos always believed was a sort of special dispensation, he was given passage.

He signed the required waiver affirming that after the war he agreed to be repatriated to his original country, even though both he and Perlman knew it was a hollow gesture. Tamos suspected that most applicants signed with no intention of ever returning to Europe – what was there to return to? – and it appeared that the JDC, at least, knew this to be the case as well.

Six days later, Béla (thanks to the last of Harry's money) was on a boat to Barcelona, like Tamos weeks earlier, only in reverse, via Sardinia and Sicily.

Tamos joined over a thousand wounded Allied soldiers and nine hundred eighty-one other refugees on the troop ship *Henry Gibbins*. In all the confusion, he had been unable to get a message to Jeri.

Tracked by Nazi air and submarine forces nearly the whole way across the eastern Atlantic, the ship docked in New York on August 3, 1944.

Tamos had been away for nearly three months.

A Bottle of Milk

AUGUST 5, 1944: FORT ONTARIO

The train slows near a large, windowless warehouse, dark and humorless, boding no warm welcome. There had been high expectations. Stopping at this warehouse, this blockhouse, imparts a wave of uncertainty through the poorly lit train car. People clamor in five or six languages – heavy, broad Slavic, animated Italian, harsh German. The passengers rise from their seats and press sallow, fatigued faces to the windows. Are we there? Is this it? Tamos Szabó looks around, unperturbed.

The train creeps on in the mid-morning light, approaching some minutes later a large encampment. No station in sight, only a large expanse filled with many long, wooden buildings laid out in orderly ranks, and a few of red-brick, all barely visible behind a long chain-link fence topped with a single row of barbed wire. At the sight of the fence there is renewed consternation. A woman cries, "A fence!" Someone else voices a fear left unsaid by many, for some unavoidable – "How can this be, in America?" says one. "Another concentration camp!" says another.

The train stops. The doors open. No one gets out. The train sits on the siding. Exclamations drop to murmurs. Still the train sits, and still no one gets out.

Townspeople gather alongside the tracks, excited, curious, chattering and shuffling, straining for a glimpse into the train cars through the dark glass. A bottle of milk is held up at arm's length by a local citizen, translucent with promise in the early morning light. The stylish red script silk-screened on one side – Byrne Dairy – accents the pure glassy white of the bottle and makes Tamos sad. Both sad and joyous, to see such a sight again, a simple thing like a bottle of milk; it looks so much like the simple bottles he delivered as a boy to the stoops and porches of the well-to-do in the streets of Budapest. And then Tamos, having arrived here so recently from the ports of New York, sees something else. Just for a moment, there is in the sight of an upraised arm holding a bright, shining object, a vision of an iconic torch held up high in the harbor, which he had seen just days before.

The bottle is an offering, an enticement, a reward. A window opens, an arm reaches out, and the milk is taken into the train car. More windows open. More milk, and cookies, and apples, and candy, and children's toys are handed up through the windows, brought in, passed around, exclaimed over, marveled at. Accepted.

Do not be afraid, these simple gifts say. Come down from the train. Come into our city. Be safe.

They all climb down.

Reunion

FORT ONTARIO EMERGENCY REFUGEE CENTER

They kissed carefully through the chain link fence, mouths barely making contact in the small space between the thick, galvanized wires. Their hands were intertwined in the links, Jeri, with her left hand, slowly spinning the gold band on Tamos's right. The sun was setting at the west end of the lake, and the red-orange light made the ring glow with promise.

"You've lost weight," she said. "Your ring barely stays on."

"Well, they are feeding us very well in here. I expect to be back to my normal pudgy self any day now."

She tried to laugh. "Oh, when were you ever 'pudgy?'"

"You should have seen me before I left Hungary for California. My Aunt Eva was a very fine cook."

"I can't wait four weeks," Jeri said, rubbing her cheek on the back of her hand. "I just can't." She pulled back and looked around, at the barbed wire topping the fence, at the guards at the entrance to the camp. "Why are they keeping you quarantined like this?"

"It's because of the War Relocation Authority, I think. It's their way of doing things. They also handle the Japanese internment camps. And because we have no legal status, no immigration status. You know how things are...they don't want us escaping and wandering around the country with no legal reason to be here."

"But my God, Tamos, we're married!"

"If only I could prove that," he said. "My name is Laszlo Kossuth, you know, not Tamos Szabó." He'd told her about the *Schutzpass* he'd obtained from Wallenberg in Hungary. "Béla, fortunately, got a pass issued in his real name. Since I had lost everything in Lisbon, well, I had to accept whatever name I was fortunate enough to inherit. I've sent word through the State Department to Caltech to confirm my identity, but there's no telling how long it will take the wartime bureaucracy will respond."

"But four weeks!"

Tamos looked up and down the fence to make sure no one was within hearing distance. "Don't worry," he said. "Some of us have already figured out how to get in and out of here without detection." He pulled a hand away and pointed in the direction of the lake. "See where the fence goes around that back corner of the Fort over there?" She nodded. "About fifty yards down the fence, just past that point, we're setting up our own 'border control station.' Meet me there at eleven o'clock tonight."

"Oh, Tamos, you're sure about this? What if you get caught leaving?"

"I can assure you that is the least of my worries," he replied, in his most formal voice.

She recognized the playfulness riding underneath the somber tone. "I can just imagine! Me, too...but, well, then what? Where will we go?"

"It is all arranged. Not the Breakers Hotel in Los Angeles, or the Ritz in New York City, but under the circumstances..."

"You've been here only two days, and already you are making deals outside the camp?"

"I'm very resourceful."

"As I have learned. Eleven o'clock?"

"On the dot. Just make your way carefully along the fence. I'll meet you just outside. You won't have any trouble finding me."

They remained standing at the fence, holding hands as best as they could through the links, speaking in low tones, for another hour or so. They finally parted without saying goodbye; neither one of them ever wanted to hear that word again.

Over the next four weeks, there were many clandestine meetings in the small room Jeri had since rented in the back of a large two-story house at the corner of E. Sixth and Cayuga – a room paid for by Harry, who, when he first heard Tamos's voice over the phone, had broken down for several minutes. The room, he'd said, when he subsequently learned of their situation, was the very least he could do.

Tamos was still in immigration limbo. The State Department had promised for over two weeks that the resolution of his case was 'immanent.' But until a ruling was made, he was stuck in the Shelter with the rest of the refugees. Even the copy of the marriage license Jeri had provided made no impression on the bureaucrats; until Tamos had been issued his official papers, he was confined to the Shelter. Harry had promised Tamos he'd do everything he could to facilitate his release.

Once the camp opened on September 1st, Jeri was able to visit Tamos in the camp, but as he still had no legal status, they couldn't risk her staying over in his apartment there. In the short times they had together, whenever Jeri could manage a visit to Oswego between her many ferry missions, he told her of his experiences in Yugoslavia and Hungary – leaving out nothing, but at the same time trying to make it sound routine – and she told him about Francey's crash, and what she'd learned from Mike, the aircraft mechanic.

Once Tamos understood the issue, he immediately agreed on their next step.

Time to call Harry.

Call from the Heartland

BISMARCK, NORTH DAKOTA

"I have your party, ma'am."

"Thank you, operator. Hello? Is this Mr. Zook's office?"

"Yes, ma'am. What can I do for you?"

"Um, is Mr. Zook in?"

"Who's calling, please?"

"This is Jeri Jillette – excuse me, this is Mrs. Szabó."

"One moment, Mrs. Szabó, I'll try to connect you."

She shuffled nervously thorough the papers littering the table, not quite sure exactly what she was going to say. She had rehearsed several conversations earlier that morning, each one laying out her plan in such convincing detail that Harry could not help but approve, and agree to help. The problem was that she had – if she were to be honest with herself – only the barest of evidence. The information Mike had provided appeared to link the incidents of failed carburetors with a particular source. But that might not mean anything. It was not just P-39s that were crashing; the accident rate in the Ferry Command was pretty high across all aircraft. But she somehow knew that these cases were unusual, that there must be something common behind the failures. And that she would be able to find it.

With Harry's help.

"One moment while I connect you," the secretary said.

There was a brief pause, and then Harry's familiar voice came on the line. "Jeri! It's good to hear your voice. Where are you?

"Hello, Harry. Um, I'm in North Dakota. Bismarck."

"Ah, the heartland! And to what do I owe the pleasure of your call?"

"Oh, Harry. We need help."

"Oh. Well, you know I'll do anything for you. Within reason, of course," he laughed.

"You might not think this is so reasonable, Harry."

"Okay, you've aroused my curiosity. What's the trouble?"

"It's hard to explain." This wasn't going as rehearsed at all. "It's about Francey."

"Francey?" Harry's heart dropped at the mention of Francey's name, as a sudden image of her as Jeri's bridesmaid flashed through his mind.

'Yes. I think I might know what caused her ship to crash."

"Well, that is…interesting." It was not like Harry to be at a loss for words, but this had caught him off guard.

"Oh, Harry, I know this sounds crazy, but I think I have evidence of…of something not right. I have a friend, an aircraft mechanic – he did the post-crash investigation – and he found something he says is very unusual. And it's not the only one that he's seen. And he has reports of other crashes, with the same failures. He thinks, that is, we think, and Tamos and I agree, that there is a common cause, something to do with the throttle body, the failures are all –"

"Whoa, hold on. Carburetors are failing?"

"Yes! Exactly. There seems to be a pattern, a common failure in all the carbs he's looked at, or that he's gotten information on. A procurement officer at the Bell Aircraft factory in Niagara Falls sent him some information, stuff he wasn't supposed to let out, I guess, and Mike, that's the mechanic, says it looks to him like faulty components."

"This 'throttle body' you mentioned?"

"Yes. Well, more specifically the aluminum throttle plate inside the throttle body. It's breaking up."

"All right, this sounds complicated. And I've got a meeting coming up in…well, I'm already fifteen minutes late. Can we talk again tonight?"

"Oh, that would be wonderful, Harry. Then I can explain everything."

"Okay. Leave a number with my receptionist, and the best time to call. You have a phone there you can use? Good. Let's see, you are two hours earlier there. That's fine; I'll call from the townhouse."

"Thank you, Harry. I can't tell you how much this means to us, and I know you are busy, and everything –"

"No problem."

BOOK VI: OUT OF TIME

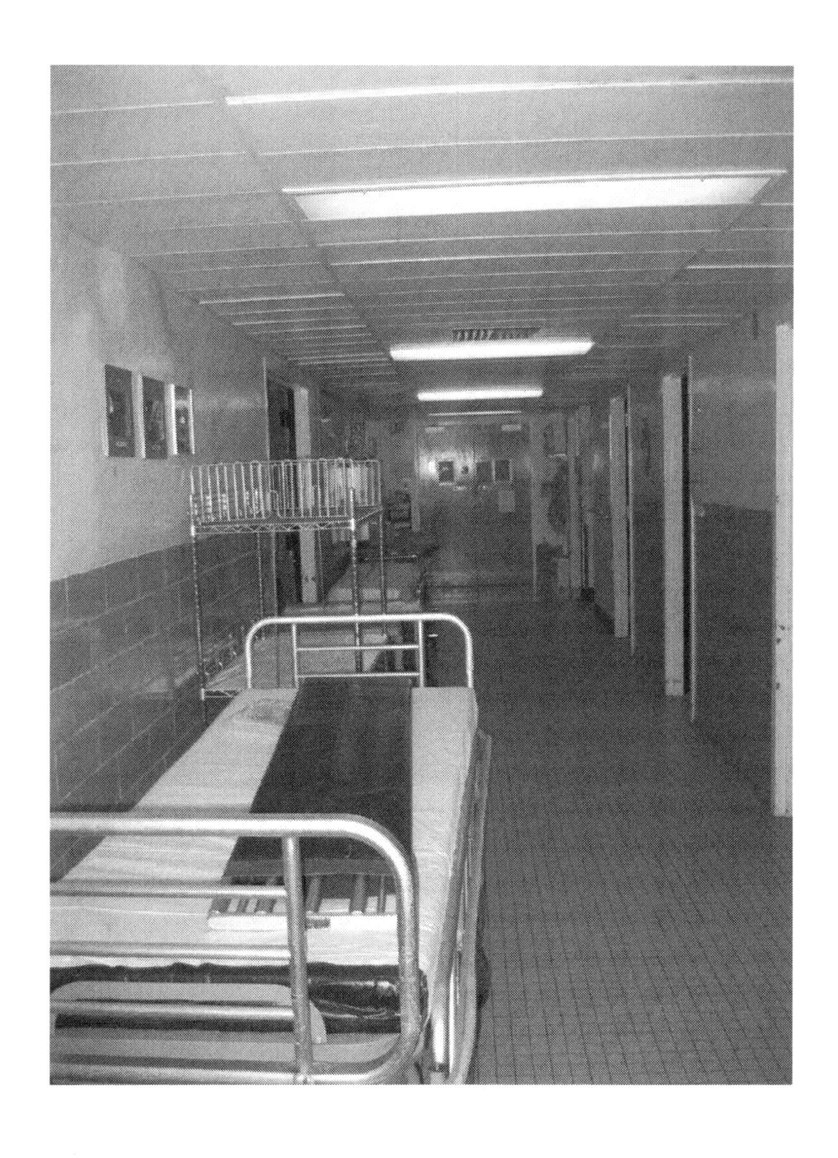

Night Visit

E. SEVENTH STREET, OSWEGO

It was well after dark. A woman dressed in dark clothing entered through the back door of the professor's house and placed a bottle of milk in the refrigerator. She'd been coming back more and more often; the milk was disappearing at a rapid rate. Which, though unexpected, was a good thing, she mused.

She moved to the basement door, looked back over her shoulder quickly, then opened the door and descended quietly into the basement. A small flashlight threw a soft beam of red-filtered light ahead of her.

A few minutes later, she returned to the kitchen, carefully closing the basement door behind her. Just as she started to the back door, she heard a noise on the steps. Another woman entered the house, carrying a casserole dish. Balancing the dish in one hand, the woman fumbled for the light switch with the other.

"Oh!" she exclaimed, as the light went on and she saw the first woman half kneeling in the dark near the door. "I didn't know anyone was here! My goodness, how you startled me. I almost dropped my dish!"

"I was just leaving," the woman said. "I had just switched off the light, and dropped my keys. I thought they would be right at my feet, but I must have kicked them away or something." She bent down behind her. "Ah, yes, here they are," she said, standing and putting a hand in the pocket of her slacks.

"I'm sorry, but I don't recognize you. Are you new to the neighborhood?"

"No, I just got into town late this afternoon. I'm an old friend."

"Oh, so you weren't at the wife's funeral the other day?"

"Unfortunately, no. I got delayed." She looked around the kitchen. "I haven't even had a chance to talk with the professor yet. I came by hoping he was home. The back door was unlocked, so –"

"Oh, yes, we're very casual in the neighborhood; we all watch out for one another."

"Yes, I can see that," the woman replied, gesturing to the casserole. "For the professor, I presume."

"Tomorrow night's dinner. Goulash. Not as good as his would be, I'm sure, but what with everything going on, he certainly doesn't have time to cook. I suppose he's over at the 1850 House tonight; he spends much of his time there, especially lately."

"The 1850 House. That's close by?"

"Up on Bridge; just a few blocks from here." The woman pointed to her left. “Up that way, Bridge and Fourth.”

“Thank you. Maybe I’ll drop by over there. See if I can catch up with him.”

“Oh, that would be lovely. Well, I have to get this in the fridge and get home.”

“Certainly; I’m sorry to have kept you.”

“Oh, no problem. I hope to see you around.”

“Perhaps. I won’t be in town long.” She moved to the door, opened it.

“Oh, well, then. Good night.”

“Good night.”

Out on the steps, she paused and looked around, then turned and walked away purposefully, to the north, away from Bridge Street, to the dark parking area where she’d left her car, at the edge of Fort Ontario Park.

Thirty minutes later, she was sitting at a table at a small, rustic bar some distance from Oswego.

She was not alone.

Running Out of Gas

E. SEVENTH STREET, OSWEGO

"*Wreck of P-39 Found in Lake Ontario*" read the headline. The subhead clarified: "*Ran Out of Gas, Say Experts.*"

Tamos carefully set the Palladian-Times aside, folded open to page six. The small headline – he'd had trouble finding the article – had made him wince painfully when he'd finally located it.

The story was nothing like what he'd given Aaron to deliver to Tiffany. Not even close.

Something was very wrong.

There were indications the article had been at least based on his story; two or three sentences that were word for word as he had written them. But he had never once mentioned the possibility that the airplane had run out of fuel. He didn't even believe that was the truth – or didn't want to believe it – but in any case, he had been at the lake that day, had seen the storm, how ferocious it had become in so short a time. He was sure that whatever had caused her to crash in the lake was certainly related to the storm.

He picked up the paper again and searched through it until he found the phone number.

"No, I already have a subscription." This was the third time he'd repeated this information, but the person on the other end seemed to have a one-track mind. "I just want to speak with one of your reporters, a Miss Tiffany Peet. Yes, I did say that earlier, before you explained, in detail, all of my subscription options, including, but not limited to, Sunday Only, Sunday with optional digital access, the Weekender – Friday, Saturday, and Sunday – and, the plan I currently have and am perfectly content with keeping, daily delivery, and no online service." He was beginning to lose patience.

"What was that number again? No, please wait a moment while I get a pen."

The new number connected him with the editor's secretary's desk. No, the editor wasn't in (he'd thought for a moment he could get the answer he needed directly, without talking to Tiffany). No, Tiffany wasn't in either. Yes, I'd like to leave a message.

Some days were like this, he knew, when everything took much longer that it should.

But he had an uncomfortable feeling that he was running out of time.

"Ah, Tiffany! Thank you for coming over!"

"Sure, Professor, no problem."

He directed her to his office, and to the stool he'd brought from the kitchen, across from his desk. He picked up the paper.

"Well, as I said in my message, I really don't understand what happened here. This is *not* the information relayed to you by Aaron."

"I've been meaning to call you and explain, but I just haven't had a chance."

"Tiffany, that article was *very* important. Very."

"Yes, I know, and I really feel bad about what happened. But there was nothing I could do about it. And I'm sorry I didn't call you sooner, it's just that –"

"That's not important now. What is important is that I understand exactly what happened."

"Yes, sir. Well, what happened is this. My editor contacted Wharton to get a clarification –"

"Wharton General Industries, WGI," Tamos confirmed.

"Yes. Anyway, like I said, my editor contacted their press office to get a comment on the allegations you made in your piece, and apparently, they had a real problem with it. A *real* problem, according to my editor."

"And?"

"Oh, like they threatened to sue us, and everything. Seriously. So, well, we couldn't run the story like you had it, and it was past deadline, so my editor ran a modified version."

"That version was provided by Wharton's press office, no doubt?"

"Yes."

"Where is the original of the article?"

"Oh, I think Aaron still has that. I made a copy."

"And that copy, where is that?"

"Oh, I threw that away when we couldn't print it; I didn't need it anymore."

"No, that's right. You didn't need it."

Tiffany squirmed on her stool. "I'm really sorry, Professor."

"Don't worry about it, Tiffany. I'll take care of it." Tamos closed his eyes for a moment, seeing his options fade. "Somehow."

He sat at his desk for quite a long time after Tiffany was gone, trying to make a plan. He'd thought he was the only one with a long memory.

But now it seemed obvious that Wharton had not forgotten, either.

He should call the Pall-Times editor, speak with him directly. What, exactly, had Wharton threatened them with? And what, if anything, had the Wharton press office revealed regarding what they knew – or believed they knew – that could be so damaging as to threaten a law suit?

The more he thought about it, the more he realized that he had reached a crossroads. He could either push on, regardless of consequences, or fall back to a safe position, wait for another opportunity to make his case. But now, after so many long years, he finally had the evidence he needed. Even if a long shot, it was the only shot he had, the shot he'd been patiently waiting for his entire life. He also knew he had to hurry.

He picked up the paper and looked again at the headline, such as it was. *Out of gas*. The thought made him nauseous.

Suddenly, literally nauseous.

He pushed himself up from his desk and staggered to the tiny bathroom.

It was to be a long night.

"Michael?"

"Professor?"

"Yes. Can you come over right away?"

Michael looked quickly at the white board on the wall next to his desk. He had a Caesarean at one-thirty. It was now just after twelve. "Right now? What's the problem?"

"I really don't feel well, Michael."

"What's going on?"

"I was very sick last night. Vomiting, dry heaves. Do you think it is too much milk?"

"Oh, I doubt it."

"Can you come over?"

Michael hesitated. "I am a little busy today, actually. Have you called your PCP?"

"They cannot get me in until tomorrow. Can you believe it? A town this size, and you still cannot see a doctor when you need to."

"How do you feel now, any better?"

"Somewhat. But my stomach is still tied in knots. I just don't know what to do."

"Okay," said Michael, thinking. "How about Maggie? Shall I call her and see if she can stop by? She's very close by."

"Oh, Michael, that would be wonderful."

There was no response when she rang the bell. A trifle alarmed, she pulled the screen door back and pushed open the front door.

"Prof?" she called.

She could barely hear the answer.

"In here."

She walked through the dim light into the professor's small bedroom.

"Prof? Are you all right?"

Tamos was lying on his bed, wrapped in blankets.

"Not so good, I'm afraid."

Maggie looked around, seeing no place to sit. "Hang on, professor; I'll get a chair." She set the medicine bag she was carrying down on the floor.

She pulled the desk chair from the other room up to the side of the bed.

"Okay, let's see what's going on here," she said, opening her bag and taking out a blood pressure cuff. "Give me your arm."

When she got back the 1850 House, A.C. was waiting.

"Well?"

"I think he's all right for now. I'm taking him over for his appointment with Dr. Linnabarger tomorrow afternoon."

"Any idea what the problem is?"

Maggie took a deep breath.

"He's very old, A.C."

The Tao of Physics

E. SEVENTH STREET, OSWEGO

Before he left for El Salvador on his medical mission, Michael stopped by the professor's house to say goodbye. Tamos was sitting up in bed, a tray nearby holding the remainders of a small lunch that had been delivered by Mrs. Gopnik from down the street.

"Yes, I am feeling much better today, Michael, thank you. Still somewhat fatigued, however."

"Well, listen to what Dr. Linnabarger tells you. And don't forget that Maggie has offered to come over and stay with you if you need help."

"Oh, yes, but I don't want to put her out like that. There is really nowhere for her to sleep."

"She told me she has an inflatable mattress. She can put it out in the front room."

"Completely unnecessary. She has enough to do without worrying about me."

"Well, let her help in other ways, then. It will make her feel better. You know how much she misses her nursing duties."

"And I appreciate everything she does for me. And A.C., too, of course."

"But he's not a nurse. Please promise me that you'll call Maggie if you need anything."

"Of course. But I still wish I didn't have to rely on Dr. Linnabarger. I really do not trust him, Michael. I think he is just in it for the Medicare money."

"Tamos, I've never heard you sound so cynical! Give him a chance."

"All right, Michael. But you'll be back soon?"

"I'll be back in two weeks."

"Well, in that case, you know you are probably going to miss all of the excitement."

"Excitement?"

"I expect to make an announcement any day now. I'm just waiting to hear back from the news media."

"Okay, Tamos. You've hooked me. What are you up to?"

"Well, since you are leaving tomorrow, I can tell you. It has to do with the P-39."

"But I thought that was all taken care of. It's on its way to the museum in Texas, right?"

"Yes, the airplane itself. But this has to do with something that was in the airplane, something I recovered. Something I have been waiting for seventy years to obtain. Something that will vindicate our efforts – mine, Jeri's, Harry's – we will be vindicated, Michael. It all has to do with the chain of chance. And with elegance."

"Tamos, you've lost me. Harry? Harry who?"

Tamos ignored Michael's question. "Do you remember our conversation on the boat? About how the chain of chance is influenced by individual effort? About how quantum entanglement could be at the root of consciousness?"

"Yes, a little, but Tamos –"

"I now have in my possession something that can change history, Michael. I know that sounds presumptuous, even mad. Oh, not history with a big 'H,' but current history, immediate history. I have been waiting seventy years, wondering if it would still matter. And, Michael, not only does it still matter, it matters more than ever. And it is up to me to make sure it matters. Individual effort, Michael. It can make all the difference. If there is anything like free will, if the choices we make are at all deterministic, in both the moral and theoretical sense, then we have an obligation, to ourselves, to each other – well, to life. An obligation to make those choices. The choices that make us who we are." He stopped to take a breath. "You know of WGI?" he asked.

"Yes, the defense contractor."

"Among other things, yes."

"They've been in the news recently. Some foreign contracts, I think."

"Yes. Well, when I'm done with them, Michael, there will be no foreign contracts." Tamos leaned back slightly.

"Good luck in El Salvador, Michael. Make your choices count."

The Reins of Power

1850 HOUSE

"It's not a sports bar!" This had been LaFleur's first reaction to Frank's suggestion that they install a flat screen TV in the bar area. But cooler, more marketing savvy heads had prevailed, and a relatively small – forty-inch – screen now hung in one corner.

Sports predominated, but it was almost always golf, with hockey making an appearance during playoff season, or, when Maggie was in the bar, whenever the Yankees were playing. The professor, when tiring of golf, would have the channel set to Turner Classic Movies, with the sound off, as he knew many of the stories well, and even much of the dialog.

It was a couple of days since the professor had left the house, but feeling somewhat better, he made the trip up to the 1850 House, to get out for some air, but primarily to watch television. This particular afternoon, it was not golf or movies Tamos was interested in, however. After settling in at his customary spot, he tuned in CNBC. He asked LaFleur to join him at his table as the press conference was getting started.

"Wharton General Industries," the announcer was saying, "was founded by patriarch Charles Wharton Sr., who at age ninety-six has, by all reports, very little say in the current business. WGI is currently one of the largest, if not the largest, infrastructure and defense contractors in the world, depending on how you crunch the numbers."

"It's been quite a dynasty," broke in a second reporter, "almost unique in American business history; not even the Rockefellers can compare. And as we previously reported, the company is now set to undergo a major transition. Charles "Chuck" Wharton, the third of the line to helm the company, has stated his intention to turn over operations to his son, Charles the Fourth."

"Operations that include some of the most important – and controversial – projects in the world," the first reporter continued. "A potential deal with Russia, for example, to complete construction of venues for FIFA 2018, has brought charges of complicity with some of the country's most infamous oligarchs. And then there are the ongoing Chinese nuclear plant construction projects. Both are touted by WGI as breakthroughs in strengthening ties between the three countries, in spite of criticism both in the press and from the current administration in Washington. In addition, WGI's secretive 'Milspec' branch is in line to become a prime contractor for the joint Navy/Air Force 6th-generation fighter aircraft."

"It appears that the Whartons are nearly ready to begin," the reporter then said, as the picture switched from their news desk to a podium set up on the steps of the WGI Tower in downtown Manhattan.

As final mike adjustments were made by Wharton's handlers, the professor leaned over in LaFleur's direction. "This is what I've been waiting for," he said.

"What's the sudden interest in finance, Prof? And why WGI?"

The professor's answer was one that LaFleur was, frankly, getting a little tired of hearing.

"All in good time." Tamos turned back to the television.

Charles Wharton III, or "Chuck," as he insisted on being called, took great pride in his humility. He often ate lunch in one of the Tower cafeterias with the "folks," usually with tie loosened and shirtsleeves rolled up. Today, however, he was impeccably dressed in a well-tailored, dark suit and red power tie. At six-feet-one, broad-chested and silver-haired, he towered over the slim young man at his side, the focus of today's transition of power.

Charles IV glanced around nervously as he stood at his father's side, looking as if he would rather be anywhere else on Earth, which was probably true. He'd lived in the shadow of his father for so long that some of his so-called friends had taken to calling him "Mossback." And so, true-to-form, he stood patiently by as Chuck made his announcement.

"I'll be brief, which I know will come as a surprise to most of you –" He paused for the obligatory chuckle from the crowd of reporters in front of him. "But by way of introduction, I'd like to remind everyone that Wharton General Industries, started by my grandfather in nineteen thirty-three, was initially just a small metal foundry in New Jersey, then known as Wharton Fabrication. By the beginning of World War II, the foundry had grown to encompass several acres along Staten Island Sound, and soon became a leading supplier of defense materials. So, at WGI, we have been investing in this country's success for over eighty years. In turning over the day-to-day operations of the company to my son, Charles," nodding in Charles IV's direction, "that tradition will continue. WGI has been, and will continue to be, at the forefront of today's most difficult – and necessary – infrastructure and defense projects, worldwide. In spite of opposition from many quarters, we will move forward in our efforts to build a global future, a future our children and grandchildren will be proud of.

"You'll be hearing more in the coming days from Charles, here," nodding in his son's direction again, but obviously not about to let Charles speak for himself as yet, "about how WGI will be instrumental in creating that future."

Here he paused, gazing at the crowd with a look of concerned benevolence. "I've made no secret of the fact that I believe this country to be on the wrong path, a path away from prosperity, away from success, away from freedom. But the business of WGI, now in the capable hands of Charles

IV, is just one aspect of what it's going to take to bring about our new vision.

"To that end, I announce today my candidacy for President of the United States."

With this, Tamos turned to A.C. "We'll see about that," he said.

LaFleur could only stare back at him, speechless.

Tequila Shooters

PULASKI, NEW YORK

"I hate these small-town bars."

She brushed back her dark, short hair, looking first at the gangly, unkempt man across the table from her, then at the short and squat, but meticulously dressed and groomed man beside her. Behind them, a couple at the bar posed for a selfie in front of a bottle of Busch Light and an overflowing shot glass.

The three of them were sitting in a sports bar located in the Salmon River fishing parking lot in beautiful downtown Pulaski, about twenty-five miles from Oswego. This left the professor's house and LaFleur's place unwatched for a short time, but the two Wharton agents hadn't seen much of anything happen in the past couple of days anyway.

Ignoring the woman's comment, the gangly man asked no one in particular, "What the hell is 'spey,' anyway?"

The well-dressed man turned to him. "What?"

"Spey. Saw a store front on the way over here. 'Tackle and Spey Shop,' it said."

"Not a fisherman, I presume?"

"Not in this lifetime. Fish should stay underwater, where they belong."

"See what I have to endure?" the other man said, turning to the dark-haired woman. He looked back at the questioner. "Spey is a type of fishing rod."

"And they need a whole shop for that?"

"Okay, enough of the local color," said the woman. "What have you found out? Did you search the house again?"

"No chance. Either the old guy's been in there, or there's people going in and out all the time."

"Yeah, he's a sort of local celebrity. It's even been hard for me to get in and out, and I have a cover."

"Yeah, but at least you *can* get in and out. So why don't you search the house?"

"Well, I did take a look around in the basement. Looks like a dead end; nothing down there, no furniture, nothing. Just an old sink. I guess I could try to take a closer look upstairs."

"Do that. We're getting heavy pressure from above. We'll concentrate on the detective and the doctor."

"You have to do your part. It's no good taking care of the old guy unless we can get the goods."

"So that reminds me; what's happening on that front?"

"Ongoing."

"The sooner the better. Why can't you step it up?"

"It's not that simple."

"Just do what you can. All right, I guess that's all. When and where do we meet next?"

"No more meetings," the woman replied, looking around. The couple at the bar behind them was doing shooters with the bar maid, laughing uproariously, and seeing her look, raised shots to the three at the table. She quickly turned back to the two men. "I'll be done here before long. If you two just get what we need, we can all get out of here."

Fox Fur

E. SEVENTH STREET, OSWEGO

"I just feel so bad that I haven't been able to do more; before now, that is," the woman said in a hushed voice. She put down a casserole dish on the counter. A neighbor from four doors down, she had been bringing in food for Tamos ever since she saw him on the local news. The refrigerator was in danger of overflowing as his celebrity spread.

"Oh, please don't worry about it," said Maggie. She and A.C. had been in the kitchen when the woman came in, waiting for the professor to return from the bathroom. "You and all of the neighbors have been wonderful."

"Well, thank you. I just hope I've helped a little, anyway. But you know, with my daughter back home again, and everything, well..." She trailed off.

"Everything you've done is more than appreciated," offered A.C.

At this, there was a noise from the hallway. Maggie took the woman by the elbow and gently ushered her out the back door. "If you'll excuse us, I need to attend to Tamos for a moment."

"Oh, yes, certainly. Oh, you're that nurse, aren't you?"

"Yes, that's right," Maggie said as the woman went out the door. "And thank you again."

"Oh, it's nothing, really."

Maggie turned and went down the narrow hallway as A.C. looked for shelf space in the fridge. "All right, Prof?" she called though the bathroom door.

"Yes, fine. I'll just be a moment."

A few minutes later, the three of them were sitting in the small living room.

"Tamos, I really think we should have a home health service come in. Just until you regain your strength," she added hastily.

"I understand your concern, Maggie, but I think I'm getting over the worst of it. It's this gastrointestinal thing, you know. I've had trouble like this before. And I don't care what Linnabarger says, it's not the milk. I need the calcium. You remember a few years ago, I had a bout of flu, fell and cracked a hip? Well, Linnabarger was the one who got me started on milk, as I recall." He shifted a bit in his chair, adjusting a pillow at his back. "In any event, I really am feeling much better."

This was immediately contradicted, however, as the professor convulsed suddenly, alarming them both. But as usual, he waved Maggie off as she rose to help. "Just some gas," he said. He sat back and closed his eyes. In a few seconds, he was asleep.

Maggie turned to A.C., a determined look on her face. "I'm calling a service, I don't care what he says," she said quietly. "He needs more constant care, at least for now. There's a good service out of Syracuse, I know a couple of the nurses working there. I'll call tomorrow."

"Probably a good idea," agreed LaFleur. "I'll talk to him, get him to go along."

They sat quietly for the next ten minutes, listening to the professor's strenuous breathing.

When Tamos woke up, he seemed surprised to see them.

"You are still here?"

"Sure, Prof. We haven't been here that long, actually."

"Ah." Tamos looked around abstractedly. "Did I ever tell you about the time I solved a crime, A.C.?"

"Well, no, I don't believe so."

"It happened in the camp. You know, no one had been able to hold on to any possessions from before, well, very few, anyway. What little they managed to bring along with them sometimes meant a great deal, even if not very meaningful or even useful. Little things, you know, a favorite broach, or a family prayer book; a shawl, something from the old life. Anyway, I remember this one woman – German, I think, she spoke German, at least, or maybe she was Polish, you know the Poles were forced to speak German all the time, maybe it was a habit – in any case, she had somehow managed to hold on to a fur, a fox pelt. And this was in summer, in Italy, so very hot, and of course it was very hot on the ship, but she wore this fox fur constantly. Never let it out of her sight. I am sure it must have had some special significance, the way she held on to it; or maybe not, who knows why people get attached to things?"

LaFleur glanced at Maggie. *Where is this going?* his raised eyebrows said. Maggie shrugged.

"One day," continued Tamos, "this woman ran into the commissary crying, 'My coat! My coat is gone!' She stood in the middle of the room, crying, murmuring 'My coat,' over and over. Well, it's hard to say, but there were a few in the camp, not so scrupulous types. Not many, but, well, out of a thousand, a bad apple here and there is to be expected, yes? Well, fox pelts were very common in those days. Many women in town had one. Or wanted one. And there was going on, what shall I call it? Commerce. Through the fence. This always happens. Even in the camps in Germany, I was told, but in any case, here she was, this woman whose coat had possibly been stolen and sold over the fence. Which is where I came in. I rather impulsively offered to get her coat back."

Tamos reached up and rubbed his eyes. "And I didn't even know this woman. I had very little to go on. It was several days later that I began to think it was going to be impossible to trace the coat, but now that I had interjected myself into this episode, I felt I had to see it through – which I did, to her great joy – even if at this point I was playing a very weak hand. I just couldn't bear to leave it unfinished."

Tamos stopped and looked at LaFleur intently. "Things I can't bear to leave unfinished. There are some things, A.C., things I have started, they must not be left unfinished." He closed his eyes. "A.C., no one plays a weak hand better than you. I have said it many times. And if something should happen to me –"

"Tamos, I'm not sure what you mean. What is unfinished?"

"You heard the press conference, in the bar the other day."

"WGI? Wharton?"

"Yes, exactly. A.C., play it out for me. You are a fine detective. You will understand. You can do this. If something happens to me, A.C., promise to play it out for me. One way or another, I'll make sure you have what you need."

"But, Tamos, I've given up on all that. I'm not really –"

"Promise me."

It was dark by the time they walked back to the 1850 House.

"What do you think he was talking about? What interest does he have in WGI?"

"I don't know," said LaFleur. "As usual, he wouldn't talk much about it. A couple of hints. But that's not what really bothers me."

Maggie stopped and turned to him. "No? What then?"

"He never told us how he got that damned fur coat back."

Mal de Ojo

SYRACUSE AIRPORT, 12:10 A.M.

The shoulder bag seemed as if it weighed at least triple its fifteen pounds; his arms were like old inner tubes, his legs sodden logs, his feet hot stones; and his luggage hadn't arrived. The flight from San Salvador had been more than four hours late, and now he faced an hour drive to Oswego. And he was due back at the hospital at ten A.M. the next morning.

Still, as fatigued as he was physically, he felt wonderful. The mission in El Salvador had gone extremely well; the weather had been good, he'd liked the doctors he'd worked with, and the children had been marvels of joyful resilience. All in all, a very rewarding experience. He could not help thinking of Tamos and his theory of the value of effort, in and of itself. Too often in this world, Michael had come to realize, effort and reward are disjointed, disconnected.

Trudging down an empty hallway, eyes on the floor, he was jarred back to reality by nearly running into a janitorial cart. The elderly woman pushing the cart gave him a hard look.

"Oh, sorry." He had stopped in front of the cart, which the woman appeared to have no intention of moving. Michael stepped back a step, unsettled. The woman looked Hispanic: Guatemalan? Perhaps even Salvadoran, she had that look about her. He couldn't say why, but he was somehow sure she was Salvadoran.

"Lo siento. No te vi. I didn't see you."

The woman continued to stare at him, her black eyes shining out from under heavy, dark eyebrows. He stepped back another half-step, and began to move around her.

"No hay problema," she said, her voice rough and leathery. She began to move away, still looking after him.

As she moved away, Michael realized that he'd stopped dead in his tracks, unable to move. His breathing sped up and his face flushed cold. He felt faint, lightheaded, almost floating.

A moment later, the feeling left as quickly as it had come.

The encounter with the old woman had triggered a feeling, an impulse; a vision? As if something dark and malevolent from the future had just passed through him, walking the opposite direction.

The evil eye. He'd just been a victim of the evil eye. From that old woman.

He shook himself, laughing at the thought. I'm just tired. More tired than

I thought.

How many times had he heard it said in El Salvador in the past two weeks, that disease, deformities, all types of afflictions, particularly among children or babies, are brought about by the forces of “the evil eye.” Some of the country people even attributed the evil eye to foreign aid workers – doctors, for example. *That must be on my mind. That’s all.*

He gathered himself, shifted his bag higher on his shoulder and made his way to the terminal exit.

Looking back over his shoulder the whole way.

The Famous Fuentes

OSWEGO HOSPITAL

In newer neighborhoods, there is little sense of community: no one knows one another; no one gossips across the back fence while hanging clothes out to dry; the kids don't bike down the middle of the street, or play soccer with tin cans set up for goals. "For sale" signs decorate every third or fourth front yard. Families come and go like locusts, leaving behind a desolate landscape of abandoned shells, two-by-four and plasterboard husks waiting for the next infestation.

The Fort Ontario neighborhood where ex-professor Tamos Szabó lived was not like that. While of course people came and went over the years, the rate of change in the neighborhood was slow, and a strong sense of continuity ran through the community. People talked on the street on the way to the park, waved to one another while they collected the morning paper, walked to church or synagogue together, brought in food when someone was ill, and checked up on the elderly occasionally, just in case.

Which was what Sylvie Podhertz was doing when she found him at about nine-thirty that night. "Mein Gott in Himmel," was all she could manage before stumbling out of the kitchen in near panic – ignoring the phone on the wall – and running back across the street to her telephone.

The 911 operator had been calm, polite, and soothing, and by the time the ambulance arrived, Sylvie's pulse and blood pressure were back to near-normal, even though her hands were still shaking with the memory of the Professor lying face down in the kitchen. Even in her shock, she could not help but to have noticed the smell; well, that part she would not describe as she told and retold her story in the coming days. The Professor had been well-known and well-liked, and she would be pressed for her story often, but would remain decorous.

The EMTs on duty that night were well-equipped to handle the situation. The lead paramedic, Ray, had just reached his sixth anniversary with the company – a hell of a long time in that business – and his secondary, while young, had aspirations of going to medical school, and so took the job seriously as well. They had both seen worse in-home incidents, but not by much. The professor was dressed, at least, and lying in the kitchen – slightly easier to deal with than the common scenario of half-dressed, falling off of the toilet – but the kitchen was a disaster. The floor was slick with a combination of vomit and diarrhea, watery and rank. A bottle of milk had been overturned on one counter and had run down onto the tile floor, adding to the mess made by the dropped casserole.

"Okay. Let's get him out of here," said Ray, pulling the stretcher through the kitchen doorway and out into the living room. His assistant swung the stretcher around in a one-eighty and booted the front screen door open, guiding the stretcher through and onto the front porch.

A small crowd had gathered, even at this time of night. Sylvie's neighbor Emma had her arm around her, holding in place the shawl she had brought over. Three or four others had joined them, and now they were all out on the lawn chattering like geese. If anyone even noticed the car just down the street pulling away from the curb a minute or so after the ambulance had gone, they were too distracted to think anything of it.

After the medics rolled the Stryker stretcher into the ER, the wide double outside doors banging behind them, a nurse rushed up to help them move Tamos from the gurney on to an exam table. As one of the EMTs rolled the stretcher back out of the room, the two nurses and the ER chief, Dr. Ladisio, began to prep the patient, stripping his pants and shirt, quickly connecting him to a multi-function monitor perched on a stand next to the table.

"What have we got, Ray?" Ladisio asked the EMT.

"Got a ninety-four-year-old man found lying face-down on the floor in the kitchen in his home – over by the Fort – we got there at 11:18 P.M.; he'd been down for an unknown period of time. Neighbor lady called it in. He was unresponsive, a moderate amount of dried vomit next to his head – we think he might have aspirated – and evidence of severe diarrhea. At the scene he was GCS 3, heart rate 120 with a weak thready pulse, BP 94 over 64, respiration 30 and shallow, no retractions or accessory muscle use, temp 35.9, blood sugar 108, and O^2 sat at 92%. On physical exam he has no signs of trauma, dry mucous membranes, chest clear, abdomen soft – non-distended – no obvious deformities or fractures. We couldn't get him intubated, so just got him on oxygen quickly with a mask and put him on the monitor. Here's his EKG; sinus tach with prolonged QT. We placed two large-bore IVs and ran 1.5 liters normal saline into him, but his condition didn't improve on the way in. Medical history and meds unknown."

"Did you get another BP on him in transit?" asked one of the nurses.

"Yes, let's see." Ray looked down at some rough notes he had written on his glove. "Um, 92 over 64, and heart rate of 126."

"Any ID found?" Ladisio asked.

"Yeah, wallet's in his pants," Ray replied, motioning to the disheveled pile of clothing now draped over a short stool off to the side.

"Okay; we'll take a look when we're through here. DNR?"

"Not that we saw; anyway, nothing on the fridge – that's usually where we find it, held up by a Disneyworld magnet."

"Yeah. Well, we'll plod on then," said Ladisio, tiredly. "Thanks a lot, Raymond. Think we've got it from here."

"No sweat, doc. See ya." Ray walked out of the ER, brushing past an unfamiliar orderly who was standing just outside the doors.

"Sorry," he said, "did the door hit you?"

"No, no problem," the woman replied. She quickly pulled up her surgical mask, which had become dislodged when Ray had come out.

As he climbed into the cab of the ambulance, he was still trying to shake off the bad feeling he had about this case; he hated leaving the ER not knowing if the patient was going to make it or not. As hungry as he was, the clammy cheeseburger and limp fries waiting for him in the ambulance were going to go down a little harder than usual tonight.

Ladisio turned to the nurse closest to him. "Kara, let's get those IVs full open and get him on a new bag, finish getting him on the monitor and I'll intubate."

"Yes, Doctor." She moved away to complete these tasks as the other nurse leaned over the patient and started yelling in a strident voice: "Sir! Can you hear me? Can you hear me?" She began vigorously rubbing his sternum, trying to get a pain response. Nothing. "He's 82 over 65, heart rate is 120," she said, glancing up at the monitor. "He's still satting at 92, and his GCS is 3."

"Okay." Ladisio turned back to the nurse at his side, quickly sweeping his hair back with one hand. "Joyce, I want an EKG, 12-lead, a chest X-ray" – he paused before rattling off a string of blood tests – "complete blood count with coags, cardiac panel, liver function, and electrolyte panel. No apparent physical trauma – this looks medical."

"On it."

"Okay. Kara, give me a hand here, let's get this oxygen mask out of the way –"

Suddenly, the old man began convulsing, his thin legs and arms twitching, chest heaving, pasty white skin blanching and mottling. The monitor, calm moments ago, began to screech in distress. Ladisio rushed up and began CPR, at the same time calmly rapping out orders. "Kara, de-fib. Joyce, epinephrine, 1-to-10 IV push."

"Code 99 in ER. Code 99 in ER."

The P.A. announcement had echoed through the empty hallways, muddy and indistinct, like a nineteen-sixties bus station announcement.

Michael, barely back from his mission in El Salvador, heard the announcement as he walked from the cafeteria back to his office. He slowed his gait to half-steps as he contemplated heading down to the emergency room. He was officially off-duty – whatever that meant around here – but Michael was burdened by the misfortune of taking his job seriously. He was also known for taking on more than his share, assisting – inappropriately intervening, as some had it – outside of his primary duties as chief anesthesiologist. In spite of the briefest hint of doubt as to whether he should respond, he almost automatically reversed direction to the elevator. A minute later, he pushed open the side door of the ER. Before he was even all the way into the room, he saw that things were not going well.

"Hey, Gus. Heard the page. Can I help?"

Ladisio looked over distractedly as Michael came in. "I doubt it. Had a hell of a time trying to intubate; probably wouldn't have made any difference, anyway. Just lost the pulse, pupils are dilated." Ladisio was obviously not thrilled to have Michael there. Ladisio was seldom thrilled about having anyone except himself there. He tolerated nurses – good nurses – and occasionally would let interns live. But just about the last person he wanted there was another doctor. Fuentes especially.

There was a momentary lull as Ladisio bent down for a final check.

"Okay, team, let's call it." He checked his watch. On cue, the nurses began unraveling the various wires and tubes that had just been employed in the failed attempt to save a life.

As Kara was removing the oxygen mask, Michael jerked back with a start.

"Oh, my God. I know this man."

"What?" asked Ladisio.

"I know him," Michael said. "It's the Prof."

"Prof? What are you talking about?"

"Tamos. Oh, my God, it's Tamos." His breath caught in his chest. He looked around at the ER staff. "Professor Tamos Szabó. Don't you recognize him?"

"Jesus, Fuentes, you're right," said Ladisio, taking a closer look at the old man's face. "Christ. What a shame."

Michael edged closer, scarcely believing it, forcing himself to remain calm. As accustomed as he was to distressing medical situations – he'd seen much worse – this was different. It was Tamos; nearly unrecognizable, even to Michael, but Tamos. *My God, Tamos.*

"What was cause of death?" Michael asked, now standing next to Ladisio.

"It's obvious, Fuentes," said Ladisio, waving a hand. "Old age. Heart failure."

Ladisio, prima donna that he was, was nevertheless an excellent emergency department chief, and had probably done a good job managing the session. But now that Michael had recognized Tamos, he was by God not going to just let it go at that. Old age was the easy out; as was declaring the cause of death as "heart failure." Well, *everyone* died of heart failure in the final analysis. That didn't make it a satisfying answer.

"Mind if I take a look?" He was still just barely maintaining his composure; he took a deep breath and clasped his hands tightly for a moment to calm himself.

"Be my guest," Ladisio said archly, then stood back, hands on his hips, scowling.

Michael moved over to the table, noticing the acrid smell for the first time since he'd entered the room, that stale reek of trauma so common to ERs, veterinary clinics, and low-end nursing homes. He was to a large degree accustomed to it – as they all were, or they couldn't keep doing what they did – but inured to it or not, it was not pleasant. He reached into his pocket and pulled out his recorder, keying it on and laying it on the edge of the table.

"Ah, the famous Fuentes," Ladisio said, barely keeping it under his breath.

Michael began examining the body, carefully noting details as he went. At the hands, he stopped. Bending low, he raised each hand into the light, turning them left and right, straightening out the fingers, tilting each fingertip up, twisting them back and forth. He reached over and switched off the recorder.

"Did you notice the fingernails, Gus?"

"What about them?"

"See the striations?"

Ladisio glanced over.

"Not really."

Michael just looked back up at him, switching the recorder back on.

"Kara, what did the EKG show when he first arrived?"

"Um, sinus tachycardia. Long QT," she replied, looking over her shoulder as she unwound an IV tube. Ladisio glared at her.

"Signs of vomitus, diarrhea?"

"Yes."

"O^2 levels?"

"Satting at 92%."

"GCS?"

"Three." On the Glasgow Coma Scale, a three was very bad, indicating little or no consciousness.

Ladisio glared at her again, threateningly this time, and growled at

Fuentes. "What the hell, Fuentes? This is my department. Get out and let us finish up here."

"Listen. I know this man. I'm not going to just let you call this and walk away from it."

"Fuentes –"

"Two minutes, Gus. Two more bloody minutes. That's all I ask."

Ladisio snorted with disgust. Michael took that as a 'yes.'

After a close examination of Tamos's arms and legs, which showed marked thickening of the skin – particularly unusual in a man of Tamos's age – he ended with a close look at the feet, also showing thick, heavy skin. Michael verbally noted "hyperkeratosis" for the recorder, then stood up. After looking up and down the body, he reached over and picked up his recorder, switching it off, then as an afterthought, bent over, and prying open the dead man's mouth, sniffed cautiously. He switched the recorder back on. "Odor of garlic from oral cavity," he said, and thumbing the recorder off, slipped it back into his pocket.

Picking up a pair of surgical scissors, Michael clipped off a small lock of the professor's hair and placed it in a sample bag, which went into his pocket with the recorder.

"I'm asking for a postmortem on this, Gus," he said.

"Like hell you are. You have no goddamned authority in here. It's my call."

"Did you see the fingernails, Ladisio?"

"What the hell is it with the goddamned fingernails, Fuentes?"

"Mees's lines. The striations across the nails. That plus other signs; the hyperkeratosis, the vomiting, the diarrhea, the vitals. It all adds up. This man was in excellent health for his age just a few weeks ago. Christ, I saw him just over two weeks ago and he was nowhere near this state of debilitation. There has to be more to this. I'm asking for a review, Ladisio. This has to go to an inquest.

"This man has been poisoned."

Ladisio just stared.

"Arsenic," said Michael.

"Fuentes, I've always known you were incompetent," Ladisio fumed, "but now you've just proven that you are also crazy." Ladisio reached out and grabbed Michael by the arm. "There will be no inquest. Not unless I say so. And I do not say so. Now, get out!" he yelled, shoving Michael away.

Stumbling back, Michael shook his head. "I don't care what you think, you stupid bastard. I'm getting an inquest. The man has been poisoned by arsenic." And with that he stalked out of the ER.

"Poisoned?!" yelled Ladisio. "Poisoned? You're insane, Fuentes!"

"Go to hell, Ladisio!" hollered Michael over his shoulder.

"Get back here, Fuentes!" Ladisio shouted, following Michael out of the ER.

"Leave me alone, Gus," Michael said, stopping to confront Ladisio in the hallway. His voice dropped to a whisper as Ladisio stood in front of him. "Just leave me the hell alone."

He pushed Ladisio to one side and walked away.

Whenever he walked down these shadowy, pale green hospital corridors this late at night, especially this night, he felt like a ten-year old at a Halloween party. At ten, a child is old enough to understand how frightening standard Halloween props can be, but not quite old enough to really, truly believe they are just that – props – and that makes it easy for the thirteen-year old brother to scare the younger out of his wits.

It had been necessary to go all the way back down to the first-floor cafeteria, at the opposite end of the hospital, to find a vending machine with a Diet Coke in it. It was a habit he'd been ridiculed for ever since he arrived in Oswego – he drank eight or ten a day – and so had accumulated an impressive collection of empty cans. He kept them neatly stacked just inside his office door, waiting until he could get around to recycling them. He turned the last corner before reaching his office and let out a low, unintentional sigh of relief.

He hadn't realized until now how much the encounter in the ER had shaken him. First, the shock of seeing Tamos lying there on the table. It had taken all of his self-control to complete his examination. *And then that pompous ass Ladisio – all right, calm down*, he told himself. *Ladisio be damned. There is going to be an inquest. I owe that much to Tamos, at least.*

He'd barely started filling out the postmortem request when he was disturbed by a slight noise out in the hallway. He looked up and out of the doorway, then went back to the form. It had not been a loud noise, rather one of those noises you hear and then two or three seconds later dismiss as a creak in the floor, a heating duct, expanding, contracting. Maybe someone at the other end of the ward below had dropped something, and the noise had arrived at his office conductively, ghostly sounds migrating through the old, tired walls and floors. Or a refrigeration pump in the basement morgue had belched, stammered to a halt, and then reluctantly restarted. All of these possibilities flashed through his mind in the seconds before he heard a loud crashing, clattering noise, very close by.

Someone had kicked over his pile of cans.

He jerked upright as a blurry figure dressed in scrubs and a surgical mask came across the desk at him. With a sharp cry, he wrenched away from the attacker. He felt the point of the scalpel glance off of his sternum, penetrating his chest cavity. A blinding pain engulfed him, red flashes, then white, pure white. He flickered in and out of consciousness for a few seconds.

I'm sorry, Tamos.

He laid his head down and closed his eyes.

BOOK VII: THE KEY

BELL KINGCOBRAS FOR RED AIR FORCE, TO BE FERRIED TO U.S.S.R. THROUGH ALASKA.

A Quick Look Around

OSWEGO HOSPITAL

12:24 A.M.

The best possible outcome of a phone call in the middle of the night is a wrong number.

This was not one of those times.

As she picked up the phone, Maggie glanced at the green, glowing caller ID display. She recognized the number: it was one of the ER nurses that she'd worked with before her retirement. They had stayed in close touch.

"Kathy?" she asked, still in a bit of a fog.

A few seconds later, Maggie sat straight up in bed.

"Oh, my God. What –"

She listened for a few more seconds. "No, no. Oh, my God. Yes, we'll be there right away."

Awakened by the conversation, A.C. raised himself on one elbow. Before he could say anything, Maggie was already out of bed and half way to the closet.

"A.C.! Get up! Michael's been stabbed!"

12:49 A.M.

Maggie came back over to where LaFleur was standing quietly, just inside the doorway of the ER. They looked over at the table where the ER doctor now on duty, a Dr. Eckard, and two nurses were working on Michael. She did not know the doctor, but had been quickly introduced as an ex-head nurse and Michael's close friend.

"It's serious," she explained to LaFleur, "but not life-threatening, thank God. The attacker apparently used a very short knife, or a scalpel; it just missed his heart."

"Serious, you said. What, exactly?"

"It penetrated a lung, collapsing it, actually, so they've got a drain inserted. They're also getting some blood into him; he lost a lot."

"But he'll make it."

"It was close, but yes, he'll make it."

"Where did it happen?"

"Upstairs in his office. A janitor working in the adjoining wing heard the commotion and rushed over. She found Michael face down on his desk. No one else was there."

LaFleur looked around.

"Have the police been here yet?"

"Good question." She turned toward the team at Michael's side. "Doctor?" she asked. "Are the police here?"

One of the nurses – Kathy, the nurse who had called Maggie – jerked her head up from finalizing an IV. "Oh, geez, Maggie! With everything going on, I forgot to call it in! Dr. Eckard, I'm sorry!"

The doctor looked up. "Please call it in, uh, Maggie, was it?"

"Right away, Doctor."

As she moved towards the phone, LaFleur pulled her to one side and leaned close.

"Give me five minutes."

She looked at him in concern. "What?"

"Okay, three minutes. A head start. It will take them ten to get here, anyway."

"But why?"

"I need to take a look at that office before they get in there and muck it all up."

She looked at the clock on the wall. "Okay. *Three* minutes. Then I call."

"Thanks." He winked. "It's what Michael would have wanted."

He slipped quietly out into the hall and walked to the elevator, feeling the adrenaline flow.

As he stepped out of the elevator, he grabbed a pair of exam gloves from a box sitting on a movable rack and slipped them on, then made his way down a hallway crowded with similar shelving units, gurneys, carts and IV stands. He made one wrong turn before doubling back to Michael's office.

"Jesus!" he cried, stepping through the door, startled by the sound of an empty soda can clattering across the floor.

"Jesus," he said again, quietly this time, as he stepped gingerly around the thickening blood pooled around the base of Michael's chair.

A scalpel was lying on the desk, covered with blood. He left it untouched. Not looking for anything in particular, he carefully lifted a few papers that had been scattered on one corner of the desk, along with a large reference book. He stepped over to a bookcase and ran his finger along the spines quickly; nothing seemed out of place. A second bookcase sat against the other wall; the books there had been pulled off the shelf and lay in a jumble on the floor. He bent down to take a closer look, and saw that, under the desk, Michael's desktop computer had been severely damaged, as if stomped on. *Not a very reliable way to destroy evidence*, he mused. Whoever had done this had been in an awful hurry.

A small wastebasket sat next to the desk. He bent down and rifled through the papers. On the bottom of the wastebasket he found a cell phone. Michael's, he presumed. He slipped it into his pocket.

Stepping back behind the desk chair, he saw Michael's coat hanging there. In one pocket, he found a small digital recorder, the type doctors use to keep notes. In the other pocket was a small plastic bag.

Hearing a noise coming from the direction of the elevator, without thinking he hurriedly put both items into his coat pocket. He got a glimpse of the police coming down the hallway just as he turned the corner at the opposite end of the hall.

1:09 A.M.

"Maggie, I'm so sorry," Kathy said, hanging her head. "I know you were close." Maggie and LaFleur had been on their way out when Kathy had motioned to them back in. "And you, too, A.C."

"But he's going to be okay, right?" asked LaFleur. "Maggie says a collapsed lung, but that's the worst of it."

"That's right, Kathy," said Maggie. "Dr. Eckard said it could be several weeks, but he's out of danger."

"Oh, no, I mean –" Kathy broke off, confused, then shook her head. "Oh, you don't know, do you. How could you?"

"Kathy, what on earth –" Maggie began.

"They brought him in earlier tonight, right before Michael was attacked," Kathy said.

"Brought *who* in?" they asked in unison.

"The professor."

They looked at one another, then back at Kathy.

"The professor?" LaFleur asked.

"Professor Szabó," Kathy replied. "They were just taking him down to the morgue when I came on duty at midnight."

Sitting Shiva

E. SEVENTH STREET, OSWEGO

"Rabbit! Remember?" asked Larry Spiegelman.

"Oh, God, yes," LaFleur answered with a chuckle. "That one April Fool's. 'Hasenpfeffer Burgers.' He nearly convinced me to make them a regular item!"

"He was always coming up with something unusual."

"Like recovering a seventy-year-old plane wreck?"

"Well, that's one of the more extreme examples, but, yes. And who else could have managed that?"

LaFleur shifted his legs, trying for a more comfortable position. The two of them were sitting on the traditional low stools, brought over for the occasion by Larry. There were three other visitors in the living room, neighbor women, conversing in low tones on the professor's couch.

"Have you ever done this before?" Larry asked LaFleur. "Attended shiva, I mean."

"Never. Sort of like an extended wake, I gather?"

"I suppose that's not a bad analogy. Without the songs or drinking. You're not Irish, are you?"

"With a name like 'LaFleur?' No, no Irish blood that I know of. Quebecois on both sides. But I've been to plenty of Irish wakes. The police department, I believe, is known to have a few members of Irish descent," he said wryly.

"You know, this is not what I would call a traditional shiva," Larry continued. "No family, for one thing. That's normally who is responsible. We'll probably cut it down to just two or three days, not the full seven. I think that will suffice. But I couldn't bear the thought of him going with no observance at all."

"What do you think about getting him relocated to Fort Ontario at some point?" LaFleur asked, after a moment.

"Next to Jeri?"

"That's my thought."

"Let me think it over. I would support it, but I think it could cause difficulties."

"Let me know."

"Well, he certainly had a long, full life," said Miriam, a woman from the synagogue.

"Yes, that's so," said Maggie. "Still, it came so unexpectedly."

"Well, he was getting up there in years. Just how old was he, do you know?"

"Ninety-four."

"Ninety-four! How wonderful."

"Yes," said Maggie. She looked around distractedly. She did not recognize any of the three other women in the living room; they'd all come together from the old Temple Adath Yeshurun in Syracuse. "Yes, I suppose so."

"Detective LaFleur?"

A.C. looked up from his stool to see Aaron standing above him, holding a manila envelope, which he then offered to LaFleur.

"Tiffany wanted you to have this. I went to the 1850 House, but they said I'd find you here, so, sorry to interrupt, but –"

"No problem, Aaron," LaFleur said, reaching up to take the envelope. "As you can see, I'm the only one here at the moment." He bent up the metal tabs holding the envelope closed and lifted the flap. "What is it?"

"It's the original of the article the Professor had given her to print in the Pall-Times. The one that never got printed. The clipping in there is what actually got into the paper."

"Oh?" Slipping on his reading glasses, LaFleur pulled out two pages of handwritten text and began reading. After a couple of minutes, he pulled out the newspaper clipping and read quickly through it. Then he looked back at the professor's text. *How did I miss that newspaper article?* he thought. *And why hadn't Tamos ever said anything about it?*

He slipped the clipping and the professor's pages back into the folder and laboriously got up off of the stool. "How much do you know about this, Aaron?"

"Just what Tiffany's told me. That the professor gave her this article for the paper, but her editor pulled it. She said someone from WGI threatened the paper, and everyone connected to the article, with a law suit. She can't afford that, Mr. LaFleur, she's only getting started, and the editor, well, he said, I mean, she said that the editor – if this gets out –"

"Don't worry, Aaron. No one will get in any trouble. I'll look at it, and get back to Tiffany if I need any more information; do you suppose that would be all right?"

"Sure, I suppose so. I'll tell her."

Aaron shifted from one foot to the other for a few seconds. "This is shiva, right?"

"Yes, that's right. Do you want to stay?"

"Oh, no, that's okay. My family, well, we never do this. I guess we're not very observant."

"Well, we're about finished with it, anyway. We're closing up the house tonight."

"Oh, well. Um, I'm really sorry about the professor."

"Thank you, Aaron. And please thank Tiffany, and tell her I might be in touch."

"Will do, sir."

As Aaron left out the back door, LaFleur took the article out of the envelope and read through it again, carefully this time.

What were you up to, Tamos?

He recalled his promise to Tamos, days after they watched the news conference with WGI. And now this, an article threatening WGI with the exposure of certain activities – wartime activities – that he promised would be extremely damaging. But no real details.

What kind of game were you playing, Prof. And what the hell do I do now?

It was late in the evening of the third and final day of shiva, and Maggie was alone in the house, doing the afternoon shift. No one had been in since nine that morning, since Aaron had come by and talked to A.C. She had not bothered to turn on the lights, and had nearly fallen asleep in the dark living room.

She got up off of the stool, stretching. She checked that the front door was closed and latched, picked up her purse, and walked back to the kitchen.

"Oh! I didn't hear you come in," Maggie said, startled at finding an unfamiliar woman standing at the refrigerator.

The woman, who had been leaning in towards the open refrigerator, jerked her head up in surprise. She was holding the door of the refrigerator open with one hand, and in the other held an empty milk bottle.

"I was…that is, I was about to go. I thought I'd come too late. I didn't think anyone was still here." She hurriedly put the bottle on top of the refrigerator and let the door close. "I mean, shiva, I guess it's over? I missed it?"

"Yes, we decided to keep it very short," Maggie said, puzzled. "I'm sorry, you are?"

"Oh, I'm from the synagogue."

"In Syracuse?" asked Maggie. "Adath Yeshurun?"

"Yes, that's right," replied the woman.

"Well, I'm sorry you came too late. Um, were you looking for something?" The woman didn't answer. "In the refrigerator, I mean."

"Oh, no. I…I was going to bring in something from the car. A large tray. I was checking to see if there was any room. You know how much food people bring to these things," she finished, rather lamely, Maggie thought.

"Well, as I said," Maggie told her, "I was just closing up the house, so, I'm sorry, but…"

"Oh, please, no, it was my mistake. I should have checked in advance." She edged sideways to the back door. "I'll be going." She nearly bolted out the door.

Well, that was odd, thought Maggie.

She locked the door on her way out, suddenly saddened at the thought that this could be the last time she'd ever be in Prof's house.

The woman cursed herself as she ran to her car, which was parked near the Fort.

Now I'll have to go back for it.

Too many mistakes.

The Lady Is a Tramp

NEW YORK CITY

"Sit down, gentlemen."

The taller of the two men slouched into his chair, crumpled jacket sleeves pushed part way up his arms; the short man smoothed the backs of his pant legs before sitting, adjusting his silk tie as he settled carefully in to the chair. Behind the large desk sat their boss, the sharp angles of his face and the bristles of a military style buzz-cut glinting in the light of a small desk lamp.

"I understand the job is complete?"

The men nodded.

"Not as clean as we might have wished, I think you would both agree?"

The men glanced at one another, still not finding their voices.

"Any fallout? Anything ongoing?" he prodded.

"Nah, the old guy is dead and buried," replied the tall man. "No inquest."

"Good. And what about your associate. Any immediate concerns?"

"Not as far as we know," said the tall man. "She should be on her way out of the country very soon."

"All right. Moving on. What about this detective, LaFleur? He seems to have inserted himself into the equation. Any issues I should be aware of?"

"Nope."

The man behind the desk repressed a sigh. "Can you elaborate? What's his current situation? Give me some background."

The portly man sat forward slightly. "Of course. Ex-detective LaFleur runs a bar and restaurant, the 1850 House. Small place, seems to be successful in a small-town sort of way. Local clientele, limited menu –"

"I don't want a Yelp review. Give me something relevant. Is there any reason to worry about this guy?"

"Sorry. We located an ex-colleague, name of Giamatti, recently retired from the Oswego Police Department. He was very forthright in his evaluation of LaFleur's character and abilities. Not favorable."

"He hates the guy's guts," the thin man said.

"Well, he doesn't think much of him, for sure," the other agreed. He pulled out a small notebook from an inside jacket pocket, flipped a few pages, and read from his notes. "According to Giamatti, LaFleur is a rummy who not only owns a bar, but lives in it. Was a lousy cop. Chronic gambler. Lives with some trampy nurse he's been involved with for a few years. Interferes constantly with local crime investigations, which always end up badly. So, we don't think he's capable of causing any trouble."

"Anyone else who could get involved in this, anyone associated with LaFleur who may be more competent?"

"There are a couple of other hangers-on. One, a geek kid, name of Blueray, of all things, comes around occasionally; minor arrest record, no significant education or employment history. Seems to be a friend of the cook at the restaurant, a guy named Frank Ivanovich. Now, Ivanovich: a little curious here. Giamatti thinks he is military but likely PTSD. We couldn't find much info about him, but he seems harmless. Has no weapon permits. Unexceptional military record. LaFleur seems to attract these reprobates like manure attracts flies. Gambling with each other seems to be their main deal. A pretty pathetic group, overall."

"And the doctor that stuck his nose in? That's an unfortunate loose end. Is he going to live?"

"Uncertain. Probably," he amended.

"That's too bad. What's our exposure there?"

"We think we've got that handled. Blame is squarely on the head ER doc, who has a history of disturbances and assault charges. As far as we can find out, he's the only suspect. There's nothing to lead to Fiorella."

"Okay, we'll need to keep a very close eye on that." He placed his hands on the desk. "What about the evidence that Szabó claimed he had? Anything new?"

The portly man sat back, looking over at his partner, who pushed his coat sleeves a little higher and shifted uncomfortably in his chair.

"Unfortunately, no. We searched the bar and house – and Fiorella poked around as best she could during her visits – but we didn't turn up a thing. Either he's hidden it somewhere no one will ever find it, or he never actually had it."

Buzz-cut leaned back. "Get back there and watch things for now. Stakes are at the highest level. We can't let anything get out of hand, especially given the, well, the complications." He sat back. "You can see yourselves out."

An hour later, another meeting took place. After providing a summary view, Wharton's principle black-ops agent sat back in expectation. He knew there were going to be difficult questions asked.

"So Szabó is safely out of the picture?" The questioner sat at a large desk in a darkened office near the top floor, his leathery, age-spotted hands clutching a small glass of amber liquid. He had not offered his visitor anything.

"That's right. Buried immediately – in accordance with Jewish law, as I understand – so we believe there is no cause for concern in that regard."

"Your people are still monitoring the situation." A statement rather than a question.

"Yes."

"And again, regarding the alleged evidence Szabó threatened to use against us? Nothing?"

"No, nothing has turned up in our searches. He either hid it away somewhere, in which case it is probably as good as lost, or perhaps he never really had it."

"But it could still be out there."

"Possibly." The man brushed a hand through his short hair, then hesitatingly asked, "But how could he have anything that could be damaging, after all these years? Isn't there a statute of limitations?"

"One would think so, wouldn't one? No, we may no longer have that protection in this case. Hence the need for drastic action. And for continued vigilance."

"Of course."

"We can take no chances. Things have already become uncomfortably complicated, given the situation left behind by your colleague."

"Yes. As to that, is there anything that –"

"You need not concern yourself. It will be taken care of."

"I understand."

With a dismissive nod, Wharton concluded the meeting, and the agent quietly left the office, unable to hide the worry in his face.

Job Security

1850 HOUSE

"Frank! Are those guys back again?" LaFleur had pulled a small side window curtain aside and was looking out at a nondescript car parked down the street. Frank had first told him about the two men watching the restaurant on the night they had celebrated the recovery of the aircraft with Tamos. At the time, he had been only mildly concerned, assuming they were interested in something related to the wreck, and would at some point make their intentions known. Lately it had become clear there was more to it than that.

Frank came out of the kitchen, wiping his hands on a towel.

"Yeah. Same guys as before, different car."

"Do we know who they are yet?"

"Tried tracing the plates on the previous car; Blueray has been helping me out with net searches, but hit a dead end at Hertz. The person on record as renting that car doesn't actually exist. At least not in the databases we've searched so far. Haven't tried tracing this car yet."

"Would the police be of any help?"

"Excuse me? Who is it I'm talking to here?"

"Just an idea. Never mind."

"They've been in here."

LaFleur jerked his head forward in surprise. "What?" It wasn't often Frank was able to shock LaFleur; he sometimes took a guiltily perverse pleasure in it.

"This morning, when we couldn't find Newton? Finally found him up on that pantry shelf?"

"Well, yeah…" LaFleur looked puzzled.

"When's the last time you remember him hiding? Never, right?"

"Son of a bitch."

"Yeah. They must have spooked him good. He held out for the good treats before he'd come down from there. And you know that back door?" Frank continued, "the one with the dodgy lock?"

"Yeah?"

"Someone jimmied it. Not that hard to do; I've been telling you it needs replacing."

"Been busy."

Frank grimaced. "Yeah, I know. Anyway, someone – not hard to guess who – spent some time in here, looking for something, from all appearances. But very carefully. They're pretty good, I'll give them that. Other than the lock, which I wasn't even sure had been jimmied, they left very few traces. If I hadn't known what to look for, or that I should be looking in the first place, I'd have never known there was anything wrong."

"What told you someone was in here?"

"Oh, no, I need some job security around here. I start giving away trade secrets –"

"Okay, okay." LaFleur turned back to the window. "God damn it. What the hell are they after? It's bad business, Frank, that's obvious. I just don't see it all, though, not yet. Whatever connection Prof had with WGI, it's created this shit storm. Prof's death, the attack on Michael. God damn it."

He jerked the curtain closed.

Fresh Brioche Buns

OSWEGO HOSPITAL

"How's he doing today, Frank?" asked LaFleur, standing outside of Michael's hospital room.

"Should be going home tomorrow, Maggie tells me."

"Wow! It's only been four days. That's good news."

"'Only four days,' the man says. Well, it'll be a relief to get off of guard duty."

"You know we appreciate it. Anything unusual happen?"

"Nope. Police have been here a couple of times, didn't stay long. Here this morning, as a matter of fact. To their credit they wouldn't tell me anything significant related to the investigation. Of course, that probably just means there isn't anything to tell. But other than that, no one other than the regular staff has been in. Besides Maggie, of course. She's practically been living here. She's here now," he said, motioning to the door.

"Yeah, I know. With you two here all the time, things have gone to hell at the 1850. Oh, well, everything'll be back to normal soon."

"Let's hope."

"Too right," LaFleur said, pulling the door open. "Talk later."

Frank nodded and turned back to face the hallway.

Maggie was sitting at Michael's bedside; Michael was asleep. LaFleur raised his eyebrows, mutely questioning Maggie on Michael's condition.

"Oh, you can talk, A.C. He's out. They've been keeping him pretty heavily sedated."

"He's doing okay?" he asked quietly.

"Yeah, they pulled the drain early this morning. He's really doing very well, considering how bad it could have been. He'll need to take it very slowly at home for several days. I'll stay with him as much as I can, and my sister has offered to come up and help out for a few days."

"Good, that will help a lot. Um, Frank says some officers were here earlier? Anyone I know?"

"Yeah, Bill O'Malley, with a younger guy I don't know."

"And?"

"Oh, they just asked the same old questions, about the argument with Gus, had there been any other incidents like that, and so on. Michael was barely awake and had a hard time concentrating. Bill pressed him on the attack itself, but Michael still can't remember much, no details at all. Just the surprise of seeing that it was someone in scrubs." She paused. "From what little he's managed to say about it, I think he's convinced it was Ladisio, A.C., and so are the police; I pulled Bill aside and he admitted that they have no other leads. Since Gus went off duty at midnight, right before the attack, he's the only suspect. At the moment, anyway."

"But nothing conclusive."

"No. But no other leads, either."

Michael shifted in bed, but did not wake up.

"I'd better go," said LaFleur.

"Okay. He'll probably sleep for another hour or so. Anyway, he'll be home tomorrow."

"Yeah, Frank told me. He's looking a little rough. He's been here the whole time."

"He won't leave! Walks Michael up and down the hall. And makes him walk on the inside, away from the windows! That man is not normal."

"He's just doing what he feels is necessary. And he knows what he's doing."

"I suppose. Can't be too careful, as they say."

"Right. Okay, I'm out of here. Let me know if anything comes up." A quick kiss, and LaFleur was out the door.

"Take care," LaFleur said, giving Frank a small pat on the shoulder as he passed by.

"Always."

1850 HOUSE

After Michael had been home a few days, with Maggie nursing him off and on, and Frank sending over food, LaFleur brought him over to the 1850 House for lunch. As soon as Michael sat down at the table, Newton jumped up onto his lap.

"Hey, Newt! Here to welcome me back to the land of the living?" Newton purred loudly in response. From that day on, he joined Michael every time he came in.

"You look like you've lost about ten pounds, Michael!" said LaFleur.

"Oh, God, A.C., don't let Frank hear you. He's been after me for days to eat more. Says he's got to get me back up to 'fighting weight.' If he thinks I'm still too thin, there's no telling how much food he'll try to stuff down me."

LaFleur glanced up as Frank came out of the kitchen carrying a tray. "Here's the first course."

Frank set down two bowls of soup – Michael's larger than LaFleur's – and announced, "English Ale Cheddar Soup." He put down a small bowl of croutons on the table. "Sprinkle a few of these on top."

"Looks wonderful, Frank," said LaFleur.

"Yeah, it's a nice golden color, isn't it? I first tried it out using Guinness, and the flavor was fantastic; smooth, rich. But the color – baby's best efforts."

"Um, well, this looks great, Frank," said Michael.

"Okay, eat up. Next course to follow soon."

After a moment, Michael suddenly put down his spoon, banging it loudly on the side of the bowl in the process.

"Something the matter, Michael?" asked LaFleur.

"Listen, A.C., you've kept me in the dark long enough. I need to know what the hell's going on. The police have been to my house three times, questioning me over the argument with Ladisio – why isn't he in jail, by the way? The coroner won't return my calls; says he been advised by the hospital administration not to communicate with me until certain issues are resolved, so I have no idea where the review stands. Both my cell phone and my recorder are missing. The police maintain that neither were in my office when they got there, so I have to assume Ladisio took them, to protect himself. And what about my diagnosis? Is there going to be an inquest? Where is Ladisio? Am I safe?" He sighed and looked at LaFleur.

"I'm really sorry I've had to keep you 'in the dark,' as you say, but it's been for your own protection. Frank has been trying to track down – ah, here he is with the second course."

Frank put down a huge platter. "Starters! Three varieties of slider: reubens, pulled pork, and fried chicken. On fresh brioche buns. Dig in!"

Michael just looked at the platter, sighing again. Frank looked over at LaFleur? "What's up?"

"Frank, have a seat. Time to bring Michael up to speed."

Frank sat down next to Michael, motioning him to his soup. "Okay, but only if you finish that soup and start in on the sliders," he said, turning to Michael.

"Okay, Frank, okay. Just tell me what is going on." Michael picked up his spoon and took a few more bites.

LaFleur reached for a slider, took a large bite, complimented Frank, put the slider on his plate, then laid his hands on the table. "All right. Here is where we are, Michael. Your questions are right on. Let's start with Ladisio. He is still the department's only suspect at this point, but there some issues. It's true that Ladisio went off shift just before the attack, and then disappeared. He was not responding to calls, no one knew where he was. He showed up for his shift just two days ago, and the police confronted him with what they believe they have against him: the argument, followed by his disappearance. The argument he passed off as 'a slight professional disagreement.' He explained his subsequent absence as taking time off for a previously scheduled hiking trip in the Adirondacks. However, the time off had not been previously authorized by hospital admin. Apparently, he's in some hot water over that. Still, he claims to have had no reason to believe there was any issue with him leaving town.

"And then there is the fact that his fingerprints were found in your office. When asked about this, he admitted that he had in fact followed you to your office right after the argument, but you were not there."

Michael looked up at this. "I didn't go directly to my office," he said. "I had to search around for a while to find a machine that had a Diet Coke in it."

"How long before you got to your office?" asked LaFleur.

"Oh, ten minutes maybe. Less than fifteen, anyway."

"So enough elapsed time for Ladisio to go to your office, miss you there, and then leave the hospital, like he says."

"I suppose so," replied Michael, reluctantly, it seemed.

"And he said he'd been in your office on other occasions, so his fingerprints could have been there from any previous visit."

Michael nodded.

"Then there is the assault and battery charge from New Jersey, from his stint at a hospital there in the nineties. The police really thought they had something there. Ladisio explained that; all charges were dropped, by the way, and no settlement ever paid. He explained that episode as a borderline-psychotic patient who became irrationally upset during an ER visit in which Ladisio had to physically restrain him, and, quote, 'verbally admonish the patient in a forceful manner,' unquote, in order to administer treatment for a self-inflicted knife wound."

"He never told me about that."

At this point, Frank nudged Michael. "You're not eating."

"Okay, Frank, hand me a pulled pork, please."

"Here you go."

"And so, Michael," LaFleur went on, "even though they have no other suspects, all they have against Ladisio is a weak circumstantial case. Really nothing to go on at all. But it's all they've got, and they'll continue to pursue it. But we believe you are safe from Ladisio."

Before Michael could say anything to this, LaFleur held up his hand. "Let's talk again about the attack. Have you remembered anything new, anything at all?"

"Like I've said, I had just filled out the review form when I heard a slight noise. Next thing I know, someone came crashing in. Dressed in scrubs. That's why I've been assuming – until now, at least – that it was Ladisio. That's really all I can remember. Oh, as I told Maggie the other day, I vaguely remember seeing her in the ER, after I was attacked. Were you there?"

"I came to the hospital, but didn't stay in the ER. Maggie assured me things were under control; they had a drain tube in your chest and were pumping the red stuff into your veins, so I took the opportunity to take a look around in your office before the police arrived."

"Jesus, you didn't! Wasn't that dangerous?"

"Ah, not really."

"What if they'd found you there?"

"That may have been a problem."

"You never cease to amaze me, A.C.," Michael said, shaking his head.

"Well. In any case, as the police told you, your office had been partially ransacked. Whoever did it was obviously in a hurry – books and papers scattered, your desktop computer smashed – the scalpel lying on the desk. I left everything exactly the way I found it, with a couple of exceptions."

"Have another slider, kid," said Frank, holding out a mini-reuben.

"All right, all right," said Michael, taking the sandwich. "What do you mean, exceptions?" he asked LaFleur.

"Your cell phone, for one."

"My cell. You have my cell." Michael looked aghast.

"Yes, well, it seemed like we should have it, rather than the police. If they had found it, you may never have gotten it back." LaFleur paused, managing to look a bit sheepish. "Oh, and I also have your recorder –"

"A.C.! Why haven't you told me any of this before now?"

"We've been looking into a couple of things. We still don't know, for example, what happened to the request for review."

"You didn't see it on my desk?"

"Well, I didn't know I was supposed to be looking for it, but no, I didn't see anything that looked like an official form. But," he said, holding up a hand, "we know you sent a message to the coroner. Just as you said." He pulled Michael's cell phone from an inside jacket pocket. "And we talked to him about it." He handed the phone to Michael.

"We had to dig though a pile of Yankee scores, stats, and commentary to find that email," said Frank. "Get a life, kid!"

"Take it easy on him, Frank. He still has the main course to go."

Frank laughed and got up from the table. "On the way."

"Why hasn't anything been done about it?" asked Michael, voice straining.

"According to the coroner, all he received is your short email message: 'Expect formal review request re: death of Tamos Szabo.' Nothing more."

"Yes, that's the message I sent," confirmed Michael. "Why hasn't the inquest gone ahead?"

"He never received the formal request, Michael. Groenik said he had no authorization to proceed. As much as he wanted to, he also said, after hearing what had happened to you. But the burial took place within twenty-four hours, as is required –"

"Oh, hell. I missed it."

"It was very perfunctory. Don't worry about it. We may do something more later, in any case. But anyway, there was no body to examine. And you were essentially comatose. Nothing legally could be done at that point."

"But my diagnosis. I made it clear to Ladisio –" He stopped abruptly as the realization hit him. "Oh."

"Exactly. Listen, Michael, until now, you have been in no shape to deal with any of this. The police see the arsenic angle as very iffy, at best. Linnabarger told the police that he believed it to be natural causes, due to extreme age. Your diagnosis – 'so-called' diagnosis, as it is being referred to – is being discredited as a hysterical reaction to a close friend's death, distorted by the hospital rumor mill and your antagonism toward Ladisio. Even the ER nurses at the hospital are playing it down, reluctant to talk about it. Cowed by Ladisio to some extent, probably, but still, no one is focused on it.

"But I have a bad feeling about the symmetry here, and it's not a good symmetry. Michael, the police still think – irrationally – that there were only two people in your office the night you were attacked. There were actually three."

"I don't get it."

"Okay. First, Ladisio. We've already covered his visit to your office that night. Apparently, you were still out on your quest for Diet Coke at the time, and he left. Nothing happened. So regardless of what the department is clinging to in their desperation to hang this thing on someone convenient, I believe we can rule him out."

"Okay, I guess I have to accept that. And the second was…?"

"Actually, the third. The janitor who found you."

"Oh, God, yes. Poor Consuela. She came to visit me the other day. She's still shaken. Burst into tears as soon as she saw me."

"I'm not surprised. She came across what must have been a pretty gruesome scene."

"So, if I understand you, that leaves, what, the second person?"

"Right."

Michael put down his third slider for a moment – he'd been hungrier than he'd thought – and asked, "So who was it?"

"The same person who killed the professor."

Michael jerked upright, giving out an involuntary cry of pain. "Oww!" He reached for his chest. "Jesus, A.C., I may have pulled a stitch!" He sat back, trying to assimilate what LaFleur had just told him.

"It makes perfect sense, if you think about it," LaFleur said.

Before Michael had a chance to respond, Frank came in with the main course.

"Up-state New York grass-fed rib-eye, medium rare; mushrooms sautéed in Bristol Cream sherry; garlic-and-gruyere mashed Yukon Gold potatoes; and fresh broccoli in a three-cheese sauce."

Michael looked up. "Are you trying to heal me or finish me off?"

Frank laughed a little uncertainly. "Well, listen, we're just trying to –"

Michael laughed in reply. "Looks great, Frank. Thanks!" He picked up the steak knife Frank had laid next to the plate and took a bite. "Wonderful!"

LaFleur let Michael enjoy his steak for a few minutes before he interrupted. "There's something else, Michael."

After taking another bite, Michael put down his knife and fork. "Okay, I'm ready for it this time, whatever it is."

"I found one more thing in your office. Along with your recorder. Oh, by the way, do you mind if I keep that for now?"

Michael shook his head. "No, that's fine. I don't need it at the moment."

"Good. Um, the other thing is something I found in one of your coat pockets. I'm not sure what to make of it."

"Yes? What is it?"

"A zip-lock bag, with a lock of hair in it." He held it up. "Is this important?"

Michael yelped again.

No Good Time

1850 HOUSE, UPSTAIRS APARTMENT

Late night was typically the only time Maggie and A.C. had a chance to talk seriously, especially as the past few weeks had been so frantic. It was always a relief to climb into bed, arrange themselves in a comfortable position, and talk.

"Larry Spiegelman is worried about you."

"What?"

"He saw you walking in circles yesterday, in the park across the street. Staring at the ground, muttering under your breath. Then you'd stop suddenly, he said, looking up and out in front of you, as if trying to look into the future, or something. He was afraid to interrupt you, so he veered off on another path."

"He should know me well enough by now –"

"Oh, he wasn't really all that worried. He's seen you like this before. I assured him you were just fine. But at the same time – he's right, isn't he? There's something preying on your mind."

"Yes."

"Okay. Walk me through it."

A.C. nestled a little closer. "Okay. We trust Michael's medical proficiency, right?"

"Of course."

"That was my starting point, as soon as I heard about the argument with Ladisio over the inquest. I've never known Michael to make frivolous accusations, or lose perspective, even in special circumstances. I can't imagine how he must have felt, coming back his first night, seeing Tamos like that. But still, I had no doubt in his diagnosis."

"What about Ladisio's reaction? Based on the accounts I've heard, it was pretty intense. And the two of them do have a history; the girls in the ER have seen it. Nothing like this, obviously, but there's been no love lost."

"Oh, I understand that. But even before it had become clear that Ladisio was just a convenient out for the department – nothing they had really sticks – I had my doubts. A disagreement like that simply would not have escalated to that level, that quickly. And when I learned that Ladisio had actually gone to Michael's office to talk, I discounted it even more."

"But Michael insists that whoever attacked him was wearing hospital scrubs. Who else but Ladisio? Certainly not one of the nurses!"

"No, you're right, that's still a puzzle. But the attack coming so close on to his diagnosis – that troubles me."

"You think they're related?"

"Well, there's a lot more than just the timing of the attack that bothers me. You know how mysterious Tamos has been acting – *had* been acting – about everything since the wreck came up. I never mentioned it, but that same afternoon he met with Larry and had him seal something in a police evidence bag. He wouldn't say what it was, just that he expected to use it in the near future, and had to make sure it had been legally sealed as evidence. But even stranger, he would not let Larry check it into the evidence room at the station. He kept it. We both argued against it, but, well –"

"Yes, I know how persuasive he could be."

"So, there's that. On top of that, he also told Jamila that afternoon to expect something from him, something related to the wreck; but once again, he would not go into detail. Just that he would need her technical expertise at some point.

"Then, last week, Tamos made a point of having me watch a news conference with him, on CNBC. It was the announcement by the head of WGI; you know, the big defense contractor? About stepping down in order to run for president. At the end of the press conference, Tamos made a very cryptic remark, cryptic even by his standards. Something related to Wharton's plans."

"What possible interest could Tamos have had in WGI? Or Wharton?"

"It made no sense to me at the time, either. But that's not all. At Prof's house, the second day of sitting shiva, Aaron brought me something Tamos had tried to get printed in the Pall-Times. An article accusing WGI of war profiteering. Or worse."

"War profiteering? Like, in the Iraq war or something?"

"World War II."

"Oh, A.C., that doesn't make any sense. That was, what, sixty-some years ago?"

"Seventy. Tamos and Jeri had just gotten married. Tamos had been to Europe and back. And then Jeri disappeared into Lake Ontario. In a P-39 with a red star painted on it."

"Oh, this is all too crazy. No wonder you've been walking in circles."

"You know the inquest Michael wanted never happened. But as he was doing his quick postmortem exam, he took a clipping of the Prof's hair. I lifted it out of his coat pocket that night, when I was in his office."

"Was that legal? I mean – oh, hell, what am I saying? Of course, you took it."

"I didn't know at the time what I had. But it's a damn good thing I did take it. I just got back the analysis from a lab in Syracuse. The results confirm Michael's diagnosis. Arsenic."

"Oh, my God. Well, we knew all along he was right, but, still. To have that confirmation! That changes everything!" She raised herself up on one elbow. "What are you going to do?"

"That's the fresh hell of it. I don't know what to do. At this point I feel like I'm no better off than the department with their fixation on Ladisio. It's all just weak circumstantial; no real evidence, just a lot of conjecture. Sure, we've got the hair analysis, and of course we could go to the department with it. But with nothing else, nothing to definitively link the arsenic poisoning to the attack on Michael, and no clue as to what Tamos had against WGI, where does that get us? Just another bizarre Oswego-style mystery, something the police treat in their usual slapdash manner, make a token attempt at solving, then quickly lose interest."

LaFleur laid back and put his hands behind his head. "No, there are still too many holes, too many missing pieces in the puzzle the Prof left behind."

"Larry must know something. Didn't you say he took care of the evidence bag for Tamos? Whatever it was."

"Yeah, that's where I was going to start. Go back through that whole deal with Larry. Maybe Tamos changed his mind and gave it back to him, or gave him more stuff to stash away for him. But then again, if he had, Larry would have told me by now. I don't know. There's got to be something we're missing."

Maggie turned to face him. "You'll figure something out. You always do. I'll help any way I can, of course. And now that Michael's safe – uh, Michael is safe, isn't he?"

LaFleur hesitated for the barest moment. "Yeah, I don't think we need to worry about that. Whoever attacked Michael did it in a panic. Not exactly a crime of opportunity, but grabbing that scalpel, the botched attack; I'm thinking it was more an act of desperation. Exactly how it relates to the Prof's death – well, that's the problem, isn't it? But anyway, I think the assailant is probably long gone by now."

He had quickly decided that this was not a good time to tell her that the 1850 House was still under surveillance, had been broken into, and that the same car that had been seen across the street on an obvious stakeout had also been seen in the parking lot of Michael's apartment complex.

No, this didn't seem like a good time at all.

Bone Density

E. SEVENTH STREET, OSWEGO

LaFleur climbed the back steps and let himself into the kitchen. The door, as usual, was unlocked.

Sylvie Podhertz had given him an extremely vivid description of the conditions she'd found in the kitchen that night – it had been cleaned up, of course, Larry had seen to it – but LaFleur still smelled death.

Too many deaths. He had thought himself well out of this, thought he'd had enough for one lifetime: the sordid yet mundane aftermath of violent ends, unknown assailants, and obscure motives.

But this was different. This was Tamos.

He looked around the small kitchen, trying to block the image out of his head; the stench, the mess. Tamos lying there, helpless.

He walked absent-mindedly around the kitchen; neighbor ladies had done a pretty good job cleaning up and clearing it out. As he turned to go into the other room, a glint of light caught his eye, from on top of the refrigerator. He stretched up to take a look, and saw it, pushed back, almost out of sight; it had apparently been overlooked. Just a milk bottle.

Then he remembered something Michael had said – the professor had been drinking a lot of milk.

Michael had said the professor's GP believed Tamos drank too much milk, and Tamos had countered by pointing to his excellent bone density levels. All due to drinking a lot of milk, he'd told Michael, no matter what his GP thought. Michael had also told LaFleur that he was surprised at how far along the professor's symptoms were at the time of his death. Normally, he said, arsenic poisoning takes weeks, sometimes even months, to manifest the signs he'd seen that night in the ER.

LaFleur reached up and took the bottle down. It was a familiar sight, with "Byrne Dairy" stenciled in red filigree script across the front of the bottle. He and Maggie had had the same milk delivered for years. Used their cream in the kitchen, their half and half on the tables. Byrne had been around as long as he could remember. The bottle was empty, but had not been rinsed out; there was thick layer of dried milk on thc bottom of the bottle. He set it aside on the counter, to take with him later. Then he made his way into the Prof's office.

There's got to be something here, he thought, as he settled into the professor's low desk chair. *Something we're all missing. And whatever it is, Prof knew he had to hide it well.*

The desk had been tidied up by Larry when he'd prepared the house for shiva guests, but Larry had assured him he'd left everything there, just arranged and straightened. Dusted. Put away pens and pencils, that sort of thing. As fastidious as the professor had been in his personal appearance, Larry had told him, it hadn't carried over to the organization of his office.

He began with a stack of loose papers at one side of the desk. Nothing out of the ordinary; miscellaneous receipts, coupons from Wal-Mart, a schedule of events at Temple Adath Yeshurun, a newsletter from the Caltech Alumni Association. He glanced briefly at each and set them aside. On the other side of the desk, Larry had arranged a small set of manila folders, some labeled, some not.

The top folder was unlabeled and contained newspaper clippings related to recent activities of Wharton General Industries. The clippings at first appeared to be very generic – some news releases, the announcement of a partnership with a segment of the Chinese nuclear industry (a quite controversial move by WGI, according to the article), the announcement of a bid for next-generation fighter aircraft, and a human-interest story, Mrs. "Chuck" Wharton at home, preparing her famous English Yorkshire Pudding – the Whartons claimed a long line of English Quakers as ancestors. Nothing to readily explain the professor's interest in WGI.

The next folder was dark blue, and had a red-bordered label attached, identified in the professor's spidery handwriting as "Hymenoptera." He opened the folder and began to leaf through the contents.

Well, this looks interesting. But what the hell does it have to do with flying insects?

The folder appeared to be a collection of scrap book items, all related to various aspects of World War II: D-Day, the liberation of Budapest, an account of the crash of a Pan Am flying boat in Lisbon Harbor. There were several pictures of Jeri, posing with a variety of aircraft. *Why had he never shown these to us?*

But what really caught his eye was a clipping at the bottom of the folder – a picture showing row upon row of P-39 fighter planes on two long parallel runways, the stars on their sides arrayed in a straight line stretching back for what looked like half a mile toward a series of low, white buildings. He had recognized the picture immediately. The same picture was hanging above the Wurlitzer juke box in the 1850 House bar. But unlike that photo – which was in black-and-white – this one was in color.

And the stars were red.

Flipping it over, he saw it had come from a magazine; the back side was a portion of an advertisement for Camel cigarettes. Also on the back side was a small, pink sticky-note, with two letters scrawled on it: *LF.*

What the hell?

Ah. This picture was meant for him.

He looked back at the label on the folder. And it hit him. The entire folder was meant for him. This is what Prof had promised, that he'd leave everything LaFleur would need. But the professor was playing this hand very cagily, from beyond the grave. Nothing was left in the open.

Hymenoptera: WASP.

Of course.

He found an old plastic grocery bag under the kitchen sink counter for the milk bottle. Carrying the bag and the blue folder, he slipped out the back door and over to Schuyler. He resisted the impulse to wave at Mutt & Jeff, as they had started to call them, sitting in their rental car in the pullout across the street. He'd just confirmed what he and Frank had known all along; these guys were not afraid of being spotted.

Which meant that they were very dangerous.

"What do you think?" The tall, thin man sounded worried.

"Looks like he only took that blue folder," answered the short, fat man, exasperated. "Nothing there to worry about."

"What was in the bag?"

"Probably found a half-empty bottle of booze. Waste not, want not, you know."

"Are we underestimating here? This is serious. If you have forgotten, highest priority."

"Listen, we already went through the old guy's desk. We looked at everything there, including the scrapbook folder. What was it, just a bunch of old magazine clippings on the war. Sentimental crap. Again, not what we are worried about."

"I suppose. But who knows with this LaFleur guy? Maybe he's not a dumb as he looks."

"Are you kidding? Did you get a good look? I'm telling you, he's got nothing."

"Not yet, anyway."

"I still think this thing's going to peter out any day now."

"Well, until it does, we keep on him. And the doc."

"Sure, sure. We'll keep on it."

"Okay. Let's get back up to the 1850 House. No telling what this guy will do next."

"Relax, will you?"

"Oh, shut up. Jesus, how do I get stuck with you every time?"

Juke Box Saturday Night

1850 HOUSE

"What does this remind you of?"

LaFleur held the picture of the line of P-39s out to Maggie, who was sitting at the bar next to him She looked at it for just a few seconds.

"It's that picture," she said, craning her neck around to look behind her. "The one above the jukebox!"

"Yeah, but in color. The stars – they're red! Just like Jeri's. And look at the caption: "BELL AIRACOBRAS FOR RED AIR FORCE, TO BE FERRIED TO U.S.S.R. THROUGH ALASKA."

Maggie got up and walked over to the jukebox, leaning close to the photo. "This isn't exactly the same picture, A.C.," she said.

"No?"

"No, there's no caption, for one thing, and it was taken from a slightly different angle." She reached over the top of the Wurlitzer and took the picture off of its hanger and walked back to the bar.

But before handing it to LaFleur, she stopped; something had caught her eye.

"Look at this!" she said, holding the photo close to the color version laying on the bar. "See here, where in the color version there are two guys climbing around on the wings of the plane in the foreground?" LaFleur nodded. "But here, in this one, look at that. Standing next to the second plane in line." She poked the picture with her finger. "That's Jeri!"

"Well, damn me for a fool. How could that have been hanging there all these years and we never noticed a woman standing there?"

"Oh, it's been there so long it was practically invisible. We never really paid any attention to it."

"No wonder the Prof always tipped his hat. He was greeting Jeri, every damned time he walked into the bar. For years."

"He was devoted. Devoted to her, and to his cause. To raise the wreck."

"The supreme effort. An elegant effort." LaFleur let out a long, low breath. "I need a drink."

He pulled two glasses off the shelf and reached for the Famous Grouse. "Ice, or neat?" he asked Maggie. She alternated, depending on mood, time of day, and season.

"Ice," she said.

As he scooped a few cubes into her glass and poured (his was neat), she went behind the bar and filled a small clear glass pitcher with bottled water. She put the pitcher on the bar and came back around to her stool.

"So that explains it," LaFleur said. "The red star. She was involved in the Russia ferry operation."

"But it doesn't explain nearly enough," Maggie retorted. "How did one of these airplanes get to New York? They were on their way to Russia. Through Alaska, according to your photo. A long way from Lake Ontario."

"Yes, a hell of a long way." He poured a little water into each of their glasses, raised his – as Maggie picked up her glass in return – and said, "To Tamos."

"To Jeri," said Maggie, tapping his glass. She put down her glass and picked up the photo. "What's this?" she asked, pointing to the corner of the frame. "There's some discoloration, some sort of creasing…?" She held the frame at a different angle. "There, in the corner. See it?"

LaFleur took the photo from her and tilted it back and forth. "Yeah. Odd."

He turned the frame over and felt along the edge. "Something hard under the backing." He used a fingernail to cut the thin brown paper along the edge of the frame, then peeled a section back.

They both jumped at the sound of a large key hitting the bar with a sharp, metallic ping.

"Curiouser and curiouser, said Alice."

"No bloody kidding."

The Tell

LARRY SPIEGELMAN'S PATIO

"Yeah, it was the damnedest thing – hidden behind the picture in the bar, the one above the juke box. We found it almost by chance. Is it a safe deposit key?"

"No, it's too large – it really is a strange looking old key – and no number. See?" Larry held the key up, turning it over and reexamining it himself. "However," he said, "I believe..." He held the key closer to LaFleur, drawing out the suspense. "I believe I *can* tell you what it is."

"Christ on a bike, Larry! If you know what it is, quit screwing around and –"

Spiegelman took a sip of his beer. LaFleur, impatiently, followed suit, taking a large draught. It was a hot day, and LaFleur would rather have been inside. Larry, however, spent as much time out on the patio as possible, sometimes into November.

"There is a safe in a New York City law office," said Larry, finally. "Now known as Penrod, Penner, Yerkes & Zook, it is the successor firm to Harry Zook's original XYZ law firm. Surprisingly enough, there is still a Yerkes attached to the firm, a descendant of the original partner, though he's been effectively retired for years now. They've kept Zook's name on the firm through the years, apparently as some sort of homage."

"And you know this, how?"

"Among the professor's papers, I found instructions to the firm regarding a particular safe located in their offices. I contacted them to confirm. It's remarkable that it's still there, after all these years, and in the same office once occupied by Harry Zook himself. Quite remarkable."

"Tamos would not be surprised."

"No, I guess not. Well, anyway – oh, by the way, have I told you I located the will?"

"No, I think that small detail may have slipped your mind."

"Don't be cynical; it reduces your normally jovial demeanor to mere conviviality."

"Reading the dictionary again?"

"It improves the mind; you should try it."

"What about the will?"

"Oh, I'm not ready to go into that just yet. I still need to clear up some issues related to the death. Let's get back to that. Anyway, where were we? Oh, yes, the safe. Since finding the document regarding the safe, I have been quite perplexed as to the whereabouts of the key, which is also mentioned, but was not among his effects."

"Well, here it is. What now? Can we get into the safe?"

"As executor, I can authorize it, yes."

"Make the call."

NEW YORK CITY

"Oh, I'm so sorry that Mr. Yerkes is not in the office today. He'll be very unhappy that he missed you. Would it be possible for you to come back tomorrow? That's the day Mr. Yerkes normally makes a trip into the city. He comes in very seldom now, you understand."

LaFleur looked around in awe. The office was right out of the nineteen forties; mahogany paneling, huge antique desk, woolen carpeting. The only things out of character were the phone and the computer. Even the secretary's hairdo reminded LaFleur of pictures of his mother from the war years – hair coiled around her ears, bangs. He felt as if he'd stepped back in time.

"Of course," he said. "But no, I'm afraid I won't be able to stay over. Please tell Mr. Yerkes I am sorry to have missed him."

"Yes, certainly. Now, as to the safe. It's in Mr. Zook's original office. It has remained there, unused by anyone except Mr. Szabó, all these years." She motioned to a small hallway to her left.

"I have Mr. Spiegelman's authorization right here," said LaFleur, pulling a paper from his inside pocket.

"Oh, that won't be necessary," said the secretary. "We do things on trust around here. If Mr. Spiegelman sent you, that's good enough for us."

The secretary got up and led LaFleur down the hall, opening the door and ushering him in as she turned on the light. She pointed to a small built-in cabinet in the back of the office. "The safe is right in there," she said. "Take your time." She closed the door behind her as she left.

LaFleur bent down on his knees and opened the cabinet door, and just as she'd said, there was the safe. He pulled the key out and inserted it into the old-style lock – he'd never seen a safe quite like this – and turned it, feeling stiff resistance. He backed off, and carefully turned it the other way. This felt better; much easier. The key turned three hundred and sixty degrees, and the door popped open.

Kneeling down even lower, LaFleur peered into the dark chamber. He swore under his breath.

Empty.

"Did you find what you were looking for, Mr. LaFleur?" asked the secretary as he came back into the reception area.

"I'm not sure," he said, cautiously. "Has anyone been here, regarding the safe?"

"Well, Professor Szabó, several weeks ago."

"Do you know if he took something out of the safe?"

"Oh, I wouldn't know. He had a briefcase with him, but I have no way of knowing if he took anything out of the safe. Or put anything in, for that matter."

"I understand. Anything else?"

She paused, as if uncertain about something. "I'm sorry. I suppose I should have told you right away. Something unusual did happen, about a week ago."

"That's all right. Something to do with the safe?"

"Yes. Someone claiming to represent a distant relation of Mr. Zook. Well, I was immediately suspicious. Mr. Zook has no known relatives that I am aware of."

"From what I know, that is correct."

"Yes. So, these two men came in –"

"Two men? Can you describe them?"

"One was tall, thin and rather shabbily dressed, I thought. His companion was shorter, but unlike the other gentleman, well-dressed, and very well-mannered. But, pardon me for saying so, he also seemed a bit, well, *sleazy*." The word was obviously not part of her usual vocabulary.

"And they were interested in the safe?"

"Oh, yes. They seemed intent on getting into it. Well, I told them in no uncertain terms that it was simply out of the question. With no authority, no credentials of any kind? As I said, out of the question."

"And what was their reaction?"

"Oh, the tall one was quite put out. He went so far as to make threatening comments; but his companion apologized for him, and they left. Did I do the right thing, Mr. LaFleur?"

"Absolutely." He paused for a moment, then asked, "Did they leave anything with you, or do or say anything else that might help identify them?"

"Well, no, they didn't say anything else. But you can see the CCTV record of their visit, if you'd like."

She said this so nonchalantly and so unexpectedly that LaFleur had a hard time masking his surprise. "Yes, please," he said, "that would be very helpful!"

It had taken just a few minutes for building security to locate the video file. It was the same goons, no doubt about it. And now he had the file on a DVD disk; hopefully Blueray could do something with it. But seeing those images really brought home just how far this had gone, even before the Prof's death.

The drive back to Oswego gave LaFleur ample time to think about what had happened in Harry Zook's old office. He kept struggling to understand why the professor would have emptied the safe, only weeks before. And then lead him to it, with the key. The Prof must have known that the contents of the safe were in jeopardy. That the same enemies he'd faced in nineteen forty-four were still a threat.

The professor had been a very good poker player, but like most players, had a "tell," a giveaway sign, a tic, a habitual gesture, a small behavioral idiosyncrasy that telegraphed to players astute enough to pick up on it exactly what type of hand was held. In the professor's case, his tell was that whenever he had a very strong hand, he would invariably under bet, making a bet too small relative to the pot or to his previous bets.

The empty safe was Prof's tell. He was betting nothing, but on a strong hand. And he had known that LaFleur would get it. Whatever had been in that safe was now back in Oswego somewhere, somewhere the Prof believed was secure.

Now he just had to find it.

Making Sense

1850 HOUSE

It was late, very late. The restaurant had closed hours before. Maggie had been asleep nearly as long. LaFleur sat at the bar, nursing a long shot of Famous Grouse.

He had hoped, when this business with the professor's search and recovery project started, to keep his involvement to a tolerable level. Support Prof in any way he could – to a reasonable extent – and wait for things to get back to normal. When Tamos had, to everyone's surprise (except of course his own) succeeded beyond what anyone had imagined – well, that had been incredible, to say the least.

And then things changed.

Never one for profound introspection, LaFleur had been trying for weeks to maintain an even disposition. He'd found in the past that prying too deeply into his own motivations more often than not led only to self-doubt, uncertainty, and a morose outlook on life, the universe, and everything. He'd found ways to avoid the worst of it, most times. In the very old family days, it was fishing, playing with the kids in the back yard, car-camping up-state. In the more recent bachelor-on-a-houseboat days, fishing, poker, and chess with Prof. More recently, Maggie had kept him sane, more or less. Still, it was easy to fall back into old habits: obsessing over details, playing out multiple scenarios over and over, driving every little thing into the ground.

And now it had begun to pile up like an Oswego lake-effect snow, threatening to bury him: the professor's death, the attack on Michael, the blocked newspaper article, the surveillance. The results of the analysis on the milk from the Prof's fridge. He'd not yet told anyone about that.

He had the blue folder in front of him. None of the items were marked with an obvious sticky note, but just as obviously Tamos had put this folder together very deliberately. LaFleur pulled out items at random.

The P-39 Airacobras sitting there on the long tarmac, lined up like Can-Can girls, noses kicked up in the air, red stars behind.

Tamos and Jeri posing together at one of the houses at Safe Haven, with a caption on the back, in Tamos's familiar scrawl, "Second Honeymoon, Fort Ontario, August 2, 1944."

An apparently original copy of an edition of the WASP newsletter, *The Fifinella Gazette* – printed on very poor ivory-tinged paper, in sky blue ink – which had, on page two, a song attributed to Jeri (her name penciled in next to the words): "Take it off, take it off / Cried the man on the ground / If you don't make it once / Then go on around / Raise the flaps, make a turn, try the pattern again / If it's clear, be sure to bring it in…" To be sung to the tune of the Andrews Sisters hit "Strip Polka," it was noted at the bottom.

A printout of a Wikipedia article on the classification, anatomy, and etymology of the order *Hymenoptera.*

The Edna St. Vincent Millay poem the professor had said was one of Jeri's favorites, *First Fig*. "My candle burns at both ends…"

A photo copy of a portion of a census of the occupants of Safe Haven, this section related, it appeared, to the Baltic countries and Greece. The name "Helaine Pterataxis" was inserted in the list (in the professor's hand?) alongside four other Greek names. An additional notation read, "One of the many Greek refugees."

LaFleur put the items back into the folder and poured another short Grouse. At least it was short by his increasingly distorted sense of volume.

Something had to start making sense.

Soon.

O Sole Mio

1850 HOUSE

The next morning came much too early. It took Frank's best efforts to get A.C. to drink a first cup of coffee.

"This isn't like you, A.C.," Frank said, solicitously.

"You're right, Frank. I can't remember the last time. Years."

"Maggie said you woke her up at four A.M."

"Yeah. Guess I made quite a ruckus coming to bed. She wasn't even talking to me this morning."

"That's what I understand."

LaFleur rubbed his eyes, muttering, "I'm getting too old for this, Frank."

Frank stood up. "Hang on about ten minutes. I'll be back."

When Frank returned, he was carrying a large platter. "Eggs Benedict Rancheros. Fix you right up. Plenty of jalapeños."

Before he'd left for New York, LaFleur had scheduled a meeting for the day after his return, with Maggie, Frank and Michael, assuming he'd have new information to go over. He had not expected to come back from the law office empty handed. Or to feel quite as lousy as he did now.

His intuition on the way home – that Tamos was trying to tell him something by leaving the safe empty – had come to nothing the night before; it now seemed like imagination working overtime. Just a few days ago, he'd felt on the brink of making sense of things – the confirmation of the poisoning, the attack on Michael, Ladisio, the goons hanging around – it all had to be related.

But at the same time, nothing bloody fit.

He'd asked Maggie to go through the professor's house and effects one more time while he was in New York City. He hoped she could find something to gain a different perspective, turn up something new.

She came up with a doozy.

By one in the afternoon, LaFleur was back with the living, but barely. Now that he felt up to it, the four of them gathered at the dining table in the upstairs apartment.

"You found these in the basement? I was down there," said LaFleur. "It was totally empty. Bare walls. The furnace. A non-functional sink."

"Oh, it is empty. But as I was wandering around down there, the old line ‘if these walls could talk’ kept running through my mind. The house is so old, has so much history. When did you say it was built?”

“Eighteen sixty-something.”

“Right. I kept thinking about what all could have happened down there over all that time. I was walking around, gazing at the walls, sort of meditating, I guess, and just as I passed that high little window at the far end, the light struck the wall just right, and I saw it.”

“Is this one of those long, drawn-out suspense novels?” said LaFleur. “Will we ever find out what the bloody hell you are talking about?” Michael and Frank laughed, but a little uncertainly.

Maggie just smiled. “You’re the one who taught me this technique, so don’t be so impatient.”

“All right, I guess I deserve that. I’ll shall attempt to be more concise in future,” he said, with an exaggerated formality.

“We can only hope. In any event,” she said, echoing a favorite expression of the professor’s, “as I passed by that section of the wall, I saw what looked like very faint scratch marks on the edges of one of the foundation stones. If the light had not been just exactly right, I never would have seen it.”

They all waited expectantly.

“There was a hidden cache in the wall. The stones were just a façade. There was a hollow behind them. And that’s where I found a small leather case. Full of letters between Tamos and Jeri from nineteen forty-four. Oh, and also her diary.” At this, she held up a stack of old envelopes that had been sitting on the table in front of her, along with a small journal.

“And they make *very* interesting reading. But we’ll get back to these later, if you don’t mind. I found something else, too.” She stood up and turned to leave. “Back in a sec.”

She returned almost immediately with a small, canvas satchel, and put it on the table

““That’s the bag Tamos had at the mortuary!” exclaimed LaFleur, as soon as he saw what she had. “Jesus, Mary, and Joseph, Maggie! Where did you find it? In the house? I never saw it there.”

“Yep. I guess you could say it was ‘hidden in plain sight.’ You know in the front of the house, that little airlock entrance that had been added on?”

“Yeah, with the steep steps up to it. Barely room to turn around in there.”

“Yeah. Well, just inside the door is a little bench; a storage bench, the kind where the bench seat lifts up?”

“I looked in there. It was empty!” said LaFleur.

“Yes, it was. But did you notice the shelf above the front door?”

“Um…no.”

“It’s easy to miss – it’s behind you when you come in, and so high that you don’t notice it when you go out. Well, I got up on the bench, and there it was, tucked way back on that shelf."

"All right!" LaFleur could barely contain his excitement. "Jesus, now we're getting somewhere. That's where Tamos put the evidence bag he had Larry seal up that afternoon. C'mon, Maggie, open it up!"

Maggie unfastened the two straps buckled across the top, then pulled the zipper open. She reached down into the bag and with a not inconsiderable effort lifted out a heavy object, placing it on the table in front of her.

Which left the others staring, some open-mouthed, some squinting in disbelief, at something totally unexpected.

A marble bust of Enrico Caruso.

"Look familiar?" Maggie asked, after letting the surprise die off for a moment or two.

"What the bejeesus was it doing in Prof's house?" asked LaFleur, obviously confused. "And in that satchel!"

"I asked myself the same question," answered Maggie. "And thinking back to the night the wreck was raised, and the sort of wake we had that night? Well, I remembered seeing Tamos come out of the restroom carrying the satchel. He bumped into me with it, actually. Of course, I never thought another thing about it. Until seeing this," she finished, pointing to the bust. "This is the bust that used to sit on top of the toilet tank in the gent's. It was there when we took over the place. I saw it every time I cleaned the john."

"And you told me a few weeks ago that it was missing," said LaFleur.

"Right. We just shrugged it off, remember? Some stupid SOB thought they had to have it more than us, I think you said."

"That's what I said," he agreed.

"But, Maggie," interjected Michael, "it still doesn't make any sense. Why would Tamos take it? It's just crazy."

"Maybe not so crazy. Once I made the connection, I brought it back here right away and went into the restroom – it was unoccupied, fortunately – and stood there, just looking around. Thinking the same thing; why on earth would he take it? Then I realized that he'd been carrying that satchel around with him all evening. Never let it out of his sight. So, I stood there, looking around, thinking, over and over, what possible reason could there be to take the bust? I stood in there at least ten minutes, just trying to make sense of it."

"And? What did you come up with?" LaFleur asked.

"Nothing. Not a damned thing. I put the bust back on the toilet tank and came out and made myself a drink."

"That's it?" LaFleur sounded edgy. "Damn poor story. A minute ago, it sounded like you were on to something. 'Not so crazy,' you said, as if you had actually figured something out." He began to stand up. "Just one more bit of nonsense in a long string. I'm going to go take a nap."

"I'm not finished."

He sat back down, glaring at her. "Okay, so we know that he took the bust that night, and hid it in his house, but we don't know why. We're still nowhere." His voice had gotten sharper.

"A.C., you're not thinking clearly. You just said it originally held the evidence bag, right? And he had it with him that night, right? In the restroom?"

He looked at her blankly. Then she saw it – the comprehension seeping slowly into his face, airbrushing out the hard angles, softening the accusatory edges.

"Son…of...a…bitch."

"Yeah."

LaFleur leaned forward. "That toilet hasn't been flushing correctly. I've been meaning to look at it." He leaned back and looked up at the ceiling. "Son of a bitch! That sneaky old bastard." He looked back at Maggie. "Go ahead," smiling now.

"Right. Well, I went back in there, moved the bust, and took the lid off the toilet tank." LaFleur was nodding, as Michael and Frank just stared at her. "And this is what I found."

She reached back down into the satchel. This time she pulled out a bulky, plastic bag. It was sealed by a bright yellow band of tape, the words "EVIDENCE SEAL" imprinted on it in large black letters.

LaFleur got up and went over to Maggie. He bent down and kissed her lightly on the cheek. "You're a genius."

"You taught me everything I know."

"Oh, you mean that ten minutes last week? Well, good thing you're a fast learner."

She craned up to kiss him back, hard and on the mouth. "I'd better get back to work."

"Thanks, Maggie."

"De nada."

After she left, LaFleur briefly explained to Frank and Michael the significance of the evidence bag – the possible significance, he corrected himself, still having no idea what was actually in it. He examined it carefully, determined that it had remained waterproof, and that Spiegelman's notations written on the exterior of the bag – the form recording the chain of evidence – were still legible.

While LaFleur had been looking at the evidence bag, Frank had gotten up and peered out the window. He came back to the table, agitated. "Boss, hate to change the subject, but there's something you need to know," he said.

LaFleur put the bag down – he'd been cradling it like a long-lost treasure ever since Maggie had left the room – and turned to him. "Shoot."

"Those two guys? The one who were hanging around last week?"

"Yeah? You mean, Mutt and Jeff?"

"Yeah. They're back."

"Back?"

"Yeah. Well, at least Jeff. I don't see the car anywhere, but one of them has planted himself on a bench in the park across the street. Looks like they have decided on non-stop surveillance. Working shifts, probably. He's there now."

"God damn it!" LaFleur shouted, jumping up from his chair, causing Frank to jump back in surprise. "God damn it! I've had enough of those assholes." He started toward the stairs.

"A.C.!" yelled Frank. "What the hell?"

"They're done, Frank. Done!"

Frank ran over to the stairway and followed LaFleur down, catching up to him just as he got the back door of the bar.

"A.C.! Stop!" Frank reached out and put a hand on LaFleur's shoulder. LaFleur brushed it off, grabbing at the door, pulling it part way open.

"Leave me alone, Frank. Those guys are done!"

Frank shoved himself between LaFleur and the door, slamming it shut. "Not on my watch."

This dumbfounded LaFleur for a second.

"What?"

"Calm down. You know you can't go out there."

By this time Michael had slowly made his way downstairs. "He's right, A.C.," he said. "You're letting your emotions get the best of you."

LaFleur moved away from the door.

"Yeah." He walked over to a table – Prof's table, he realized with a pang – and sat down. "Yeah, of course, you're right. You're both right. Christ, what was I thinking? We've got to be smart here. First Tamos, then you, Michael. And here I am, about to go out and bring them down on the rest of us?"

Frank and Michael came over and sat down next to him. The commotion brought Maggie in from the dining room.

"What is going on back here? It sounded like the place was being torn apart."

"Tensions running a bit high, that's all," said Frank.

LaFleur gave a small laugh. "High, indeed." He looked up. "Have a seat, Maggie?"

She pulled out a chair and sat down with them, eyeing LaFleur suspiciously. "Everything's okay, then?"

LaFleur just nodded.

They sat quietly for several minutes, not quite looking at one another, not quite avoiding looking at one another, no one sure of what was to be the next step.

LaFleur finally broke the silence.

"All right, damn it." He stood up. "To paraphrase one of Prof's favorite authors: the fucking game is afoot."

They all knew A.C. had finally been pushed over the limit. What remained unspoken between them was the knowledge – something Tamos had known all along – that A.C. was now the only one who could keep them all safe.

And to do that, he was going to have to solve the professor's final puzzle.

BOOK VIII: HYMENOPTERA

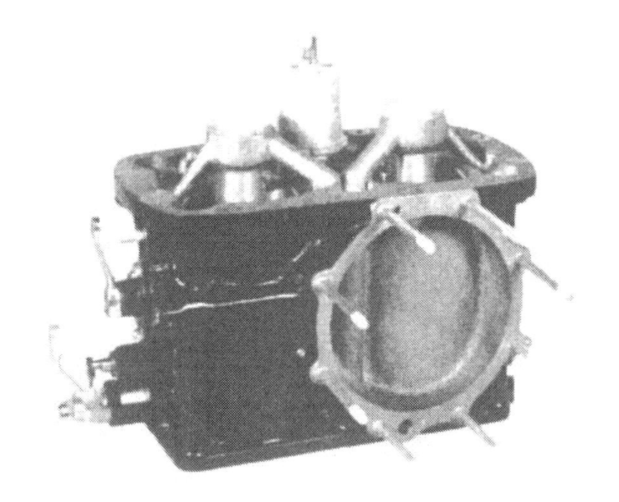

No Tickee, No Washee

KIM'S DRY CLEANING

James Kim was a third-generation Korean-American who operated the dry-cleaning shop two doors down, in the same block-long building as the 1850 House. He had long grown used to being stereotyped as the local "Chinese" laundryman. He and LaFleur had made a running joke out of it.

"Charlie Chan!" LaFleur said to Kim as he entered the shop, carrying an armload of shirts. "Just the person who can help me out."

"Oh, so now I'm a famous detective? I thought that was you!"

"Not even close."

"Well, at least I'm not Number One Son, but Charlie himself! Last month I was only Kato, so this is a real step up."

"Oh, yeah, you've had a big promotion. I need a sharp detective to help me out with something." He threw the pile of shirts on the counter.

Kim looked at the shirts with an exaggerated frown. "Not tablecloths? You always have tablecloths, all these years, and never any shirts."

"Oh, there will always be tablecloths, just not today. In fact, these shirts are actually clean, but I needed an excuse to come in here. I'll still leave them."

Kim took a quick look. "Well, they probably *are* clean, but I can make them look…well, uh, a lot better…uh, less, well, less dingy," he finished, apologetically.

LaFleur laughed. "I'm sure you can. Probably should have started bringing them in long ago."

"So, what's the real reason you're here, A.C.?" Kim asked, moving the shirts off to the side. "You said you need a detective?"

"Well, actually, an accomplice."

"Oh, now I'm back to being Kato again?"

"Not exactly. More like Number One Son, after all, I guess. Kim, you know the passages down in the basements?"

"Sure, the old bootleggers' tunnel. They connected the cellars down there to move their hooch around, back when the 1850 House was a speakeasy, wasn't it?"

"Yeah, exactly. Is your access to the cellar still in good shape? I mean, can you get down to your passageway okay?"

"Well, I think so. No one's been down there for quite a while. What the hell is this all about?"

"I may need to use the tunnel to get in and out of the 1850 House for a few days. Come up in your shop, here, and out the back."

"That tells me *what* you want to do, but not *why*."

"Afraid I can't say why, just yet. I don't mean to be overly dramatic, but I don't want to put you into any danger."

"This is starting to sound like an old B-movie."

"Oh, just wait until you hear my next request."

"Go ahead."

"I'd also like the use of one of your delivery trucks. To hide in, as I come and go, to various places. Um, I'll also need a driver. You got anyone needing some extra time? I'll pay well. And I won't need it too often; I don't want to disrupt your business."

Kim shook his head, laughing. "And I thought things were interesting around here when old Joe ran the 1850!" He handed LaFleur the claim ticket he'd made out for the shirts. "Sure, A.C. Just let me know when you need to get in and out. I'm sure we can work something out."

"Thanks a lot, Jimmy, you're a good friend. I knew I could count on you. And I'll explain everything, as soon as I can, I promise. I'll let you know when I need to get out; and I'd like to make a trial run in the tunnel, just to make sure I can get from my place into your back room. How about fifteen minutes? I'll knock on the door. I assume it's set up the same way as mine?"

Kim nodded. "Probably. There's a small door in back, with a narrow stairway down to the passageway. Like I said, we never use it, but I'll go check the door now."

"Okay. You'll see me soon." He turned to go. "And no one else will!"

Doohickey

LARRY SPIEGELMAN'S

"Well, where is it?" Larry sounded unhappy.

"It's back where Tamos hid it," LaFleur replied.

"Which is?"

"It's at the 1850 House. In the toilet tank."

"It really needs to go the police evidence room, you know."

"I can't do that, not after the way Tamos reacted to that suggestion. And that's the only reason we even have it now. Anyway, I agree with him, I don't think it would be safe there."

"But it's safe now, at the restaurant?"

"For now," LaFleur assured him. "I'll want to find someplace else for it at some point."

"You said when you got here that it needs to be opened, examined."

"That's right."

"How can I do that if I don't have it?"

"I can't risk taking it out of the restaurant."

"Then I'll go there."

"I don't want you to be seen going there."

"Seen? By whom?"

"We're being watched. It's complicated, but it has to do with whatever Tamos put into that evidence bag. I don't want to put you into any danger."

"Now you're beginning to alarm me."

"As long as I manage this properly, there's nothing to worry about."

"You'll have to convince me."

"You'll have to trust me on this, Larry. And I still need you to open that bag."

A.C.," Larry said, sounding unhappier by the minute, "if you won't bring it here, and I can't go there..."

"I have it all arranged. Do you have any dry cleaning that needs to be picked up?"

LaFleur and Spiegelman were sitting in the back of one of Kim's laundry vans. LaFleur had emailed instructions to Larry the night before – not trusting that the 1850 House phone wasn't tapped – and had had the driver back up into the driveway close to the house. Larry had brought out an armload of clothing, ducking into the open door of the van at the last second as the driver put the clothes in the back. LaFleur was sure they had not been followed, but could not be entirely certain that one of the goons wasn't watching Larry's house. The driver, a young relative of Jimmy Kim's, was totally into the James Bond routine, and had assured LaFleur that he could be trusted to the death. Too many spy novels, LaFleur thought, but was glad of the boy's enthusiasm.

Squinting in the dim light, LaFleur carefully unwrapped the oilskin cloth; seventy years under water had turned it into a covering as delicate as the skin on the back of a nonagenarian's hand; a hand he had been picturing for days now, a hand holding cards. He knew he had barely started the long process of missing the Prof.

What LaFleur had revealed under the thin skin of its protective cover were two objects – three, rather, as one had been broken in two. The smaller of the objects, the broken one, was an aluminum plate, something that apparently belonged to a larger mechanism of some kind. The larger was equally mysterious: a black, metal box-like thing about the size of a brick, or rather two bricks stacked on top of one another, with various levers, ports, studs, and what LaFleur could only think of as doohickeys, protruding from it.

"This could be," he said, slowly, still trying to work out the ramifications, "what Tamos intended for Jamila. He mentioned that he would have something technical for her to look at that afternoon at Henderson Bay, when the wreck first came up." He turned to Larry. "How should we proceed? Do we need to reseal the bag now, then reopen it for Jamila?"

"That would probably be the safest course," Larry replied. "We don't want there to be any question as to the validity of the evidence, should it come to that."

"I agree. Okay, let's put it back together, and I'll let you out of here."

A Very Good Chicken Spiedie

RIT

"What have you got for me here, A.C.?" asked Jamila. LaFleur had also arranged their meeting by email, still not trusting the 1850 House phone or his cell, and he didn't know where he could even find a pay phone these days.

"Remember the afternoon at Henderson Bay, just as they brought the wreck in? I recall Prof telling you he'd have 'something technical' for you to look at. This is it."

LaFleur had taken the precaution of bringing Larry Spiegelman along with him to record the transfer of the evidence to RIT. LaFleur had gone by laundry truck to The Knights Inn out on West Seneca, a regular Kim's Dry-Cleaning customer, and Larry had picked him up there and driven down to RIT.

They had just opened the evidence bag, laying the contents on a small table in Jamila's lab, as she looked on in bemusement. LaFleur unwrapped the fragile oilskin covering, revealing the pieces of aluminum and the accompanying mechanism.

"At the risk of repeating myself," said Jamila, "what is it?"

"That's what we need you to tell *us*," said LaFleur. "All I can tell you is that it was found in the cockpit, along with some other personal items. For some reason, the Prof insisted that these items – nothing else – be secured as evidence. For what reason, we don't know."

"Let me get one of my engineering students in here this afternoon," Jamila said, hefting the larger object. "He loves this kind of stuff."

SODUS POINT

A second meeting with Jamila, arranged the same way as the first, came two days later. LaFleur had them meet at a small dockside café in Sodus Point. He'd highly recommended their chicken spiedies. He'd come alone this time; Larry had left a car for him at the Knights Inn.

"What did we ever do before the internet?" Jamila asked. "I can't imagine how long it would have taken us to track this down if we were still plodding through, ugh, physical books in libraries."

LaFleur chuckled. "I hear that from Blueray all the time," he said.

"Blueray?"

"Oh, yeah. You haven't met Blueray. Raymond Levine, more commonly known as 'Blueray.' He's helping us out with some rather complicated, uh, I'll call them 'internet activities.' He's a young kid, self-taught computer wizard, a genius in many ways, even though he barely finished high school. He's helped me on cases several times, ever since – as Maggie so quaintly puts it – I 'took him under my wing.' We're helping him fund a computer science degree at SUNY.

"Anyway, I still enjoy slogging along with physical clues. And that reminds me: I need to warn you," and here his voice lowered, "please don't give me any details over the phone, or even email, related to what you've found, or will find in the future."

This was met by silence.

"Jamila?" LaFleur finally asked.

"Sorry, A.C.; I was just reminded of a short conversation I had with Red, at the lake that day."

"What about?"

"We wondered, based on the professor's behavior and a couple of things he'd said earlier, whether the discovery of the wreck might have, um, 'serious repercussions,' I think we said."

"That's your answer."

She nodded. "I understand. Well, I don't *really* understand, but I assume that will be forthcoming?"

"You'll be the first to know. Ah, looks like our sandwiches are ready," he said, noticing the counterman signaling to him. He went to the counter and picked up the spiedies, brought them to the table, and sat down.

"You made quick work of it," he said, as Jamila pulled a manila folder from her briefcase.

"Oh, knowing it came from the wreck gave us a huge head start. After looking at it, my engineer said he thought it was some sort of engine part; we assumed P-39, and found the basic information pretty quickly. We also tracked down detailed specs, located at MIT, and had those scanned and sent over."

LaFleur put down his sandwich and wiped his fingers on a napkin. "What is it, exactly?" he asked, pulling the documents out of the folder.

"It's part of a Bendix-Stromberg carburetor, used on Allison V-12 aircraft engines. As in P-39s, among others. Specifically, it's a part called a throttle body; it regulates the flow of fuel into the carburetor." She reached across and thumbed through the documents, pulling a spec sheet out and setting it on the table between them. "Here," she said, pointing out the part on the drawing.

"And the broken piece?"

"That's a key functional component of the body, called the throttle plate. We compared it to the plate in the body; they look identical."

"Well, that's a good start, anyway." He began putting the specs back into the folder.

"A.C.?"

"Yeah?"

"Why did the professor want the parts sealed in an evidence bag? Evidence of what?"

"Well, yes. That's the question, isn't it?"

Word Games

1850 HOUSE

LaFleur sat staring at the contents of the Hymenoptera folder, spread out in front of him on the bar. The restaurant had closed two hours earlier, but he hadn't been able to sleep, and had not wanted to disturb Maggie. And for some reason, he seemed to be able to think better in the bar. Even without Grouse; tonight, he was sticking with mineral water.

He'd told Jamila what the professor had told him, that he'd have 'everything he needed' to carry out whatever it was the professor expected of him.

The answer – at least the path to an answer – was hidden somewhere in the information in front of him.

Start at the beginning. Hymenoptera. He'd already made the connection to WASP, but all that told him was that the folder was related to Jeri, or the WASPs, or both, and that the information in the folder was all related somehow. So what else might it mean?

He resorted to Maggie's iPad, reluctantly at first, but was soon rewarded. He started with the root meaning of Hymenoptera, according to Wikipedia: "All references agree that the derivation involves the Ancient Greek πτερόν (*pteron*) for wing;" the professor's search had started in earnest right after he'd found the wing tip hanging on the wall of the 1850 House. He read on: "…a key characteristic of this order is that the hind wings are connected to the fore wings by a series of hooks. Thus, another plausible etymology involves Hymen, the Ancient Greek god of marriage, as these insects have "married wings" in flight." More confirmation that wherever this was leading was directly related to aircraft flown by the WASPs, and particularly by Jeri. But they'd already sort of known that, just by the photo.

But the photo also told him that what he was looking for had to do with the P-39s at Great Falls, Montana. The ones with the red stars.

In a few minutes, he had the connection; those airplanes were on their way to Russia, via Alaska, through Lend Lease. So how in the hell did one of them, Jeri's, end up in Lake Ontario? Back to the folder. There is the partial list of refugee names, one name, Helaine Pterataxis, marked with an arrow to insert it into the list as "one of the many Greek refugees." But there are only four Greek names in the list. Helaine Pterataxis had been added in what LaFleur recognized as the professor's spidery, European script. So there has to be some other meaning. Since Prof seemed to be playing with words here, he started with the name Helaine, the Greek form of Helen. Which, he quickly found, means "shining one," or "torch."

Well, that makes no sense.

What about "Pterataxis?" Obviously, "ptera" (or optera), once more, "wing." Well, yeah, Prof, I'm bloody well winging it here, that's for damn sure. Then there was the suffix, "-taxis." A quick search yielded "movement of an organism in response to a stimulus: aerotaxis, electrotaxis, geotaxis."

Prodding me to action, eh, Tamos? Well, I'm giving it a go. You'll have to help me out, here, though. We've got your evidence, but don't know it's significance, and so far, we've got almost nothing else. What are you trying to lead me to?

He shuffled through the pages of the folder once more. There was the St. Vincent Millay poem, the one about burning the candle. Sort of a torch, I guess. Something about this poem? He read through it slowly. One phrase suddenly caught his eye: "But ah, my foes…"

The throttle body was evidence. Evidence to be used against someone, somehow.

Against a foe.

New Lights

1850 HOUSE

“Son of a bitch! In the milk!” Michael picked up the bottle LaFleur had placed on the table.

“High levels of arsenic. The goons must have seen all of the deliveries he was getting and realized it was the perfect way to administer it. They must have started weeks ago, as soon as the Prof began to make threats against WGI.”

“But he was always so vague about that. He never made any specific charges, at least that I know of. And you say that he never gave you any more details, either. So why would that take such extreme measures?”

“That had me flummoxed, too. Until Aaron cleared things up, though unknowingly.” LaFleur handed Michael the article Aaron had given him that afternoon while LaFleur was sitting shiva.

“But I never saw this in the paper,” said Michael, after reading through the article.

“That’s because it never made it into the paper,” replied LaFleur. “The editor contacted WGI for a reaction, before going to press. WGI clamped down immediately, threatening lawsuits. It wasn’t long after that Prof began to slide downhill quickly.”

“Son of a bitch,” Michael repeated, softly, shaking his head.

Maggie had her hands folded and placed on top of a small stack of letters, as if to keep them from floating away, the letters she’d found hidden in the professor’s basement wall. She and A.C. were sitting at the small dining table in the upstairs apartment and had just finished reading them together, Maggie for the third time, A.C. for the first.

“Well,” LaFleur finally said, “that certainly puts a new light on things.” He looked up at the ceiling searchingly, as if expecting to see an explanation displayed there like a PowerPoint slide. “What was it she said about the evidence she had?”

She shuffled through the envelopes until she located the one she wanted. “Let’s see,” she said, pulling the letter out and skimming the pages. “Yes, here it is: ‘*With what I’m bringing to you, once we match it up with all of the documentation, we should be able to proceed with the accusations.*’ That certainly sounds like she’s referring to the device you gave to Jamila.”

“Yeah. And that really caught my attention, the reference to documentation. You know, when we found that key, the one to Harry’s old safe, I was sure we were going to find the rest of what Tamos intended me to have. Seeing that safe empty was quite a shock. I'd let my expectations build unreasonably, I guess. But now we know the documents exist; at least they did at one time."

"And the Prof surely would have preserved them, like he did these letters, and in a safe place."

LaFleur jerked upright, as if receiving an actual electrical shock. "A safe place." He chuckled. "Get it?"

Maggie looked puzzled, looking back at the letter as if searching for a clue as to what LaFleur was talking about.

"Word games," LaFleur went on. "Remember I told you how Prof kept saying how well I always played a weak hand? I think he even said 'empty hand' at one point. And my idea that the empty safe was a kind of a tell?"

LaFleur got up and went to his desk in the corner of the room. When he came back to the table he had the Hymenoptera folder in his hand, waving it back and forth. "It's all here." He put the folder down, opened it, and pulled out the refugee list. "Look, here," he said, spinning the page around for Maggie to see. "Helaine Pterataxis. A non-existent Greek refugee." He could hardly contain his excitement.

"I don't understand."

"It's simple. The documents? The ones that used to be in Harry's safe? I know where they are."

Maggie leaned forward expectantly, but LaFleur waved a hand to put her off. "But there's another thing these letters help explain: the red star." He motioned to the stack of envelopes. "That last letter. Read it to me again."

Maggie picked up the letter on the top of the stack and pulled out a single page, written on Great Falls Army Air Base stationary. "Let's see, first she talks about how much she misses –"

She stopped abruptly, putting a hand to her mouth. "Oh, A.C., this is probably the last letter she ever wrote to him." She thrust the letter at him. "You read it."

LaFleur, no less touched by Maggie's sudden thought, cleared his throat awkwardly as he began to read a passage near the end. "*'I'm truly in danger here. So, the sooner I get back to New York, the better. Thank goodness that I'm not military, I'd be court-martialed for sure – Harry says that as it is, I'll be lucky to get off, even if we succeed against Wharton. But he knows some very good lawyers. So, I head out first thing tomorrow morning...on a wing and a prayer. I'll circle the Fort and waggle my wings at you before I land at Syracuse. Love always, Jeri.*' So," said LaFleur, after a moment's reflection, "this letter not only confirms what we suspected, that the plane came from Great Falls, it tells us it was an act of desperation."

"But something went wrong."

“And she ended up at the bottom of Lake Ontario.”

There were no more words. Not for some time.

BOOK IX: A PLAN

Fer. Div. Form No. 75-10E 24 April 1944

RESTRICTED

AIRCRAFT DELIVERY MEMORANDUM

Bell Aircraft Corporation
Ferrying Division Installation

Niagara Falls, New York.
Location

TO J. Jillette Date 11-13-44 Memo No [illegible]
Pilot

Co-pilot Engineer

Navigator Radio Operator

Deliver aircraft described below to destination indicated.
Additional instructions:

Upon completion of delivery, crew will report to 7th F. G. Operations Officer, GREAT FALLS, MONTANA.

Signed Capt John R. [illegible] Control Officer
Name & Rank Official Position

AAF Form No. AIRCRAFT DELIVERY RECEIPT

1. Aircraft: P-39[illegible] Model [illegible] Serial No.
Russian Account; Pri [illegible] Proj. No. or Block Priority; Flight Order No. (if applicable)

CLASSIFIED EQUIPMENT INSTALLED ON AIRCRAFT:

OTHER EQUIPMENT AS LISTED ON A.C. FORMS NO. 263A AND 263B (Cross out 263B if not applicable)

2. Delivery

To: C O Great Falls AAB
Recipient Organization

At: GREAT FALLS, MONTANA Delivery Point; [illegible] 1944 Date

From: 55[illegible] AAF Base Unit (3d Fer. Grp.), Romulus, Michigan
Releasor

At: Niagara Falls, N. Y.
(Pick-up Point)

3. Receipt: I acknowledge receipt of aircraft with contents as noted above, and Forms 263A and 263B (Cross out 263B if not applicable)

Recipient Organization

[signature]
Signature of person authorized to sign for Recipient Organization

Rank and official position of signer

Distribution:
Copy 1 - Home Station of Pilot
Copy 2 - Pilot
Copy 3 - Aircraft Recipient
Copy 4 - Office issuing memorandum

RESTRICTED

SHIPPING & RECEIVING AGENCY
AAATC, STATION NO. 6
GREAT FALLS, MONTANA

Two Chumps, Same Bluff

1944: NEW YORK, NEW YORK

The Sportwing watercolor hung prominently on the wall of the library, to the left of Harry's desk. He sat there gazing at it now, remembering the night he'd opened the Christmas package, and how unimpressed his Wall Street friends had been, expecting a Matisse, a Gauguin. But Harry prized the painting more than anything else that adorned the walls of the apartment. He always made a point of showing it off to visitors, telling the story of how he'd met Jeri, and bragging like a proud father on her latest exploits as a Ferry Command pilot.

A military courier had delivered a packet of documents earlier that day, as Jeri had promised him in their call two weeks earlier. She'd also done her best at describing what the mechanic, Mike, believed the problem to be, stressing the failure of the aluminum plate, but told Harry that the information she'd sent would provide more detail than she could provide over the phone. Harry sat thumbing through the papers, looking for an angle. There was *always* an angle; sometimes it just took a while to hit on it.

Having helped negotiate the design and production of the Grumman Goose floatplane that he and his neighbors used to commute into the city from Lloyd Neck out in Long Island, Harry knew a bit, quite a bit, about aircraft manufacturing. Now it was just a matter of narrowing down the possibilities.

The key was obviously the throttle plate. Jeri had even had the base photographer take a picture of the broken plate for her. The documents provided by the Bell factory source were surprisingly comprehensive. They included not only specifications, but also procurement records for both the complete carburetor and for various associated parts, including the throttle body and throttle plate. The carburetor model numbers were complex. As Jeri had explained it, each model number contained codes related to the application, that is, the specific engine and airframe, a revision number, and a list number that specified all the parts associated with the carburetor. Some of the part numbers referred to the name of a supplier Harry recognized.

According to the records, Wharton Fabricating, in Elizabeth, New Jersey, was currently providing parts to Bendix-Stromberg. Wharton had been one of the suppliers used by Grumman during the manufacture of the Goose. He'd met Charles Wharton, the owner, a couple of times during production, but had never been to the Wharton plant. From the address, it appeared to be located in the industrial waterfront at the west end of the Goethals Bridge.

In any case, he had what looked like a very promising lead. He'd have to come up with a good excuse to meet with Wharton – calling it a "ruse" wouldn't be exaggerating, he thought to himself – and try to finagle the records he needed; copies of purchase orders, perhaps, or some other record of Wharton's relationship to the manufacturer. He'd at the very least need to get some idea of how to proceed. It wasn't much, but it was a place to start. He'd call Charlie Wharton in the morning, hoping to get over there soon, before heading back to the estate in Lloyd Neck for the weekend.

He sat back, a feeling of sudden exhaustion descending on him. One of Churchill's "black dogs" of depression coming after me, he though absently. It had been happening more often lately, more often than he admitted to anyone. Sort of a relief to have remained unmarried, no one to burden with these periodic slumps. Then he thought of Jeri and Tamos. Thank God Tamos had returned safely. Harry had refrained from ever confiding to Jeri his deep doubts about Tamos's chances of ever coming home.

His thoughts shifted back to the task at hand. It certainly appeared that Jeri had come up with something. How was he to make sense of it? He was just a lawyer – a damn good lawyer, he knew – but this was well out of his realm of experience.

Then it hit him. Tamos! Of course! Harry had never met anyone quite as smart as Tamos Szabó. And even though his academic career at Caltech had been interrupted by the war, Harry was sure that Tamos would have the scientific capability to take on this challenge.

He slipped the papers back into the mailbag, stood up, took a deep breath, and with a last look at Jeri's painting, turned off the desk lamp and made his way to bed, a determination in his step that he hadn't felt for quite some time.

Harry woke up with a plan. He'd had a slight twinge of conscience while contemplating what he'd need to do – it would involve some level of misrepresentation – but the stakes were high, and it was wartime.

As soon as he got in to the office, Harry called Wharton directly, thinking his Grumman connection was a good way in; the personal touch, Harry found, more often than not greased the skids.

It didn't quite work as expected this time.

"Yes, Zook, Harry Zook. I worked with Charles on a project at Grumman Aircraft. I'm sure he'll remember me. No, I don't have an appointment; as I indicated earlier, I'd like to *make* an appointment. Yes, I'm sure Mr. Wharton is very busy. Well, could I leave a message? Please tell him I'd like to speak with him concerning a possible investment in the company. Yes, an investment in Wharton Fabricating. Yes, please have him call me at his earliest convenience. Zook. Of Xerxes, Yerkes, and Zook." Harry gave the receptionist his office number. "Yes, as soon as possible. Thank you so much."

When Wharton finally called back, Harry told him that he was representing a client interested in investing in a war-related industry, preferably something easily acquired, perhaps raw materials, and that he'd remembered a conversation he'd had with Wharton along these lines at one of the Grumman production meetings. (He didn't, actually, but then, he was betting that neither would Wharton.) Promoting war bonds was fine, Harry explained, but if you could support the war in some direct manner, it made pretty good publicity. And didn't hurt the bottom line any. He thought Charlie might have some good leads.

Harry's suggestion produced the desired response. Wharton mentioned a few possibilities, including steel, aluminum, and asbestos. At the mention of aluminum, Harry's ears practically twitched.

The throttle plate was made of aluminum.

Harry hinted to Wharton that he'd already been thinking of aluminum. Wharton agreed that aluminum probably had greatest potential at the moment. Any specific vendors? Harry asked. Well, Wharton said, we deal primarily with a company called Allied Aluminum. But there are other possibilities. He'd be glad to talk to Harry about it in more detail. Sure, for you, Harry, Friday would be fine. Ten o'clock?

As soon as he got off the phone with Wharton, Harry called a commodities trader he knew. The trader confirmed that Allied Aluminum did indeed do business with Wharton Fabricating, quite a bit of business. Harry thanked him and buzzed his secretary.

"I know it's short notice," he said. "It doesn't have to be top management. Just try to get me an appointment at Allied Aluminum with someone who can confirm business dealings with Wharton Fabricating. Yeah, as soon as possible; tomorrow, if you can. Tell them it's part of an ongoing negotiation for a third party or something, investment potential, business opportunities, you know the lingo. Doesn't have to be specific; whenever a lawyer shows up, people tend to divulge things they shouldn't, fearing the worst. Or best." He paused. "Yes, buzz me as soon as you have something arranged. Thanks."

While he waited, Harry finished his roll and coffee. It was no more than fifteen minutes later that Marge came in to his office.

"Okay, Harry, you're set to meet with a Mr. Bowles of the Allied Aluminum sales department, at eleven tomorrow morning. I'll have a train ticket for you this afternoon; they're located in Trenton."

"Marge, you are a wonder. Thanks." As she turned to go, Harry called her back. "Forgot to tell you, I have an out-of-office appointment on Friday at ten. Can you adjust my schedule?" She made a face. "Yeah, I know, I'm a tyrant."

Harry knew that Allied would have no knowledge of any problems with throttle bodies; after all, they were just in the business of supplying aluminum blanks. No, it had to be something happening at Wharton that was behind the failures. But what, exactly?

And how to prove it?

Harry rehearsed his story on the train all the way to Trenton, so that by the time he got there he almost believed it himself.

After a few minutes in an anteroom, Harry was escorted into the office of Bertram Bowles, sales director.

"How can I help you, Mr., um, Zook, is it?" said Bowles, offering his hand as he came around his desk. A portly man dressed in an ill-fitting blue suit and brown shoes, with a greasy comb-over and beads of perspiration dotting his forehead, Bowles did not look the part of a director of a successful company. Harry's source, however, had praised Allied.

"Yes, Harry Zook, Xerxes, Yerkes, and Zook, New York City. Pleased to meet you." Bowles indicated that Harry should sit.

"And how can I help you, Mr. Zook?"

"Well, I'll get right to it. My firm has been asked to put together some data regarding raw material production –"

"Are you with the WPB?" Bowles interrupted.

"The WPB? Oh, the War Production Board. No, well, not directly, no. We have a client interested in investing in a customer of yours, Wharton Fabricating, and I'm here to do some due diligence. Our client is particularly interested in the aluminum production capabilities at the plant here. Wharton has an eye to ramping up their production of certain aircraft-related parts, but before they move forward with any expansion they need to be sure they have a reliable source of raw materials. It's my understanding that Wharton has purchased a considerable amount of aluminum stock recently," he went on. "If possible, we'd like an assurance that Allied has the wherewithal to ramp up production, by perhaps thirty or forty percent, maybe even more. Should the need arise."

Bowles hesitated. "I'm not sure I should discuss our production capabilities," he said, "without authorization from our managing director."

"Ah, well, that is understandable. As a matter of fact, I do have a dual purpose in coming here today, which I believe may require talking with someone in a position to discuss more complicated business issues, rather than strictly production."

"And that purpose might be?"

"To be frank, my client may actually be interested in acquiring Wharton Fabricating outright. Apparently – and this is confidential, of course –" Bowles nodded knowingly as Harry continued his spiel. "Wharton is having, well, some financial difficulties at the moment, and our client feels this presents an opportunity. So, I'm sure you can see that makes it even more imperative that we understand the nature of Allied's business relationship with them."

"And your client. May I ask who you are representing?" said Bowles.

"Ah, I'm sorry. I can't reveal that at the moment."

Bowles looked perturbed, but continued. "You just said you have certain financial information related to Wharton, information that would be significant in terms of our dealings with them. Can you provide specifics?"

"Again, I have to plead client confidentiality at this point. If in the future, however, we see a way forward, our firm may – for a very nominal fee – be in a position to facilitate such dealings, perhaps even bring Allied in on the deal?"

At this suggestion, Bowled leaned forward anxiously. Harry paused, considering his next move. "To that end," he went on, "and with an eye to moving forward quickly, would it be possible to get some confirmation of the extent of Allied's business with Wharton? Copies of pertinent purchase orders, for example?" He was really winging it now.

"Please excuse me for a moment?" Bowles picked up his phone and motioned that Harry was free to leave the room.

"Of course. I'll just wait outside..." Harry closed the door behind him.

A few minutes later Bowles gestured through the office window for Harry to come back into the office. "We may be interested in pursuing some sort of business arrangement," he said, as Harry came back in, "but before we go any further I'll need to have a discussion with our president and other members of the board. As to providing the business information you alluded to, I have been authorized to provide an example of a recent Wharton contract, specifically related to aluminum purchases. I believe this should satisfy the immediate requirements of your client?"

"Absolutely," replied Harry, trying to mask the relief in his voice. "I believe that will be adequate."

"Please see my secretary on your way out. She will provide you with the pertinent documents. Now, I really must get back to other matters."

"Of course, sir. Thank you for taking the time to see me on such short notice; I appreciate it."

"Certainly, certainly," said Bowles expansively. "Hope we can do business."

Harry pulled up to the front entrance of Wharton Fabricating at precisely 9:55 A.M. Friday morning.

The plant was much larger than he'd expected. Nestled in amongst scrap yards and long rows of warehouses, it took up most of a large block, with what looked like extended facilities branching off along the small streets at the terminus of the bridge.

The receptionist looked past Harry pointedly, obviously making note of the large black Packard town car sitting in front of the main office entrance. Harry reached into his vest pocket and pulled out a business card with a flourish; the habits of some of his more flamboyant Broadway clients were rubbing off on him, he realized, but a grand entrance almost never went unrewarded.

"Harrison Zook, of Xerxes, Yerkes, and Zook. I spoke with Charlie earlier; I believe he's expecting me?"

"If you mean *Mr. Wharton*, then yes, I believe you may have an appointment." She started thumbing through what looked like an appointment book.

Uh, oh. This gal's pretty hard-boiled. Can't push her.

"Ah, yes, thank you. I hope I'm not inconveniently early?"

She closed the book, and in a marginally warmer voice, replied, "No, you're right on time. I'll buzz Mr. Wharton. One moment."

"Thank you."

"Harry! Great to see you!" gushed Charles Wharton as Harry was shown in. "You look fantastic. What a suit! You show biz guys…always look smart." Charlie Wharton acted as if Harry were his long-lost brother, a technique Harry had all but given up. It was just too transparent, even among his Broadway crowd. *Oh, well, just have to go along with it.*

"Charlie! You're looking great, too, how long has it been? Say, thanks for seeing me on such short notice. I know you must be up to your ass in production issues. Everybody needs everything, and then more of everything, and they want it yesterday, right?"

"Too right, Harry. Enough is never enough in this business."

"So, I won't waste your time. You mentioned aluminum yesterday morning –"

"Up and coming. Steel, of course, that's the bread and butter of the war effort, but aluminum, now; some things can't be done using anything else. We're using a lot of the stuff."

"Well, I'm glad to hear it. After we talked yesterday I contacted a Wall Street associate – no, no names," Harry said, waving his hand "and he's very bullish on Allied Aluminum. Says they are nipping at Alcoa's heels but may be prime for a takeover. And it sounds like just the thing my client is looking for. So, I need to do a little due diligence."

"Harry, I need a little more to go on. What exactly are you after?"

"Like I said, due diligence. Confirmation of existing contracts, ongoing business. Nothing confidential, mind you, just the same kind of thing you'd report to your shareholders, say. It would help quantify what we're – that is, what my client – is looking for, in terms of their future revenue prospects."

"Why should I give you information that might compromise our business with a supplier?"

"Well, like I said, the firm looks to be a perfect candidate for a buyout." Harry sweetened the pot. "Confidentially, Charlie, they may be in trouble. My associate says they've been shopping loans." Harry inwardly cringed; this kind of double-dealing was not his normal operating procedure. He forged ahead. "We don't want to lose the opportunity to make a play before they go somewhere else."

"Of course." Wharton leaned back, striking a pose of contemplation. "Well, I'm not so sure we should be sharing that kind of information –"

"Based on what I find, we'd be perfectly willing to share whatever we come up with related to their position. And we'd certainly bring you on board."

"Well...I suppose there's no harm in doing some preliminary investigation." Wharton stood up, now all business. "Let me make a quick visit to the contracts department."

As Wharton left the office, Harry couldn't believe his luck. At the same time, he couldn't help wondering, *what is this guy really up to?*

Wharton was gone more than ten minutes, leading Harry to doubt even more that his fishing expedition was going to turn up anything. When Wharton returned, he was all smiles. "All set," he said. "Just ask the receptionist to take you to the contracts room. She'll know where to look."

Harry stood and offered his hand. "Thanks, Charlie. I'm sure this could be mutually beneficial."

"I hope so, Harry. No, I'm *sure* so." He let go of Harry's hand. "Just see the receptionist. She'll take care of you. Stop back in when you're done and we'll talk more."

"Will do."

As soon as Harry left the room. Wharton picked up the phone. "Sarah? Get me Lloyd."

A few minutes later, a tall man in an exquisitely tailored pin-striped suit came into Wharton's office. "Charles. You needed to see me?"

"Ah, Lloyd." Wharton motioned to the man to take a seat. "I've just had a very interesting conversation with Harry Zook. Know him?"

"New York lawyer, right? But the firm's not too reputable, as I hear it."

"Right. Xerxes, Yerkes, and Zook. Jewish immigrant firm, upstarts. They call them XYZ on the street. Zook's a show-biz lawyer, and, no surprise, the firm has close ties to big money."

"And what does this have to do with me?"

"Well, Lloyd, as 'President' of the company, I thought you'd be interested in a little deal I'm cooking up." Charles Wharton held the majority interest in the fabrication firm, but for both personal and political reasons preferred to stay in the background. Lloyd Worthington made the prefect front man. A Boston Brahmin on the outs with his family and relocated to the big city to make his own fortune, Worthington had the credentials and social network that Wharton needed to further his ambitions. "Zook just brought me an opportunity. You know Allied Aluminum?"

"Sure. One of our big suppliers."

"Right. Well, Harry tells me they are in trouble, possibly up for sale. Outright, or maybe loan to own. If I play my cards right, I think we can parlay this into a sweet deal. A year ago, we were paying an arm and a leg for aluminum. Our arrangement with Allied has been a godsend. And now we have a chance to actually own it. Jesus, I can't bear to think of the margins. If you think we've been doing well on our aluminum stock purchases lately, wait until I'm done with Harry Zook and his big investment deal."

Fifteen minutes later, Sarah ushered Harry into Wharton's office for the second time.

"Sarah, did you get Mr. Zook everything he needed?"

"Yes, sir. I mimeographed several pages of contracts for Mr. Zook."

"Thank you, Sarah. That will be all for now."

"Yes, thank you very much, Sarah," added Harry. Sarah glared at Harry, dipped her head to Wharton, and retreated.

"Please, Harry, sit," Wharton gestured. "I've been thinking about how we might expand our partnership in this little venture of yours."

"Oh?" said Harry, warily.

"Perhaps you've heard the rumors? We're unhappy with our current corporate law representation."

"I hadn't heard that, actually."

"Well, they aren't that well known, I suppose. Burton, Burton, and Warburton, of Stamford, Connecticut. No? Well, certainly not as well-known as XYZ, but, in any case, we've just terminated our contract with them."

Harry sat silently, wondering where this was leading.

"If your information on Allied is correct – and I trust that it is – it could be extremely beneficial on both sides to have a much closer relationship. Especially now that we are in need of new legal representation. Do you get my drift?"

"Well, if I understand you correctly, I'm not sure that we can ethically..."

"Oh, come now, Harry. We both know how the world works."

Harry couldn't believe it. Wharton actually winked at him! This guy should be on Broadway.

"C'mon, Harry. Who's your client? Hollywood? Or is it old Long Island money?" Wharton's envy practically washed the room with a green haze.

"Well, I really shouldn't be letting this out, but, well, the first name is Joe, if that helps."

Wharton looked smug. "Last name wouldn't start with 'K,' would it?"

"Could be. Not saying it *is*, mind you."

"Then we'll need to move quickly. If you'll excuse me?"

Harry knew he had him.

After Harry was safely in his town car and down the road, Wharton called Worthington back in.

"You didn't! Client contracts?" Worthington was astute enough to know he may be a figurehead, but he still took what little responsibility he had seriously.

"Hey, he only got what I wanted him to get. Enough to convince him that we have an interest in buying out Allied. And now we have an inside track. He's willing to cooperate in a takeover deal."

"But, Charles, what confidence do you have that he won't just take the information to his client and cut us out?"

"Ah, that's the beautiful part. I told him we needed a new law firm, to replace Burton. We'll work in tandem, I told him. More in it for all of us. Pretty sure he is interested."

"You can't mean we're going to hire those Yids!"

"Calm down, Worthy. Of course not. But now we're in the cat bird seat. I can't wait to see Harry's face when he reads the financial pages a few weeks from now. 'Allied Aluminum Purchased by Wharton Fabricating.' Not to mention the fact that now we will be in a hell of a good position regarding getting in on the B-29. They were already *that close* to signing; now it's a done deal. Do you realize how big that program is, Worthy? Do you? Fortunes are waiting to be made! We can be as big as Boeing!" He smiled.

Worthington had heard it before. "And you trust this Zook character?"

"Oh, hell, Worthington, don't look so pessimistic. This is exactly the chance we've been waiting for." Wharton's smile widened. "And don't worry; I've got Zook over a barrel."

7075

NEW YORK, NEW YORK

Harry sat at his desk staring down at two nearly identical purchase orders for aluminum stock; one from Wharton, and one from Allied. The dates were the same; the quantities matched; in every detail but one, the P.O.s looked the same.

On one P.O., the one from Allied, the aluminum specified was termed "2420." The Wharton P.O. specified a different number, "7075."

Harry picked up the phone.

"Operator? Yes, I'd like to place a call to the Emergency Refugee Center at Fort Ontario, New York. Yes, the number is Circle-7-2288. The administrative office, Building 104. Yes, I'll hold."

Harry knew it would be at least an hour before the message he left got to Tamos, and sometime after that for Tamos to call back, an hour or maybe more if there was a line at the telephone. The residents were only allowed a limited amount of time for outside phone calls, and they had to have good reason to make the call. Making a call back to someone who had called in to the center was easier than initiating a call, so Harry knew Tamos would eventually get back to him.

Two other calls came in while Harry waited, each one raising his level of anxiety. The third call was from Tamos.

"Harry! Hello!"

"Hello, Tamos. How are you?"

"Good, Harry. I had a very busy day today. We are organizing a Boy Scout troop, right here in the camp, can you believe it?"

"That's wonderful, Tamos! Let me know if I can help in any way – uniforms, equipment, whatever you need."

"Harry, thank you. I will let you know. We are getting a lot of help from the town, of course; they are very anxious to help everyone in here feel like a part of the community. But why did you call?"

"Tamos, I need some advice. I've made some progress in terms of figuring out some of the details of carburetor components, but I came across something that might or might not be an issue. It has to do the grade of aluminum used to manufacture the throttle bodies, or throttle plates, I guess. The plate is the critical component, is that right?"

"Yes. As far as we know from what Jeri and Mike have sent you, that is what is failing."

"Okay, here's my question. I have copies of what look like identical purchase orders for aluminum, from both sides of the transaction, Wharton and Allied. But the Wharton P.O. specifies one material specification number for the aluminum stock, and the Allied order, the order that was actually filled, shows a different number. Could that be significant?"

"Harry, off hand, I cannot say. Depending on what those numbers mean, I guess it could be significant. It is certainly worth looking into. Can you get more information from Allied on exactly what it is they are supplying to Wharton? Who have you been dealing with there?"

"My meeting was with one of their sales directors. I'm trying to pull the wool over their eyes; convince both of them is that one is interested in buying out the other."

"Sounds very lawyerly. No, you need to talk to an engineer, or at least a production manager. They will know the technical details."

"Ah, Tamos, I knew you'd get right to the nub."

"Okay, well, I've got to get off the phone now; let me know what you find out as soon as possible."

"Will do, Tamos. And don't forget to tell me what your Scout troop needs."

"Certainly, Harry."

The Allied Aluminum manager of production, who introduced himself as Hank Morton, Junior, was a surprisingly young-looking fellow, tall and thin, and dressed in factory coveralls, to Harry's surprise. When Harry commented on this fact, Morton looked up and down at Harry's Lloyd & Taylor suit and said, "No favoritism here, Mr. Zook. We're all in this war together."

"To be sure, young man. Very commendable."

Morton turned and led Harry to a large glass encased office sitting above the factory floor.

Harry turned to Morton, holding out the copies of both the Wharton and Allied purchase orders. "So, Mr. Morton, as I indicated in our call earlier today, I'm interested in pinning down some final details concerning our ongoing negotiations with Wharton Fabricating. I believe Mr. Bowles has filled you in?" Morton nodded. "So, what I have here," he said, as Morton took the copies, "are two copies of the same contract, the same P.O. But they have different specification numbers listed. I just need to confirm that the orders are in fact the same."

Morton took the copies from Harry and began to carefully read through them. An intense, studious look came over his face as he examined each contract. After looking at the purchase orders, he looked up.

"There's something here I don't understand. The Wharton copy of the

P.O. specifies 7075T6."

Harry blinked. "What?"

"The alloy specified on their copy of the purchase order. It's 7075T6. We don't ship that to Wharton."

Harry blinked again. "No?"

"No, sir. That's very high-grade stuff. New. No, what we've been selling to Wharton is a different alloy, 2420T3."

"Ah. I see." Harry tried to gather his thoughts. This was unexpected. "So, there is a difference in...what was ordered and what was shipped?"

"No, sir. The Allied order here is correct. That's what Wharton ordered and that's what we shipped."

"And the alloy on the Allied P.O., the twenty-four..."

"2420T3."

"Yes, the 2420T3. Is there a difference between that and the, the other one, the seven-something?"

"Seventy seventy-five tee-six. Well, for one thing, the twenty-four twenty is cheaper. Much cheaper, in fact."

"Really?" He paused. "And what, well, what would the difference be in terms of how it's used? Are they, well, interchangeable?"

"Oh, depending on the application, it might not make any difference at all which one you used. But, you see, the twenty-four twenty is a slightly different alloy."

"And that could be an issue?"

"Possibly. Now, I'm not an engineer, but I would say that the twenty-four twenty tee-three is fine for most applications, especially if treated the way we do with a surface layer of pure aluminum; that's to prevent corrosion. You can check with our engineering department, but as for me? I would be concerned about how the twenty-four twenty is being used. I'd sure ask Wharton about it."

The production manager paused and looked closely again at the two copies, shaking his head, and then handed them both to Harry. "I still don't understand how the Wharton P.O. could specify the seventy seventy-five. There has to be some sort of clerical error. Yeah, that's probably it. Some clerk at Wharton just entered the wrong details in this copy of the contract or something like that. They must get their seventy seventy-five from another vendor, and some entry clerk has made an error."

"Yes," said Harry, thoughtfully. "Yes, that's probably it."

Several days following the meeting with Harry, Worthington walked into Wharton's office without warning, something he'd rarely, if ever, done. Wharton tended to keep him at arm's length. Worthy was essentially just window dressing, after all.

"I just got off the phone with Mr. Brentwood Morris at Allied," Worthington said, referring to that company's president. "He did not sound happy."

"What are you doing calling them?" Wharton snapped back. "I'm taking care of that."

"He called us. You were busy. Told Sarah 'no calls,' as you typically do, but he was insistent, so she transferred the call to me. He wants to know, I quote, 'What the hell is the idea?' end quote."

"Just tell me what he said, without the theatrics, please."

"Okay, I'll paraphrase. Why the hell are you spreading rumors of financial problems at Allied, and what the hell is the idea of sending a lawyer sniffing around?"

"Lawyer?"

"Yeah. None other than Mr. Harry Zook. He was there last week. Day before he met with you. Talked to a director, with some story about assessing their capabilities. And that's not all. He practically offered them an inside track – to buy us out!"

Wharton looked down at his desk, fists clenched on his knees.

"That son of a bitch!" He brought his balled-up fists up, slowly banging them up and down on the desk. "Shit! We've got to get this sorted out with Morris right away. Let's hope he didn't fall too hard for Harry's bullshit. You want to make the initial call, or shall I?"

When Worthington didn't answer, just stood there gazing out the window, Wharton turned to him. "Worthington! We've got to get in touch with Morris. Find out what that bastard Zook told them and whether he believes it or not."

"Wharton, what Morris believes or doesn't believe is the least of our worries."

"What the hell are you talking about now?"

"Come to my office." Worthington turned to go, but Wharton just sat at his desk, fuming. "Charles? You'd best come to my office. It's not good, Charles. Not good at all."

A few minutes later, Wharton sat across from Worthington with a stunned look. "Someone at the Bell factory?"

"Yes. They say they have had several recent inquiries related to materials procurements."

Wharton squirmed in his chair. "Shit. What's our exposure?"

"The subpar aluminum stock, Charles. Obviously. And who knows what Zook was really doing at Allied, or what he knows. He's obviously poking around, looking for something. Morris said he even came back later and talked with one of their production managers, maybe even someone in engineering."

"Shit. But just as soon as we land the Allied deal, Boeing is right behind. We won't need to use the down-grade stuff any longer. And anyway, all of the P-39s with the bad parts are going to Russia on Lend-Lease. Who gives a damn?"

"Not everything is going to Russia."

"What do you mean?"

"I mean, that not every subpar throttle body went to Russia in a P-39. We supplied a secondary contractor, as well."

"And just how did that happen?"

"A procurement order came through. It was filled. As soon as I found out, I took care of it. But some number had already gone out."

"Some number?"

"At least fifty. Maybe many more. We're checking."

"But we've got it covered, right?"

"Only if we're lucky."

"And that means?"

"That means, if we are not lucky, if any of this is traced to us, they can hang us, Charles. Especially if Zook has info on the aluminum."

Wharton stood up, sat back down again. "Who do we have inside at Bell?"

"Russo."

"Get him on the horn. We've got to take care of this thing before it goes any farther." He sat back, frown deepening.

"And put a tail on that god damned Harry Zook."

Khandajar

LONG NECK, NEW YORK

The refugees weren't "prisoners," exactly, just undocumented aliens in wartime. Tamos was in the rather peculiar position of having once had a legitimate U.S. visa, while living in California, along with his Hungarian papers, but his passport and other documents had all been lost in the crash in Lisbon. But the bureaucracy in his case was grinding along even more slowly than usual, and in the meantime, he remained just another refugee, subject to the same requirements and travel limitations imposed on everyone else in the camp.

After the quarantine period ended, many of the refugees had taken part-time jobs in town, or were attending local schools. Conducting business, making friends, making connections. But their access to the outside world was still nominally controlled; passes were required, limited to preapproved activities only. It was ironic that Tamos, one of the very few refugees to actually have legitimate immigration status, was trapped in the Shelter.

An unauthorized trip to New York City required some level of subterfuge. Fortunately, as Jeri and Tamos had been getting together regularly, they knew it was not particularly hard to get out of the camp.

Tamos met Jeri using his unofficial exit, and they hopped an early evening train to the city.

Of course, they had known that Harry was wealthy. They just didn't grasp how wealthy until they arrived – having been chauffeured directly from the Penn Street station – at his estate in Long Neck. The mansion was even *named*, Tamos had been somewhat surprised to learn, just like baronial estates in Britain or Europe, but more exotically: *Khandajar*. The walls were lined with big game trophies and exotic artifacts from all over the world.

After a warm greeting and a brief tour of the main house, they were shown to their room – a suite larger than their entire apartment in California had been – with instructions to meet Harry for breakfast in the conservatory at nine o'clock sharp.

Breakfast was soft-boiled eggs, bacon, toast, and real coffee.

Jeri gaped. "Harry, I haven't had a fresh egg in weeks! And bacon!"

"Well, I used up quite a few coupons, but figured you kids need the protein. And you're going to have to work for it, let me tell you. But before we get to work, let's just enjoy breakfast. Tamos, how's your uncle Béla getting along in Spain?"

Surrounded by citrus trees and palms under the greenhouse glass, they chatted about family, friends, ferry missions, barracks hijinks, camp life, Harry's past exploits in Africa. As the dishes were being cleared, Harry pulled the mailbag out from under the table and unloaded a pile of documents on to the center of the table.

"Okay, to work. Tamos, here's what we've got. It's up to you to make sense of it."

Harry laid out two documents. "Here's what I'm calling 'Exhibit A,' the purchase orders from Wharton and Allied." He leaned over and indicated a specific line item on one sheet. "Here, on the Wharton P.O., they specify 7075T6-grade aluminum. But here," he pointed to the Allied P.O., "the P.O. provided by Allied's contract department, the aluminum actually delivered – this P.O. shows 2420T3-grade aluminum."

He slid the two papers to one side and brought out a photograph. "Here's 'Exhibit B,' the photo of the broken throttle plate." Harry went on to describe some additional documents. "These are the documents provided by Jeri's contact at the Bell factory. The carburetor specifications, the Request for Proposal, every related document calls for 7075T6-grade aluminum."

Harry then recalled the Allied production manager's comment. "Tamos, the manager at Allied said that he'd be 'very concerned' about how this aluminum was being used. What do you think?"

"Harry, from what I've already learned, I would agree. I would, however, like to get verification regarding these particular grade designations. Can you get me to the New York City public library?"

The afternoon meeting, held in Harry's office, was short and somber. Tamos had learned a lot in a short time.

"So, I've been able to verify my suspicions," he began. "To begin with, 2420T3 has a much higher percentage of copper in it compared to the 7075T6. Um, something around two to four times as much. This changes the characteristics of the metal in various ways. The stress characteristics, for one thing. Now, in some applications, this doesn't matter. But if used as material to fabricate a part subjected to high pressures and vibration – a throttle plate, for example – it would make a significant difference."

Tamos pulled the photo of the broken part out of the pile of documents lying on Harry's desk and held it up for them to see.

"See this fracture line? It is at what's called a stress riser area, near the center of the axes of rotation, where the metal goes from thick to thin. Like I said, this is subject to extreme pressures in the carburetor, and because of the relative weakness of this alloy, it is prone to metal fatigue. And fracture, just as you see here. Jeri had already guessed much of this, by the way." She smiled at the compliment as he tossed the photo on the desk.

"So, this is it. We have our smoking gun," said Harry.

"As far as I am concerned," said Tamos, "absolutely."

"What now?" asked Jeri.

"Good question," replied Harry. "I've been thinking about this. As I see it, there's certainly something actionable here, but on what basis? There are three possible explanations: incompetence, sabotage, or profiteering. Let's take them one at a time.

"First, incompetence. With production schedules pushed through the roof and manpower strained to the limit, the best person for the job is not always the one doing it. Could the difference in the purchase orders be a simple clerical error, as suggested by Allied's production manager? Possible, surely, but probable?" He held up his hand as Jeri began to comment. "No, let me finish, then we'll go over it.

"Second, sabotage. Jeri, you've said that your colleagues see a saboteur behind every bush." Jeri nodded. "But I don't think this looks like sabotage; no sand in the carburetor, for example, which I think you mentioned to me once. No, there are just too many variables, and nothing in the factory documents hint at a conspiracy of that kind.

"The last candidate is profiteering. All too common, from what I've been reading. The recent scandal over that engine plant in Lockland, Ohio; B-25 bombers coming off the line with engines failing, and not just a few, and not in subtle ways. The investigation so far points to widespread manufacturing, production, and inspection problems, with collusion from military brass, sad to say." He paused. "Okay. Comments?"

They all agreed that the anomalous Wharton P.O. pointed to profiteering, that the purchase orders had been intentionally altered. Why? Because 2420-grade aluminum was cheap. "Much cheaper" than the 7075-grade, Allied had told Harry.

"Okay," said Harry. "I think we all agree that it is definitely profiteering. I also believe that what we have so far is only the tip of the iceberg. Wharton has a multitude of contracts throughout the defense industry. Who knows how many more cases like this they are involved in? The sooner we can get an investigation opened up, the better.

"The next question is how to proceed to prosecution? Will the documents on their own stand up? What proof do we have that these particular purchase orders were altered? And even if they have been, what is to prevent Wharton from simply claiming clerical error, on either their or Allied's side, or from submitting alternate documents?"

"What about physical evidence?" Tamos asked.

"Well, we have the broken throttle body that Mike gave Jeri. But we don't have any provenance for it." He thought for a moment. *If he had both the documentation and the plate – prima facie!*

"We need a known bad carburetor," said Harry, "that is, a new carburetor but with a known bad throttle body." Before Jeri or Tamos could respond, Harry voiced what they were both thinking.

"And we need it before the engine it is attached to becomes the object of another crash investigation."

Waiting On CAVU

VARIOUS LOCATIONS

"What have you got?" Wharton fidgeted impatiently.

"One, I bamboozled the secretary at Allied into giving up some information. She says she made copies of work orders for Harry Zook."

"Damn it all! What the hell did they think they were doing? Damn it. Well, what else?"

"Harry Zook has visitors, out in Long Neck. Man, what a layout!"

"Yeah, yeah, I'm sure it's swell. So, what about these visitors?"

"Okay, one male, young, dark hair, looked foreign, dressed kinda shabby. The other was a woman, some sort of military."

"Military? What branch?"

"Hard to say. Wearing khakis and a sort of cap. Oh, and she was wearing a flight jacket."

"Follow them."

Jeri had been to the factory many times, of course, just never in this particular facility.

In the past, it had always been just a matter of reporting to the local commander, signing off on a ship – they were held responsible for the airplane they were delivering until it had been signed for at the other end – and taking off.

Today she was a bit off limits.

"Excuse me, where can I find Technical Sergeant Upfield?"

"Um, let me check the duty roster." The clerk ostentatiously busied herself with a sheaf of papers. Trying to make her job look more important than it really was, Jeri thought. *Oh, give the poor girl a break; just because she didn't fly fighter planes didn't make her job any less valuable.*

"Yeah, he's here today." The clerk pointed down a long corridor to the left of her desk. "Down there, uh, 49-B."

"Thanks very much." Jeri strode down the hallway displaying much more confidence than she really felt.

The door to 49-B was open. A young air force sergeant wearing wire-rimmed glasses sat behind a drab metal desk, poring over a paper, one of many, apparently; Jeri saw a huge pile of documents on one side of the desk, a smaller pile on the other. She remained in the open doorway for a moment. The sergeant didn't look up. Jeri cleared her throat, trying to sound nonthreatening. The sergeant still did not look up. Jeri edged herself slightly into the doorway.

"Excuse me?"

At her voice, the man jerked his head up quickly.

"Yes?"

"Sergeant Upfield?"

"Yes."

"Um, are you busy?"

Upfield looked pointedly at the piles of documents on his desk. "Well, yes, actually."

"Oh. I'm so sorry to interrupt you." An awkward silence prompted Jeri to continue. "I was hoping you could help me. I'm a friend of Mike's – ah, Sergeant Zebrowski, in Bismarck?"

Upfield blinked slowly behind his think lenses. "You're here about the carburetors."

"Well, yes."

"I've already sent everything I had. Everything I could, that is."

"Oh, and it has been extremely useful. Very valuable. It's just that, well, now that we have the documents…"

"Yes, well?" Upfield was not making this easy.

"Is there any way…that is, would it be possible to, well, requisition, let's say, a carburetor? A carburetor from a particular, um, that is, with a particular model number?"

The sergeant looked at the ceiling. "And you would have authorization from whom?"

"Yes, well, that's the problem."

Upfield looked over at the wall, back up the ceiling, back to Jeri. He opened a drawer and pulled out a form. He picked up pen, bent over, and laboriously filled the form out. When he had finished, he thrust it out to Jeri, avoiding eye contact.

"This what you're looking for?"

She examined the form, recognized the Wharton model codes.

"Yes, that's it exactly."

"You didn't get this from me."

"Oh, no, sir." Jeri had found it useful to address all military men as "sir" regardless of rank. On the other hand, most military men typically treated her as an officer, being equally unsure of her rank, of which she actually had none. It all evened out in the end, she thought.

Upfield shook the form in his hand. "Take this to procurement, down that way. They'll take care of you."

Jeri resisted the urge to salute as she backed out of the office. "Thank you, sir," she said.

He waved her away, looking back at his document.

Jeri walked quickly down the corridor in the direction Upfield had indicated. *What was it Harry had said? Prima facie!*

"The guy went to Fort Ontario."

"Fort Ontario?"

"Yeah, in Oswego. New York. Some sort of detention camp; barbed wire, guards at the gates. Anyways, that's where this guy went, like he's being held there. Have this second hand from Whitey, so don't know much more about it."

"Do we know who he is?"

"No clue."

"How did he get out in order to go to New York?"

"How do I know? I've told you everything Whitey told me."

"Never mind. We can get back to that later. What about the woman?"

"The military dame went to Niagara Falls. To the Bell aircraft factory. When she left, she was lugging a big crate with her. Had a hard time getting it into her car. From there she went to a hotel in Buffalo, the Lenox."

"Any word from Russo at Bell?"

"Yeah, he says she met there with a sergeant, um, a Technical Sergeant Upfield, in the parts procurement division, he says."

"Okay. Don't spend a lot of time on the other guy for now; let Whitey handle that. As long as the guy's in a detention camp, he probably can't create too much trouble. But stay with the woman, no matter what it takes. Find out who she is. I have the feeling she's key in this."

"Anything else?"

"No, just don't lose that woman. In the meantime, I'll take care of Upfield."

The crate looked enormous sitting in the small room at the Lenox. The bell boy had acted a bit put out when she handed him a half-dollar, but she'd thought that very generous. She'd managed to get it all the way here from Niagara Falls, after all.

There's no way I can get this thing to New York, she thought; it's just too big. She'd just have to take it with her, and then get it to Harry however she could. And besides that, she had to get back to Romulus. She'd have to drive all night.

She had an idea, and got on the phone to Bismarck.

Forty minutes later, following Mike's instructions, she had dismantled the carburetor. She wrapped the throttle body – a part about the size of a thick cigar box – along with the broken plate in oilskin, for protection and cushioning, and put them into her travel bag. The rest she put back in the crate, which went into the trunk of the car. The travel bag with the throttle body was just small enough to fit in the cockpit behind her seat.

She might have to leave the dress and nylons behind this time.

"Wharton? Yeah, it's me. The dame turns out to be something called a 'Wasp.' A pilot in sort of a women's air corps, from what I can learn from the desk clerk; I guess they come to the Lenox all the time. Anyways, she's a pilot, Army Air Corps, or whatever. They fly airplanes around the country in place of male pilots, the clerk said, since they're all being sent to the front lines, I guess. Name of Jeri Jillette. Anyways, that was the name she used at the hotel. But she's married now, to a Thomas Szabó. And guess what, he's the guy in the detention center in Oswego. Say, that place is a hell of a thing. They took a whole bunch of Jewish refugees there, in August."

"You're kidding me. They're bringing Jews in now? Don't we have enough already? And how in holy hell did he get married to an American? God damn it. Okay, never mind. Where is this pilot – this Jillette woman?"

"I'm not sure."

"What do you mean, 'you're not sure?' Where the hell did she go when she left Niagara?"

"I was able to follow her as far as Romulus Army Airfield."

"Where the hell is that?"

"Detroit."

"So, fine. She's at the Romulus air base. Keep on her."

A few hours later, Wharton's phone rang again.

"Me again."

"Just a second." Wharton stood and moved to the door of his office, took a quick look around, then closed the door and sat back down at his desk. "Okay. Got anything new?"

"Managed to get the dope on this place from an off-duty airman in a bar. The women based here mostly fly airplanes out of Niagara Falls."

"God damn, the Bell factory. P-39s."

"You got it. Anyways, they take an Army Air Force transport plane from here to Buffalo, then go out to the Niagara airfield to pick up their P-39. From there they fly it to Montana."

"Great Falls."

"Right."

"That makes sense. Going from there to Russia. "

"Yeah, that's what this guy said, too. But, they also fly P-40s, and other stuff, out of the airfield here. Take them all over the damned country."

"So? Is she still there, at Romulus? Or has she flown off somewhere?"

"Can't say. Got turned back at the gate."

"God damn it. Figure out a way to get in there and find out where she is."

"Listen, Wharton, this is a god damned Army base, for Christ sakes. How am I supposed to find out where she's gone now?"

"I don't give a damn how you do it, just find her."

"Aren't you listening, Wharton? It can't be done. You don't pay me enough to spy on the god damned U.S. Army. Go to hell."

6:45 PM

Got out of Niagara Falls with no problems. Weather good all the way, until we got here. I just made it in, very late, before it closed in. Not even minimums of 2500 and three miles this morning. All the girls are anxious. Will see Mike later tonight.

"Upfield's missing." Mike looked pensive.

"What?" Jeri scowled in concern. "What do you mean?"

"I've been trying to call him for two days, ever since you left Niagara."

"But where do they say he is?" Jeri still wasn't quite following.

"That's just it. He's *missing*. Didn't show up for his regular duty shift. Day after you left with the carb."

6:50 AM

Weather still bad. Can't fly. No word from Niagara. Mike not in the hanger this morning. Left a message for Harry about Sgt. Upfield, and to call me ASAP. I have a very bad feeling.

"Jeri?"

"Yes, is that you Harry? The connection is bad."

"Listen, Jeri, I've put out feelers; we can't locate your sergeant in Niagara."

"Oh, God, Harry. What's going on?"

"Not sure, kiddo. But it doesn't look good."
"What should I do?"
"Nothing for now. Let me keep on it. Do you know yet when you'll be leaving Bismarck?"
"No, darn it. We may be stuck here for another two days, at least. Waiting on CAVU."
"On what?"
"Ceiling and Visibility Unlimited. That's what they require for us to fly."
"Oh, yeah, okay."
"But, anyway, so far, we've not even gotten close to our minimums. I swear, Harry, they put so many restrictions on us. I mean, really. We can fly in this stuff."
"I'm sure you can. But this might be good, you staying put until we know what's going on."
"Oh, I guess so, Harry. But I'm worried."
"Me, too, kiddo. Just hang in there. Let me know the instant you find out you can fly."
"Will do."

9.15 PM
I've been trying to call Tamos all day, but the camp operator says he's out in town somewhere. His Scout troop? Harry not returning calls either.
No CAVU.

She finally got through to Tamos very late that night. He did not have good news.
"Jeri, Harry's apartment in New York was broken into last night. His desk was rifled, drawers searched. Very little stolen, just enough to make it look like a burglary, in Harry's opinion."
"Does he think it's related to the bad carburetors?"
"Yes. He is pretty sure Wharton is on to him. It appears that Wharton and Allied compared notes and realized that there is no deal to be made on either side. Wharton won't return Harry's calls. And now this. He is afraid he may have pushed Wharton too far, and now Wharton suspects – or knows – that Harry has information he shouldn't have."
"Oh, my God, Tamos, what's going on?"
"Do not worry, Harry thinks he can deal with it. We should know more by tomorrow."

"You'll call me?"

"Yes. Now, just be careful; you'll hear from one of us again soon."

At six A.M. the next morning, Blage called Jeri into his office.

"Oh, my God. No. No, it can't be."

Blage rubbed his eyes, sighed loudly, twice, as if his exhalations could somehow alter reality, change what it was he was telling Jeri.

"I'm so sorry to be the one to tell you. I hear that you two were, well, close."

"What? No, no, we were friends, yes, but, oh, my God."

Blage shifted in his chair. "Yes, well. Terrible."

"How did it happen, again?"

"As far as we know – from what the MPs reported – he was attacked behind the Wagon Wheel bar. Maybe around midnight."

"The Wagon Wheel?"

"That's what they said."

"But he *hated* that bar. He never went there."

"Well, be that as it may. Witnesses said he came in asking for someone who'd left a message for him, but all he had was a first name. Joe, if you can believe that. One of the same witnesses reported an altercation in the bar a little while later, between Mike and a stranger. Said Mike got very belligerent. No one knows who the other guy was."

"But that's not like Mike. Not at all."

"Didn't sound like it to me, either. Anyway, that's the report."

Jeri closed her eyes. "And how did it…I mean, how did he –"

"Are you sure you want to hear the rest?"

"Of course," she said, eyes still closed.

Blage picked up the form that had been lying on his desk. "Multiple knife wounds, it says. Apparently, he bled to death while lying in the alley."

Tamos tried to keep his voice from telegraphing his concern. He needed her to stay focused.

"Only one? You are sure?"

Jeri had hardly been able to talk when she'd first gotten Tamos on the phone; she was slowly calming down. "Yes, I think so. Anyway, he's the only one I saw."

"What did he say, exactly?"

"Oh, I don't know, it was so unexpected. He came up behind me, and leaned in over my shoulder. All I really heard clearly was 'you could be next,' and he was gone."

"You never got a good look at him?"

"No."

"What on earth were you doing, going over to that bar?" Tamos asked.

"I just had to see where it happened. And I thought maybe I could find out something. The local police are acting like it's strictly an Army issue, and the Army is trying to pass it off on them. No one seems to take it seriously. Just another bar fight gone bad. I couldn't let it go at that."

"I understand how you must feel, but you cannot take risks like that."

There was a long pause. "That's not all," Jeri finally said. "When I got back to the base, there was a car sitting off to the side of the road, just in sight of the gate, but far enough back so as not to be too conspicuous. I think it was the same guy."

Tamos very uncharacteristically swore. "Damn it, Jeri!"

"What should I do?"

"Just stay in the barracks as much as you can, and do not go anywhere alone, not even to the mess hall." He paused. "How soon do you think you can get out of there?"

"The weather is lifting. We can probably go on to Great Falls tomorrow."

"Okay. Call me just as soon as you get to Great Falls. I'll try to think of something in the meantime."

"I'm scared, Tamos."

"I know. So am I. But we will work this out. We just have to act fast, and get Wharton shut down before he has a chance to get to any of us."

Tamos had a sudden thought. "Jeri, is your P-39 safe? Does it have one of the good carburetors?"

"Yes, Mike is sure it's okay, though of course he can't guarantee that there isn't something else – oh, Tamos. Mike never hurt anyone! How could they –"

"They are obviously desperate, Jeri. Which proves that we are right. And that you need to get back here with that throttle body as soon as it's safe. Now, get a good night's sleep, if you can, and we'll talk again soon."

It was very late at night, but she hadn't been able to sleep.

Now it was her turn to propose a plan.

"That is insane!" said Tamos, after she'd explained her idea.

"I have no choice."

"We can come up with something else. Let me talk to Harry."

"We don't have time. They know where I am, where I'm going. I won't be safe at Great Falls, either, Tamos. They killed Mike, and probably killed poor Upfield. We have to do something."

He didn't know what to say. She was right, but at the same time what she was proposing was outlandish. It would never work.

"Jeri, you can't do this."

"Let me call Harry."

Jeri looked back over her shoulder to make sure, once more, that the door to the phone room was tightly closed. "We have an idea, but we'll need your help, Harry."

"Go on."

"Well. Like I said a minute ago, I first thought I could just grab the first SNAFU back to Romulus and bring the evidence with me. But we've heard that there will be no SNAFU flights available out of Great Falls for at least a week, maybe more."

"Isn't that unusual? To have to wait that long. I mean."

"Yes, but it happens."

"Okay, what's your idea?"

"I'll fly a P-39 back to Syracuse. As soon as I get to Great Falls. It's almost certain we'll go tomorrow morning. The next day, I can fly back to New York."

"But aren't all those airplanes supposed to go on somewhere from Great Falls? To, well, some other delivery point?"

"Yes, they're all destined for Russia, through Alaska. The ships we're flying have no insignia – as soon as we deliver one, the Soviet Air Force insignia gets painted on, overnight. They've been staging ships up there for a couple of weeks now. Once we deliver this batch tomorrow, they'll all go out the next day to Alaska."

"Wait, this is not making sense. If they're on their way to Alaska, to Russia, how can you bring one back to New York?"

"It's a little complicated, but I've been thinking about this for a long time. Normally, WASPs are not allowed to take the ships on from there; only male pilots, or Russian pilots, fly from there to Siberia. But none of us like that. We think we should be able to take them all the way to the last drop off point in Alaska. Hell, Harry, we're checked on more planes than most male pilots, even ships they are afraid to fly. And we don't get the credit for it. So, some of us have been talking, idly, until now – wouldn't it be something if one of us managed to sneak off in one of these P-39s with the group going to Alaska? That would show them we're capable. I'm pretty sure a couple of the gals here would help me."

"But how does that get you here?"

"I takeoff, wait until I'm out of sight, then turn around."

"Wait a minute. Won't you be missed?"

"Oh, sure, eventually. But it's a really big group going out; in all the hustle and confusion, I'll probably be overlooked. It happens once in a while."

"This sounds crazy."

"That's what Tamos said. But, Harry, I'm afraid to stay here." She'd already told him of the dire warning at the bar, the stalking at the base.

"Yes, yes, of course."

She waited through a long silence, then asked anxiously, "Harry, are you still there?"

"Yes, just thinking it over." Jeri could almost see him running his hands through his hair, that way he did when he was worried, trying to work out a problem.

"Harry?" she asked again.

"And you and Tamos worked this out together? You agree on this?"

"Yes." *As soon as you agree to it.*

"What do you need me to do?"

Form 23

GREAT FALLS, MONTANA

Normally Jeri did the Niagara to Great Falls ferry trip over two or three days, with RONs along the way. But there was no time for that. She'd have to fly nearly nonstop, perhaps grabbing a quick bite and resting while getting refueled.

Straight-line distance from Great Falls to Syracuse was about seventeen hundred miles. But Jeri would have to wend around a bit, from one small airstrip to another, so the actual distance was going to be closer to eighteen hundred. Finding airstrips with runways suitable for the P-39, and at the same time not too close to a large military field had been tricky, but they'd identified several small, out of the way fields they could use.

Finding suitable runways, however, also provided a solution to a larger problem: the availability of 100 octane fuel. With wartime fuel rationing and no private aircraft allowed to fly, they'd first thought this was going to be a deal breaker. But the fields they'd found, like many small private airfields all over the country, had been turned into impromptu AAF training fields. By landing at these ad hoc training fields, Jeri (hopefully) would be able to land, refuel, and continue on, before the local airfield operator had a chance to question it. They'd worked up a couple of only marginally fantastic cover stories, relying on both the novelty of a woman piloting a pursuit fighter (decorated with a red star, no less!), and the Army's nearly phobic need for secrecy. As added insurance, Jeri had fabricated authorization papers that if not examined too closely should pass as official, and that she would use as a last resort.

Based on the approximately five-hundred-mile safe range of the P-39, they had planned four stops, each leg averaging between four and five hundred miles. Flying time, at three hundred and fifty MPH, just under top speed, would be a little over five hours. Total time including takeoffs and landings, and some time on the ground, they figured at seven hours. Since she would be flying against the sun, she'd have to leave Great Falls nearly at first light in order to get to Syracuse before it got too dark.

It was a very tight schedule. The last leg would push the edge of the fighter's maximum range. But they were confident in Harry's calculations – he'd flown solo around the world, after all – and in Jeri's flying abilities.

The Army Air Forces flight suit Jeri had cadged was a bit large on her, but she just rolled up the pant legs and cinched in the waist. If anyone happened to see her, they would not notice anything unusual as she climbed into her ship.

The biggest problem they faced was getting the final flight release form completed – the ubiquitous Form 23, used to control all flights – and accepted by the flight line crewman. Her accomplices had done their own midnight requisitions, in the form of two ground control uniforms. They would be on the runway flagging Jeri, and were confident that they could slip her Form 23 into the pile without a problem, given the number of flights leaving the next morning. These operations were typically confused even at the best of times, and this would be to their favor. And it would be hours before anyone could know there was anything amiss.

The rising sun illuminated the controlled chaos taking place at Great Falls Army Airbase. P-39s were taking off every two to three minutes, as fast as they could roll up to the active runway.

Before sunrise, Jeri and her friends went out to pull her P-39, the one she'd flown in from Bismarck, from behind the maintenance hangar. It was the ship that Mike had certified in Bismarck as airworthy, just a few days ago.

It wasn't there.

Damn. Why did someone have to choose this particular time to be conscientious? It had already been pulled into the flight line.

Suddenly unsure of what to do now, she went back to the barracks with the other two WASPs. Once there, she decided she'd call Tamos a little earlier than planned. He was at Harry's Park Avenue apartment, having taken a night train from Oswego up to the city. They were expecting her to call at her first stop, later that morning.

Tamos's first reaction was about what she'd expected. "Okay, we must call it off," he said, flatly. "We will have to think of something else."

"But everything is in place, we're ready to go," countered Jeri. "There's no reason I can't take some other ship."

"You do not know if another ship will have a good carburetor."

"The odds are good that whatever plane I take, it will be perfectly sound. I think I should go ahead with the plan."

After a short silence, she heard Tamos speak away from the mouthpiece. "Harry, talk to her. Get her to see reason."

"Jeri, you can't go through with this," Harry told her as soon as he got on the phone. "Let Tamos think of an alternative. He can figure a way out of almost any problem; I'm sure he can come up with something now."

"But Tamos is not here this time, Harry, and I am, and I'm sure this will work."

"I still say it's too dangerous. What if you get a ship that's unsafe? You could experience engine failure, crash land somewhere, out in the middle of nowhere."

"Harry, I've made emergency landings in places even *you* wouldn't try. Cornfields. Country roads. I even landed on the grounds of an Indian school in the desert in New Mexico once. Harry, I can land anywhere."

"Okay, I can't deny that you could probably land safely in just about any situation. But, still, Tamos is right, it's just not worth the risk."

"Put Tamos back on, please, Harry."

"Okay. Here he is."

Before Jeri could say anything, Tamos repeated what Harry had just said. "Jeri, it's just too risky. You cannot know if the plane you take is mechanically sound."

"No, you're right, I can't. But, Tamos, everything is a risk. What about the terrible chances you took in going to Hungary?"

"That was different. It was a matter of life and death."

"So is this. I'm in danger if I stay here, now."

Tamos didn't respond right away, and when he did, his voice was low. "You're determined to go through with this?"

"Yes, I am. Tamos, I'm in danger no matter what I do. But I'll be in even more danger if I stay here."

There was a long silence. "Alright, Jeri," he finally said. "Keep Harry up to date all along the way, and he'll relay your progress to me.

"I'll see you in New York."

She had quickly modified her Form 23 to match the number of the plane they'd selected, one at the end of a long lineup. This would give one of the other WASPs time to slip into the control area with the modified form as Jeri did her run-up. Not optimal, but as she'd learned from Tamos, improvisation was an extremely valuable skill.

While she ran though her checklist, Jeri simultaneously gave herself a short pep talk. *I can do this. I'll get the evidence to Tamos and Harry. They will prove beyond doubt that Wharton and his cohorts, whoever they may be, are actively involved in war profiteering, an act of treason.*

But she also had no illusions. There would surely be serious consequences for her actions today. She was, after all, essentially stealing an airplane, an advanced pursuit fighter, the property (at least temporarily) of the U.S. government, war matériel allocated to the effort to crush Hitler on his second front at Stalingrad, at Minsk, in the cold wastelands of Mother Russia. Would the resulting, hopefully successful, prosecution of a local war criminal – which may or may not have a significant impact on the outcome of the global conflict – would this be worth the personal sacrifice she was about to make?

She pressed the starter pedal, felt the shake and rumble as the massive Allison engine came to life; she finished her startup procedure and maneuvered the ship into the line.

Her turn, sooner than she had expected. “This candle –” she automatically started to say, and released the mike button with a start. Then, in a low voice, a feeble attempt at disguise, she knew, she contacted the tower again.

“Ready for takeoff.”

“Cleared.”

Throttle at three thousand, right full rudder. Rumble down the tarmac. Into the air.

The ground dropped below her quickly as she gained altitude, the effect as usual creating a split second of vertigo as her brain tried to make sense of what was happening; then all fell into place and she was soaring ‘into the blue,’ at one with the open sky around her.

Reality intruded as she spied a ship off to her right making a shallow turn to the northwest. She strained her neck to get a better look at the weather around her; light cirrus, with a bit of low haze to the north. Not optimal, considering her objective. Better stay with the group a little longer.

A few minutes later she spotted a lake below and to the left – Freezeout Lake, if she remembered the chart correctly – and some small cumulus building low just to the south. That should do. She angled away from the lake and into the clouds. And then she was flying east.

Flying in the wrong direction, without authorization, in an Army fighter plane bearing the insignia of the Soviet Air Force.

Her panic subsided at the thought of seeing Tamos in a few hours. She trimmed tabs, adjusted the cooling shutters, checked her temps.

She got back to her mission.

In the Book

WASHINGTON, D.C.

"Where are we on the Zook business? Taken care of?"

"The mechanic and the parts guy at Bell are out of the picture; nothing to worry about from that end. Done."

"Good. And the dame, the pilot?"

"Whereabouts unknown."

"Shit, give me a break, are you some kind of movie detective? 'Out of the picture.' 'Whereabouts unknown.' What the hell?"

"Okay. The pilot was last seen at a diner in Bismarck, North Dakota. And let me tell you, that was no easy thing, following her out there. You know where Bismarck, North Dakota is?"

"Lord Jesus, help me in my hour of need. Can't you just answer a simple question? Does she have anything that can hurt us?"

"Possibly."

A third voice entered the conversation. "So, what's the next move?"

"You tell me."

"What about Zook himself? Take him out?"

"No, too risky. He's a player. Goddam Jew deserves it, but there you go."

"At the risk of repeating myself – what next?"

"I say we fall back for now."

"And if we do fall back, as you say, that does not obviate the need for continued observation. In fact, I would say that this must of necessity become a permanent operation."

"Permanent? How?"

"As in, as long as it takes."

"Like, what, forever?"

"Didn't I just say 'as long as it takes?' This goes into the book, gentlemen."

Off the Beam

EN ROUTE

Her first stop was Spearfish, South Dakota. The operator there, as at the other planned stops, had been warned in advance to expect something unusual, had been given hints of "classified" operations, demanding utmost discretion. As hoped, the elderly man who came out to refuel the plane treated her with deference, almost embarrassingly so. He could hardly bring himself to look her in the face. Perhaps the shock of seeing a woman climb out of the cockpit had addled him. Jeri could just imagine his anguish over the next few days as he labored to keep the secret of her visit, which she had stressed was of immense importance.

"Yes, Ma'am, no worry about that. No, Ma'am. No worry." He winked conspiratorially. "Loose lips, and so on."

"Yes, indeed."

Thirty minutes later she was in the air, on her way to Mason City, Iowa. A similar experience at Mason City gave her a much-needed boost of confidence. Only a short hop to Kokomo, Indiana, and then on to Syracuse.

The P-39 sat on the apron of the runway at Kokomo, red star on the fuselage glowing in the afternoon light.

It truly was a sight to behold, at least based on the look of the airport mechanic servicing the plane. Jeri sat on a dilapidated wooden bench outside the small airport office, once more wondering at the sheer insanity of what she was doing. She stood and stretched, forced herself to focus on the leg ahead. The last segment, Kokomo to Syracuse, was a long one, still within range, but she'd have to fly a bit slower to conserve fuel. The weather appeared to be holding – she'd been very lucky so far – but it didn't look quite as good ahead of her. An ominous dark line ran along the horizon to the north. But fairly far to the north, she judged.

Once in the air, and with just about two hours to go, her worries vanished. Soon, she'd be in Syracuse, and an hour after that, at Fort Ontario, with Tamos.

Safe.

She'd been flying on visual much of the way; none of the small airports she needed were broadcasting the LFR radio range navigation beacon she'd normally be following. She had been able to use the airport beacons from time to time, but would break off as she neared the larger airfield. She'd just flown along the south shore of Lake Erie, using Buffalo LFR, and now skirted the edge of Lake Ontario, near Rochester. About a hundred miles from Syracuse, she was finally able to rely on "the beam."

She adjusted her headset slightly to maximize the signal, a modulation of the Morse code signals for "A" and "N", which, if on course, overlapped to create a steady tone – the beam, a virtual path more than three miles wide. When she eventually passed directly over the airport, the signal would disappear, and she would then go into the LFR holding pattern, make her final approach, and land. In the meantime, if she wandered to the left of the beam she heard the separate code for "N", *dah-dit, dah-dit*; if she drifted to the right she heard an "A", *dit-dah, dit-dah*. Hear an "N," turn right. Hear an "A," turn left. Simple.

But not foolproof.

The dark line of weather she'd worried about earlier had moved south, into her flight path. Static from the associated thunderstorms crackled and popped in her headset, at times making it difficult to hear the signal, to stay on the beam. But she had been managing, in spite of the worsening weather, in spite of the interference, constantly adjusting her course to keep the signal modulated.

One thing she didn't know, however – the electromagnetic interference created by the approaching thunderstorms was causing the "A" signal to skip into the "N" quadrant. So, when she heard an "A", meaning shift course left, she should have been hearing an "N," which meant shift right, you're too far north. Instead, she kept hearing an "A," and kept edging the plane to the left, searching for the beam.

The clouds broke for a moment, revealing the shore of Lake Ontario just off to her left.

Oh, hell. What is going on? I'm much too far north.

Banking sharply to the right, she turned to the southeast, away from the lake, west of Sodus Point, which lay about midway between Rochester and Oswego. Of course, she didn't yet know exactly where she was; and since she was now flying practically blind, through rain and fog, she desperately needed to relocate the beam to Syracuse. As soon as she got back on track, she could follow it straight to the airport.

As the weather worsened, she'd quickly abandoned her planned flyover of Fort Ontario. Tamos would understand.

She continued southeast, still not hearing the *dah-dit, dah-dit* that should have located her in relation to the beam. Even though she'd been a star instrument student while training blind – "under the hood," they called it – she'd never really liked it. And WASP ferrying was done almost exclusively under CAVU conditions; whether or not they had an instrument rating, the Army considered it unwise to have WASP pilots flying on instruments, unless unavoidable due to changing conditions. Her abilities were now being strained to the limit.

She broke out of the clouds and at the same time picked up the LFR signal again near the small town of Lyons. Right below her she saw the unmistakable contour of the Erie Canal, which quickly vanished as the clouds thickened around her.

She banked sharply east. First drifting to the left and then to the right, "A" to "N" then "N" to "A," she finally settled on the solid beam. Which abruptly vanished, replaced by a strong *dah-dit, dah-dit.* She began to correct to the right, when the signal shifted again, to "A." The new *dit-dah, dit-dah* remained loud and steady, so she continued left, to the north again.

She flew on for some time, still hearing the *dit-dah* urging her north. She made a wide circle in what she thought was the right direction, trying to pick up the solid signal, the beam.

Then she saw the fuel gauge.

Had she used that much extra fuel while searching for the beam? Or had the last operator shorted her, skimmed off fuel to resell? Was there profiteering everywhere?

She leaned over and quickly switched the fuel selector to "reserve." How much time did she have? The reserve should be plenty to get her to Syracuse; they'd left ample leeway, she was sure.

She continued circling. Nothing but static. No *dah-dit, no dit-dah,* simply a crackling hiss, punctuated by loud pops. Desperate now, she circled back to what she thought must be north, where the beam should be. The clouds were unrelentingly dense, not a hint of a break. She checked her altimeter, pushed the stick forward, dropping another one thousand feet, looking for a break, any break, in the cover.

She'd completely lost the beam.

The wind and rain intensified, heavy rain and sleet lashing the cockpit, the small plane buffeted by strong gusts. She could barely see her instruments in the darkening cockpit. She'd already turned on the cockpit light, but it just seemed to add to the gloom.

She strained against her harness, trying to lean forward to read her gauges. First pulling off her headset, she reached down and released the harness lock, which let her get closer to the instrument panel. She checked the altimeter first, and gasped when she saw she had dropped to six hundred feet. *Can that be right?* She pulled back on the stick, leveled off at one thousand. She also saw that she'd been seduced into turning almost directly to the north by what she now realized must have been a scrambled LFR signal, distorted by the fierce electrical energy of the storm. They'd been warned of such things in training, a "swinging beam," but only briefly, and as a mere technicality, nothing to really concern themselves over.

And then the clouds opened up, and the lake appeared below her. She'd already dropped back down to six hundred feet.

She grabbed the throttle, pulling it wide open. *Just like those Russian night witches. Full on or nothing.* She pulled back on the yoke as the huge Allison roared.

There was a short, sharp backfire, like a gun firing.

The engine died.

The silence in the cockpit was profound.

When the plane hit the water, she was thrown violently forward. Since in her desperation she'd forgotten to relock her harness, her head hit the stick with considerable force, killing her instantly.

And so she did not know that only one small section of the wing had torn off on impact, and that the rest of the ship remained intact as it sank into the dark water.

Or that it slowly drifted quite some distance, caught in the lake's slow circulating gyre, to finally settle, gently, about ninety feet deep, onto the side of Duck-Galloo Ridge.

ROMULUS, MICHIGAN

"I'm sorry, Mr. Szabo, there's nothing more I can do."

Tamos looked around at the drab walls of the Romulus base commander's office, trying to focus his thoughts. How could anyone work in here? It's stifling. The barracks at the camp are more cheerful. What did he say a few minutes ago, about the flight plan?

"But you have to admit that it is possible," said Tamos, "given the circumstances. Something similar happened in Long Beach, a few months ago. The Army did not know that a P-51 was missing for four days! And I am telling you I know where Jeri went!"

"Mr. Szabó, I can assure you we've done a thorough review of the flight line procedures in Great Falls, and have a very good idea of what happened. The two WASP pilots who abetted Mrs. Jillette – excuse me, Mrs. Szabó – in commandeering the P-39 in question have been interviewed, and their accounts agree in all particulars. They have, by the way, been severely disciplined. It's a very unfortunate turn of events, I agree. But the fact remains that as far as the Army is concerned, Mrs. Szabó's aircraft was lost during an unauthorized mission, somewhere between Great Falls and Kamloops, British Columbia. We have no reason to believe otherwise."

NEW YORK, NEW YORK

"Harry, they do not believe me.

"Would you, if in their shoes?" Harry asked. "This is the Army, in war time. They have their hands full, believe me. The war is winding down, sure, but in the overall scheme of things? I'm sure that in their minds, what's one more lost WASP?"

"My God, Harry, how can you say that?" Tamos exclaimed, nearly jumping up out of his chair.

"Please forgive me for being so brutal, Tamos. I loved her too, you know, like a daughter. Like a daughter," he repeated, his voice low. "Just as I love you like a son. I'm just not sure anymore what anything means. How to cope with the chaos around us. What this all means," he said, waving his hand around the ornate library in the Park Avenue apartment. "What good is all of this, in the end? What have I really accomplished? I had hoped that we – the three of us – were going to do something important, something true.

Bring down those bastards. But now, well, now I guess that is all over. Perhaps I am just becoming jaded in my old age, but it seems like the harder you try, the harder you fall."

"What will we do, Harry?" Tamos tried, but failed, to keep the anguish out of his voice. He was very close to breaking down completely.

"Ah, Tamos. I wish I knew. Maybe it's time to give up. Any efforts from this point on I fear will not be very fruitful. In my experience – admittedly, not in corporate law, but I have seen a few things in my day, and have been communicating with colleagues – going head to head with a large company is extremely difficult. Maybe even close to impossible. Wasted effort."

"Ah, but it is the effort that sustains me, Harry."

"Tamos," Harry replied, thoughtfully, "you know, I've never known anyone with your intelligence, your determination, and your concept of the value, and meaning, of effort. It makes you a truly uncommon man." Harry paused.

"God help us both."

Six months later, Harry Zook was dead.

He had continued to try, with Tamos, even as his illness progressed, to get the Army to expand their investigation into the loss of Jeri's aircraft, and into the use of substandard aluminum alloys in critical engine components, which continued to cause engine failures in P-39s across the country, and no doubt in the Soviet Union. And who could tell what else? Unable to procure additional carburetor parts from Bell Aircraft as evidence, and stonewalled by Wharton Fabricating at every turn, they had eventually given up. Wharton had won.

It had all been for nothing.

It was Malta Fever – Brucellosis – that brought Harry down. Picked up on one of his safaris in Africa, or perhaps on the flight around the world, no one was certain.

Harry was not one to abandon hope altogether. It was true that without the physical evidence Jeri had been transporting, they had no real case. But the documentation they had gathered – the specifications, the purchase orders, the photographs – Harry had, before he died, put into an office safe, to be administered in perpetuity by the law firm Xerxes & Yerkes, or their successors. Tamos now had the only key. In addition, Harry left quite a sizable sum to Tamos, to be used to continue his schooling, and to support and further his continued efforts for Jeri, and for all WASPs.

Tamos Szabó, like Harry Zook, was also not one to abandon hope. His only failing, despite all efforts, was that he ultimately did not live to see it through to the end.

BOOK X: END GAME

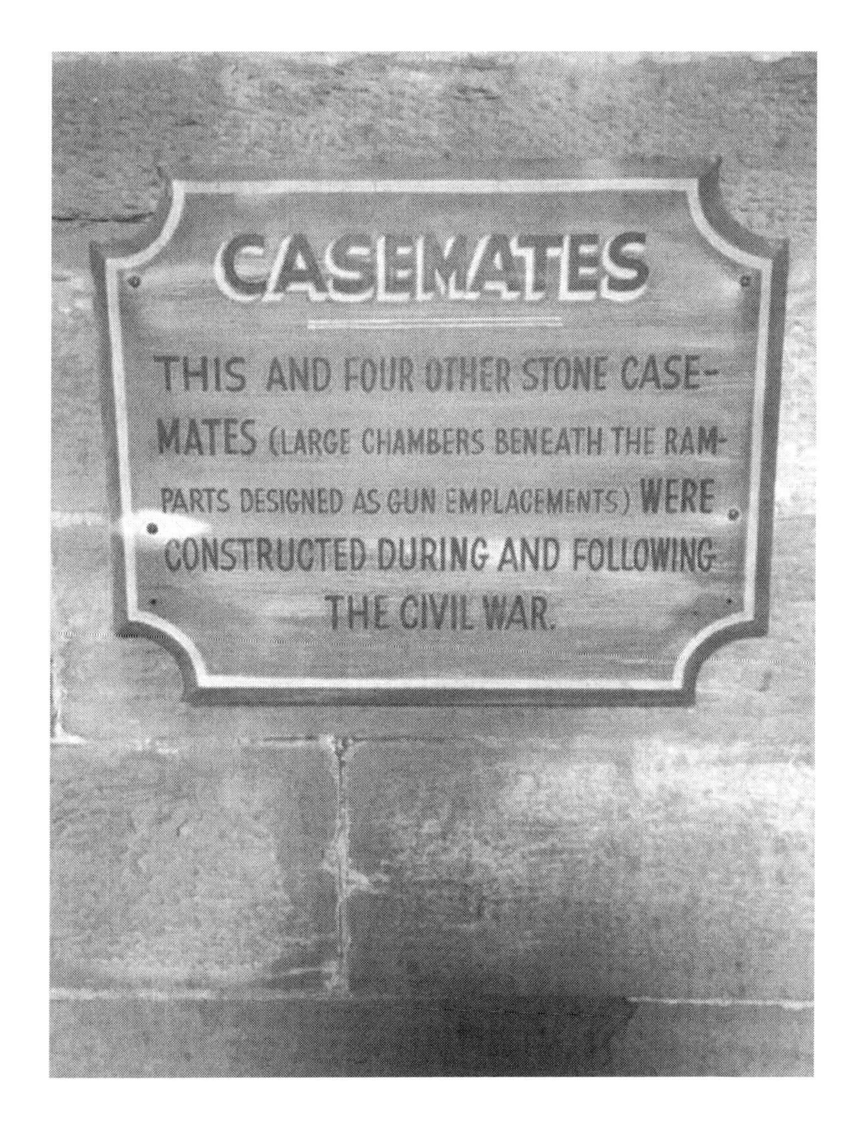

It's Greek To Me

SAFE HAVEN MUSEUM, FORT ONTARIO

Jimmy Kim insisted that he himself drive LaFleur and Maggie this time, perhaps sensing LaFleur's anxiety. "Why should my cousin's kids have all the fun?" he complained. "Besides, you told me I was Number One Son, remember?"

"Okay, Jimmy, you're right. I wouldn't want to trust this one to just anybody."

"Where to?" Jimmy asked.

LaFleur turned to Maggie, smiling.

"The Safe Haven Museum."

"Oh, yes, I remember you," said Mrs. Rothstein, warmly, it seemed. Perhaps she was more congenial with return visitors. "Would you like another tour? Or just look around?" She looked at LaFleur pointedly. "It's still five dollars per person, tour or no," she said.

"Oh, that's fine," said Maggie, opening her purse for the money. As Mrs. Rothstein took the ten dollars, she asked again about a tour.

"No, not this time, thanks," said LaFleur. "We're actually here for, well, I guess you could say, research. We're trying to track down some information related to a Professor Tamos Szabó."

"Ah, Professor Szabó. Oh, I knew him when I was just a little girl, in the camp." She shook her head sadly. "Such a shame."

"Yes, it was," said Maggie. "It's surprising how many people who were in the camp are still in the area."

"Oh, no, there are not that many, really," replied Mrs. Rothstein. "A handful."

"So, we have been lucky, then, to meet those we have."

"Who else do you know who was at Safe Haven?" she asked.

"Well, there's Jamila Sayvetz," said LaFleur, "Sarah Weismann's granddaughter."

"Oh, yes, I knew Sarah. We had a sewing circle. But you are not here to listen to me reminisce. What is it you are looking for, exactly? Something about Professor Szabó, you said?"

"Not about the professor himself, actually," replied LaFleur, carefully. "I have some...notes...from the professor relating to another refugee. I wondered if it would be possible to look through your archives. You mentioned when we were here last that you have an extensive collection of data – personal histories, and so on."

"Yes, that's true, although we typically do not allow access unless formally requested in advance, for example through an academic institution."

"I'm sorry, we should have introduced ourselves earlier. My name is LaFleur. I was a detective for the Oswego Police Department for many years. Retired now," he added. "This is Maggie Malone," he said, tilting his head in her direction. "She was head nurse at Oswego Hospital until she retired, just a couple of years ago. While we don't have any official authorization, I'd really appreciate it if we could just have a brief look at your files. We have a specific set of names we're interested in."

"Well, Detective, since you knew Tamos, the professor, that is, I suppose it would be alright." She turned. "This way."

As soon as Mrs. Rothstein left them alone in the file room, LaFleur pulled out the copy of the list he'd found in the Hymenoptera folder. "We might as well start with the Greek name; there's just four of them listed, a single family, apparently. Maybe he stashed the documents in with that file, but I'll be surprised if it's that easy." He peered at the page. "Kouzouca."

Maggie pulled open a large drawer marked "H-K" and flipped through a few file folders. "Here it is." She lifted the folder out and opened it, laying it out on a small table in the corner of the room. "Atanasia, the mother, and three daughters, Meropi, Evangela, and Stella." LaFleur stood by as she rifled through the contents. "Nope. Nothing out of the ordinary." She closed the folder and replaced it in the cabinet. "What next?"

"The name he wrote in is Helaine Pterataxis. The key there, I believe, is 'Ptera.' Try that."

Maggie opened another drawer. "No, nothing," she said, after looking through the folders.

"Okay. Try under O for Optera."

"Should be right here," she said. "Nope, only five names under O, and Optera is not one of them."

LaFleur stood back. "Let's try to think like the Prof was thinking, when he set this puzzle up," he said. "Look under H. For 'Hymenoptera.' Maybe it's not as difficult as I'm trying to make it."

Maggie moved back to the H-K drawer. After only a few seconds, she stood up, a thick folder in her hand. "Ta-da!" She handed it to LaFleur.

"Optera, Hymen," he read from the tab.

"And *not* filed under O, but under H. The foxy old devil," said Maggie, handing the file to LaFleur. He laid the file on the table and opened it. It only took one quick look.

"This is it, Maggie," LaFleur said. "The mother lode." He looked over at the door into the museum lobby. "Can you engage Mrs. Rothstein for a few minutes while I figure out how to get this stuff out of here?"

"Are you finished, Mrs. Malone?" Mrs. Rothstein asked Maggie as she came out into the lobby.

"Oh, it's not 'Mrs.,' that is, we're not, I mean, I'm not married."

"Oh, I apologize. But did you find what you wanted?"

"Um, Mr. LaFleur is taking one last look, but, no, it doesn't look like it. We must have had some misleading information."

"I'm sorry to hear that. If you ever need to come back, please don't hesitate to ask."

"Thanks very much, that's very generous."

"The more interest people take in the museum, the better, I always say."

"Well, we will certainly come back again. We may come across something more related to the professor. We're still learning a lot about him that we never knew."

"You know, even though I was only a small girl, I have very fond memories of the professor from the camp. He was a real favorite with the children. And the older boys, too. Did you know he started a Safe Haven Boy Scout Troop?"

"Yes, I had heard that," said Maggie. "He was quite a popular character, apparently."

"Oh, yes, I would say so! He was always making deals around the camp, trading, buying and selling, bringing in things from outside. Oh," she said, catching the concerned look on Maggie's face, "oh, no, nothing illegal! It was just a game with him, and us kids loved it. He loved games, and hiding things. Why, we even knew his so-called secret hiding place. But we never let on, he had too much fun with it."

"Where was this hiding place, Mrs. Rothstein?" asked Maggie

"Oh, in one of the casemates. There are gun emplacements, recesses in the walls, which made a perfect hiding place. He used to use one of those recesses, in particular. Not too many people knew about it."

"I'd love to see it!" said Maggie. "Now that I know the story behind it."

"Well," said Mrs. Rothstein in a low voice, looking around, "you know, the casemates are haunted."

"Haunted! Really!" Maggie was delighted to hear this.

"Yes. Not someplace you should be after dark." Mrs. Rothstein looked up guiltily as LaFleur came back in to the room. He was walking a little stiffly.

"Well, I guess we're done here," LaFleur said.

"I'm sorry you didn't find what you were looking for, Mr. LaFleur," said Mrs. Rothstein.

"Oh, that's all right," he said. He winked at Maggie. "In my business, we often come up empty handed."

Even assuming that the goons had not followed the laundry truck, LaFleur and Maggie made sure they were careful when leaving the museum. Jimmy Kim was parked at the far end of the small lot across from the museum. At LaFleur's signal, he pulled around to the back of the building, where Maggie and LaFleur could climb in to the back of the van unobserved.

"Where are the documents, A.C.?" Maggie asked quietly, as they climbed in.

LaFleur patted his chest, back, and legs, which made a flat slapping noise. "All here. I feel like I'm wearing body armor." He flopped on to a stack of towels and closed the van door behind them.

"Now the real work starts."

T & S

SODUS POINT: THE NEXT DAY

"These specs match what my engineer located at MIT, I'm sure of it," said Jamila, wiping spiedie sauce from her fingers. "But what is really interesting are the purchase orders for the aluminum blanks. We didn't really know what direction to go with this. Now we know."

"What exactly do these purchase orders tell you?" asked LaFleur.

"At this point? All I can see is that Wharton was perhaps purchasing two forms of aluminum. I can't say yet what this means. We'll have to do further analysis on the parts you provided us. That shouldn't take too long."

"Well, we don't have much time."

"I know. It's the 'old man in a hurry' syndrome."

"How right you are."

"I'll let you know as soon as I have something."

"I've eaten more spiedies in the past few days than I've had in my entire life."

"They're good for you."

"I surely hope so."

"What did you find out?"

"Well – and this was a very clever thing on my part, I want you to know – I've done both atomic emission spectroscopy and mass spectroscopy on the broken parts, as well as on the undamaged plate in the throttle body."

"Very 'T and S,'" said LaFleur.

"Pardon?"

"Technical and Scientific."

"Well, obviously," replied Jamila, smiling. "It's my job, you know. So, anyway, ready or not, here are the gory details. The alloy being purchased by Wharton from Allied in nineteen forty-three – the blanks they used to manufacture the throttle plates – was termed 24ST, now known as 2420T3. This was a formulation widely used in the war and would have been readily available. However, this alloy, which contains a relatively high percentage of copper –"

Jamila paused to look at her notes. "Um, 4.3-4.5% copper, to be exact. This formulation was highly subject to corrosion. To prevent this corrosion, they applied a surface coating of nearly pure aluminum, easy and cheap to do. This unfortunately also made the resulting material prone to fatigue cracking. A serious problem in this case. The vibration of the big V-12 engine in a P-39 could cause the throttle plate to break apart and get sucked into the engine intake manifold. This, in turn, could lead to anything from a rough running engine – which would not run all that long – to what my engineer called a 'detonating' cylinder, a catastrophic failure, almost certainly leading to an immediate crash.

"The aluminum they should have been using –" Jamila paused again and looked up. "Still with me?"

LaFleur nodded. "So far. Go ahead."

"Okay. The aluminum they should have been using was a new formulation called 7075, which was, ironically enough, secretly developed by the Japanese, but newly available in the U.S. as well. This composition contains only 1.2–1.6% copper, which makes it much less prone to fatigue. In addition, it was typically heat treated – tempered – to increase the strength. I could go into the details of dispersion of eta and eta-prime precipitates along grain boundaries, but I doubt that would be useful?"

"Correct."

"Bottom line, then, the new tempered alloy – 7075T6, the safe one – was very expensive. The old alloy – 2420T3 – was cheap and readily available. That's the path they chose to take."

"Apparently covering it up with falsified purchase orders."

Jamila raised her eyebrows as that registered. "War profiteering."

"Exactly."

Immediately following her meeting with LaFleur, Jamila sent a request to the director of the P-39 restoration project at the museum in Texas, asking for a report on the state of the carburetor. Later that day, he replied.

The throttle plate was broken in half.

Score One for the DOJ

LARRY SPIEGELMAN'S

"We've got to stop meeting like this," said Larry, after watching LaFleur climb out of the back of a laundry truck yet again.

"I hope that happens sooner than later," replied LaFleur. "Actually, I think we have everything we need to go ahead."

"You still haven't explained exactly what 'going ahead' means."

"Okay. We've managed, with luck, and by deciphering a set of rather obscure clues Prof left behind, to gather a collection of technical and photographic evidence he was planning to use against Wharton General Industries. I'm sure that what we have is sound. What I'm not sure of is, where do we stand legally? That's where you come in."

"You know I'll do whatever is necessary, if I can."

"Well, we would never have gotten this far without you, so I'm sure you'll know what to do here."

"Walk me through it."

LaFleur opened the folder and laid out several pages of documentation on Larry's dining room table, along with a photo of a throttle body and broken throttle plate, and the spectroscopy reports from Jamila.

"Some quick background, before we get to the technical issues," LaFleur began. "We don't know the complete story, but Jeri was flying back to New York from Great Falls, Montana, carrying the physical evidence that the professor and Harry were waiting for. Once they had it all in one place, they apparently planned to go public and take their evidence to a military or government office. Because what they had gathered was evidence of war profiteering on the part of the original WGI company, Wharton Fabrication, of New Jersey."

"And the documents you have here prove profiteering?"

"Along with the physical evidence, yes, I believe so. As did Tamos." He went back to the folder and extracted another piece of paper. "This is an article Tamos gave to the Pall-Times, laying out his accusations. But it never got printed. WGI got wind of it and blocked publication." He handed it to Larry, who spent a couple of minutes reading through it.

"This is related to the P-39? The one from the lake?"

"Not specifically. We also have information, gathered by Jeri and Harry Zook – falsified purchase orders, shipping documents, and multiple P-39 crash reports – we'll go through it all – showing a pattern of mechanical failure and cover-up, leading directly back to Wharton. All of this had been stored in the safe in Harry Zook's old New York office until fairly recently.

Tamos went to New York some weeks before he died and cleared out the safe. We found everything hidden in a filing cabinet at the Safe Haven Museum."

"The hell you say!"

"I know, pretty unlikely scenario. But as Tamos used to say, 'chance favors the bold.' We were very lucky to have found all of this, given the Prof's care in hiding it. He was obviously afraid to leave it all in one place, and hid some of it very elaborately – as you saw with the evidence bag – and may have feared for his life."

"Perhaps not soon enough," murmured Larry.

"No. And we know that the attack on Michael was directly related to Prof's death. And that some or all of us are still in danger."

"Let's have a drink."

Larry reread the article Tamos had wanted published, simultaneously going over the documentary evidence LaFleur had spread out.

"He was really serious," he said, with a sort of awe in his voice. "These are not idle threats," he said, holding up the article. "He was making specific charges against Wharton Sr., the original head of Wharton Fabrication, and the legacy company. I mean, serious threats."

"Yes, I know," said LaFleur. "Remarkable. But this is where it gets confusing. Why would WGI be so afraid of this, now? This all happened, what, seventy years ago." He pointed to the documents scattered around the table. "And there's a copy of a letter," he shuffled through a small set of papers still in the folder, "from Harry Zook to another attorney, a criminal lawyer – Harry was an entertainment lawyer, I found out – anyway, in this letter Harry is asking advice as to the prosecutorial strength of their case, which they had planned to bring to the Senate Special Committee – the Truman Commission – hoping to charge Wharton with war profiteering under something called the False Claims Act. Even in nineteen forty-four, he apparently had his doubts."

"From what I've seen here," Larry said, "I would think they had a very strong case. Do you have the criminal lawyer's reply?"

"Unfortunately, no. But what's really bothering me is the statute of limitations. Surely, by now this is no longer prosecutable? And wouldn't Tamos have known that? Why risk everything on such a weak hand?"

Larry rubbed his chin as he read the letter. "You're right. Tamos wouldn't have done this without being sure of his chances." He handed the letter back and reached for his iPad. "Give me a minute to double check on something."

LaFleur gathered up the documents, sorted them, put them back into the folder, and sat back, waiting for Larry's verdict.

Spiegelman looked up a few minutes later. "It's just as I thought, A.C. I recall reading about this not long ago. In 1942, Congress passed the Wartime Suspension of Limitations Act, WSLA. This effectively removed the statute of limitations on all FCA cases for fraud against the government. Which this certainly was, as the final product went to the manufacture of war matériel. There was a provision in the law specifying that such suspension of limitations expired five years 'after termination of hostilities.'"

"But it's been seventy years! Wouldn't that mean the statute of limitations is in effect?"

"Ah," said Larry, "that's where it gets interesting." Larry referred back to his tablet. "A few years ago, the Department of Justice decided, since we were at war in Iraq and Afghanistan, the WSLA was back in force, allowing them to bring cases that normally would have been disallowed. The DOJ's position was upheld by more than one appeals court."

"But those wars are over, too. I'm confused."

"So were a lot of people, so much so that it went to the Supreme Court. And in 2015 they ruled – well, it's complicated, dealing with civil and criminal cases slightly differently, but essentially what it means is that the professor's claims under the FCA – the fraud, the profiteering – are, in fact, not subject to the statute of limitations."

LaFleur leaned forward, gripping the edge of the table as if afraid of falling off of his chair. "So, you're telling me..."

"God damned right, A.C. You've got the bastards."

You're on Candid Camera

1850 HOUSE

"It's not a matter of *if.* It's *when* and *where*. They're going to hit again, they've made that obvious. First here, a few days ago; now Michael's. Was there much damage, Michael?"

"No, A.C., they just 'tossed the place,' as I think you coppers call it. No lasting damage. And there was nothing there to find."

"Well, we truly understand now what the stakes are. They suspect we've got it, and they want it. We've got to get moving quickly. We can't afford to sit on it for even seven days, not to mention seventy years. Wharton's actions could escalate quickly – they've already committed murder – and as Frank commented earlier, recent events would appear to make them even more intent on stopping us."

"That's right, A.C.; my military contacts don't have all the details, but it's obvious there's something big in the works."

"Along with Chuck Wharton's political ambitions. The situation is quickly becoming very volatile."

LaFleur looked around at the group. They were all huddled around the upstairs apartment dining room table: Maggie, Michael, Larry, Frank, and the new member of the team, (as LaFleur was starting to think of them), Blueray. Frank had called Blueray in to help with the online aspects – he had already started trolling CCTV footage, looking for anything that related to the attacks on the professor and Michael.

"We have two main issues here, as I see it," LaFleur went on, "listed not necessarily in order of importance. One, protect the data. If we lose that, we're hosed. It's what Wharton wants, more than anything else, and what the professor fought to retain, all these years. We can't let him down. Two, and this is intimately connected with the first, we have to protect ourselves. We know what they are capable of; the professor's grave is evidence of that. It's just pure luck that Michael survived. And the moral of that story is, you can never drink enough Diet Coke."

Michael responded with an appropriately grim smile.

"Oh, and by the way, the police have officially dropped the investigation into Dr. Ladisio, but have not initiated any follow-up. As expected." He turned to Blueray. "Blueray, thanks for helping out on short notice. We hope this won't interfere with your studies."

"A.C., if not for you, there would *be* no studies."

"Well, this one could be more dangerous. But hopefully we'll get through it in short order. Anyway, as to the first priority. I call it a priority, in the sense that there is a difference between *important* and *urgent*. Both tasks we have in front of us are important; vital, in fact. But the most urgent, in my view, is to protect the data we have so fortunately and laboriously obtained. I mentioned earlier that they had already been here, in the 1850 House, but came away with nothing. We can't assume that our luck will hold. A toilet tank, as clever as it was on the professor's part, on short notice, well, it's not all that secure a hiding place; just think back to all the drug cartel movies you've seen; there's always something in the toilet tank. Maybe drugs, maybe a gun. Anyway, I don't trust it any longer.

"The professor was also very careful not keep everything in one place. Which is the situation we have now; all of the documents are sitting over on that desk at the moment, and the throttle body is back in the tank downstairs. Unacceptable."

LaFleur looked around the table. "Any suggestions? Where can we stash the evidence?"

After an appropriate awkward silence, Maggie raised her hand. "I know the perfect place." She smiled.

"And that is?"

"Inside Fort Ontario, of course."

The group was suitably impressed with Maggie's suggested hiding place. Now it was just a matter of logistics. But that would be the subject for a slightly later discussion. For now, LaFleur turned to priority number two.

"Do we have anything on these guys yet? Mutt and Jeff, as they are so affectionately known these days. Anything operable?"

Blueray glanced at Frank for permission to speak; Frank nodded.

"Um, A.C., we don't think the goons are the only problem."

"Elaborate."

"We've been deeply scanning the net for CCTV images, starting several weeks before the professor's death, and the days following, all the way up to the present; the hospital, the professor's house, the 1850 House, local hotels, airports. We've come up with some footage you should see. We'd have shown you sooner, but, well, you've been busy riding around in the back of a dry-cleaning truck."

"Apologies accepted. What have you got?"

Blueray stood up and carried his laptop over to where A.C. and Maggie were sitting. "We thought we'd do this in chronological order, to show how things fit together, although that wasn't at all clear to us at the start."

"Go ahead."

The first images were a series of aerial shots of what looked like a typical Oswego neighborhood. It took LaFleur only a few seconds to recognize it as the professor's block – E. Seventh Street, next to the Fort.

"We got this from a real estate site; they're promoting a house a couple of doors down from the professor's. They're highlighting the proximity to the park, obviously," he said, as the video panned up and out over the Fort, then back into the neighborhood. He pointed at the screen. "There's the professor's house. Nothing unusual. But these agencies typically take a lot of footage, and only post a very small portion of it. So, we contacted them and asked to see it all." He switched to a different screen. "We've edited what they gave us to highlight the interesting segments."

LaFleur watched as a woman in dark clothes came up to the back door, at about dusk, it appeared. She looked around quickly and went in. She was carrying something, unidentifiable in the video. In less than a minute she exited out the back and made her way towards the park.

"We spotted her in no less than four videos," said Blueray. "All at about the same time at night. Fortunately, the agent's drone videographer seems to have been practicing, or something, going back and doing these shots over and over, to get them right, we guess. Otherwise we wouldn't have known she was there multiple times. Also, remember we're telling you this with the knowledge of hindsight."

"Understood. Go on."

Frank leaned over the table. "Hospital next, Blueray?"

"Yep. A.C., this is the night the professor came into the ER. The night Michael was attacked," he added, looking over at him. He switched to a new screen. "This is the CCTV camera mounted right outside the ER doors."

Michael stood up and moved closer to the other end of the table to get a better view.

"This is that night?" he asked. "What time? Oh, there it is, in the corner. 11:39?"

"That's right."

They watched as the EMTs pushed the gurney through the double doors into the ER. There was someone standing off to the side, dressed in scrubs, wearing a surgical mask.

"Who's that?" asked Michael.

"Just watch."

There was no action for a few minutes, as the EMTs transferred their patient – Tamos – to the ER staff. Then the doors suddenly opened as they brought the gurney back out. The person standing near the door was startled, and jerked back out of the way.

The surgical mask dropped, just for a second. Blueray froze the video at that point.

Maggie gasped.

"My God. I've seen that woman!"

Please Support Your National Parks

FORT ONTARIO: ABOUT 8 P.M.

Maggie's conversation with Mrs. Rothstein had provided the hiding place, but since they couldn't be seen in daylight carrying things into the Fort, they needed a cover.

The timing couldn't have been better. Maggie had read about it only a few days earlier: New York Senators Schumer and Gillibrand had recently announced legislation to determine if Fort Ontario, together with the Safe Haven Museum, should be designated a national park. To this end, they had arranged for a group tour of the Fort, museum, and graveyard by relevant VIPs to drum up support, scheduled for that night.

LaFleur immediately had Maggie arrange to have dinner with Larry Spiegelman at Canale's, a popular Italian restaurant – and main competitor to the 1850 House – over on W. Utica.

LaFleur had Jimmy drop him off at Canale's as laundry. From there, he and Maggie drove Larry's car to the Fort for the festivities. Given how casual social events tended to be in Oswego, LaFleur had no doubt that they could infiltrate the tour with ease.

It was just as they'd hoped. No one noticed when they joined one of the sub-groups meandering through the various sites on the Fort grounds. LaFleur carried what appeared to be a laptop bag. As there were several others carrying similar bags, no one took any notice.

When they got to the casemate in question – Maggie had scouted it out in advance – they lagged behind until everyone was out of range. While Maggie kept a discrete watch at the entrance, LaFleur quickly located the chamber, stuffed in the contents of the bag, and was back out on the grounds in less than two minutes.

As they strolled back to the car, arm in arm, LaFleur turned to Maggie. "Okay, now for some really good Italian food!"

Black Widow

1850 HOUSE: THE NEXT MORNING

Maggie had indeed recognized the woman in the ER. It was the same woman she'd seen in the professor's kitchen during shiva. The one who'd identified herself as being from the synagogue.

It had shaken them all. She may be, or even probably, was still in the area. And having failed to silence Michael, possibly desperate. Her employers would not be happy about the current state of affairs. There was no predicting what she'd do next.

"Frank and Blueray are running facial recognition software on the ER image, along with images they have from the airport and the rental car counter in Syracuse. In both cases, she obviously knows there are cameras on her, and she tries to avoid a full-frontal view, but this facial recognition stuff is getting scary, so we have hopes. Don't ask Frank how he has access to the software, he'd have to –"

"Don't say it, LaFleur," said Frank, holding up a hand. "The NSA takes a dim view of stale jokes."

Blueray spoke up. "I found a partial trace back to a computer bot that was apparently keyed on the professor's name, anything to do with World War II fighter aircraft, P-39s in particular, some other stuff. Unfortunately, the trail ran cold as I got close to a particularly well-protected server. I could identify only that it seems to be – *seems* – to be located in Washington D.C. That could explain how WGI got such an early start on the professor. They probably started watching him as soon the wreck was located."

"That would explain a lot," said Michael. "You need time to kill someone by arsenic poisoning. And now we know it wasn't the goons after all, but a Black Widow. Maybe it's her signature method. Just like an old pot boiler." He stopped, his face showing a new realization. "When she overheard my argument with Ladisio in the ER, she must have panicked. Followed me to my office." Then he shivered, as if reliving the attack.

"I'm sure you're right, Michael," said LaFleur. "In any case, Frank and Blueray have a chance, they say, of getting some sort of match. Then again, we may never know who she is, other than as the professor's killer." He stood up.

"It's time to make our move."

Bombshell

FORT ONTARIO

He had not meant to upstage the honorable senators from New York, not intentionally.

But upstage them, he did.

LaFleur had scheduled his press conference – which by rights belonged to Tamos – for just three days after the senators' VIP tours. The less time the evidence sat in that wall, the better, he felt, but it had taken time to line up the media. Mutt and Jeff had mysteriously vanished the day before, which Frank thought somewhat ominous, but still, having the evidence well-hidden had allowed them more freedom, and LaFleur had dispensed with the dry-cleaning subterfuge.

Larry Spiegelman had spent the three days frantically coordinating with the Department of Justice, while LaFleur worked with the FBI and the local police department regarding the professor's death and the attack on Michael. They felt fully prepared, if still anxious. Hopefully they were also prepared for the aftermath.

It was to be the press conference to end all press conferences, LaFleur had told Maggie the night before. He'd had been able to arrange ample pre-publicity, even in such a short time, some of it quite sensationalistic, primarily tied to the recovery of the P-39, but also to the untimely death of the professor. He expected it to be quite a show.

A dais sat in front of the original enlisted men's barracks, facing northwest toward the lake. It was flanked by four chairs, two on each side. Maggie and Larry sat on one side; Michael stood behind them. On the other side were two empty chairs, both draped in black.

In the front row facing the dais were representatives from the Oswego Palladium-Times, the Syracuse Post-Standard, and the Albany Times-Union, as well as a raft of small, local papers from around the area. (LaFleur had made sure that Tiffany Peet, the Palladium-Times reporter whose story had been blocked, would get a byline in each of the regional papers.) With the newspaper crews sat reporters from Syracuse WSYR and Albany WNYT television news. Each station had cameras set up at strategic points.

At exactly ten o'clock that morning, LaFleur came out of the casemate, which sat not far from the main building where they'd staged the conference. He was carrying a small, canvas bag. As he made his way over to the area, he could hear the crowd buzzing. Even though this crowd had gathered only within the past thirty minutes or so, it sounded like an audience who had been left waiting several hours for a favorite rock star to appear. It was not a comforting sound.

But he could not help smiling when he saw four laundry trucks arrayed on the small road surrounding the perimeter of the central area. Jimmy Kim had told him the night before that he'd offered to provide (with the approval of his good friend Police Chief Boyko) the services of his "East Side Security Team," all trusted members of his family. LaFleur had demurred, but Jimmy had insisted.

When LaFleur reached the podium, he set the bag down and looked around with obvious trepidation. Not only had the local news and regional media come out in force, he'd just been informed by Frank that not only were reporters from several national media outlets present, one was allegedly from Russia 24, the state-owned news channel.

Well, this is what we wanted.

First glancing briefly at his notes, he tilted the podium mike up a bit higher, and leaning forward, began.

Here we go, Prof.

"Hello. My name is A.C. LaFleur. I'm a retired Oswego police detective. With me here today are Ms. Margaret Malone," he motioned to his left, "and attorney Lawrence J. Spiegelman, both of Oswego, and who are intimately involved in this case. Not with me today," he continued, indicating the two empty chairs, "are the two persons actually responsible for this press conference.

"One of these empty chairs represents someone who was honored on these very grounds just a few weeks ago, Women's Air Service Pilot Jeri Jillette Szabó. You probably read about it – she was the pilot of the World War II fighter plane, a P-39, recently recovered from Lake Ontario. She's buried just over there, in the Fort Ontario military cemetery, the first person so privileged in over seventy years.

"Those of you who have been in Oswego a long time, or who recall the recent story of the recovery of the P-39, will recognize Jeri's last name: Szabó. The second empty chair is there for Professor Tamos Szabó, who spearheaded the search and recovery effort that led to the discovery of the lost aircraft, and his wife. Professor Szabó died just under two weeks ago. His death was attributed, perhaps naturally, since he was ninety-four years old, to simply 'old age.' That was not, however the cause of death.

"Professor Szabó was murdered."

After the commotion died down, LaFleur continued.

"To continue: Professor Szabó was poisoned, by arsenic, over the course of several weeks. As the dose was steadily increased during that time, he grew increasing ill, and finally died late one night in the emergency room of

Oswego Hospital.

"Dr. Michael Fuentes, standing to my left, was present at the time, and was the first to diagnose the poisoning, but his diagnosis was unfortunately ignored before it could be thoroughly investigated. The doctor himself was viciously attacked and nearly killed the same night the professor died, most probably by the same person who killed the professor.

"I know these must sound like preposterous claims. And what on earth does it have to do with the recovery of the P-39? Why hold this press conference in Fort Ontario, for that matter? Well, this bag, here," he said as he held it up, "contains the answers."

He put the bag down and opened it, carefully removed the yellow plastic evidence bag containing the carburetor parts, then removed a sheaf of documents.

"This is what Jeri died for," he said, holding up the evidence bag. "It was November of 1944. Jeri, in desperation and fearing for her life, was carrying what is contained in this bag, which subsequently ended up at the bottom of Lake Ontario. The bag was removed from the wreck of the P-39 and immediately sealed and warranted as evidence by Mr. Spiegelman. And why Lake Ontario? Professor Szabó was interred here in Fort Ontario as a refugee, in Safe Haven. Jeri had planned a flyover of the camp to let him know she had arrived safely, before continuing to Syracuse to land. Something went wrong.

"While we don't know, and will never know, the details of that crash, we *can* be certain that the recovery of this evidence led directly to Professor Szabó's murder."

At this point he put the evidence down on the dais and raised his hands, trying to subdue the audience, who had again burst into a confused clamor, even startling the geese wandering around on the lawn behind them.

"Please bear with me for a moment. Please," he said as he made calming motions with his hands, "please let me continue. There will be time for questions at the conclusion of my remarks." He took a deep breath. *Okay, Prof, time to knock their pants down around their ankles.*

"You've heard me claim, twice now, I believe, that Professor Szabó was murdered. Let me explain.

"The items I have here," he said, gesturing, "are evidence of deliberate and methodical war profiteering. That is, defrauding the United States government during a time of war. At the time of Jeri's death, she and Tamos, working with an attorney in New York City, Harrison Zook –" he paused to look at his notes – "were preparing a case to present to the Truman Commission, under the False Claims Act covering such actions, establishing that a clear pattern of deception had been undertaken in order to maximize profit on certain components used in the manufacture of aircraft carburetors.

To reiterate: the physical evidence I have here, recovered from the wreck of the P-39 piloted by Jeri Szabó, is corroborated by documentation gathered at the time by Mr. Zook and preserved by Professor Szabó since that time."

He looked up. "This profiteering led directly to not only Jeri Szabó's death – the recovered P-39 contains additional evidence – but to the deaths of an unknown number of other pilots, here and overseas. We also have ample reason to believe that, once an investigation is reopened, as we intend to do, additional instances of profiteering, unrelated to P-39s, will be uncovered.

"The perpetrator of these acts – and the force behind the murder of Professor Szabó – was the parent company of Wharton General Industries, then known as Wharton Fabrication, under the direction of the founder, Charles Wharton, Senior."

This time it took more than several minutes to restore order.

After things had finally calmed down, LaFleur introduced Larry Spiegelman, who briefly explained the relevance of the Wartime Suspension of Limitations Act. LaFleur then described Maggie's role as an eye witness, and additional circumstances surrounding the attack on Michael. He then began fielding questions, calling out reporters as if in a White House news conference.

"Yes, you in the striped shirt, go ahead. Yes, as Mr. Spiegelman explained, the WSLA, as interpreted by Supreme Court rulings in 2015, provides the legal basis for our suits. The Department of Justice concurs. We are confident we are on solid ground here."

He continued to call on various reporters, somehow not surprised that their questions had for the most part already been answered in his original remarks; everyone wanted a moment in the sun, apparently.

"Yes, that's right: Ms. Malone was the only one to actually witness the murder suspect, some time before the professor's death. She has been working closely with the FBI and local law enforcement. We're hopeful that something will turn up soon."

"As I said, the assault on Dr. Fuentes took place immediately after the professor's death in the ER, within fifteen or twenty minutes. Chief Boyko of the Oswego Police Department" – here LaFleur nodded in his direction (might as well try to stay on his good side) – "has reopened the investigation into the attack, and is also working closely with the FBI. We're almost certain it was the same person."

"Yes, I did say that many P-39s saw use overseas. A great many P-39s, P-40s and other aircraft were delivered to Russia under the Lend Lease program, to be used in air defense in Eastern Russia. Let me give you some numbers," he said, looking down at his notes quickly. "Yes, here it is: nearly five thousand P-39s, out of around ninety-five hundred built, were flown to

Siberia, via Alaska. Many of these aircraft, though we can't know how many, certainly crashed due to defective carburetors, that is, sub-standard carburetors containing parts supplied by Wharton Fabrication. I think I failed to mention a distinctive feature of Jeri's P-39, the one recovered from Lake Ontario, that has some significance – it had been marked with a red star, the insignia of the Soviet Air Forces. So, it was certainly one of the P-39s earmarked for Russia."

Then a request for recognition came out of left field. "Mr. LaFleur!" As LaFleur acknowledged the questioner, he saw Giamatti standing next to him.

Now what? "Name and organization, please?"

"Yeah, Smith, AP (something, something)," the reporter half-slurred, evidently not wanting to make himself heard. "Isn't this all just a grandstand attempt at some sort of personal ego gratification? Trying to make up for past failures? It's more or less common knowledge that you have a record of interfering in open, ongoing investigations, and making a shamble of them."

"Is there a question here? If not, I suggest –"

"My question is this: why should anyone pay attention to you and your cohorts? You, now just a glorified bar tender; an ex-nurse generally frowned upon by the community for her loose morals; a small-town doctor with behavioral issues; and a backwater attorney willing to forego all standards of protocol in dealing with what you claim is evidence. And who are your heroes? A senile, chronically ill, and bitter old man, probably an illegal immigrant, and an apparently incompetent and hysterical woman pilot who ran her airplane out of gas and had to ditch it in the lake. It's no surprise that this town is the only place you could get an audience for such a ridiculous story."

While the man was ranting, Tiffany Peet had run frantically to the podium and leaned over to LaFleur. As she scurried away, he turned to the accuser.

"Well, Mr. Smith, since you are not actually a reporter at all, but the WGI thug who tried to bury this story weeks ago, I will tell you that no matter how hard WGI tries to block this, our evidence *will* speak for the dead. And as for your characterizations of me and my colleagues, I have just three words for your employers: Just try us."

He had to almost yell to be heard over the subsequent furor. "No, I'm sorry, that's all I have for now. No, we're not prepared to go into any more detail at this time. The full story, as well as periodic press releases, will be issued as our efforts and the various investigations proceed.

"Thank you all for coming."

In the News

Washington, D.C., Wharton General Industries [WGI]. For Immediate Release. "While not wishing to impugn the motives of Mr. LaFleur or his associates, we vehemently deny any wrong doing on the part of Mr. Wharton, Senior; the original Wharton companies; or any other party or parties associated with WGI or its affiliates which may be targeted by Mr. LaFleur. He has, for apparently personal reasons, from whatever so-called evidence he believes he has, concocted a ridiculous fantasy. We trust that these ludicrous allegations will be given the scant attention they deserve."

Washington, D.C., Wharton General Industries [WGI]. For Immediate Release. "Wharton General Industries [WGI] has announced a $100,000 grant, to be presented to the Director of the National WASP WWII Museum, Sweetwater, Texas later this week. Charles Wharton IV, the new CEO of WGI, said yesterday, "We've long admired the women of World War II, and in particular the contributions made by the Women's Air Force Service Pilots. This grant has been in the works for several months, and we're glad to finally have the opportunity to further the goals of this fine organization."

CNBC: "WGI, reeling from accusations that its parent company and founder, Charles Wharton, Senior, were involved in war profiteering during the late stages of World War II, has released a strong refutation today, in addition formally charging the accuser, A.C. LaFleur, with slander [...]"

The New York Times "The Russian government today cancelled a prior agreement with Wharton General Industries for the completion of several newly constructed FIFA 2018 World Cup stadiums. A FIFA spokesman declined to speculate on the possible reason for Russia's withdrawal from the contracts, saying only that the venues would still be completed in time for the event. WGI did not respond to inquiries, however it is thought [...]"

CNBC: "The Chinese government has unexpectedly awarded its latest nuclear plant construction contract to General Electric. The contract had been slated to go to Wharton General Industries. A Chinese government spokesman cited 'financing difficulties' as one reason for the sudden change. WGI declined to comment in detail on the announcement, saying only that projects of this scale often run into temporary setbacks [...]"

The Sweetwater Reporter, Sweetwater, Texas. "The National WASP WWII Museum located here in Sweetwater has declined an offer by

Wharton General Industries to fund an upcoming construction project, citing recent negative publicity. On a related but more positive note, the P-39 pursuit plane recently recovered from Lake Ontario, New York, is scheduled to go on limited display during its restoration. Interest is extremely high, and the museum expects large crowds [...]"

CNBC: "The stock price of beleaguered Wharton General Industries continued its freefall today, losing another 12% since the open, on news that the Department of Justice has opened an investigation into what it termed "disturbing anomalies" in a number of government contracts related to the production of sixth-generation fighter aircraft. The stock has fallen more than 45% in the last two weeks, following allegations of war profiteering during the Second World War [...]"

Russia 24 television: "In an unprecedented motion at the U.N. today, Russia envoys demanded that a formal apology be issued by Wharton General Industries acknowledging their culpability in the deaths of an unknown number of Russian fighter pilots, most of them women, who flew Bell Aircraft Airacobras, affectionately called by the women, *Kobrushka*, or Little Cobra. Known by the Nazis during the war as Night Witches, the Russian women pilots were formidable foes against German ground troops throughout the Eastern Front [...]"

WSYR, Syracuse: "Charles 'Chuck' Wharton, current candidate for President, today reportedly refused to appear before a Senate Select Committee formed to investigate allegations of past and present corruption at Wharton General Industries. A spokesman for Mr. Wharton referred our reporter to the Select Committee for comment. The Committee has so far not responded to our requests for more information. Turning to sports [...]"

CBN: "Two persons suspected of being involved in the murder of an Oswego, New York, professor and a related attack on a doctor at the hospital there, have been detained by Canadian Border Services Officers as they attempted to enter the country at Thousand Island Bridge using false identity papers. The two are being interrogated currently, according to a Border Services official, and a determination will be made shortly as to their eventual disposition."

The Washington Post: "Charles 'Chuck' Wharton's difficulties mounted today, as it was revealed that he had not previously disclosed a blind trust, worth tens of millions of dollars, as required by Federal election laws. It is uncertain as to the implications of this revelation, as he recently withdrew from the race. The Department of Justice, however, has not ruled out possible future prosecution […]"

The Palladium-Times, Oswego, New York. By Tiffany Peet. [Also carried by all AP and UPI news outlets.] "Detective A.C. LaFleur of Oswego, New York, today released copies of previously unknown documents showing that in late 1945, Wharton Fabrication had tried to recover known defective carburetors from the Bell Aircraft factory in Niagara Falls, New York, after discovering that New York lawyer Harrison Zook had information implicating the company in fraudulent practices related to their manufacture. In addition, evidence is mounting that the extent of the fraud goes far beyond the Bell Aircraft facility, and potentially affected the manufacture of a large number of critical structural aircraft components, all using substandard materials sourced from Wharton Fabrication. Detective LaFleur said the documents were uncovered during extensive searches of government files under the Freedom of Information Act. LaFleur further said these documents only add to the already substantial collection of evidence supporting the claims made against Wharton General Industries only two weeks ago."

Washington, D.C., the office of Charles Wharton III. For Immediate Release. "Charles Wharton III has formally withdrawn his bid for nomination for President of the United States, effective immediately. A spokesman for the Wharton campaign said a statement will be made by Mr. Wharton personally at his campaign headquarters in Washington. That statement is expected at 8:00 PM Eastern time."

CNN: "Breaking News: The FBI has just released images of the woman thought to be the infamous 'Black Widow' assassin responsible for the poisoning death of Professor Tamos Szabó in Oswego, New York. She was arrested at New York's LaGuardia airport as she was attempting to board a plane to Barbados. She is being held without bail awaiting arraignment in a New York federal court. In a separate report, the FBI announced today that Professor Szabó's body has been exhumed and arsenic poisoning confirmed."

All media outlets: "Charles Wharton, Senior, founder and chairman emeritus of Wharton General Industries, has been indicted on two counts of conspiracy to murder in the poisoning death of Professor Tamos Szabó, of Oswego, New York, in addition to multiple counts of obstruction of justice and related charges.

"A WGI spokesman declined to comment."

Endings and Beginnings

1850 HOUSE

"I can't think of a more appropriate place for the reading of the will" said Larry, "than here at the 1850 House bar, where Tamos spent so much of his latter days, watched over by Jeri and her P-39 in Great Falls, with the juke box playing *Sentimental Journey*." Which it was playing even now, over and over. Blueray, to no one's real surprise, had extensive electromechanical as well as computer skills, and had rigged the Wurlitzer with a repeat function.

The small assembly was gathered at the back of the bar. Maggie and LaFleur were with Larry and Arlene at Tamos's table; Frank, Blueray and Red were huddled at another table deep into a conversation on ethical computer hacking; Michael and Jamila shared a smaller table. The restaurant was closed for the night, a sign in the front window reading, "Closed for Private Party."

"It's a very simple will," Larry continued, "with just three provisions. One, all liquid assets, other than the house, are to be divided equally. Fifty percent is to go to the National WASP Museum in Sweetwater, Texas, earmarked for the restoration of Jeri's P-39." A quick round of applause followed this announcement. "The other fifty percent is to go to the Safe Haven Holocaust Refugee Shelter Museum. The latter, it seems to me, is of particular importance. If I may editorialize for a moment?"

"As if we could stop you," interjected LaFleur.

"Thank you. As I was about to say, before being so humorously interrupted, since the Fort and the museum are soon to be become part of the National Park Service, and while that certainly imparts a much needed and appreciated mark of status, the Park Service is not well-funded, being kept by the Federal government on what we will politely call an ungenerous budget. So, this money will, I hope, be utilized quickly and effectively."

"I'm sure Mrs. Rothstein is up to the task," said Maggie.

"No question of it," responded LaFleur. He raised his glass. "To the museums! Long may they prosper!" Glasses were raised all around.

"Second, the house," Larry continued. He looked over at Jamila. "It's yours."

Jamila's eyes widened in surprise. "Seriously? He left me that darling house? Oh, my." She looked around. "You don't know how wonderful that is. And how timely. I've just accepted a position at SUNY Oswego, and I had no idea where I was going to live. This is so like Tamos."

"Well, Jamila, welcome to Oswego!" said LaFleur, seconded by the rest of the group. "But, Larry," he went on, "you've only given us two provisions, the bequests to the museums and Jamila's house," said LaFleur. "You said there were three. What's the last provision?"

Larry settled back in his chair. "It's something rather special, I believe. For you, A.C." He pulled a small envelope out of his inside coat pocket and put it on the table. "Oh, but before I forget," said Larry, "I have another piece of very good news. I've gotten approval from both Fort Ontario and Adath Yeshurun to inter Tamos's remains alongside Jeri at the Fort cemetery."

"The hell you say!" exclaimed LaFleur. "How soon can we get him interred? Nothing elaborate, I think we would all agree?" There was general assent from around the room.

"I'll speak with Abruzzo first thing tomorrow and see when we can arrange it," replied Spiegelman. "Probably within the next few days."

"That's great, Larry," said Maggie. "Thank you."

"Yes," agreed Jamila, "that will be very appropriate." Jamila said. "He was cheated out of so much; his life with Jeri, most of all."

"And for so many years, to be denied real justice," said Maggie. "If he were here today, he would be extremely pleased with what you've done, A.C., as difficult as it was."

"What we've all done, together," LaFleur interjected.

"Yes, that's right," said Maggie. "And playing a weak hand, yet again. Why does it seem we're always playing that weak hand, A.C.? Always against the odds. Trying to figure out how it matters. Or if it matters at all."

LaFleur looked down and stared into his drink for a moment. When he looked back up, he had a determined look on his face. "You know, sometimes I feel like I'm barely holding on, by pure force of effort, and it's only the effort that matters." He looked around, his face brightening. "But now here we are, Maggie, living in a castle built in 1850, after being chauffeured around town all week in white limousines" – Maggie laughed at this and reached out for LaFleur's hand – "surrounded by friends, and celebrating our success."

"Not to mention celebrating the lives of two extraordinary people," said Maggie, soberly, "for whom no effort was too great, and who lost their lives pursuing justice."

"Well said, Maggie," affirmed LaFleur. "And that calls for another toast!" As he picked up his glass, he noticed Jamila looking around awkwardly. "Oh, damn, Jamila, you don't have a drink. What a lousy bartender I am."

"As we heard at the press conference," said Michael.

"Watch it, Michael, or all you'll get the rest of the night is Diet Coke." He got up and went behind the bar. "What's your pleasure, Jamila?"

"Um, do you actually have any, well…Diet Coke?"

LaFleur burst out laughing. "Watch out, Michael. I think this may be a clever ploy to attract your interest. The way to Michael's heart is through his diet soda, Jamila."

"Oh, my God, A.C., that's the worst joke you've ever made!" cried Michael, clutching at his chest.

Amid the general laughter, LaFleur bent down behind the bar and extracted a Diet Coke from the cooler. After pouring it over ice, he brought it over to Jamila at the table and sat back down next to Maggie.

"All right," said Larry. "The last bequest." He picked up the envelope, opened it, and carefully took out a small gold ring. Holding it up he asked, "Do you recognize this?"

Maggie's hand went to her throat. "It's Prof's wedding band," she said, weakly. "The one he wore on his right hand." The room had grown quiet.

Larry turned to LaFleur. "He left it to you, A.C." He handed LaFleur the ring. "Along with this." He took a second, smaller ring from the envelope, a simple gold ring with a small diamond. "Jeri's," he said, softly. "No specific instructions, but..."

LaFleur held up the rings, gripping them tightly, as if he thought they might vanish at any second.

"Maggie," he said.

"Yes," she said.

Two and a half weeks later, a small wedding was held beneath the trees surrounding the Fort Ontario cemetery, on the grassy area next to the war memorial.

Jeri and Tamos, attending posthumously, could not have been more pleased.

EPILOGUE: THE ELEGANCE OF EFFORT

In the weeks following the recovery of the wreck, Tamos often walks out to the Fort. His memory of that long-ago afternoon by the lake has over the years taken on an almost independent existence, like something forgotten but then found to be graspable, real, and lucid. A memory not of the past, but of the timeless.

It is one of those muggy summer nights that seem to stop the stars in their tracks. Tamos sits at the edge of the lake. The moist air is calm and heavy, draped like a blanket over the quiet park. He stares out to where he knows the horizon must be, an ineluctable line between water and sky at the limits of the visible, between light and darkness.

He is on a small knoll at the northern edge of the Fort Ontario grounds, below one of the five stone points of the old fortification. He sits there for a long time, feeling the cooling night air seep into his back, a slow, sweet ache, the ache of longing. He anxiously turns the thin gold band on his right index finger around and around, first one way, then the other. A slight tremor runs up and down his arm. After a few minutes, twisting the ring calms him.

This quest he is on is not one of vengeance, but of justice. Justice long delayed, and for anyone else seemingly unattainable. He has no doubt that his current efforts to finish the task will prove successful. Still, he is running out of time.

He looks up at the stars.

We are all made out of star dust, he muses, infinitesimal bits of exploded suns momentarily defying entropy in a random universe, matter in some distant time to return to star dust – and therefore, some say, nothing much matters at all. But do not those relationships we forge during the course of our lives cause matter and energy to entangle in some unfathomable way? As unfathomable as what we sometimes, hopefully, sentimentally, call love? If so, then everything matters.

And it is the elegance of effort that makes it true.

NOTES

While not a historical novel in the strict sense, many elements of our story are based on actual facts or events. The following is a brief summary of those elements, along with references where appropriate, and an indication of where we have strayed from, or otherwise embellished, the truth.

Recovery of military artifacts.

The recovery of all sunken military artifacts, regardless of origin or location, is strictly controlled by the Department of the Navy. While we have gestured in the direction of the regulations, the professor's efforts to raise the wreck of the P-39 would certainly have required a much more extensive permitting process than we have described.

The regulations are found in the Department of the Navy document, *Guidelines for Permitting Archaeological Investigations and Other Activities Directed at Sunken Military Craft and Terrestrial Military Craft Under the Jurisdiction of the Department of the Navy.*

https://www.federalregister.gov/documents/2014/01/06/2013-31068/guidelines-for-permitting-archaeological-investigations-and-other-activities-directed-at-sunken

The story of the recovery of the Russian P-39 is true; it was found intact and preserved as described. http://www.airspacemag.com/military-aviation/lieutenant-ivan-baranovskys-p-39-41818469/?no-ist

The Yankee Clipper.

Pan American flight #PA9035 crashed into the Targus River at Lisbon on February 22, 1943. The aircraft was carrying several celebrities, including the famous band singer Jane Froman, who was seriously injured. The cause of the crash was not a fire, as we have described, but the "inadvertent contact of the left wingtip of the aircraft with the water." The record of the crash is available at

http://www.baaa-acro.com/1943/archives/crash-of-a-boeing-314-clipper-in-lisbon-24-killed/

Japanese spies were not uncommon throughout Europe during the war, including in Lisbon, which was often called "the Capital of Espionage." Information from operatives was routed through the Japanese Embassy in Madrid.

Jeri's aviation and WASP experiences.

The inspiration for Jeri Jillette is one of the author's (Steve's) mother-in-law, Mary Catherine "Jary" Johnson McKay. Jary was part of the second graduating class of 1943 (43-W-2). Many of the historical references and journal entries (including the flight from New York to Los Angeles), military orders, and the radio show *The Army Hour* were adapted from actual documents and transcripts. The WASP killed on takeoff at Bismarck, N.D., was Jary's best friend, Dottie Nichols.

The official WASP archive is maintained by the University of Texas at https://www.twu.edu/library/womans-collection/featured-collections/women-airforce-service-pilots-wasp/

The National WASP WWII Museum in Sweetwater, Texas, also has extensive materials and exhibits related to the WASP organization, http://waspmuseum.org/

War profiteering and the Wartime Suspension of Limitations Act.

War profiteering during WWII, while not common, did occur, and sometimes on a large scale. The most infamous case is that of the Curtis Aeronautical plant in Lockland, Ohio, which produced large numbers of known defective aircraft engines, approved for use using fraudulent inspection procedures. Several company and military officials were prosecuted as a result of an investigation by the Truman Commission.

While correct in all technical details, our scenario of defective P-39 carburetors is a fabrication.

The Wartime Suspension of Limitations Act, or WSLA, was originally intended to allow the prosecution of war profiteering during WWII (suspending the statute of limitations regarding such offenses) until "the end of hostilities." Subsequent rulings by several courts, up to the Supreme Court, have extended the time limit of the suspension of limitations in certain cases.

Raoul Wallenberg.

The Swedish diplomat Raoul Wallenberg was indeed as intrepid and fearless as we have described, and was personally responsible for the rescue of thousands of Hungarian Jews. The story of Wallenberg rescuing the Jews from the train is a true story, fictionalized for our purposes. An excellent account of Wallenberg's efforts can be found in John Bierman's Righteous Gentile: The Story of Raoul Wallenberg, Missing Hero of the Holocaust.

Fort Ontario Emergency Refugee Center (Safe Haven)

The only refugee center ever established during WWII in the United States, the Emergency Refugee Center at Fort Ontario (also known as Safe Haven), came about primarily through the singular efforts of a remarkable woman named Ruth Gruber. She details the whole story in her book, Haven: The Dramatic Story of 1,000 World War II Refugees and How They Came to America.

The Safe Haven Holocaust Refugee Shelter Museum in Fort Ontario, Oswego, New York, is well worth a visit. http://safehavenmuseum.com/

Lake Ontario Bathymetic Sounding Data Image

The image used for the cover was obtained from the National Oceanic and Atmospheric Administration (NOAA).

https://data.nodc.noaa.gov/cgi-bin/iso?id=gov.noaa.ngdc.mgg.dem:282

ACKNOWLEDGMENTS

As always, we want to thank the friends and family members who have helped us throughout the entire process of writing the book; without their support, encouragement, and engagement, it would never have been completed.

As in the past, we've had invaluable assistance from several key contributors. Kurt "Chicken" Schmitt and Arthur "Caruso" Handley provided many excellent plot suggestions. We must thank Pete "Danger" Huisveld for providing crucial technical material and story elements, along with Thomas "The Tree" Fountain and Michael MacFadden for technical advice and background on RIT. Emergency room procedures and additional medical advice came from Dr. Michael Luckow. A beautiful, four-color, polyconic soundings chart of Lake Ontario was provided by Liz Mauer.

Our principal proofreaders were Sandy Fountain and Debbie Abbott, whose careful review and valuable suggestions improved the manuscript markedly. Sarah Massey-Warren reviewed nearly every chapter as it was written and saved us from many blunders. Adrienne Abbott also aided in the review, as did Bill and Nancy Baer. Many thanks to all. Any remaining errors are, of course, ours alone.

Once again, we cannot give enough thanks to Bill Reilly and Mindy Ostrow for their continued support, and for providing the premiere outlet for our books: the river's end bookstore, located at 19 West Bridge Street, Oswego, New York, online at http://www.riversendbookstore.com.

ABOUT THE AUTHORS

Dr. John Fountain, after graduating from Wayne State University School of Medicine in Detroit, Michigan, traveled overseas to do his initial residencies, first spending two years in Dunedin, New Zealand, followed by two years in Perth, Scotland, where he met his wife, Sandy, a nurse. They returned to the U.S., where John did a third residency in Lexington, Kentucky. They then moved to Oswego, New York, where John practiced as an anesthesiologist for nearly twenty-five years, followed by two years as Chief of Anesthesiology at Adirondack Medical Center in Lake Placid, New York.

A few years ago, John and Sandy retired to Big Sky, Montana, where they enjoy frequent visits by their three children and two grandchildren. John has recently embarked on a rigorous three-part athletic program: 100 days of fishing, 100 days of skiing, and 100 days of golf. The other 65 days he spends conjuring up ideas for another book.

Steve Abbott is a Colorado native, and lives with his wife Adrienne on the outskirts of Boulder, Colorado. He graduated from the University of Colorado, where he and John were roommates during their undergraduate years. After over twenty-five years in the computer industry, a few years ago he returned to CU to obtain a Master's degree in English Literature.

Steve has since retired and spends his time reading, writing, and playing poker, with the goal of eventually playing a weak hand as well as A.C. LaFleur.

Made in the USA
Columbia, SC
01 September 2020